GUILD OF TOKENS

GUILD OF TOKENS

JON AUERBACH

NYC
QUESTING
GUILD

I

GUILD OF TOKENS
Copyright © 2019, 2021 by Jon Auerbach. All rights reserved.

No part of this book may be reproduced in any form or by any electronic or mechanical means, including information storage and retrieval systems, without written permission from the author, except for the use of brief quotations in a book review.

Cover illustration: Felix Ortiz
Cover design and interior layout: STK•Kreations
Character portraits and guild recruitment poster by Rebecca Sorge Jensen
Vignettes by Danusko Campos
Chapter header illustrations by Tom Parker
Maps by Soraya Corcoran
Memoria copyediting by Nicole Evans

Hardcover ISBN: 978-1-7347990-1-9
Trade paperback ISBN: 978-1-7347990-2-6
Worldwide Rights.

Published by ARC Worlds Publishing
www.jonauerbach.com

Also by Jon Auerbach
***NYC Questing Guild* Series**
Guild of Tokens (#1)
Guild of Magic (#2) - Coming soon

Guild of Tokens: Origins
Trainee (#0.1)
Enforcer (#0.2)
Relic Hunter (#0.3)
Memoria (#1.1)

CONTENTS

MAP OF NEW NETHERLAND
ix

GUILD OF TOKENS
1

MAP OF MANHATTAN
407

TRAINEE
409

MEMORIA
435

ENFORCER
541

RELIC HUNTER
571

GALLERY
609

ACKNOWLEDGMENTS
616

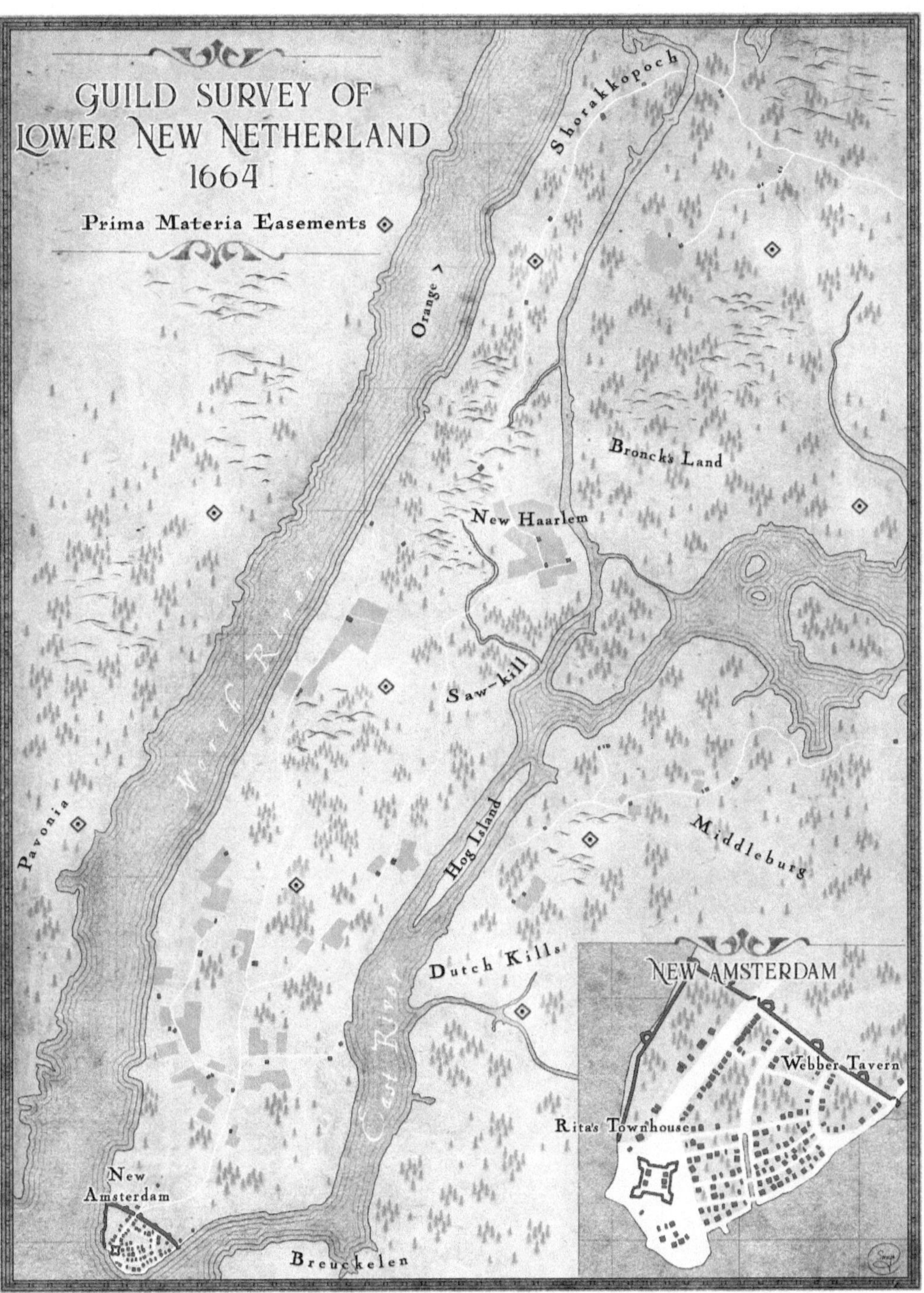

GUILD SURVEY OF
LOWER NEW NETHERLAND
1664
Prima Materia Easements
Shorakkopoch
Orange
Broncks Land
New Haarlem
Saw-kill
North River
Hog Island
Pavonia
East River
Middleburg
Dutch Kills
New Amsterdam
Breuckelen
NEW AMSTERDAM
Webber Tavern
Rita's Townhouse

GUILD OF TOKENS

WAIT THREE DAYS
BETWEEN QUESTS

The first Quest was simple.

I went to Chelsea Market during lunch, bought a handful of blueberries, a tillandsia, an apple popsicle, and three pounds of 90/10 ground beef. I left the goods in the windowsill of a brownstone on West 9th Street and then headed to Central Park, where the Requester had taped a plain, white envelope under a random bench. Inside was a wooden token, the size of a half dollar, with the number one intricately carved in the middle. I quickly hid it in one of my desk drawers, then proceeded to get absolutely no work done for the rest of the day.

The second Quest was slightly more taxing. I waited the required three days before checking the Quest Board again. There didn't seem to be any enforcement mechanism of the waiting time, but not wanting to upset anyone, I did as instructed. When I logged onto the Quest Board, the screen flooded with fresh Quests waiting to be undertaken. I soon found myself perched over the Hudson River, trying to fish out five small stones without falling in the disgusting brown water. My footing was sure, so I didn't have to explain to my co-workers why I smelled like rotten garbage. The stones I placed in a brown leather pouch, which I left next to a fire hydrant in Chinatown. This time, I had to fetch my reward out of an unlocked mailbox up in the Bronx. I secreted away the token in the bottom of an old pair of shoes so that my nosy roommate wouldn't find it and began the countdown again.

The third Quest was another straightforward one. The headline was misleading-a promise to visit a quirky, forgotten shop-but when the full instructions arrived in my inbox, I sulked. A quick trip into Grand Central was all it took to find the cheap plastic bracelet, which I deposited in a garbage can on Track 18. This time, the token was close by, stuck between the pages of an issue of *Nintendo Power*.

The fourth Quest was nostalgic. I again gathered up another weird menagerie of items and went back to the brownstone on West 9th Street. The items from the first Quest were gone, save for the popsicle stick, and I hoped that whoever had fetched them had gotten there before the popsicle had turned into a pile of mush. Or maybe they wanted the mush. Who knows. Another envelope awaited me when I returned to the same Central Park bench. Later, I pulled out the first token and set it aside the new one. The craftsmanship was undeniable. Maybe at some point, I would get to meet their creator.

The fifth Quest was the most challenging by far. The instructions were multi-tiered and required precise timing. First, I had to board the last car of a downtown 6 train at 51st Street at 9:47 AM. I then had to exit the train at 33rd Street and re-enter the third car of that same train. Needless to say, I drew a multitude of stares when I burst through the closing doors of the third car. Second, I needed to exit the train at 14th Street and board a crosstown bus going west, standing in the middle of the bus without holding a handrail. Third, I had to exit the bus at 7th Avenue through the front door and take the first available taxi all the way down to Battery Park. These steps needed to be completed in no more than 47 minutes door-to-door. I arrived at Battery Park with minutes to spare, only to realize that the original instructions had stopped after this step. Dejected, I almost left to go home, but a small, intricately painted arrow on a sign caught the corner of my eye. I walked in the direction of the arrow, only to find another arrow on a second sign. That arrow led to several more (I lost count after the 11th one), as I zigzagged across the park. The final arrow pointed me to a set of stairs leading down underground. At the bottom was an imposing wooden door sporting a large iron knocker. I hesitated slightly before banging the knocker three times. Nothing happened. I waited. Still nothing. After several minutes of contemplating the exact number of knocks needed, a small portion of the door slid aside to reveal a pair of piercing, golden eyes.

"You're late." The voice was raspy and deep-toned.

"I'm sorry?"

"Tokens, please."

The Quest made no mention of bringing my tokens with me, but on a hunch, I had collected them from their various hiding places. I drew them out and a small, sooty hand reached through the slot and grabbed them from me. Before I could say anything, the slot closed suddenly with a thud. I stared at the door. Was this all some kind of stupid trick by a crazy person with too much time on their hands? Before my anger could get the best of me, the slot opened again and the hand reached out to give me something small and round. Another token I realized. But it was iron, not wood. The same number one was in the middle, etched elegantly into the metal. I grabbed the token greedily and without another word, the man's hand withdrew back into the door and the slot closed again. Tucking the token away into my jacket, I danced happily up the stairs and into the mid-morning sun.

When I logged onto the Quest Board again three days later, a new section had appeared. "Epic Quests," it said. "Requires 185 gold tokens."

CHAPTER ONE

IN WHICH I DISCOVER THE WORLD OF QUESTING

*"We traveled across the ocean in search of a new beginning.
What we found was something entirely different."*
— RITA VAN ASCH, JANUARY 1, 1777

I didn't click the link at first.

You wouldn't have blamed me if I'd ignored it.

The email looked spammy: every word was misspelled, the sender's name sounded Eastern European, and it ended with an exhortation to "klik hear!"

I had left the office just after midnight, after an exhausting 48-hour sprint cleaning up code that my jerk-of-a-co-worker Russ dumped on my lap so he could take a four-day weekend. The perils of being the only female programmer at a startup, I guess.

And a pushover.

Well, I'd show him, I thought.

I'd do such an amazing job that it would force my boss, who was so used to Russ's crap code, to marvel at my elegant functions. Or, more likely, he'd compliment Russ for taking time to rejuvenate himself so he could come back to work refreshed and ready to kick butt. Or he'd pat Russ on the back for giving someone like me the chance to do some "important" work. Maybe both.

Anyway, I was flipping through my work email on the cab ride home when I saw it. "Epic quests 4 u!" the subject said. Probably one of those MMORPG ripoffs, I thought, but I opened it anyway, only so I could relegate the sender to the spam bin forever. With that accomplished, I drifted off as the cab sped down the FDR.

Three weeks later, it showed up again.

Unsurprisingly, Russ had taken all the credit for my hard work and then announced that he'd accepted a new job at our biggest rival in Silicon Valley. I worked through his goodbye party, documenting all of Russ's code from the three pages of handwritten chicken scratch he had given me so we wouldn't be flying blind once Russ the Great departed.

"Epic Questers wanted!" this one said. Well, at least their spelling improved this time. I opened it and read on.

"Adventurous individuals needed. Complete Quests for treasure and glory. Click here!"

In college, when no one was looking, I became obsessed with *Warriors of Olympus*, an online role-playing game where you fought for your chosen Greek god or goddess, completing quests, killing legendary monsters, collecting loot, that sort of thing. I fought for love. That is, the goddess of love, Aphrodite. It was exhausting. Not just because of the late nights I spent holed up in my room building my standing in the Aphrodite Guild, but also because I had to take great pains to make sure I never, ever, ever said anything about this nerdy passion to my friends, who wouldn't be caught in the same state with such a game.

I read the email over again for some clue as to why this mysterious game was worthy of my (virtual) blood, sweat, and tears, and my real time, money, and sanity, but no such clue was forthcoming. Off to the Mines of Moria with you then, foul email.

It was another three months before the final email arrived.

We were now in perpetual crunch mode, working around the clock, seven days a week, to ship a game months behind schedule that was lacking 60% of the features we promised in our Kickstarter campaign. But no worries, because all of our backers had gotten their t-shirts and posters and other crap that we had wasted 20% of our funds on. Money that could have been used to pay me, as I was now doing both my job and Russ's job. Or to buy snacks for the office. Really, I would have settled for supermarket-brand bottled water.

I had fallen asleep at my desk, the keys of my mechanical keyboard pressed into my face, when the ping of a new email roused me from my coma. It was 3:43 on a Sunday morning.

"This is your final chance, Jen."

Great, now they know my name.

"This is not a game. The Quests are real. The rewards are real. The glory is real. Do you have what it takes?"

These jerks were relentless. They must only follow-up with the people who opened the earlier emails. Clever bastards. Well, now they finally had my attention.

I clicked the link.

My screens went dark. So did the ones to my left, the ones to my right, and all the ones in the row in front of me. If anyone else had been in the office, they would be losing their minds right now. Of course it was the girl who clicked on the ransomware email, they would say. Of course it was the girl who willingly pushed millions of lines of code into an encrypted lockbox that would cost the rest of the company's cash to retrieve because she was so tired one night and got distracted by an email. An email of all things! I stared at my screens, waiting in the pitch black room for something to happen. Anything. But the gentle whirring of the computer fans had gone silent, leaving me utterly alone.

It was then that the Quests appeared.

The blinking cursor materialized first on my screen. Then rows of random characters whizzed by, as they moved up the black screen and out of sight. Finally, a set of letters formed. It looked like the beginning of one of those old school text-adventure games, before actual computer graphics, where everything had to be made out of ASCII characters.

It said:

```
"Welcome to the Quest Board, new Quester!
There are three rules.
1. Wait three days between Quests.
2. Finish what you start.
3. Always Quest alone.
May the light of adventure guide you.
Happy Questing,
The Council"
```

I blinked, and the message was gone, and in its place was a prompt.

```
"Enter your handle:"
```

I paused to think of something appropriate. In my *Warriors of Olympus* days, I was JadePhoenix42. I rose quickly through the ranks and pretty soon was running the whole shebang. Then one day, a new player came along and turned the whole guild against me, got me kicked me out, and tried to get me banned from the game for good measure. After that, I retired the handle and stopped gaming altogether. But that was seven years ago, and maybe it was time to bring back the phoenix.

I hit enter and then a list with ten numbered entries formed. I read the first one:

```
"1. Wanted: a MetroCard receipt from the West 4th
St station. Not your own. Leave on the top step.
Reward: One wood"
```

Then the next:

```
"2. Pls give me some red leaves from Prospect Park.
Reward: Eight wood"
```

Then the next:

```
"3. A Polaroid shot of the Raging Bull statue. Tape
it on the construction wall at 1571 Second Avenue
at exactly 5:32 PM tomorrow. Reward: One iron"
```

Then finally:

```
"4. Hi! Could you be a dear, and fetch me a handful
of blueberries, a tillandsia, an orange popsicle,
and three pounds of 80/20 ground beef from Chelsea
Market? Leave in the windowsill of 194 West 9th
Street. Thanks! Reward: One wood"
```

I moved the cursor down until I reached the bottom of the list, where further instructions awaited.

> "Select your Quest, or press A for the next page, B
> to submit your own, C for Q-mail or Esc to quit."

That MetroCard receipt Quest seemed easy, so I went to hit 1, but before I could, it blinked out of existence and everything moved up one slot. The old number two seemed stupid and the new number two too precise, so I quickly hit 3 and pressed enter, as I wanted to go to the Market anyway to get some vegan sushi. The Quest list faded, except for my selection, and a new message appeared:

> "Remember your Quest. Skylarose101 is counting on
> you, JadePhoenix42!"

With that exhortation, the Quest Board dissolved and I was left alone again in the dark. But only for a moment. In another blink, all the screens were back on and my stupid company wasn't going to kill me after all. I put a reminder in my phone for tomorrow's trip-sorry, Quest!-to Chelsea Market, grabbed my bag, and headed home, a new skip in my step, ready to grind my way to the top of whatever this crazy thing was. I was JadePhoenix42, reborn again.

CHAPTER TWO

GIRLS WHO
QUEST

"The natives called this island 'Manna-hatta,' the Island of Many Hills.
A more appropriate name would have been the Island of Many Secrets."

The dragon bowed before my might, the sword an extension of myself. I moved it with the fluidity of a dancer, the swiftness of a hummingbird, and the strength of an ox. The sword tore into the dragon's flesh, yellow blood bursting out, drenching the stone floor of the castle tower. The blood-stained weapon fell from my hands, and it clanged against the cold stones. I felt my knees go weak as I too fell to the ground.

When I opened my eyes, the rat was dead and the blood-smeared shovel next to it. I didn't want to look at what I had wrought in the alleyway, the carnage I had unleashed for the sake of a few tokens. No, I wanted to leave the shovel and the dead rat and retreat back upstairs to the comfort of my railroad apartment. But I knew I couldn't. It would be a waste.

I regretted taking the Quest immediately.

"Kill a rat with a shovel," it said. "Reward: three wood tokens, but make sure you bring the rat to Washington Square Park within 15 minutes after you kill it or I don't want it."

The first time I read it, it seemed like a win-win. There was a rat that lived in the alleyway next to my building and there was a shovel that the super usually left in the lobby. I would throw some leftovers into the alley, lure the rat out into the open, and then smash its stupid head open, ridding me of the anxiety that surfaced every time I heard that clash of claws on concrete and earning me some tokens in the process.

Then I accepted the Quest and everything changed. I suddenly remembered that I went running the other way when I saw so much as an ant and had the athletic skills and coordination of a manatee to boot. There was no way I was going to stare down a disgusting rat and kill it with a shovel and carry it to Washington Square Park within 15 minutes.

Maybe Duncan could do it. I mean, that's what boyfriends are for, right? But he was in Hong Kong (again) raising money for his boss's newest fund. As he had been for much of our relationship.

We met at work actually. He and one of the fund's senior partners had come to the office two years ago to meet the engineering team as the initial part of their due diligence. There were only three engineers on the team then: me, Russ, and Andrew, who earned a PhD in comp sci from CalTech at 21. What he was doing at our rinky-dink startup I still wasn't sure.

Duncan and the senior partner impressed upon us that they made a point of investing in "diverse" companies and I was going to say that one white girl and nine white dudes hardly constituted diversity, but thought better of it and kept my mouth shut. As they made their rounds through the three rows of desks, Duncan kept turning his head back at me when he thought I wasn't looking. I proceeded to look away so that our eyes wouldn't meet, then eventually ran off to the bathroom to avoid further interaction.

When I emerged 30 minutes later, Duncan was gone. He had, however, left his business card under my keyboard, with a short note scrawled at the bottom:

"Going to be a pass, sorry, but ditching Bret to grab a drink tonight at Rigby's if you're not inclined to pass on me ;)"

As far as pick-up lines went, it was pretty terrible. But I hadn't had a date in months and we were just out of another crunch period, so I wasn't surprised later when my feet carried me west on that rainy evening to Chelsea instead of east to the subway.

The bar was packed when I arrived, and by the time I weaved my way through the thronging masses to Duncan, there was a drink waiting in front of the empty stool next to him.

"Macallan 12, neat," he said, gesturing to the drink.

I locked eyes with him and then at the drink, before picking it up and swirling the brown liquid around counterclockwise.

"Trying to see if I poisoned you?"

I stopped the glass, the scotch cresting against the side and spilling slightly over the breech.

"No, just pondering why I am here, in this bar, contemplating a sip of a scotch that I absolutely hate, with you, who seemed more interested in doing due diligence on what's underneath my sweater. Honestly, did you spend your entire time at RPGLab staring at me?"

I put the glass down and slid it toward the bar, waving over the bartender.

"Laphroaig 25, on the rocks, and put it on his tab, please."

The bartender obliged, and a few moments later, I sipped my new cold scotch.

"You know," said Duncan with a grin, "it's rude to drink without cheers-ing first."

I stared at him, debating whether to chew him out again or to go along with the banter. I chose the latter.

"You're right, how rude of me. What should we toast to?"

Duncan thought for a minute before he raised his glass towards mine.

"To not missing out on a promising investment," he said.

Our glasses clinked and I took a sip. The whiskey burned my throat as it went down, enough to make me forget for a second Duncan's second lame attempt at a pick-up line. I began to reply and that was when a cab drove right through a huge puddle behind me, the resulting wake drenching me from head to toe.

I was still outside the bar. Duncan, inside.

Our conversation: within the confines of my head.

I had not actually gone in, but had stopped to look through the window of the bar, trying to work up the courage to walk in and make the bold entrance that had just played out in my mind.

Duncan turned toward the window and I darted out of his view. Whatever courage remained had been washed away by the dirty rain water wave. And so I retreated.

The next day, I was in the middle of debugging the new inventory APIs when I felt a tap on my shoulder. I swiveled to see Duncan, who had grabbed a chair and was sitting directly behind me. I yelped.

"W-what are you doing here?" I stammered out. "Don't you know it's rude to sneak up on someone?"

Duncan chuckled.

"And don't you know it's rude to stand someone up? I had to cook up a really good explanation for my boss as to why I couldn't take the early flight out this morning."

I stood up and stared down at Duncan, trying to gain control by talking down to him as so many men had done to me.

"It doesn't count as standing someone up if the invitation was unsolicited and not accepted. You're the one who chose to wait there, not knowing if I was going to come. Which I couldn't, because I was here last night until 12:30 making up the work I could have been doing if we didn't have to spend three days getting a build ready for you and Bret. For all the good that did anyway, seeing as how you're more interested in me than my code."

I cringed at that last line. Not only because it made me sound like a 16-year-old, but also because my boss would be furious if he found out I told off a potential investor.

There was a silence between us for only a few moments, but it dragged on for what seemed like ages. Then Duncan got up from his chair and we stood, facing each other eye to eye.

"You're right. I shouldn't have presumed anything and it was wrong of me to come back here after you clearly weren't interested in me." His eyes shifted from mine to the floor, and then back again. I considered him again during this moment of vulnerability. He was cute in a used-to-be-dorky-in-high-school-but-then-became-an-investment-banker-sort-of-way. His dirty blond hair was an unkempt mess and I didn't really like the sweater-vest/button-down combo he was rocking, but he had done what a lot of guys would never do: admit that he had made a mistake. I decided to relieve him of some of his guilt.

"Well," I said. "You weren't completely wrong."

Our actual first date did not go down like I had imagined it. He insisted on buying me a proper dinner and we ended up closing the place down. Then, the next day, in what would be an annoying pattern that still persisted to this day, Duncan left town. He did come back, but never for more than a week or two at a time. He even convinced his boss to throw in a bit of money in the end. And so our relationship had proceeded at a glacial pace, despite it being a year and a half that we'd "officially" been together.

So he was not there when I (eventually) decided to confront the dragon. I took the leftovers from my fridge, grabbed the shovel from the lobby, and then waited in the alley for the beast to appear. It did, and my first attempts were not pretty. The rat was quicker than I expected, it ignored the food, and the super's shovel was too heavy, so that every time I swung, the little bastard just scurried away. I discarded my coat for added mobility, leaving me in the alley with nothing but a ratty old t-shirt, but the increased speed was not enough. Eventually I just chucked the shovel blindly, hoping that the vermin wouldn't expect a flying projectile attack, but the shovel just skirted harmlessly across the pavement. This Quest was going to get the best of me, it seemed.

I collapsed to the ground, exhausted. As I did though, the locket around my neck fell free from my t-shirt. It had been my mother's and she had given it to me for my 11th birthday as my sole present. At the time I thought it was a pretty terrible gift, but now she was gone and I just had the locket.

That's when it hit me. You couldn't just give the dragon some crappy food and expect it to turn away so you could stab it in the back. No, it wanted something valuable, something special. And suddenly I realized what I had to do.

I unclasped the locket from around my neck and held it in my hands. It was silver, the size of a dollar coin, and the clasp had long since rusted over. I don't remember if I opened it at the time my mother gave it to me and if I had, its contents were now lost in my memory along with the rest of my childhood.

The rat's squeak interrupted my reminiscing and I refocused on the task at hand. It was now or never. I skipped the locket down the alley like a stone on a lake. The sound it made bouncing against the pavement made me cringe. Was this even worth it?

My opponent didn't care about my moral crisis and finally emerged from the shadows. It studied the locket for a few seconds before deciding that it was more appetizing than the actual food offering I had made earlier and sunk its teeth into the silver.

With cat-like stealth, I crept along the alley walls to my discarded shovel, grabbed it in-stride, and with one last lunge brought the head down into the rodent's flesh. It was over.

But not really. The rat corpse needed transporting, and there was the matter of retrieving my locket from the jaws of the dead creature. So I did what any normal 27-year old woman did on a Tuesday night: I stuck my hand in a rat's mouth and pulled.

CHAPTER THREE

KANSAS CITY SHUFFLE

"We bought the island for the equivalent of 60 guilders,
an absolute bargain."

There was not enough silver polish in the world to remove the rat essence from my mother's locket and after the 14th time I had buffed every arc and curve, I contemplated shutting it away in a drawer with the three stupid tokens it had earned me.

But I couldn't and back it went around my neck. One day soon I hoped not to remember in crystal-clear detail what I had gone through to get it back, but that day had not yet come.

The momentary burst of courage I felt when I faced down the rat hadn't taken root and so I was skittish in my selection of the next few Quests, staying within the safe parameters of fetching tchotchkes from random stores around town. It was boring and I knew it, but I couldn't bring myself to venture outside of my Questing comfort zone.

Besides, what was the point of this whole exercise? I was still half-convinced that this was an elaborate marketing campaign for some new game (maybe even my own company's) and if so, I probably wouldn't even have cared. Any game that spent this much on advertising was probably going to be something incredible. Or a PR nightmare. "Woman sues gaming company after catching rabies from rat." Heh.

But I was growing tired of the fetch Quests for random junk. And I was tired of watching my stack of wooden and iron tokens grow taller bit by bit with absolutely no idea of what to do with them. Fortunately, good things come to those who wait, because one night when I went to check the Quests, there was a new section:

```
"D. Quester Profile"
```

I hit D and a new screen appeared:

```
"Quester: JadePhoenix42
Quests completed: 11
Tokens earned: 23 wood, 2 iron
Level: 1
Token experience: 27
Level up: 30"
```

Now we're talking! If there's one thing that will get someone to keep playing a game, it's the sense of making progress. It doesn't matter if it's steps on an endless, meaningless ladder, people will continue to climb even after their fingers are numb and their wallets are empty.

It's one of the directives we received from the higher-ups at work: keep the fish coming back for more.

And now they had a hook in me too. As much as I wanted to think that I was immune to such tactics, in truth it activated the same dopamine trigger in my brain like everyone else. Show me that I'm three experience away from the next level and I'll play all night to get there.

I clicked from the profile screen to the Quest list to look for something that would get me there in one hit: either a three wood for three experience or a two iron for four. I scrolled through several pages, looking for the perfect Quest that would elevate me. Finally, on the fifth page, I found one that stood apart from all the others:

```
"Testing out a new shell game in Times Square. If
you win, or even if you don't, I'll give you two
iron. Come by the northwest corner of 47th and
Broadway tomorrow at 2 PM."
```

I clicked quickly to accept. Two iron for losing at an obvious con game was a no-brainer, and I didn't want anyone to grab it first. Plus, I would actually get to meet a fellow Quester in the flesh.

Eleven Quests in and I still hadn't made contact with the people whose Quests I had completed, or Requesters, as I had dubbed them. My standard operating procedure was to have the token sent to the front desk of my office building, which was 70 stories tall and afforded me anonymity from potentially crazy Requesters.

I had to sweet talk the security guy to be on the lookout for envelopes addressed to JadePhoenix42. It took a bunch of cups of coffee, plus some borderline flirting, but he finally agreed. I'm sure he thought the whole thing was a poor attempt at covering up a pot delivery, but thankfully he never opened any of the envelopes. And, after all, this was Manhattan, the land where people hired other people to do every menial task they couldn't be bothered with.

Now I know the Quest said that win or lose, I would still get the two iron, but that didn't stop me from looking up all ways to win the shell game or its cousin, three-card monte.

You could just refuse to play the game, knowing that you were going to be cheated, but that didn't seem appropriate. You could delusionally convince yourself that you could follow the correct shell all the way to the end, but somewhere along the way you would miss the trick and lose everything. Or, you could just trust your fate to the goddess of chance and guess a shell at random. That seemed to be the best option at the end of the day.

I sat at my desk all morning, watching the minutes tick by, until finally it was 1:30, and I darted out to the subway. When I got to the Times Square station, I bounded up the stairs and into the madness of thousands of people looking up at giant billboards while walking very slowly. Finally, I arrived at the designated corner. Which was empty. I looked at my watch and then at my phone to make sure I wasn't late. I wasn't. In fact, it was precisely 2:00 on the dot. I pulled out my phone again, trying to access the Quest Board to see if I had misread the Quest when I suddenly felt something sharp push into my back.

I turned and looked down, half expecting to see a bloody knife sticking out of me, but it was just a cardboard box. A sharp box at that, but still only a box. Phew. I stepped back as the box was lowered to the ground by its owner, who I could now see was a young girl who couldn't have been more than 12.

"Oh, hey! Sorry about that! Are you Jade?" the girl asked cheerfully. She was on the shorter side, with blond hair done up in pigtails, big gold hoops in her ears, and a denim knapsack on her back.

"Umm, yeah, that's me, and you are?"

"I'm Polly!"

The girl stuck out her hand, which I reluctantly took, and she gave me a vigorous handshake.

"Of course you are," I said. "Aren't you a little, err, young to be trying to scam people out here? I was expecting someone who looked a little more like your typical grifter. You know, worn face, missing teeth, poorly made leather jacket."

She frowned, and let go of my hand.

"I'm not so young, I'll be 11 next week!"

"OK, OK, sorry I asked. And happy birthday I guess. So, are you going to show me this trick of yours, or what? I need to head back to work soon."

Polly bent down to push the box toward the Starbucks near the corner and I walked with her as she positioned it just so.

"Yes, yes, have a little patience, lady. I need a few minutes to set up."

Polly plopped down her backpack on the box and began rummaging inside. I tried to look away to avoid the passing judgment of the Starbucks patrons filtering in and out of the store, but no one seemed to pay any attention to us.

"So, Polly. You been Questing long?"

The girl looked up at me as if I was her grandma asking how to use an iPhone.

"Whatever gave you the idea that I was *that* desperate?"

"Well, uh, because you're posting Quests on the Board?"

"Right, exactly. I'm paying you. Not the other way around. If one day we ran out of money then I gueesssss I would have to start from the bottom like you. But if that ever happens, shoot me. Can you imagine, me, a Janssen, Questing? Ridiculous."

Ohhh-kay then. Obviously what I thought was a simple question was actually laced with insulting underpinnings. This girl's family was evidently a big deal in the Questing social circle, but what that circle even was, I had no clue, and was a tiny bit scared to ask more. I didn't get the chance though, as Polly had finished setting up, and on the cardboard box were three identical shells, painted in bright pink. In front of them was a little blue ball that I guessed fit under the shells.

"All right, Jade. Time to play. Now, I'm not sure if I got all the kinks out, so that's why I'm giving you two iron even if you lose. Which you probably will, just going to warn you."

"I know, don't worry about my ego. So how do I play?"

Polly smiled.

"Easy. I'm going to put the ball under one of these shells, like so." She covered the ball with the leftmost shell. "Then I'll shuffle all the shells around." Her hands deftly swapped the leftmost and rightmost shells, then further swapped the rightmost shell, which had the ball, with the middle shell. "And now you guess under which shell the ball is hiding. This first one's easy, so you should get it ... if you're not a total idiot."

"Thanks for the vote of confidence. The middle one." I tapped it twice with my index finger for extra emphasis and she turned it over, revealing the ball.

"Very good! Well, not really. That's the warm-up, the one you do to show the mar-errr, contestant that they have a chance. Now I'll speed it up a bit, to see what you've got."

Polly put the ball back under the middle shell and then began swapping at random with blazing speed. Sometimes she would move the shell to a different spot; other times, she would move it right back to where it was. Luckily my years of gaming had trained my eyes well and I spotted all of her feints and swaps with relative ease. So when the shells stopped and I pointed to the left one, I wasn't surprised to see the ball underneath.

"Well done, lady. Most people usually can't follow me that quickly. I think it's time, though, for the real game to begin."

The ball disappeared back under the left shell and off it went. The speed was even greater and I felt myself losing the ball several times. It was then that I noticed the tell. To move the shell with the ball required just a little more energy, which Polly's hand betrayed ever so slightly. With that piece of intel, I stopped watching the shells and focused only on Polly's hands. But when I confidently tapped the rightmost shell at the end of the round, it was empty.

"Ooh, so close. Care to go again?"

I cursed under my breath. I was not going to let this little punk best me so easily.

"Yes, let's do it."

This time I had the benefit of my hidden edge the whole round and, again, I felt sure that I had tapped the correct shell, only to come up empty-handed a second time.

"Again," I said.

Polly just smiled as the shells began their dance anew.

Finally, after countless more rounds, I relented.

"Enough, enough. You are something else."

"Why thank you Jade," said Polly with a smile dripping in condescension. "You were watching my hands, weren't you? That's smart, but it won't do you any good with these particular shells."

"And why's that?"

"Oh come now. If I told you that, I'd have to kill you, now wouldn't I?"

I stared at her as she made her pronouncement with a matter-of-fact tone.

"Just kidding. Geez, can't you take a joke? Tell you what, I'll make you a deal. If you can win the next round, I'll not only show you how the shells work, but I'll double your tokens. If you lose, you get nothing, plus you'll owe me a favor. Do we have a deal?"

I didn't give it a second thought.

"Done."

CHAPTER FOUR

THE TIES THAT BIND

"Then the English sailed four ships into the harbor and took it from us. We crushed their navy in response, but let them keep the island anyway in exchange for some nutmeg trees halfway around the world. You tell me who got the better deal."

I read too many stories growing up about naive would-be heroes, who think they can outwit a demigod or a mischievous dwarf or some other creature but only end up indebted and forced into their service. Even knowing that, I still agreed to Polly's terms.

"Ooh, I like your style, Jade. Most people would at least ask what the favor is first before agreeing, but you're bold. Anyway, here we go."

I didn't think it was possible, but Polly's hands moved even faster this time and I could barely keep up as the shells whirled around and around. I tried looking at her hands and the shells at the same time to keep track, but it was no use, and I resigned myself to owing this little girl what was hopefully a minor favor, like pretending to be her older sister to get her out of school early. As the shells slowed though, I noticed a new pattern in her hands. I could still see the extra exertion in one hand, but as the shells swapped places, so too did the tell. It was as if she was throwing the ball between shells, the receiving hand straining just a bit as the other hand relaxed. I watched the pattern repeat itself until finally Polly stopped and the shells were displayed in front of me to choose.

"The middle one," I said.

Polly's cheerful demeanor faded in an instant, as she uncovered the shell to reveal the ball.

"Well, I'll be darned. You won. I don't believe it."

I smiled.

"Neither do I. Now pay up, please."

Polly bent down to dig something out of her backpack and then set two iron tokens on the box.

"Where are the other two?"

"See, the thing is, I never expected you to win the double-or-nothing and so I don't have the other two."

"Well then, I think that you are now in the position of owing me a favor."

Polly frowned.

"I don't give out favors willy nilly, especially not for this small a debt. Come back here tomorrow and I'll have your tokens."

"No, I don't think so. How about this: I'll forgive the debt, but after you show me how your little game works, I get to ask you one question and you have to answer it truthfully."

We stared at each other while Polly considered my offer. Several times she opened her mouth as if she were about to say something, only to stop short. I was half-expecting a lucrative offer to play the game again, but I think she was scared that I had actually deduced the secret. Finally, she sighed and started flipping over the shells.

"The thing about you noobs-you're a noob, aren't you?-is that you think this is all a game out of some Rumpelstiltskin fairy tale. Well, it's not. And ordinarily, there's no way I'd agree to answer your question. But I'm a Janssen and we keep our word. Plus, I still can't believe you won, so I'll indulge you. Now, watch closely."

Polly tapped the two outer shells together, and then took the ball and dropped it in the left shell. She stood back with her hands in her pockets. I bent forward and looked into it, only to find nothing there.

"Try the right one," said Polly.

I looked in that one and there was the ball.

"But, you didn't … how?"

"Watch again." Polly took the ball out of the right shell, tapped the center and right shells together, and then put the ball back in the right shell. I peered into the right shell and it was now empty. Instead, the middle one held the ball.

"It's some sort of false bottom, right? You tap the shells together to open it?"

Polly shook her head.

"Any ol' person could do that, Jade. You should know better than… oh. I see."

"What?"

"What level are you?"

"Umm, err."

I didn't want to admit that the girl was right and that I was a noob. Nothing was more embarrassing than being that player who had no idea what they're doing and who stumbled around like a fool, playing the game so poorly that their own teammates try to off them so they didn't get in the way. But I knew so little as it was and if I tried to pass myself off as someone more experienced, I was certain that Polly would not tell me anything at all.

"So, I'm about to be level two, once you give me the tokens. I've only been Questing for a few weeks though."

Polly hit her forehead with her palm.

"Unbelievable. Lost to a friggin' baby noob." The girl shook her head, and a look of disgust formed on her face. "Look, I'm still going to show you how the trick actually works, but just tell me how you won. Tell me it was blind luck and I'll sleep a little better tonight."

I told her how I noticed the muscles in her hand flex and relax as the ball moved from one shell to the other and she nodded, a slight smile on her face.

"All right, I'm sorry I called you a noob. You clearly have some clue what you're doing and next time I do this, I definitely need to wear gloves. And, you're not entirely wrong about the false bottom. But, there's only one ball. Here, hold these."

Polly handed me the middle and right shells after fishing the ball out first. I looked inside them but didn't see anything out of the ordinary.

"Tap them together."

I did, and felt a tingling sensation in my hands, as if the shells were now connected with an invisible tether.

"Now, here comes the important part."

Polly flicked the ball into middle shell with a graceful throw and I caught it, only it never arrived at the bottom of the shell. Instead, I looked down into the right shell to see the ball rolling lazily around the bottom.

"Impossible. How … you couldn't have … I mean, I saw the ball go into the middle shell."

I held the shells in my hand, the tension between them gone. Without asking first, I quickly tapped them together, and the tension returned but just as quickly faded.

"Look in the middle shell again."

I did and there was the ball. I tapped them together again and the ball went to the other shell. To an outside observer, I must have looked like a crazy person, tapping shells together next to a middle schooler.

"You done or do you want to wear a hole in them? Those weren't cheap, you know."

I handed the shells back to Polly, who put them back on the box.

"I give up," I said. "How does it work?"

"Well," said Polly, "not sure I should actually be telling you, given your level. I mean, the Council came up with those for a reason. But, a promise is a promise, I guess."

She turned the shells on their side so the insides faced me, and then tapped two of them together. The formerly opaque bottoms had changed somehow, a silvery circle in their place.

"Promise you won't scream?" she asked me. I nodded quickly, not wanting to miss out on what she was about to show me.

"OK then. Stick your finger in one all the way to the bottom."

I stuck my index finger into the bottom of one shell, only to see it emerge from the other one several inches away. As if not believing what I was seeing, my brain told my finger to move, and the floating finger tip obliged.

I broke my promise and screamed.

CHAPTER FIVE

LEVEL UP

"The English, in their stupidity, let us stay. We've been paying
them back for that favor ever since."

There are moments in my life that are so vivid, I only need to close my eyes and think briefly about them before all the details come flooding up to the surface.

Me locked in the middle school bathroom, sobbing for hours.

My mother's body draped in a sheet on the morgue table.

There were others, too few of them happy.

And now, I would have to add this one to the list.

The next thing I remembered was Polly grabbing my wrist and pulling it away from the shell, as if I was a child who had touched a hot stove. I brought my hand up to my face and wiggled my index finger to make sure that it was still attached. It was. But before I could dwell on the stunning development of the magic shells, Polly began pulling me down the street.

"W-what are you doing?"

I yanked myself free and we continued walking away from the corner.

"What does it look like I'm doing? Getting us the hell out of there. You promised you wouldn't scream, remember?"

"I did, but you could have warned me!"

We walked to a grocery store at the end of the block and I followed Polly inside. Only when we had reached the middle of the cereal aisle did Polly finally stop and set down her bag, into which she tossed the shells.

"I didn't think I needed to. It looked like you had figured it out on your own."

"You said it yourself though; I'm newer than a noob; how was I supposed to know that you somehow created a tiny rip in the fabric of the space-time continuum?"

"The what?"

"You know, a wormhole."

Polly shook her head.

"I don't know what the heck you're talking about. It's just some vervorium painted on the bottom of each shell."

Oh, of course. Some vervorium painted on the shells. Her tone made it sound like she was describing how to make a sandwich.

"I don't mean to sound like an idiot, but what is vervorium, exactly?"

"Vervorium, Jade, is a very rare but incredibly useful prima materia used to link two places together. It's hard to make and you need a lot of ingredients. Like the spleen of a freshly killed rat, for one."

She did it again. Prima materia. Available in your local bodega next to a can of chili.

"So that was you I was delivering the rat to?"

Polly smirked.

"Nope. This vervorium I stol-err, borrowed from my dad. Whoever wanted your rat was someone else and not necessarily to make vervorium. Rats are very useful. We keep a ton in our garage."

A clerk walked by with a cart full of cereal and we headed in the opposite direction towards the freezer section. I tried to process these new revelations and wanted to ask a million more questions. Was this real magic? Or some incredibly complex science that had been concealed from the world by a select few? At some level, it didn't really matter, as one of my favorite authors, Arthur C. Clarke, had once opined, "any sufficiently advanced technology is indistinguishable from magic." Polly still owed me the answer to one question, so I wracked my brain for one that would reveal the most information.

"All right, time for my question." We stopped in front of a case of frozen fish sticks. "So the Quests are just some cheap labor to fetch ingredients for your magic potions, is that it?"

I had formulated my inquiry with just the right level of ridiculousness in the hopes that Polly would relish the opportunity to disabuse me of my misconceptions by talking too much. But to my disappointment, she did not take the bait.

"No," was all she replied. I waited for more but she suddenly turned quiet and began drawing doodles on the freezer case.

"That's it?" I said.

"Look, uhh, I've already told you way too much for a level one. Here's your iron. Good luck to you." She forced the tokens into my hand and then ran off before I could say anything more. For a second I contemplated chasing her out of the store, but realized the optics of that were abysmal and would likely get me arrested.

I kicked myself for asking too big of a question. There was clearly something greater going on here than just a bunch of random fetching;

my finger tip floating in mid-air was proof of that, but all that I had to go on was a bunch of tokens, a crazy message board, and an even crazier story about a teleporting ball.

With a sigh, I started to walk out of the store when something on the freezer case caught my attention. What I had thought were mere doodles were actually numbers, six numbers in fact, separated in the middle by a period. It read "949.278."

I stared at them, trying to figure out what they could mean, then kicked myself for not recognizing the sequence immediately. After all, I had spent every summer since I was 15 through college working in the Borough Park Library. I could hear my old boss Ms. Bakadet's voice in the back of my mind, berating me for not remembering the Dewey Decimal classification for 17th century Celtic literature, and I couldn't imagine how many months of stack duty she would have assigned me for my transgression just now.

But thanks to those hours she spent hammering into my brain every single Dewey Decimal number, I was sure I could figure out at least part of this one without resorting to what Ms. Bakadet referred to as the "idiot terminal."

900 was history. 940 was the history of Europe. 949 was the catch-all for the random parts of Europe that people didn't care too much about. But the three numbers after the decimal remained a mystery, as there was only so much information I could store in my brain. And having not worked at the library in five years, there was no reason to remember this stuff any longer. The 2 would be the country, but which one I had no clue. The 78 would be some other topic and time period as it related to this country, though again I was stumped.

I pulled out my phone to cheat, only to be bombarded with a flurry of Slack messages. Evidently, Ross, Russ's replacement, had picked up Russ's bad habit of fixing one bug by introducing two more. I quickly answered that I was on my way back from a doctor's appointment and ran out of the store, but not before snapping a picture of the cryptic numerals and then wiping the glass clean.

It took me the rest of the afternoon and well into the evening to undo Ross's mishap and between that and the haunting visage of my finger that appeared whenever I closed my eyes for more than a second, I had no motivation to tread back into the world of library numbering systems. But, I still wanted to see if my level-up had gone through and so I clicked over to the Quest Board and logged in.

I took out the two iron and set them in front of my keyboard, as if offering them to the Questing gods. My profile screen loaded and a big pop-up window appeared in front.

"Congratulations! You've reached level two!" it said in fancy green script. I closed the window to check out my new stats:

```
"Quests completed: 12
Tokens earned: 23 wood, 4 iron
Level: 2
Token experience: 31
Level up: 100"
```

One hundred experience to get to level three? What the heck! It had taken me 10 weeks just to get this far. I didn't want to count how many more rats I would have to bludgeon to get close to level three. There had to be some way to take on more rewarding Quests or I would be stuck getting sneered at by the Pollys of the world for the next three years. But, to do that, I would have to get smarter on the subject of Questing.

So, the next day, on my way to work, I stopped at the midtown library to look up the mystery number. I wasn't sure how a book about the history of some random country was going to help, but I had a hunch that the decimal was chosen more for its obscurity than for its relevance to the subject matter.

My theory was spot on, as a search of the library's digital holdings yielded nothing with that number. Not a good sign. But knowing how the library system worked, I was sure that their hard-copy card catalog was lurking around the building somewhere.

After several annoyed librarians gave me conflicting answers, I finally found the six-foot tall structure in a poorly lit corner of the basement. The handwritten labels were brown and peeling, and of course the drawer I wanted was just out of my reach, so I located a rickety wooden chair, leaned it against the cabinet, and stepped up. It held.

A cloud of dust sprayed my face upon opening the relevant drawer and I began flicking through the cards. Finally, I reached 949.278 and was rewarded for my diligence. I pulled out the section number and the two cards that followed it, carefully stepped down from the chair, and took my prize over to a small table nestled between two stacks.

Someone had written the name of the section on the first card in cursive, the blue ink of the letters scrunched together so that they barely took up any space. I studied the writing several times before I could make out what it said:

"The history of Dutch settlement in North America."

That was … not what I was expecting. I looked at the other two cards, hoping the book titles would shed some light on the relevance of what was turning into a wild goose chase. But instead of titles like I was expecting, there were only numbers.

Fine, I thought. I'll just go back to the stupid computer upstairs and type in the numbers and voila, books located. But the computer failed me again, bringing back nothing at all.

Finally, I gave up and went to the reference desk. My run of luck continued, as a woman who could have been Ms. Bakadet's twin was hammering away at her keyboard when I approached. I stood in front of her, remembering my training well.

"Never interrupt a librarian mid-thought!" Ms. Bakadet had said. "She could be on the verge of locating a long-lost book that the next Nobel Prize winner needs to complete their master work!"

As much as I highly doubted that this scenario had ever occurred, I waited patiently until the clacking ceased.

"Umm, excuse me?"

The librarian turned and glared at me above the spectacles on her nose, as if it weren't her job to help people locate books.

"Yes?"

"I was wondering if you could help me locate these two books." I handed her the two cards. "I searched the regular catalog but couldn't find anything."

She snatched the cards out of my hand with the speed of a cobra.

"Where did you get these?"

"I, umm, they were in the card catalog in the basement."

"And you just decided to rummage around in the meticulously organized card catalog that dozens of librarians spent years creating and maintaining?"

Uh oh. It was becoming apparent that I had unknowingly walked into a bear trap and I needed to pull my foot free before this woman attacked me with the ferocity of a rabid dog.

"Well, uh, no. I just looked at these two cards. And I used to work at the Borough Park Library, so I know how important it-"

"Oh, so you think because you used to work in a library, you can just waltz down to our card catalog and take out cards to your heart's content?"

"No, but, umm, look, I'll just put them back, so they don't get los-"

"You will do no such thing, young lady! I don't want you anywhere near my card catalog. The fact that-"

"Look, are you going to help me or not?"

The rudeness of my question knocked the wind out of Ms. Bakadet's twin and she just stared at me, unblinking, for several seconds. Then, in what I could only chalk up to a minor miracle, she relented and began searching for the numbers on the cards on her computer.

"Hmm, I can see why these didn't come up for you. Someone must have transposed the book numbers incorrectly in the computer system. Fortunately for you, I've seen this before, or you would be out of luck. Ah, here we go. Oh."

"What happened?"

"So, I found your books. It's just that I don't know where they are."

That made not one lick of sense to me, but maybe it did in librarian speak.

"So, they're lost?"

The librarian glared at me.

"We don't lose books. These two happen to be checked out at the moment, but by who and for how long, I don't know. It might have been a week or two or 12 years. Whoever loaned these books out did us both the disservice of not properly documenting those transactions. But, I'll put you on the waitlist and when they do come back in, we'll let you know. Have a good day."

"I, uhh, OK. Thank you very much."

As much as I wanted to find out more about these missing books, I knew when I had overstayed my welcome and walked out of the library with even more questions and no answers.

CHAPTER SIX

QUESTAHOLICS ANONYMOUS

"We kept to ourselves, mostly, as the English never paid us much attention. Neither did the so-called Americans. Not that they knew the truth. If they did, maybe things would have turned out differently."

"Hi, my name is SteveSonOfSteve and I'm a Questaholic."

"Hi, Steve."

The voices echoed around the church basement, despite the small crowd seated in only one corner of the room. That other people had actually showed up quelled some of my remaining paranoia that I was the subject of a Harry Potter-obsessed lunatic's idea of an elaborate joke, but maybe everyone here was in on it too? That still wouldn't explain Polly's stupid shell, so I brushed such thoughts aside as I tried to listen to the confessional.

Steve quickly launched into a sad and sordid tale about how he had broken his clavicle falling into the Gowanus Canal while collecting moss and that after a couple of months of recuperating, he had finally attempted to complete the Quest only to fall again into the Canal. By the time he had gotten around to his sixth attempt at collecting the moss, I had largely tuned him out. Unlike the rest of the motley crew sitting in dingy chairs in the barely-lit room, I had not come to achieve catharsis. No, this was an information-gathering mission.

It had been several weeks since my visit to the library and I still hadn't received any word on the mystery books. I had a sneaking suspicion that the friendly librarian had tossed my waitlist request into the garbage and that I would never find out what Polly was trying to tell me.

Then I caught a lucky break. I should have realized after the Questing profile appeared randomly that there was more to the Board than just the Quests themselves. Because now when I opened the main menu, there was a new option, E, labeled "Q-Board."

I hit E and a new screen popped up. It was a rudimentary message board. The excitement bubbled inside me as I began scrolling through the posts. Here they were, the memoirs of the legendary heroine recounting her trials, tribulations, and defeat of the ancient evil that had ushered in this golden age of prosperity!

Or the Quest equivalent of spam. Awesome. Even membership in a secret underground magic world did little to slake humanity's innate compulsion to spam everyone else apparently. But at least I was a member of the club. And, given the lack of a Missed Connections section on the Quest Board, this spam was all I had to dive deeper.

After checking to see that no one was looking over my shoulder, I printed out each post, stuffed the papers into my purse and ran down to the Treehouse. No, it was not one of our conference rooms (ours were all named after *Final Fantasy* characters), but rather the woman's bathroom, my preferred place for silent reflection. As the rest of the engineers were arguing about some nitpick in last night's episode of *Arrow*, no one noticed as I scurried past them into the Treehouse and locked the door. Finally alone, I pulled the papers out of my purse and set them down on the marble counter to study.

There were token banks, where scrupulous individuals would watch over your tokens for free (and probably loan them out to seedy goblins played by Warwick Davis), advertisements for how-to pamphlets (where to find the most frequent Quest-requested items, creative excuses for work absences, and more), and then some of the posts had printed out completely blank as far as I could tell.

It was all very exciting. But where to start? As much as I wanted to check out the token bank, they would probably laugh me out of the room for bringing my meager hoard. I was also convinced that it was merely a cover for robbing gullible idiots. And my lack of money also made the how-to pamphlets cost-prohibitive. I was about to stuff everything back in my purse when I noticed the last piece of paper, which I thought had been blank.

"Ignoring your spouse to dumpster dive for trash behind the 7-11 at three in the morning?

Skipping work meetings to meet Quest scalpers outside Madison Square Garden?

Stealing half-eaten ice cream cones for kids because you think they're worth a couple of wood?

These aren't the signs of healthy Questing.

No, they may be the symptoms of a Questaholic.

But you're not alone.

We've been there.

And we can help.

We're Questaholics Anonymous.

Next meeting on Thursday at 700 E. 3rd St, Grace Church basement."

It was the perfect opportunity for an undercover operation because, after all, I had few tokens to my name but a lifetime of sob stories to really inject some desperation into my fake descent into Questaholism.

I tucked the papers back in my purse and perused the Quest Board on my phone for Quests I could pretend to have failed. Outside, I could hear the engineers hypothesizing what the title of *Star Wars Episode IX* should be, but inside the Treehouse, all was peaceful.

The other Questaholics drank in Steve's story, nodding at his misfortune while pretending to listen. I surveyed them as a sociologist would.

Compared to the rest of the group, Steve could pass for normal. Some were disheveled, a cocktail of odors emanating from their bodies and mixing together to form an even more horrid stench. Some stared off into space as if they were observing a parallel reality. One woman wore an empty baby carrier across her front and would from time to time pat the head of the not-there baby. I didn't have to try hard to imagine how far she had fallen off the wagon.

I soon realized that my rehearsed tale of woe was not going to be sufficient. These people were far more broken and screwed up than I was going to pretend to be or actually was. If I was going to avoid the fate of a Size 0 showing up at an Overeaters Anonymous meeting, I needed to kick it up a notch.

Luckily I ended up being last in the circle, so when it came to my turn, I had my story ready.

"Hi, my name is Jade and I'm a Questaholic."

"Hi, Jade."

"I stopped at the Park Slope Farmers' Market on my way home from work to pick up an empty lobster tail shell. Digging through piles of discarded shellfish, I found the perfect one, or so I thought. As I exited into the alley next to the seafood stand - a shortcut I had found during a previous Questing foray - I was beset upon by a band of teenagers, who circled around me with menace in their eyes. I was about to reach into my pocket to offer them my wallet, when a smile appeared on one of their faces.

'Keep your filthy norm-money, it's your tokens we're after.'

I was never one to carry my tokens on me, but I knew that wasn't going to be a satisfactory answer, so I stalled for time.

'This lobster tail shell is worth five wooden tokens if you throw it in the sewer grate on the corner of Baltic and Bond. That's all I have.'

I held out the shell with trepidation. The leader of the group walked toward me with a smile and took the offering. As he turned to walk away, I breathed a sigh of relief. But in that moment, I let my guard down and thus didn't hear his compatriot sneak up behind me. As I looked down, a gleaming serrated blade held audience with my throat, its edges just a thin gap of air away from spilling my blood.

It was then that the first ruffian turned back towards me, a glint of metal reflecting from his knuckle.

I stood there, paralyzed, as he punched me in the gut three times. The knife wielder withdrew and I collapsed to the ground, gasping for breath. Still smiling, my attacker, barely more than a boy, bent down until he was squatting in front of me.

'No one comes questing near the Market without our assistance. If I see you snooping around here without any tokens on ya, the hurt you're experiencing now will feel like a summer breeze compared to next time. Ya follow?'

I nodded slowly, which satisfied him and the rest of the group. By the time I got to my feet, they were gone."

I looked around the circle, waiting to see the group's reaction. Finally, a woman in her sixties with greying brown hair smacked her fist into her palm.

"The Council's gotta put a stop to these attacks before someone gets hurt! I'll bring a petition to the next meeting that we can all sign."

Most of the other people nodded in agreement, as I breathed a sigh of relief. But then a troubling thought bubbled up in my brain. This manufactured gang might not have been as fake as I had thought and that made my heart beat a little faster.

"Is there some sort of map charting out the safe spaces where we won't be attacked or robbed?" I asked.

If I was actually going to be set upon by marauding teens, I might as well know where the no-go zones were. The brown-haired woman's brow furrowed for a second at the question.

"Can't say that there is, but it would be a good idea to pool our findings. Let me talk to some of the other meeting groups and maybe we can't just get something whipped up."

The meeting finished soon after and I made my exit quickly after grabbing a powdered donut, lest anyone hit me up for more information about the non-existent gang.

I was nearly up the stairs to street level before Steve caught up to me.

"Interesting story back there," he said, with a hint of mockery in his voice. "If I didn't know better, I'd say you just carved yourself a nice little slice of territory where no one else is going to intrude."

My eyes widened. I hadn't even thought of that. I was just trying to sound troubled.

"I don't know what you're talkin--"

"Save it, newbie. I'm not going to rat you out to Ms. Concerned Citizen down there, but next time, try to come up with something that doesn't sound like it was taken from a bad 80's movie that you watched on cable last night."

We reached the top of the stairs and Steve starting walking away.

"Wait!" I cried. This guy obviously knew a lot and I would be stupid not to try to milk him for whatever information he would tell me. Steve stopped and turned around, and I jogged over to him.

"Look, I'm only a level 2 and honestly I just want to know more about what the hell this whole thing is. An iron for your story? I'll throw in the first drink too."

I held out the token in my palm and stood there in silence while he considered my offer. I only had four iron, but this seemed like a good use of the tokens. Plus I really had no idea at this point what else I would spend them on. Finally, Steve shook his head and pushed my hand away.

"Keep your tokens. Don't need 'em. But," he said, giving me a look up and down with a creepy smile that made the hair on the back of my neck stand on end, "I do need a drink and some company after the day I've had."

On second thought, maybe this wasn't such a good idea. Did he think I was hitting on him in a weird roundabout way or something? Gross.

But then that stupid shell flashed in my mind again. I had to know more, even if it meant enduring the stares of this creepazoid for a few hours.

CHAPTER SEVEN

TALES FROM THE CANTINA

*"When the war broke out, we didn't want to get involved.
The Guild had played both sides for so long, why take a risk now?"*

After the third subway transfer, I was beginning to suspect that letting Steve pick the bar had not been a good idea. When we finally walked down from the train platform at Ditmars Boulevard in Astoria, it had taken the better part of the evening and despite the long trip, Steve had barely said a word to me.

"Where exactly are we going?" I said, finally breaking the silence. Steve ignored me and we continued weaving through the crowded sidewalk, passing one bar after the other. He abruptly turned off the main drag onto a side street, where he quickened his pace. I followed, but my danger radar was about to reach its boiling point.

Thankfully, we had finally reached our destination: a three-story brick building with a boarded up storefront. Someone had tagged the boards with black spray paint and the second floor windows were all dark. So much for a night out at a trendy cocktail lounge.

"Look, I'm sorry if I gave you the wrong idea, but there's no way I'm stepping foot in your apartment. Why don't we just go back to one of the 15 bars we already walked by?"

Steve ignored me and hit a buzzer next to the door, which after a few seconds swung open on its own accord.

"You coming or not?" he asked.

Not waiting for my response, he walked into the building.

I could have walked away then. It would only have cost me a wasted evening. But, against my better judgment, I ran to the door before it swung shut. The interior opened almost immediately into a set of stairs dimly lit by rusty light fixtures that lined the walls and Steve was already close to the top landing. I caught up to him and saw that there was someone else there, a woman who looked to be in her seventies, sitting on a metal folding chair.

She would not have looked out of place at the Questaholics Anonymous meeting, her grey hair bushy and unwashed, a pair of reading glasses dangling from a chain around her neck. If she and Steve knew each other, they didn't acknowledge it. Steve pressed onward through a red door at the end of a short hallway and I followed, the woman paying no mind to me either. I hoped they weren't paying her a lot to be the bouncer because she was doing a terrible job.

The red door swung backward after Steve went through and I paused to let it rebound before pushing it back. If what waited for me on the other side was some sort of torture dungeon, at least I would be able to quickly escape.

But all of my trepidation vanished, as I stepped foot into a crowded, noisy bar. I blinked, waiting for the illusion to vanish, but it didn't.

In contrast to the woman outside, all of the people here looked, dare I say, normal. The bar itself was in the center of the room, a huge square manned by four bartenders who were efficiently serving up drinks to the dozens of patrons on all sides. A balcony ringed the room above, with tables spaced around a metal railing. If I hadn't just spent the last 90 minutes trekking across the city to a random, abandoned-looking building, I would have thought it was indistinguishable from the bars I frequented in my post-college, finally-on-her-own-in-the-big-city days.

Steve walked past the bar to a small spiral staircase that led up to the balcony. The upper level was quieter, the crowd from downstairs evidently not preferring the intimate tables. We sat down at one of them and the long journey finally was over.

I waved over a waitress so I could fulfill my promise to buy the first round, only to realize that I had no idea if I even had enough tokens to cover one drink.

"Umm, Steve, I know I said I would get the first round, but uhh, how many tokens does a drink usually cost?"

Steve snickered.

"Where do you think we are? Some secret Quester bar?" He shook his head. "This is just a regular bar pretending to be a Prohibition-era speakeasy. Only difference is the extra $2 a drink for the 'ambiance.'"

The waitress arrived and we gave her our order. Now that I knew we were no place special, I held my Quest talk until she had dropped off the drinks a few minutes later.

"Oh. But, if this is just some random bar, then why did you make me trek all the way out here?"

"Been meaning to try this place and wasn't sure they would let me in without a pretty face."

He grinned and I shuddered internally. Did he think that was a compliment?

"So, Jade, why were you at the meeting? I thought I was the only one who liked to feel better about myself by listening to those sob stories."

"Wait, so you didn't break your clavicle trying to get some moss?"

"Of course not. It just sounds so pathetic and, to be honest, most people don't know what a clavicle is, which means I don't have to show up to the meeting in a fake cast."

"Oh."

This guy was turning into a real scumbag, but I tried not to let my disgust show.

"Got it. So you just Quest as a hobby, or...?"

Steve took a sip of his drink, put the glass back down, and then began stirring the tiny little straw in a clockwise rotation.

"Something like that. Let's just say that my father, also a Steve if you hadn't figured that out from my handle, was so wildly successful in certain pursuits that we wouldn't have to Quest for several generations even if we spent our tokens like a bunch of drunken sailors in a whorehouse."

This conversation was leaving me more and more confused by the minute. Unless there was a whole underground economy run on tokens, what was the point of stockpiling these things when we were living in the real world and needed real money to pay for our real world needs, like food and shelter for instance?

"Right, right," I said, as if I knew what I was talking about. "I wish I didn't have to Quest, but my parents wanted nothing to do with me after high school, so now I'm starting from square one."

The lie was believable, or so I thought. I had already given away too much, I realized, when I asked Steve for help, but I thought that he might tell me more if he thought I was one of them, a member of the Questing fraternity, rather than some random person who opened an email one night.

"That's a shame," he said. "I couldn't imagine if my kid had to work her way up from the bottom. Not that a little hard work wouldn't do her some good, mind you, but I'll bet it's been tough out there since they opened the floodgates."

"What do you mean?"

"You must have noticed, or maybe you hadn't, because you're so new, but it didn't used to be like this."

"Like what?"

"Quests done for a couple of wood. Not to sound like an old man, but when I was a kid, there weren't any wood tokens. They started at iron, and a Quester wouldn't walk out the door for less than 20 iron. And that was for something basic. Now that the Council has brought in so much riff-raff, the bottom fell out, and you can source pretty much anything for a few wood."

Steve paused to finish his drink in one long sip and then flagged down the waitress for a second Old Fashioned, which she brought over quickly. It was always a good sign when someone got so agitated that they felt like drinking more; it meant that I was on the right track and just needed to keep needling.

"But people aren't just going to keep Questing for wood, right? I mean, what good are they if they're not even worth so much experience?"

"Experience. Ha! Another recent invention by the Council. They thought that making the whole thing like a game, peeling things back level by level, would help them find what they are looking for. But no, all it's gotten them is that motley crew in the church basement. A bunch of people who couldn't find the Philosopher's Stone if it was lying on the ground in front of them."

So I wasn't so far off in thinking this whole thing was a huge manipulation of everyone's dopamine triggers. I would have found the whole thing diabolical if I wasn't so impressed with the execution.

"So what is the Council looking for?" I asked. I didn't know who or what the Council was, but it seemed like the next logical question.

Steve took a big swig of his second drink and then perused the drink specials placard on our table until the waitress walked by.

"Two grogs, please," he told her, which, according to the menu, was a drink that contained one or more of the following: rum, cider, beer head, pineapple whiskey, lemon juice, water, cinnamon, and red dye #2. It sounded disgustingly sweet, the kind of drink that would give you a hangover before the night was over.

"What are they looking for? That's easy. New blood."

The grogs arrived in big glass mugs with intricately decorated handles. I had barely touched my scotch, as I wanted to maintain my facilities during this conversation, so I hoped that the grog wasn't too strong. The bartender must have put in copious amounts of red dye #2 (which I thought was a joke) because the liquid was a shimmering red.

"Cheers," said Steve as he raised his mug towards me. I clinked mine in response and we both took a sip of the grog.

Imagine the most foul concoction of spirits, beer, and wine and then multiply that by 30 and you still wouldn't be halfway to how bad this tasted. For all the simpleness of the ingredients, it felt like the liquid was going to burn a hole in my esophagus, if it didn't eat through the glass first.

"New blood for what though? To go on epic Quests?"

"Epic Quests, ha. Just the Council trying to be creative. You know how many lifetimes it would take to get 185 gold tokens? I've never even met someone who had one. No, the Council's goal is much simpler."

Somehow Steve had already drunk the entire mug of grog and was eyeing mine lustily. I wanted to pour the whole thing into his glass, but we weren't close enough for that yet. I also wanted him to get to the point of this conversation before I lost it. It was like he was taking long sips on purpose to avoid getting to the climax.

"What?" I asked.

"To find more magic."

CHAPTER EIGHT

SUFFICIENTLY ADVANCED TECHNOLOGY

"But war makes strange bedfellows and too many of our number threw in with the British. So the rest had no choice but to help the new Americans."

"I'm sorry, what?"

Steve hiccuped, his cheeks alcohol red.

"S-surely your parents showed you-BWAAAP!"

The sound and the smell of the loud burp made me cringe. I looked around to see if anyone was paying attention to us, but thankfully, we remained safely anonymous.

"Excuse me. Hooo. The grog is strong tonight, amirite? That needed to come out. Anyway, what was I saying?"

Steve pulled something out of his pocket and popped it in his mouth. As he chewed, his demeanor began to change almost instantaneously, the drunken sloppiness of the previous few minutes fading to the background and his cheeks returning to their normal color.

"You were saying that the Council was bringing in new blood to find more magic. What magic?"

"Oh. Right. You know about magic, yeah? Real magic? Not wave-your-wand-and-say-a-stupid-word magic?"

No, I didn't. But please, continue.

"Ummm, sort of. My parents weren't exactly the talkative type."

"Oh. Hmm. Maybe I shouldn't have said anything then. But how awful of your own family to keep you in the dark like that! I mean, I told my daughter the truth when she turned six, although if I known how that was going to turn out, maybe I would have waited."

"Your daughter wouldn't by chance be an 11-year old girl with blond pigtails named Polly, would she?"

Steve's face lit up with excitement and I instantly regretted making this connection.

"Yes, that's her! How do you know her? Is she mentoring you or something? I told her that she should be helping people instead of trying to scam everyone. The little scoundrel. What a small world. I mean it's not like there are thousands of Questers in the city, but still!"

Ah crap. I had just broken open the dam of this whole secret world and now we were going to get sidetracked into a discussion on how great little 'ol Polly was. If Steve only knew how she had raided his stash of vervorium, then he might not be so eager to sing her praises. Which gave me an idea.

"No, nothing like that. I did a Quest for her a few weeks back. She wanted to test out a new game she was working on. Cute kid but…"

I stopped and reluctantly took a swig of the grog, causing me to shiver involuntarily as the liquid cascaded down my throat.

"But what? What did she do this time?"

"I don't want to get her in trouble or anything. I mean she paid me what she said she would, but…no. I shouldn't."

"Yes, you should. You've already said enough to get her in trouble, so you might as well tell me so I know how serious this is."

"OK. Fine. I'll tell you. But you go first. Something about 'real magic?'"

"Oh. Right. So. Magic. Maybe that's a bad word for it. It's not something you're born with or can learn by practicing. That's just some fairy tale that Hollywood cooked up to sell movie tickets. No, magic is something that's literally a part of the earth. Think of it as this big source of power that's running through the entire planet, like a river. It's in everything. It can become part of anything. It's the most valuable natural resource in history and most of the world doesn't even know it exists."

I stared at Steve, not knowing what to say, my pulse quickening and my stomach churning, like the day I got that call from the detective about my mom. I wanted to throw up. What insanity had I gotten myself into?

"What? I … I don't understand," I stuttered. "So you're saying that there's literally magic coming out of the ground?"

"Well, yes. And no. The days of pure magic spouting from the earth like a fountain are long, long gone. If those days ever existed in the first place."

"Oh. But… I'm so confused. I mean, I've seen some things, but I thought maybe…"

"That you were losing your mind?"

"Yes!"

"You're not. This is why you're not supposed to know the truth until level 25. By then, you would have completed enough Quests to realize there was more going on than people asking random strangers to do weird errands."

"Right. Well, I appreciate the truth, I guess. So the items people are fetching on the Quests..."

"... have magic in them. Yes. Not much, mind you. Like any natural resource, magic is not infinite. It can be used up, hence the current predicament. We can't rely on the old sources anymore. We've had to be resourceful, to figure out new wells to draw from. Some of which are inconvenient and messy."

"Like the spleen of a rat?"

Steve nodded.

"Yes. Yes, exactly! Picture all of the different places a rat goes. The different things a rat eats. It's a collector of sorts. Of germs and disease, but also, trace amounts of magic."

"Wouldn't that mean that there was magic in people too?"

"Hmm. Probably. But the amount that could be pulled from a person is not worth the price of admission, if you know what I'm saying. Far easier to kill a rat. Or even a pigeon."

I didn't know whether to feel excitement at this incredible discovery or absolute horror. If magic was real, marvelous, and amazing, that meant that other things could be real too. Like ancient evil monsters sleeping within the earth's crust waiting for the appointed day to rise up and lay waste to humanity in an ocean of blood. It made my heart race even faster.

"I can tell by your silence that I've probably already told you too much. It's a lot to process, I'm sure. That's why those that know try to tell their kids early enough so it's something they think of as part of their everyday world. Your folks did you a real disservice by hiding it from you."

"Seems like it. But, to be honest, this whole thing sounds like a far-fetched fairy tale from a guy who's had too much to drink. I don't mean to be rude, but you're what, four drinks in?"

Steve smiled and reached into his pocket, pulling out something small in a bright green wrapper, which he put on the table.

"You're right about the number of drinks but wrong about everything else. Finish your grog and your scotch and then take this and you'll see what I mean."

That sounded like a terrible idea: get extremely drunk and then pop a who-knows-what from a complete stranger. Yet the next thing I knew, my mug and glass were empty and my hands were fussing with the mystery object on the table.

The sudden influx of alcohol had already hampered my fine motor skills and so it took almost a minute for me to unwind the green wrapping, which revealed an even brighter orange square gummy.

I popped it in my mouth and began to chew. Contrary to its outward appearance, the gummy tasted like a rotting piece of fish with the consistency of an uncut cherry tomato. Fortunately it was small enough that the disgusting taste soon faded and I waited for something to happen.

I began to feel light-headed, the two drinks I had imbibed in successive fashion no doubt working their destructive force inside my liver, and I felt my already-churned stomach getting ready to release its content back up my throat.

"Can you excuse me for a-"

Steve shook his head.

"Just give it a second."

My head began to spin and I gripped the table, expecting the worse. But then, like a flick of a switch, my sober mind was back and my stomach calm. I sat back down.

"W-what just happened?"

Steve smiled.

"Just a little concoction I whipped up using some basic alchemy. Nothing too fancy. Here, take another for your next night out."

He slid another green-wrapped gummy across the table and I pocketed it.

"That was something else. How did you make that? What else can those gummies do? What are the ingredients? Do you need any special equipment? What's alchemy?"

"Hmm. Seems like it's a causing a weird side effect on you. It'll probably go away in a few minutes. But pretty impressive, right?"

It was impressive. Something like that could be worth millions, if not billions, of dollars. But at the same time, it seemed so mundane. What Polly had shown me was something I couldn't have thought possible.

"Anyway, what was it that you didn't want to tell me about Polly?"

"Oh. That. Well, the thing is, she borrowed a bit of your vervorium, whatever that is. Not a lot, according to her. Just enough to create a portal between two shells for a three-card monte scam. It was actually quite clever. I screamed so loud when I put my finger in-"

The grog mug came down on the table and shattered into a dozen pieces. I looked at Steve, whose forehead now sported several popping veins.

"I'm sorry, I need to go. Thanks for the drink." He tossed some crumpled-up dollars on the table and headed down the stairs. I dug a similar handful of money out of my purse, hoped it was enough, and ran after him. Steve had stopped at the bar, where he had pulled out another wad of cash and placed it on the counter.

"Sorry about the mess."

The bartender looked at him quizzically but Steve didn't stay to explain, as he continued to the door, down the stairs, and out onto the street.

"Why are you in such a hurry?" I yelled at him. He stopped and turned back to me, and I made up the distance.

"Because my daughter is in more trouble than I realized. Now good night."

He started off again but I wasn't ready to let him go.

"I know about the books. Polly told me," I said. Technically that was true. I did *know* about them, just not what they were or where they were.

"She did?"

"Yes."

I didn't say more, hoping he would spill some more secrets.

"Bullshit. My daughter may be many things but she's not stupid enough to give away the Compendium to someone like you."

The Compendium. The word dripped with mystery and lore. Now that I knew its name, I had to redouble my efforts to find it.

"She didn't give it away. It was a fair trade. I won her little game and she gave me the call number for the Compendium. But a lot of good that did me. Someone else checked it out of the library first."

Steve chuckled.

"The Compendium isn't in any library. No, I'm afraid my daughter was playing another trick on you. Wouldn't be the first time. She has bad habit of messing with noobs."

"Then what…"

"Damned if I know. Listen, I really need to get home. Try to stay out of trouble. Especially the alleyway behind Trader Joe's in Union Square. That's the Black Vultures' domain and you don't want to mess with them."

"Umm, OK. And why is that?"

Steve pulled up the bottom of his sweater, revealing a jagged scar that pulsed with a faint, otherworldy green glow. The vomit that should have come earlier finally rose in my throat and as I stooped over to finish retching, I could hear Steve laughing as he retreated into the distance.

CHAPTER NINE

GIRLS'
NIGHT OUT

*"I was one of the last holdouts. Most of the men in power were spoken for and it is
hard to predict, even for me, who will be pivotal and who will be pitiful.
But I eventually found someone suitable."*

"I canNOT wait to try this food. Lisa, you have to taste this dip. It. Will. Change. Your Life."

"Ooh ooh, looks yummy, pass it over here, Stace."

"Wait a sec, just need to get a pic for Insta first. OK, one sec.

#cheatday, #omgsogood, #girlsnightout, #besties. With @lisatees and @jjacs42.

OK posted. Here you go."

"Thanks Stace. Wow, that is good. Try mine. Wait, let me get a Snap."

On and on this went for the entire first course. Next time I should remember not to agree to go to a tapas place until the world runs out of rare earth metals and we don't have any smartphones left. My own food sat uneaten in front of me, not because I was trying to match Lisa and Stacy's social media whoring, but because I hadn't been able to keep anything down since yesterday's fateful evening with Steve.

It should have been a momentous occasion: the discovery that the world wasn't what it seemed, that there was something greater lurking underneath the veneer of everyday life. But no, Steve had to leave me with that final parting gift.

The jerk hadn't even bothered to see if I was OK after the vomiting subsided. When I finally regained strength enough to stand, he was gone and I was alone. In fact, I had probably never felt more alone. And that was saying something.

I spent the entire night staring at the ceiling in my bedroom, afraid to fall asleep lest that green glow trap me in a never-waking nightmare. Why couldn't he have let me enjoy the discovery of the truth for even a few hours, without revealing the darker, horrific side of magic?

I dragged myself to the office, exhausted, and spent the day trying to forget what I had learned and what I had seen. It didn't work, no matter how many lines of code my eyes scanned through. I think I fell asleep in the Treehouse for at least an hour at some point, which was good, I guess. But back at my desk, the Quest Board was calling to me.

My mind had shifted into grief mode, a familiar setting, to process this new reality and I had already moved past denial and anger to bargaining.

"What if I just played it safe?" I asked myself. "I won't go milling about in dark alleys late at night," I declared. "You can't get stabbed with a mystical knife if you don't hang around in an area where the knife wielders are likely to be." It was just another version of being street smart.

My mind continued warring with itself the rest of the day, one side never gaining enough will to either command my hand to click over to the Quest Board or delete the bookmark forever.

When the texts from Stacy and Lisa began pouring in about our dinner, I broke the stalemate and rushed out the door to meet them.

This was what I needed. A night of distraction. Even if I couldn't tell them what was going on, just being with other people was enough for the moment, despite them probably ignoring me for most of the evening.

"JJ, have you lost weight? You look great!" cooed Lisa.

I hated that nickname. It's not like my last name was long or unusual. It's Jacobs, how much more nondescript could you get?

And yes, I had lost weight, thank you very much, all in the last 20 hours. I wish I never had met Steve.

"Oh, maybe just a little. Trying to eat smaller portions, you know." I said sheepishly.

"Well whatever you're doing, keep it up! Anyway, Stace, you should have seen the look on Brad's face when he saw this month's credit card bill, I swear…"

I tuned out Lisa's latest wedding planning squabbling while moving the spoonful of orzo around on my plate. It had only been four months since their engagement, but it felt like that movie *The Five-Year Engagement*, what with the number of dress fittings, celebration drinks, celebration brunches, and other assorted celebrations that Lisa had concocted. For some reason, news of these outings always managed to trickle my way at the last minute, but I learned long ago that as the member of the trio with the least social capital, I should just be thankful that they were still even friends with me.

"JJ, what do you think of my new haircut? I'm trying something out for the wedding."

I looked at Lisa's hair, which looked indistinguishable from its normal look, but I knew better than to say that, so I studied her perfectly coiffed do for a few more seconds before answering.

"It looks cute!" I said with as much enthusiasm as I could muster.

"No!" Lisa pushed away the rice balls she was eating in disgust. "I told the hairdresser I wanted to look hot, not cute! UGGH! I have half a mind to storm down to that salon right now and demand a refund. I swear, if they're going to charge $650 for a cut, they damn well better…"

I ignored Lisa as she launched into a cavalcade of explicit and violent things she was going to do to her hairdresser, who, based on my three-word review, had done terrible, life-shattering damage to both Lisa's hair and psyche. I sighed.

These were my friends. Not just my friends. My two best friends. My two only friends. Shoot me please. I only had myself to blame. Most people would jettison a bunch of self-centered vapid friends at the first opportunity. But not me. You know how sometimes the first people you meet freshman year of college end up being the ones that stick around the rest of your life? Yeah, well, I had the unfortunate privilege of running into these two during my first 20 minutes in Ann Arbor. They had ambushed me by my dorm room as I was fumbling with all of my luggage.

"Hi! I'm Stacy and this is Lisa."

I had looked them over warily. They looked like they belonged to the popular set: hair and makeup perfect even though they had just spent hours unpacking, just in case someone important or cute walked by. I meanwhile looked like I had just woken up after a nine-hour bus ride.

"Hi, I'm Jen. Jen Jacobs."

"Nice to meet you, JJ," Lisa said. "Can I call you JJ? You look like a JJ."

"Umm, sure, I guess. My mom used to call me J-"

"Perfect, then it's settled. JJ, you're coming with us. We spotted some cute boys hanging out in the lounge upstairs"

I relished these girls at first. Really. I had no one else in my life then except an aunt I hadn't seen since I was a kid and some neighbors who made sure I wasn't getting into any trouble those last few months before I left for college.

And they were nice to me. At least at first. They let me borrow their clothes, taught me about boys, and tried to be the older sisters I didn't have. I perversely felt a sense of superiority whenever the three of us were strolling through campus.

But over time, the compliments turned backhanded, the slights started mounting, and my standing in the group began to decline. But I held on, as much as I could. What other choice did I have? There was no one else.

I felt a buzz in my pants pocket.

I pulled out my phone and nearly dropped it on the floor. The Quest Board had somehow opened on my phone and was displaying blinding, blinking pink text.

"Time for a new Quest?" it said.

I put my phone back in my pocket, my hand trembling. What was happening? It was like the Board knew what I had learned and was determined to wrap its tentacles around me and not let go.

My mind wandered back to the internal battle I had been putting off earlier. It was a bad habit I had accidentally picked up during a meditation class in college; instead of focusing on my breathing, I inevitably created an intense visualization about something that was giving me anxiety and this time it was no different.

It was single-combat: the old, normal me versus the new, magic me.

The normal me was dressed in a hooded sweatshirt and jeans, and I held a wooden staff and shield for some reason. The magic me was dressed as a valkyrie, with a shining metal helm and an axe at my side.

It was not the bloodbath I was expecting. Normal Jen wielded the staff with discipline and efficiency. Valkyrie Jen was the opposite: erratic and emotional. She swung her axe with too much force time and again, allowing Normal Jen to step to the side. This went on for several rounds, until a wicked grin appeared on Valkyrie Jen's face, and she suddenly lurched forward and struck the ground in front of Normal Jen with the axe.

The earth sundered, a crack forming under Normal Jen's feet. As the ground split apart, Normal Jen tried to jump to one side, but slipped and fell, her fingers digging into the dirt atop the deepening chasm. Valkyrie Jen walked over to the edge, surveyed her opponent for a few seconds, and then, without warning, sliced the girl's hands clean off, sending Normal Jen tumbling into the depths.

Back at the table, a small smile began to form on my lips. This was the last time I was going to sit with these two and feel sorry for myself, I thought. I was destined for greater things than being the third wheel to two vapid women.

I took my phone out of my pocket again and looked down. My hand twitched, the burst of confidence expended. The blinking message was still there and I quickly tapped it with one finger, bringing up a single Quest.

"Please bring five three-quarters eaten portions of food to 1690 Bleeker St. in the next 20 minutes. But it can't be your food. Tricky, I know. Also, a stolen lipstick. Reward: 2 iron tokens."

I stared at the Quest, which seemed to have been written by the guy sitting at the booth behind me. If I hadn't just been put through the ringer by Steve and his stupid scar, I would have been totally weirded out and refused to take it. But what would have bothered me yesterday morning wouldn't even register today in my new reality.

Now that I knew at least some of the truth about the Quests, the requested items didn't seem like they were destined for some intricate magical concoction. No, if I had to guess, the Requester was hungry and had some spare tokens lying around. Iron being fairly worthless, it was like getting food and lipstick for free. So of course I accepted the Quest without giving it another thought.

"Ugh, this sucks!" I said, still staring at my phone.

"What happened?" asked Lisa.

"My boss just emailed me. Some new investors are coming in tomorrow and he needs some more hand holding on the new code we just finished up. I gotta run, I'm sorry, girls!" I pushed my plate away and began inching out of the booth.

"Oh that stinks, JJ! Let's have them wrap up some stuff for you to go. I'm done eating anyway, don't want to add any more inches to my figure since I already had my last fitting. Excuse me?" Lisa snapped her fingers at a passing waitress as I exited the booth, knocking over Stacy's purse "accidentally" in the process, the contents spewing all over the floor.

"Shoot, my bad Stace! Let me clean that up for you." I got down on my knees and began scooping up the fallen items, pocketing a neon red shade of lipstick for myself.

I grabbed the food from the waitress and raced out of the restaurant. Ten minutes later, the items were safely deposited on the stoop of a seemingly abandoned townhouse and I was enjoying a leisurely evening stroll back to my apartment.

My mind wandered back to the aftermath of the battle. Valkyrie Jen stood alone at the edge of the chasm, before walking a few paces to pick up the wooden shield that Normal Jen had been holding. She stared at the depictions on the front, and I observed them too.

There was me, staring at a computer screen, my eyes bloodshot; me, waiting for Duncan to FaceTime from Hong Kong; me, trying to pay attention at dinner tonight. Valkyrie Jen shook her head and let out a loud guffaw. Then, with a flourish, she tossed the shield into the air, grabbed her axe from her side with the other hand, and, with a perfectly timed swing, obliterated the shield as it began falling to the ground.

Despite the earlier violence that I had witnessed, this display of wanton destruction raised a little seed of doubt within me. Had I made the right choice? As if sensing the growing moral quandary, the pieces of the shield on the ground began shaking as if they were trying to put themselves back together.

Valkyrie Jen however was having none of it. She snapped her fingers and a column of flame erupted around the broken shield. The flames vanished and when the smoke dissipated, all that was left was a pile of ash. Satisfied with her destruction, Valkyrie Jen then turned her gaze skyward, as if she could see me, as if I was a goddess watching her creation from above. The proud warrior grinned at the sky, clapped the dust off her hands, and walked away.

The scene dissolved into a hazy mist and when I reoriented to my surroundings, I found myself in front of my apartment. A grin had formed on my face, the same grin worn by the valkyrie.

In the end, I didn't need the battle to convince me which path was the right one. Why? Because for all my fear and doubt, it was really a simple choice between the drudgery and loneliness of my prior life and the chance to be part of something fantastical and extraordinary.

What other choice did I have?

CHAPTER TEN

FARHAMPTON

"As far as husbands went, and I've had too many to count,
Henry was one of the better ones."

The pie crust turned a golden brown as I watched anxiously through the oven window. I waited a few more minutes and then, mitts in hand, I removed the pie and set on the windowsill in the kitchen, the cool autumn air drafting in through a crack.

Quest complete. Well, almost. Just needed to drop this baby off under a bench in town and the tokens would be mine.

No, really.

It was early Saturday afternoon and the house was quiet. Duncan was upstairs sleeping, having landed early this morning from Hong Kong and needing to get rested for his boss's party tonight. We had rented a small house for the weekend in Northampton, a very old East

End hamlet with a very new name. Evidently an enterprising real estate agent had started advertising his listings as being located in the then non-existent town of Northampton to foreign buyers looking to stash their cash in the U.S. and suddenly, prices began skyrocketing, trendy shops began filling the downtown strip, and the town council was considering multiple petitions to change the town's name.

Fortunately, the new eight-figure homes that had popped up hadn't yet fully pushed out the quaint cottages that dotted the town's winding roads, it had only made their owners jack up the weekend rental price. But Duncan didn't flinch at the cost, his most recent bonus plentiful enough to absorb the hit.

Speaking of, the man had still not made his way downstairs. Which gave me time to make another pie. I cut up the apples I had picked earlier into slices, poured the sugary filling into the crust, and laid the top over the whole thing. I slid it into of the oven and pulled up the details of the Quest:

"One apple pie, made with Mutsu apples picked from the 17th row of trees at Running Brook Orchard. Reward: Seven iron."

I wasn't planning on Questing this weekend, as I needed a break from, well, everything. The last four months had been an unrelenting grind. If not for the mandatory three-day wait between Quests, I would have tried to do one every single day. Even with the gaps, I still managed to rake in 40 wood and 16 iron for a grand total of 72 experience, leaving me just a hair over level three. The day I reached that milestone should have been a happy one, but Duncan had been away and I hadn't felt like drinking by myself (again). So I splurged on a spa day and tried to forget that to get to level four, at my current rate, would take at least eight months. If the Council, whoever they were, wanted some new blood, this incessant grinding was not the way to go about it.

And I hadn't had any luck tracking down the mystery library books either. Several visits to branches in all five boroughs had yielded nothing, hours of online searching had been fruitless, and if I set foot in another used bookstore, I was going to shoot myself.

So it was a nice surprise when I woke up to an email from Duncan the other day that not only would he be coming home a few days early, we were going away for the weekend to boot. A whole weekend with Duncan was a rare occurrence and I wanted to be present, rather than thinking about alchemy, prima materia, and the scar.

Unfortunately, my curiosity and boredom got the best of me after five minutes, as I really had nothing else to do when I got to the house yesterday evening. I had innocently pulled up the Quest Board to see if there was anyone out here who had taken the red pill. Turned out that the East End was not a Questing hotbed, with only a smattering of rinky-dink fetch Quests offering a few iron at most. I wouldn't get out of bed for less than six iron, so seven iron was right on the line, but the opportunity to take in the fresh fall air at a scenic farm was enough of an incentive for me, so I accepted.

The orchard was practically empty when I arrived and I paid the ridiculous $40 for the right to fill a bag with more apples than I would be able to eat in a month and set off for the designated row. The few orchard employees out among the trees eyed me suspiciously. I suspected that they were used to seeing happy couples arm-in-arm, or parents swinging their kids in the air as they meandered about. The pathetic sight of a girl picking apples by herself at 8:45 in the morning couldn't be countered by an argument that the apples tasted better or there was something satisfying about foraging for your own food.

But I didn't need to justify my presence; I just needed to find the frakking trees so I could go make my pies.

Yes, pies, plural. If this wasn't yet another errand for someone, then there was something different about these apples and I was damn sure going to figure out what that was. Which was easy enough. I would just make a second pie, take a bite, and see what happened.

I walked down the path that ran through the center of the rows of trees, until I reached a very threatening piece of yellow tape that was strung across the gap at the 17th row. I looked around to see if anyone was nearby and seeing no one I stepped leisurely over the tape and into the forbidden section.

I knew something was wrong immediately when my right foot sunk into the soil down to my ankle as soon as it hit the ground. My left foot remained planted on the other side, and I stood there, stradling the tape, trying to reclaim my foot and my freedom. But the soil had turned rock hard, almost as if it was cement. I struggled without success for a minute or two, all the while looking back to see if anyone had noticed my predicament. Luckily I remained undetected, but unluckily for my favorite hiking boots, I quickly determined that the only way to wrest myself free was to leave my right boot trapped in the dirt.

I gave the trapped boot a good pull just in case the dirt had decided to play nice, but it wouldn't budge and I reluctantly parted ways with it and walked away from the yellow tape.

The ground was slightly damp from recent rains and my right sock soon was covered in dirt. I contemplated wrapping the empty apple bag around my foot and trudging back to the front of the orchard, but the sight of stray apples in the grass gave me an idea.

I backtracked one row and took a hard left away from the center path. The trees in the 17th row abutted their siblings in the 16th row, the only difference being there was no yellow tape separating the two. Apples littered the ground at the base of the trees. I stopped at a random spot and pushed my way in as far as I could manage. The corresponding tree in the 17th row was still a bit out of reach, but luckily, its fallen apples weren't. Careful not to step too close to the weird soil, I began collecting the Mutsu until I had a decently full bag and then retreated to safety.

I looked down at my spoils. The apples were green like regular green apples. I put the bag down and removed one of the apples. It weighed what you would expect an apple to weigh, no magic golden apples here. I brought it up to my mouth, held it there for a few seconds, and then took a small bite.

Nothing happened.

I swallowed and took another bite, swirling the apple pieces around in my mouth like a sip of wine.

Still nothing.

Maybe it was one of those slow-acting apples. You know the ones where you take a bite, go to sleep, and then don't wake up for a hundred years. Well, if that was the case, the damage was already done. Or maybe the apples needed to be heated for the effects to kick in, hence the request for a pie. In any event, my facilities remained unimpaired so I figured I might as well get the hell out of Dodge before I was discovered. I put the half-eaten apple back in my bag, stopped at a row of trees with yellow apples to cover over the Mutsu, and trudged off back to the rental car. It was late enough in the morning now that the throngs of apple pickers had began to arrive, and so none of the staff noticed the one-booted girl slip by with a bag of potentially magic apples.

When I arrived back at the house, I laid out my haul on the counter: 14 Mutsu apples, enough for two pies with a few leftover. I set to work, nibbling on the extras as I went, all the while hoping that whatever magic they held would kick in eventually. If necessary, I was prepared to eat the whole pie, stomach consequences be damned, to figure out what was so special about these apples. I imagined the answers neatly laid out in the Compendium, hidden on a shelf somewhere in the city.

There would be pages of maps, showing the location of flora and fauna that had magical properties. Tables of recipes and experiments on how to mix disparate ingredients to make something new. A whole chapter on the uses of rats. The pages would be brown and make a satisfying crinkly noise as you turned them. I imagined that each family had a copy that had been passed down from generation to generation, each successive one scribbling notes in the margin with new ideas and new things they'd tried.

Without the Compendium, though, I would need to figure everything out for myself, one Quest at a time. The first pie would be for the Quest and the second one for me (and Duncan if he ever woke up). Just a few more minutes and I would be able to find out if these apples were worth losing my boot over.

The creak of the old wooden stairs betrayed Duncan's descent into the kitchen. He wore a tattered t-shirt and sweats, the back of his hair was sticking up, and I'm sure he hadn't brushed his teeth yet, but I didn't care. It had been so long that I almost had forgotten what it was like to have someone else in my life.

Duncan surveyed the scene in the kitchen with a quizzical look.

"One day in the country and you've gone domestic on me."

"And hello to you too. I didn't think you were going to wake up in time for the party."

Duncan walked over to me and gave me a kiss. It was short, more than a peck but less than a haven't-seen-your-longtime-girlfriend-in-three-weeks type of kiss. He pulled back slightly and I wondered if he was waiting for me to press forward, as if testing me to see if I would continue the kiss, to see if I had missed him more than he had missed me. But then suddenly his hands were around my waist, his lips back against mine, his fingers trying to untie the apron. Our lips never parted as we made our way up to the bedroom, and the distance that had separated us was gone.

We lay together in bed afterward, the sheets and blankets strewn about haphazardly, my head resting on his shoulder, his arm around me. For the first time in a while, I felt content and calm, as if the world outside the room didn't exist, as if the Quests were just a bizarre daydream I had created. I closed my eyes and pretended that this could last as long as I didn't open them.

But the kitchen smoke detector had other plans.

CHAPTER ELEVEN

AN APPLE PIE
FROM SCRATCH

*"Over the years, my methods have evolved as my talents have waxed and waned.
For the foreseeable future, I will have to rely on my marriage, my pen, and my ink."*

Duncan raced out of the room, still naked, and scampered down the stairs. I threw on half of my clothes quickly, grabbed some of Duncan's, and followed. The kitchen was full of smoke billowing from the oven when I entered, and the sight of him wearing nothing but oven mitts trying to fish a pie out of the oven was too much so I let out a chuckle.

Duncan looked up, his face red from either the heat or anger, and stopped what he was doing.

"It's not funny, Jen. You could have burned down the whole house!"

"Oh please. It's just a bit of smoke! Plus the window's open, so it mostly went outside already."

I plopped his clothes on the counter and shooed him away from the oven to survey the damage.

My spare pie was burnt to a crisp, the upper crust charred a deep black and rock hard. Crap. I looked over at my remaining apples on the counter. Just two, not enough for another pie and damned if I was going to go back to that orchard again. I found a fork in one of the drawers and poked the top of the pie with it. It did not give way. I kept poking until finally a chunk of the crust sunk into the apple filling below.

"Umm, Jen, what are you doing?"

Duncan had managed to put on his underwear and t-shirt and so looked a little less ridiculous than before, but he was clearly annoyed that I had ruined the second round of hooking up that he was likely hoping for.

"Trying to see if any part of this pie is salvageable. It took me a long time to make."

I managed to break away more of the crust so that I could retrieve a good-size bite of the center. The extra heat didn't seem to have affected the interior of the pie, which was odd and I brought the filling up to my nose. It smelled normal, so I took the plunge and stuck the whole thing in my mouth.

The urge to vomit began almost immediately as I swallowed the last bit. I dropped the fork and raced out of the kitchen to the nearest bathroom. Squatting over the open toilet, I began dry heaving involuntarily and waited for the bile to rise in my throat. But then, just as quick as it had come, the compulsion faded.

When I returned to the kitchen, Duncan was seconds away from cutting into the first pie.

"What are you doing?!?" I said, almost screaming.

"Having some pie, what does it look like? I was so confused as to why you even tried the burnt one when you had a perfectly good-"

"Don't eat that, please," was all I could say before snatching the pie away from Duncan's grasp.

"What do you mean? Why else did you make it if we weren't going to eat it?"

Duncan looked at me like I was a crazy person and he was only half wrong unfortunately.

"Because, umm, well…"

This was not the moment I planned on revealing my secret. I mean, what a dumb way for him to find out, right? I would have rather been caught drinking some arcane concoction, or walking out of the bar with Steve, or even looking at the Quest Board on my computer. But to give it all away for the sake of a stupid pie was absolutely ridiculous. At the same time though, I wanted those tokens and I didn't care what Duncan thought.

"… because I was baking it for your boss's party tonight."

The expression on Duncan's face held steady for a few seconds before finally settling back to normal.

"Oh, ok. Why didn't you say so?"

"Sorry; it's just I worked really hard on this. I picked the apples myself this morning and everything."

"It's fine. But you know, there are like farms everywhere here. You could have just bought a pie instead of going through all this trouble."

"I know. But sometimes it's good to get your hands dirty."

Duncan smiled and put his arm around me.

"Say, since we were so rudely interrupted before, why don't we…"

Without warning, Duncan lifted me onto the counter and began pulling up my shirt while kissing my neck.

"Baby, it's, oh, that tickles, I told your boss's wife that I'd drop the pie off soon though. You know how she gets."

Duncan halted his advance, my shirt already up to my neck. I pulled it back down and slid off the counter.

"Okay, I guess. But you owe me a raincheck, Jellybean."

"It's a date."

I gave him a peck on the cheek and ran upstairs to get my clothes. Alone in the bedroom, I realized that my lie had now spawned several subsidiary lies, such as why the pie wouldn't be on the dessert table later. Fortunately Duncan was never one for remembering every little thing and in a few hours he'd be so jetlagged and drunk that he would forget all about the pie. But one step at a time.

I parked a few spots down from the bench and waited in my car for several minutes on the off chance the Requester was still nearby. No one appeared and, anxious to get back to the house, I walked over to the bench and sat down. I had placed the pie inside several layers of plastic bags, which were tied into a tangled knot. I hoped it was enough protection from the elements and so I leaned forward and slid the pie underneath the bench.

Evidently the Requester was very trusting, as the tokens were already waiting in an envelope taped under the bench. I ripped the envelope free and tore it open. Seven iron tokens. Not that I cared so much about the tokens themselves. With the whole level ladder revealed to be a fraud by Steve, it didn't matter how slowly I was progressing through the ranks. Besides, I already knew more than someone at level 25 and my aim at this point was knowledge, not these worthless tokens.

I sat there, still hoping the Requester would show him or herself, but after several minutes it seemed like a lost cause, so I decamped for the car and began the slow, winding drive back to the house. As I meandered by horse farms and neatly planted fields, I speculated on what should have happened when I had tasted the pie.

In *Warriors of Olympus*, there were magic fruit you could find while exploring. Some restored your health, another cured you if you had been poisoned, and still others bestowed some temporary benefit, like being able to run quicker for a few minutes.

Any of those would be earth-shattering revelations if real. But the cheap reward for the Quest made me suspect that the effect was more mundane than that. I mean, if the orchard was hiding apples that could bring someone back from the dead, the reward should have been a lot more than seven iron. My mind considered the opposite proposition: what if the apples *were* that amazing but setting the reward further up the token spectrum would have drawn attention to their value and everyone would have just tried to take the apples for themselves. Uggh. This was making my head hurt. I tried to stop the guessing game but my brain had already leaped to the next possibility: the apples were only deadly if you baked them into a pie and by eating said pie, I had unwittingly poisoned myself and would soon die a horrible death.

Thankfully I reached the house before I could dream up any more awful pie scenarios. What's done was done, I supposed, so I shifted my anxiety to surviving the night's festivities.

"I hope you'll at least try to talk to someone tonight."

It was dark and we were lost in the woods. The roads twisted and turned as our car lurched forward. I didn't know if it was the jet lag or if he had already forgotten the afternoon's, err, activities, but Duncan was in a foul mood and, as usual, taking it out on me.

"But of course, Professor Higgins, your etiquette lessons have been most helpful. I'm ever so excited for this party."

Duncan rolled his eyes.

"I think we made a wrong turn. Did you come this way earlier?"

From what I had Google-stalked, Duncan's boss's house was something to behold. Twelve bedrooms. Two pools. A private dock. If only

I actually had brought the pie over earlier, I might have convinced someone to give me a tour.

"Umm, maybe? I'm not sure. The GPS was working earlier and it wasn't dark."

After a few more silent minutes, the woods melted away and we were driving between eight-foot-tall perfectly manicured hedges. Finally, rows of tail lights appeared and we pulled up in the enormous gravel driveway to wait our turn to valet.

"Look, there are going to be some important investors here. Just shake hands and smile and don't make me look bad."

I resented the implication that I was a boor from the wrong side of the tracks who couldn't be trusted to have a normal conversation with another human being. But one bad night at one of Duncan's work dinners had evidently given Duncan the impression that I was always on the brink of embarrassing him. Tonight I would comply and be the perfect little New England boarding school-Ivy League alumna that he thought he should be dating, but we would definitely be having a talk about this later.

We walked up the steps to an immense wooden door, which opened into a huge foyer with marble floors and twin staircases leading up to a landing. Duncan's boss Jeff and his wife Plastic Surgery Face (not her real name) were greeting people in the middle of the room.

"Duncan! Recovered from last night's festivities?"

"Hey, Jeff. Yeah, the usual Dramamine-Hong Kong overnight flight combo, plus I took another nap this morning at the house we rented."

"Good, good. And hello there Jen. Good to see you. Sorry for keeping your boyfriend away all the time. But he says you're working round the clock anyway. Hopefully so you can make us all some money soon?"

Great. Five seconds into the party and I was already forced to bite my tongue. Yes, thanks to the generous investment by The Jeff

Fund, we would make it to the end of the year. But, in the process, all of my stock options had been so diluted that at our current valuation, I would maybe net minimum wage this year, while Jeff would make out like a bandit. And Duncan would get nothing because of the conflict. A win-win-win.

"Good to see you too, Jeff. Yeah, we've been slammed reworking the engine. It's been really tou-"

"Marcus! My man!"

The next sycophant walked in behind us, which gave me the perfect excuse to slip away. Besides, Duncan and I both knew that I was a deadweight in these conversations. I would show my face a few times, laugh at someone's jokes, and my duties for the night would be satisfied. So I excused myself to use the facilities and walked away.

The foyer led into a gigantic kitchen, with dozens of waiters milling about waiting for appetizers to come out of the various ovens. I maneuvered around them to the open glass doors at the back that led out onto the deck. The cool fall air was kept at bay by tall heat lamps placed every few feet. I found a spot at an empty cocktail table, flagged down a waiter for a drink, and waited to see if Duncan would eventually find me.

He didn't, so I spent the next half hour people watching and admiring the view out onto the bay. It was quite breathtaking. But I could only stare out at the water for so long and despite our earlier conversation, it would look bad if I kept my distance from Duncan the whole night. The kitchen was even more packed than before, a new set of people already laying out dessert on a giant table. I barely managed to squeeze past it when something on the table caught my eye.

My pie.

CHAPTER TWELVE

THE FRUIT OF
GOOD AND EVIL

*"My letters have been intercepted, and the results have been as expected.
Henry and General Washington continue to be astounded at Howe's inexplicable
refusal to finish off the Continental Army. It makes me smile."*

I stared at the pie way too long to convince myself that it wasn't mine. But there was no mistaking the small impressions that my fingers had left on the crust that were now baked in to the finished product.

"Can I help you with something?" One of the waitresses was setting down a big tray of apples next to my pie. Her jacket was covered in some kind of dust, her blond hair was frazzled, and she looked like she hadn't slept in days.

"No, no. Was just admiring the dessert selection."

"Yeah it is something else. Well, we'll be bringing it out to the patio a bit later, so…"

"Thanks."

I walked out of the kitchen reluctantly and went to find Duncan. He hadn't even made it out of the foyer, where he was talking to a group of people whom I didn't recognize.

"There you are, Jen. I was wondering where you had run off to. This is Tad, one of the LPs of our newest fund and his wife Julia."

"Nice to meet you."

I proceeded to nod along as Tad recounted in great detail their summer in the south of France. Eventually, the waiters appeared with little plates of Petit fours, so I knew it was time to go pie hunting.

The bigger desserts had been arranged in a buffet out on the deck and by the time I got to the pie, it was already half gone. I grabbed two slices and went to find Duncan.

"Here Dunc, some of my delicious homemade pie."

Duncan looked at me quizzically.

"Oh, right. I almost forgot you brought that over. An odd choice by Jeff to have the dessert be potluck, but he's always looking for weird ways to save money."

"Yeah, strange. Well, cheers!"

We clinked our forks together and each took a bite. The filling was soft and warm and actually tasted good. If this programming gig didn't work out, maybe I had a second career as a hipster baker.

I took a second bite of just the crust and froze. It tasted like streusel. Streusel that wasn't on the pie when I left it under the bench earlier. I resisted the urge to spit everything back onto the plate and slowly chewed the crust, the chomping of my teeth amplified with every movement of my jaw up and down. Finally, the bite was gone but my heart was racing. What the heck was going on here?

That's when the voices started.

"Mmm, this is good pie."

"I hope Julia didn't see me talking to Abby."

"It actually worked."

I clutched my ears and nearly fell over. The light din of conversation in the foyer had suddenly exploded into a cacophony of voices. If I concentrated hard enough, I could pick out the individual strands, if only for a moment.

"Time for another drink."

"This house is so pedestrian."

"Next party I need to have Barbara pick out something for Jen to wear. It's embarrassing."

That last voice I recognized. I stared up at Duncan, who was chowing down on the rest of the pie slice, seemingly unaffected by the voices and oblivious to the fact that he had just insulted me.

"Dunc, what do you think of my dress? Lisa lent it to me." A lie. This dress had been in my closet since college. It was a miracle it still fit.

Duncan nearly spit out the pie, which sparked a coughing fit that continued for over a minute.

"Whoa, sorry. Wrong pipe. Your dress? It looks great, babe. You look good in anything."

I glared at him, not sure whether to accept the compliment or call him on the-

"What are you doing?"

A woman's voice cut through the others and I looked around the room to see who was yelling at me.

"I said, what are you doing?"

The voice hit me again a second time and I nearly fell to the ground. A chair was set nearby and I staggered over to it and sat down.

"Jen, what's wrong?"

"Probably had too much to drink, she's always been a lightweight."

Duncan's words and thoughts hit me back-to-back, but I didn't want to deal with him right now. I just wanted the voices to go away.

"Just a bit of a headache. I'll catch up to you in a bit."

He nodded and walked away, leaving me alone with my thoughts and everyone else's apparently.

"Don't ignore me, I asked you a question."

"Who, me?" I said out loud.

"Yes, you. But you don't need to shout. I can hear you even if you don't speak."

"Oh." I thought. "What do you mean, what am I doing? I'm being bombarded with the thoughts of half the people at this party."

"Yes, I know. And you almost ruined a perfectly good experiment."

"Umm, sorry?"

The sensation of talking with someone in my mind was incredibly disorienting and-

"Stop that. You know I can hear what you're thinking, right? I just didn't think you would be able to hear me back. That has made things … interesting."

"Glad I could help."

"I'm not sure I would go that far. But you've piqued my curiosity, so I'll let this go a little more before I get rid of you."

Crap. Crap. Crap. I knew I shouldn't have eaten some of the apples. Wait, could she hear this? I needed to come with a plan bef-

"Too late. I heard it. I told you, it's like you're shouting in my ears from a foot away. So you're JadePhoenix42. Kind of a dumb handle if you ask me. But I guess a small thanks is in order, though, for baking such a delicious pie. And for solving the mystery of why you can hear everyone too. That would have been bugg.."

I shut my eyes tightly and blocked out the rest of the voices. Instead of trying to block my tormentor's thoughts too, I would channel them into a place where I was in control, my anti-meditation skills finally proving their usefulness.

I imagined myself in a bare room with no doors. Without warning a big sheet of glass appeared on one wall that looked out into another room. I could vaguely see the contents of that room and the formless shadow of my tormenter, who was perched at the glass trying to listen. If my thoughts were loud, my "voice" would carry through the glass and she could hear me. But if I whispered, then she was cut off and my thoughts were still my own.

Excellent.

Now to figure out how to get rid of this woman. So I asked what I thought she would think was a stupid question.

"Because of the apples? When I ate them earlier, nothing happened."

I saw the shadow of the figure behind the glass move, but then the figure disappeared and a new image appeared on the glass. It was the fuzzy outline of someone walking through Running Brook Orchard. The image vanished as quickly as it appeared and I forced myself not to think about it further.

"*Of course not. Did you let your boyfriend over there have some?*"

"No."

"*Right. Then there would have been nothing for you to hear. The apples create the link that allows thoughts to travel from one mind to the other.*"

The mention of the apples again triggered another scene to start playing on the screen. But it wasn't like watching a movie. I was reliving a memory through *her* eyes. It was the orchard, except this time at night. I watched for a few seconds as she walked down the familiar rows of trees, before the memory flickered off again.

"Oh, that makes sense. Like the vervorium linking places."

"*Yes, exactly. Now, if you don't mind, I need to get going and you–*"

"Wait, but then what about the pie?"

"*Do I need to lay everything out for you like a kindergartner? When you baked the pie, you degraded the apples so that the linkage between minds only*" *went in one direction. Like a one-way mirror. At least, that was my theory before tonight and now that I've proven it, I-"*

"Ah, now I got it. But hold on a second. There was streusel on the pie that I didn't put there. Was that part of it too?"

"Don't be stupid. Your pie just looked so bland, so I needed to make it more appetizing. Anyway, I'm glad we cleared this whole thing up, and I really do need to get on with the mind wiping and all so-"

"But why didn't you just go get the apples yourself?"

The memory resumed and this time I could feel what Beatrice was feeling too. I didn't know if that was her name, but I needed to call her something other than "that woman" or the "mind reader," and it was the first thing that came to mind.

I felt the thrill of sneaking into the orchard at night, felt that thrill turn to terror as her feet submerged into the same soil that my foot had been trapped in, felt that terror turn to fear and desperation as she struggled to free herself.

"Well, because you so helpfully agreed to get them for me for seven iron. What an asinine question. Quit stalling so I can-"

"Not buying it. If I knew about these apples and what they did, there's no way I would let some random person know that there was something different about them."

"You'd be surprised at how desperate some people are for tokens. They don't ask questions and are just happy to have the chance to get-"

"No. I think that you would have gotten them yourself but you were afraid of going back to the orchard."

The memory flickered off but it gave me an idea. It was a wisp of a thought, a puff of smoke, there and gone in an instant. I couldn't risk Beatrice hearing it and ruining the plan before I could execute.

"What? Don't be ridiculous. It's an apple orchard, not a torture chamber. You know, you are starting-"

In my mind, I ran over to the glass wall and started "shouting" as loud and fast as I could.

"You got stuck, just like I did. Well, probably worse. You went at night and no one found you until the next morning. I can just imagine the state you were in when they dug your feet out of the ground."

And as I recounted what I had just seen back to Beatrice, I felt the same feelings resurface in her mind and the linkage between us began to weaken, the joined rooms becoming fuzzy.

"You were cold and tired, your pants were soiled, and then, for good measure, they dropped you on the dirt and gave you a few nice whacks in the stomach. Then they stood you up, walked you out of the orchard, and tossed you onto the road. Guessing they banned you for life, not that you would ever go back, the trauma-"

"STOP IT!"

The force of her voice pushed me out of the room in my mind and nearly out of the actual chair I was sitting on in the real world. I straightened myself up and tried to refocus on the room, only for the voice to-

"You know, I was going to go easy on you, just push you to drink a little too much so by tomorrow you wouldn't be sure if this was real or not. But now you've really pissed me off."

The rooms snapped back into focus, except, this time, instead of the glass divider, there was an old wooden door between my mind and her mind. As the knob began to jiggle slowly, I retreated to the back of my room.

"Oh have I? The way I see it, we wouldn't even be having this conversation if it wasn't for me."

I tried to keep up my confident front, but I could feel the fierceness of her anger increasing like a shark that smelled blood.

"Not a great way to repay someone who helped you out, now is it?"

"You got paid what you agreed to," she yelled through the door. It began to open, but the wood was warped and Beatrice had trouble pushing all the way through.

"Maybe so. But had I known when I agreed to your Quest what I was really fetching, well…"

"Well nothing. I found the apples. You're just a pair of hands. A pair that has overstayed its welcome, so if you don't mind, I think you'll be going now…"

The door flung open and I saw her for the first time. Except it wasn't the first time, I realized. I had thought Beatrice was likely the snooty wife of one of Jeff's investors, but this made much more sense. The perfect way to infiltrate a party full of rich people with lots of secrets to be purloined.

Because no one ever pays attention to the help.

The avatar Beatrice presented in my mind was different than the frazzled waitress I had seen in the kitchen. The dusty jacket was replaced with a long black gown, her blond hair was long and stick straight, and there were no bags under her piercing green eyes. She stared at me, cowering at the back of this room I'd constructed and smiled.

"Nowhere to run, Jade," she said, as she slowly walked the length of the room toward me.

She was right. I had nowhere to run. My back was against the wall and the only thing separating me from her was time.

Wait.

That was the answer.

If I couldn't run away, then I would make her keep running to me. Because after all, this whole room was of a construction of my own making. It could be as long as I wanted it to be.

As the thought finished, the room exploded and I felt myself being flung backward. When the dust settled, I was still against the same wall, except instead I was now at the end of a very long hallway.

"*Neat trick,*" Beatrice yelled from the other end. "*But I'm going to catch up to you eventually, so all that you've done is postponed the inevitable.*"

Beatrice trudged down the hallway in her heels but that gave me precious moments to think of how to stop her. With the orchard memory used up, I didn't have any of her own pain left to use against her.

That was OK, though, because I had plenty of my own to spare.

"Can I tell you a story?" I shouted.

"It won't take long. I'll be done by the time you reach me. I was having a drink with a dear, dear friend the other day and he was telling me about he got into a right nasty scuffle with a bunch of street toughs and things got ugly. One of them had a knife, you see. And not one of your everyday, run-of-the-mill knives that just stabs someone and makes all the blood come out. No, this knife was different."

"*Enough.*" She was getting closer, maybe only 10 feet away. "*Get out of this house now or–*"

"It left a mark on its victim that just wouldn't go away. And then my friend, who loves a good joke, pulled up his shirt and…"

I pulled up the bottom of my dress while calling up the image of Steve's green scar. It was as horrifying as I had remembered it, and I felt a shudder ripple through my body. I looked down and there was the scar, criss-crossing my stomach like a lightning bolt, its otherworldly glow casting the hallway with an eerie light. I looked up to see Beatrice only a foot in front of me, and the last thing I remember before the floor dissolved underneath us was the small purple stone around her neck shimmering softly as we fell into a black abyss.

CHAPTER THIRTEEN

MIND READER

"General Washington continues to evade Howe but for how long, I do not know. Winter approaches and I am running low on ink."

I opened my eyes. The party was still in full swing around me, as if no time had passed. I squinted at the harsh light of the real world and I felt beads of sweat dripping down my forehead. Whether the people around me were actually talking out loud or if I was still hearing their thoughts, I wasn't sure, and I felt a growing urge to vomit for the second time that day. Suddenly, one of the waiters ran past me toward the kitchen. I took that as a sign that Beatrice had caused some sort of commotion and I staggered off to the front door. Luckily, the valet stand was not crowded and I was soon winding my way back through the dark country roads.

I was halfway back to the house when I was sure the voices had stopped, which was about 10 minutes before I realized I left Duncan at the party with no car. I had bigger problems to deal with now though. I finally pulled into the unlit driveway of the rental and found my phone flooded with dozens of texts from Duncan, who had been scouring the party looking for me.

"Sorry, Dunc. Felt sick so needed to get out of there," I texted him. Also, you're a dick for thinking that I can't dress myself.

"U could have told me," he wrote back.

"I know. But didn't want u to feel obligated to leave"

"It's fine. Some stupid waitress knocked into Clarice and she smacked her face against the marble counter. Blood everywhere. Jeff took her to the hospital."

"Oh. Wow. Is she OK?"

"Not sure. Might need another nose job."

"Haha."

"Wasn't trying to be funny."

"Oh"

"i need to stay until Jeff gets back."

"OK."

I got out of the car and walked to the front door. The night was quiet and starless, the only sound coming from the crunching of my heels on the gravel walkway. It was a marked change from earlier, when the combined chatter of the partygoers' thoughts had threatened to overwhelm my sanity. I sat down on the stoop and stared out into the darkness, letting the silence wash over me and clear my head, but my thoughts kept drifting back to those stupid apples.

That's when I remembered I still had two in the kitchen. I headed inside to the kitchen counter where I had left them. I picked them both up and weighed them in my hands, as if they now were the golden apples of Eris. What were they truly capable of? And what else was out there, lurking in plain sight? I put them in the freezer, climbed the rickety stairs, and collapsed on the bed.

————

I woke up to an empty bed and a text from Duncan that he had stayed over at Jeff's and was getting a ride back with him to the city. Whatever. He would be on his way back to Hong Kong tomorrow and by the time he came back, last night would be ancient history. Well, nothing to do now but pack up and head back home myself.

It was a long, lonely ride west and I spent most of the time trying not to replay my encounter with Beatrice. Looking back, it was a miracle I had escaped from her clutches unscathed. If she was actually capable of controlling my mind, there's no telling what she would have made me do.

As I sat in traffic approaching the Midtown Tunnel, I felt like I was trapped on a small boat in the middle of a rushing river with only a worn wooden paddle to navigate, while Steve and Polly and Beatrice and everyone else passed me by on fancy yachts or huge clipper ships. The wake from their boats made my pathetic dinghy rock from side to side. I tried to steady myself with the stupid paddle but it was so useless, I chucked it in the river and just gave myself to the whims of the river.

After what seemed like hours, I finally reached home to find the door to my apartment slightly ajar and the noise from the TV filtering out into the hallway. That wasn't anything out of the ordinary, as my roommate had a bad habit of leaving the door open with her keys still in the lock.

"Marnie, you left the door open again," I called out as I entered the apartment. She didn't respond.

Great, I thought. I just went through a hellish weekend only to come home and find out we've been robbed. Or worse, Beatrice had tracked me down and was waiting for me on the couch watching *Real Housewives*. A quick search of the apartment revealed nothing other than my roommate's stupidity, so I retreated to my room, shut the door, and pulled out my laptop.

Before I realized what I was doing, the familiar whizzing of the Quest list appeared on my screen. I began scrolling through the text looking for promising leads, discarding Quests that were too easy or too cheap, and was about to accept one to fetch some Khat leaves when I stopped myself. What the hell was I doing? Any one of these Quests could deliver me right into the arms of another psychopath. Or the same psychopath. I couldn't stay away though. I had taken the red pill and I needed to keep going down the rabbit hole to see where it went.

The ping of my regular inbox interrupted my moral quandary and I clicked over to see who was bothering me. An email from the New York Public Library was waiting for me with the subject "Book on hold available."

My eyes widened. Had someone finally returned one of the mystery books? I put all thoughts of Questing on hold and ran out the door to find out.

It was unexpectedly pouring when I exited the subway and I sprinted the last few blocks to avoid getting drenched. After waiting behind an old man trying to return a DVD for 20 minutes, it was finally my turn at the circulation desk. A familiar visage greeted me as I stepped forward: the librarian from my first visit. She looked at me with unknowing eyes and quickly walked to a room in the back after wordlessly looking up my hold on the computer, returning a few minutes later with a large book wrapped in a plastic dust jacket.

"Here you go. Due in two weeks. Next!"

I grabbed the book and scurried away before she changed her mind, retreating to a carrel in the basement to inspect my prize.

The outside was hardened leather and had no discernible title. The bottom of the spine had a small piece of paper taped under the dust jacket: the call number that matched the one Polly had written out on the freezer case so many months ago. I opened the cover to the first page. The texture of the paper was coarse and the weight of the page substantial. Three words and a number were written in dark green ink:

Rita van Asch, 1777

The pages that followed were similarly handwritten in the same dark green ink. Some of the ink had faded. Other pages were incomplete, either with pieces torn out or with the writing stopping halfway down the page. I read the beginning few lines of a couple of random pages, which seemed to recount the history of the settlement of New Amsterdam/New York, although not one that I had ever read.

I flipped to the last page, which sported an entry dated December 31, 1777 and read the first few lines.

"Finally arrived at Valley Forge with some of the other officers' wives. British army retreated back to Philadelphia. According to Henry, we will be camped here for the better part of the winter. The area has good natural defenses and my survey yesterday indicated the presence of several promising sources. Hid Compendium in the usual place before I left, which is unfortunate, but troops will provide plentiful supply of testing subjects. Any resulting deaths can be blamed on starvation."

I closed the book. The account was cold, methodical, and it made my head spin. This woman, whoever she was, sounded like a sociopath, like someone who would throw away lives as if they were lab rats. In short, she sounded like a certain person with a penchant for apple pie. I shuddered and turned the last page over to see if there was another entry on the opposite side, only to be greeted with an envelope taped to the inside back cover. An envelope with one word written on it.

"Jen."

I felt my insides turn to jelly as I traced my finger across my name. What the heck was going on? Maybe Polly had had the book this whole time and was waiting to see if I was worthy enough to receive it. That made sense. If I were her, I wouldn't have trusted this book to me either.

I ripped the envelope from the book and carefully opened it to find a piece of paper folded in three. Unfurling it revealed a short handwritten note with something taped to the bottom.

"Jen,

Yes, I know your name isn't Jade. That's what happens when you join minds with someone, things are bound to leak through that you didn't expect. It's how you probably know my name too. It's also how I knew you were looking for this book. Consider it a gesture of good-will on my part.

Because I have great plans for you, Jen. You see, I've reached an inflection point in my Questing progression. I've come a long way since I fetched that 90/10 beef, tillandsia, apple popsicle, and the handful of blueberries all those years ago. But I need help to keep climbing the mountain, to take on the Guild. And after searching for a long time, I think I've found the person who's going to help get me there.

See you soon,

Beatrice"

My eyes drifted to the bottom of the letter, where the writing continued in a darker black ink.

"PS: Put this ring on."

A simple silver ring was taped to the letter just below the words, which suddenly began echoing in my head, in Beatrice's voice. They got louder and louder and louder, until my own thoughts were suffocating under their weight, and the only thing I could do was comply, and I watched as my left hand ripped the ring from the paper and place it on my right index finger.

Beatrice's voice immediately faded into the back of my mind until my own thoughts resurfaced, and I stared at the ring now adorning my finger. The initials RvA were inscribed along the band. Horrified, I grabbed the ring with my left hand and began to pull, only to hear Beatrice's voice rise again in my mind, commanding me to put on the ring. I stopped pulling and the voice subsided. Three additional attempts yielded the same result.

Just then, I felt my phone buzz in my pocket. I pulled it out to see a new text message from a number I didn't recognize.

"You can't take it off, Jen. So don't try. See u soon. Love, B."

What had I done?

NEVER
QUEST ALONE

The first Quest was simple.

I went to Chelsea Market, bought a handful of raspberries, a tillandsia, a grape popsicle, and three pounds of 75/25 ground beef. I left the goods in the windowsill of a brownstone on West 9th Street and then headed to Prospect Park, where a plain, white envelope was waiting for me under a random bench. Inside was a wooden token, the size of a half dollar, with the number one intricately carved in the middle. I quickly tucked it into my pocket and began the long trek back to my office, a new swing in my step.

I progressed quickly through the next series of Quests. It was as if someone had copied down the tutorial section of *World of Warcraft* and was playing it out in real life.

Kill three pigeons.

Fetch some random plant.

Buy two rats from a particular pet shop.

They were a fun diversion at first and luckily I had no girlfriend at the moment to distract me, but I didn't see the point. Sure, I was quickly earning experience points, but what were they for? Some sort of secret contest, where the guy who racked up the most XP got a year's subscription to the newest MMORPG? I mean, that did sound awesome, but was it really worth my time? Yes, yes, it was.

One day, about a year since I'd discovered this whole thing, I was minding my own business, picking which Quest to tackle on my way home from work, when I saw a message waiting for me in my Q-mail inbox.

```
"Twelv3_parsecs,

Congrats. You've passed my test. If you're ready
to take your Questing to the next level, then go
to the NYU library and bring me the book at call
number 949.278.01. I'll be waiting for you at
Bleecker St. Grounds on Monday morning at 10:30.
See you soon,

Trinity"
```

I read the note over a second time. Then a third. And then probably six more times after that. It's no secret that I loved *The Matrix*, so now to be getting a cryptic note from someone named Trinity was making my head spin. I had to find that book, so I could meet her. If it even was a her.

The task seemed simple enough, except the book had been checked out of the library by a patron with no name the day before. I tracked down all the library employees to see if someone remembered who it had been, but all that got me was a vague description of a man in his seventies with a tweed jacket. I pressed on though, and after some subterfuge and a lot of phone calls, I was walking out of the smelly professor's office with the book in hand and only an hour to spare.

My breath was nearly gone by the time I made it to the coffee shop downtown, but there she was, waiting for me. Her hair was blond and her eyes were green and when she looked at me that first time and smiled, I swear my knees almost gave way.

I tried to play it cool at first. Girls don't like a braggart; they want a confident, suave guy, or so I'd read on the Internet. So I downplayed how hard it was to find the diary and she seemed impressed at my Questing skills. But the whole time my heart was racing and I felt the sweat pooling on the back of my neck. Man, I wished I had talked to more girls in college.

She asked if I had read the diary and I told her that I'd only just retrieved it.

"Oh," she said. "Then you don't know the truth."

"What truth?" I asked.

"The truth about magic."

She then launched into a tale so ridiculous, so out of this world, that it made me feel like the sane one, and I was the guy who had been running around town fetching stuff in exchange for weird tokens for a year. But then she took out a small plastic container from her bag and placed it on the table.

Inside was a tiny brown mouse, scurrying about. Next, she produced an ornate dagger sheathed in leather. She withdrew the gleaming blade, popped the lid off the container, and then, without warning, plunged it into the little rodent and then removed it just as quickly.

My eyes went wide and I was about to get out of my chair and run away, but she pointed into the container and I looked inside. There was the mouse, except instead of a furry creature, there was a stone statue of a mouse in its place. She lifted it out of the container and put it on the table, and I cringed.

"Magic," she explained "is everywhere. It's in the soil, in the water, in the plants, and even in the metals in the ground. This blade," she said, as she resheathed it and placed it back in her purse, "being just one example."

She kept going, explaining how she had uncovered the truth on her own, how she had developed a knack for alchemy and amassed a collection of rare prima materia that she still needed to experiment on, but how she had hit a wall in her progression up the Questing ladder.

I stared at her in silence, trying to take in this new world she was revealing, but I couldn't help noticing the dimples in her cheeks, the way her hair fell on her face, and the sparkle of the mid-morning sun in her eyes.

It was literally something out of a movie: the dorky yet secretly brave and heroic and awesome main character being chosen by the drop-dead gorgeous but also brilliant and funny girl of his dreams to learn the truth.

I took that as a sign that she liked me. I mean, if you learned there was a secret magical world, you wouldn't go around telling every idiot on the street, would you? Of course not.

I was so absorbed with her entire being that I didn't actually hear the question the first time.

"Will you be my new trainee?"

"Y-yes," I said without a second thought. If she had asked me to cut out one of my kidneys and lay it on the table, I probably also would have said yes.

It was only later that I found out she was taken.

We were at her apartment, fresh off our first successful Raid, and she had just revealed the secret room hidden behind a bookcase where she hid her alchemy lab from the rest of her life. The room was stocked with shelves and bookcases full of vials and jars, and she began explaining what everything was. I tried to pay attention but it was all just so much to take in, on top of the fact that I was actually alone with her in her apartment.

But before I could try to make a move, I saw the picture out of the corner of my eye.

"Oh," I said, pointing at it. "Is that your brother?"

It wasn't.

Worse, the guy was a jerk. It wasn't that hard to figure out that he was cheating on Trinity. And I only followed him for one day. She must have known, but I held my tongue. Well, for a while anyway.

It took me a couple of months to work up the courage to tell her, and when I did, you'd think she would have thanked me. But she didn't. No, she pretended I hadn't said anything and then abruptly left the coffee shop. I waited a few days before reaching out and wondered how long I should wait before asking her out. After so long with that dipshit, she would want a change, I was sure of it, but I wanted to give her some space.

Six weeks later though, she showed up at our usual table at the coffee shop with a rock on her finger. That should have been the end of it. I should have pushed down my feelings and moved on. We could still work together. I didn't want that to end, because I was learning so much about alchemy and prima materia and magic and, well, I couldn't go back to how it was before. When I was just grinding up a down escalator with no hope of getting to the top.

But the heart leads and the brain follows. It started small at first. I began stopping by her apartment building each morning, waiting across the street until she went out for her morning jog. God, she looked good even in sweats. I figured out her running route after a few weeks, and then one day ran into her "by accident." She was a little weirded out, but I explained that I had started exercising and the West Side Highway was really the best place to run near my apartment.

Next, I started following her to her tutoring appointments at our coffee shop. I showed up at one of them and pretended that I thought we were meeting that day. She gave me an awkward hello and then told me I was mistaken. Finally, I executed the last part of my plan: confront the cheater head on. I took a break from tailing Trinity to document that scumbag's extracurricular activities, printed out all the evidence, and then waited for the perfect opportunity.

I waited outside a restaurant where they were having dinner, dressed in my finest suit. When they were done with their entrees, I strode up to their table and plopped the folder of pictures down.

"You deserve better than him," I said. She went white as a ghost while he turned beet red. The entire restaurant was staring but I stood my ground and waited for her to say something. Except she didn't. She just sat there, refusing to look me in the eye, until finally her fiancé got up and cocked me in the face with a right hook. The next thing I knew, I was out on the pavement, stars swirling in my vision. She never came out.

I realized on the way home that the whole plan had been so inartful. If I really wanted to win her over, embarrassing her in public was not the answer. I just needed to tell her how I felt.

I penned a long missive and sent it over Q-Mail to her. She didn't respond. So I wrote another one, then another, and then another. The last one may have been too over the top, and I immediately regretted what I had called her. I quickly wrote a follow-up note profusely apologizing and asking if we could meet, so I could sort this whole thing out.

"Hello, Doug."

It's the day after my last note and I'm making up some work that I had blown off in one of the public atriums on 6 ½ Avenue. I look up and she is standing at the doorway.

She is stunning. Even more so than usual. A long black dress hugs her figure and her heels clack along the marble floor as she walks toward my little table. I quickly get up to leave, afraid that the cops are going to jump out from behind the corner, but she motions me to stay.

"H-hi Trinity," I say.

"You can call me Beatrice."

"OK, Beatrice."

"Can I join you?" she asks.

"S-su-sure you can, please."

I get up and pull out the other chair for her and she sits down. She stares at me in a way she's never looked at me before and I feel my heartbeat quicken.

"H-how did you know I'd be here?"

"You're not the only one good at stalking."

I start to protest, but she holds up her hand.

"No. It's fine. I understand. You were just looking out for me. It was sweet. In a way."

There is something tender in her voice now, and I know that my notes must have finally gotten through to her.

"I just wanted to say that you were right about everything," she says, leaning in close to my face, so that our mouths are just inches apart and I can see the sheen on her lips. "And, well…"

She leans forward suddenly and we're kissing. After about half a minute, I open my eyes a crack to convince myself that this was real, that this was actually happening, and there she is. Kissing me of all people. Her lips taste like strawberries on a summer's day and her perfume smells like lavender and I just want this moment to continue on forever.

But finally, she breaks away, and I sit back in my chair and let out a deep breath. I can still taste her on my lips, and I run my tongue over them to experience that feeling again. But when I do, the strawberries are gone and in their place is something foul, something I remember from that first visit to her apartment all those months ago.

"Goodbye, Doug," I hear her say, as my throat starts to swell and my vision becomes blurry, and the last thing I see is her in that black dress, walking through the empty atrium and into the night.

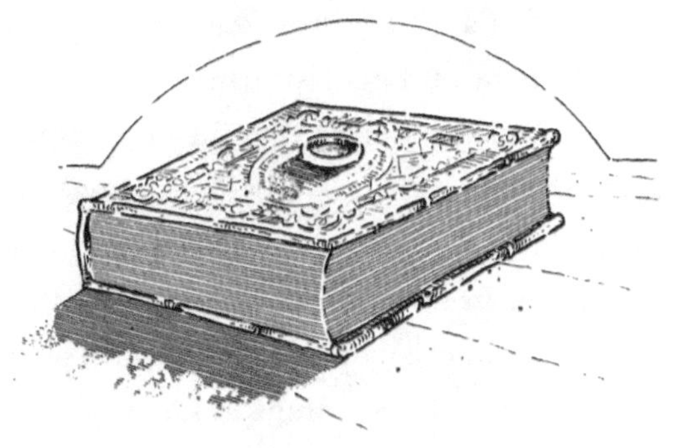

CHAPTER FOURTEEN

AND IN THE DARKNESS BIND THEM

"Some write to remember. I write to forget."
— RITA VAN ASCH, JANUARY 1, 1787

Once upon a time, I was a normal girl living in a normal world with normal friends, a normal job, and in love with a normal boyfriend.

I still had those things today. The normal friends, who were catty and shallow and who used me for their own ends. The normal job, that was doing its best to grind me into the ground. The normal boyfriend, who had chosen to stay in Hong Kong for two months instead of coming home for a week in between like he normally did.

Once upon a time, I also clicked a link in a random email, discovered a secret world, completed Quests, survived a fight to the death, and found a magic ring.

But it wasn't as thrilling as it sounded. The secret world, it was turning more sinister by the day. The Quests, well, they had led me straight into the mind of a mad woman. And the ring, it was trapped on my finger, put there by said mad woman.

That ring had adorned my right ring finger for three weeks, but as for the woman who put it there, well, she had gone radio silent.

As soon as I had returned from the library, I had locked the dusty book away in a drawer in my bedroom, along with the top half of Beatrice's note. I didn't want any part of Rita van Asch, didn't want to know what she had done, didn't want to know why the diary was so important.

No, I had a constant reminder of Rita on my finger at all times, and that was enough.

The bottom portion of the note, with those words that had compelled me to put the ring on, I had placed in an envelope, which I had then put inside a second envelope and then inside a still larger third envelope for good measure. I had buried the Russian doll of envelopes under a smattering of old clothes in a box in the corner of my closet, where hopefully no one would find it.

I had waited a day before attempting to take the ring off again, and when I did, Beatrice's voice returned, commanding me to put the ring on. I complied, and the voice stopped once more. This became my morning routine, but every result was the same. Some days I lasted a minute before succumbing and other days I had given up before the voice could even finish the sentence.

One random morning a week ago, I had resolved to hold out as long as possible.

In one fluid motion, I had pulled the ring off my finger, dropped it into the same drawer that held the diary, and then quickly closed and locked it again. But the command returned, as if a set of speakers were held up to my ears, and I writhed on the floor for what seemed like an eternity trying to resist its pull. In the end, I had lasted a total of 75 seconds. There was no text from Beatrice afterward though. Did she know what I was attempting to do? Or was she so confident in the command's power over me that she didn't feel the need to check on me?

And if her torments during my waking hours weren't enough, there was no refuge in sleep either. It had taken about a week for me to realize that the weird dreams I had been having weren't dreams at all, but more of Beatrice's memories that had seeped into my mind during our encounter at the party.

Each morning, I tried to write down whatever I could recall but all I produced were meaningless fragments: a baby's cry, a deserted path in a park on a moonless night, a woman reading a newspaper at a coffee shop.

Tonight, as I continued my new nightly ritual of numbing myself with scotch and trying to speedrun through *A Link to the Past* before my midnight FaceTime with Duncan, I read over the unintelligible scribblings and searched for a deeper meaning. I didn't find it.

The time on my laptop flicked to 12:00 and I clicked on Duncan's number in the chat window and waited for his visage to appear. But the pinging noise continued on with no response from him halfway around the world.

The bottle of Bruichladdich and a shot glass were already next to my computer from last night, so while I waited for Duncan to answer, I pulled up the Quest Board, clicked on a random Quest, and then took a shot. I clicked back to FaceTime and then back to the Board to open a different Quest, and took another shot. By the fifth shot, my mouse hand could barely move the cursor over the End Call button, so I took that as a sign to retire for the evening, Duncan be damned. I laid down in my bed, closed my eyes, and waited for sleep to claim me.

I opened my eyes. A bottle of red wine was in front of me and I was sitting on an unfamiliar couch in an unfamiliar apartment. A phone next to me vibrated several times before I picked it up and brought it into a kitchen full of marble and stainless steel. As I set it down, it vibrated again and I read the messages that appeared on the screen.

An inexplicable jolt of anger suddenly flared up inside me, but I didn't know why. I blinked and I was now standing in a doorway in front of a man in his boxers, who was sitting on a bed. I held up the phone so he could see it before letting it fall from my hand and storming out of the apartment.

On my cab ride to somewhere, I pulled out a different phone and began texting random numbers until one responded. I blinked again and I was in a bar, a drink in my hand, an older man in the seat next to me. I blinked a third time and we were in bed together, our bodies pressed against each other. A fourth blink and I "awoke" sat up in that same bed to find the man from the bar lying asleep next to me. My head was pounding, so I rose and walked to the bathroom. I rubbed my eyes and stared at myself in the mirror. Except it wasn't me.

It was her.

Beatrice.

The reflection of Beatrice stared back at me. My eyes (or were they hers?) were weary with the weight of a thousand problems, my lips were tinged with sadness, and I let out a low sigh.

Suddenly, the face in the mirror frowned. Then without warning, the woman in the reflection cocked her ring-adorned fist and smashed the mirror to pieces.

I awoke again, this time in my own bed. My hair was matted with sweat, my sheets, the same. What had I just seen? A distant memory from Beatrice's life or something that had just happened last night? Whatever it was, I hoped that the next time I drifted off to sleep, my dreams would be my own.

My phone suddenly buzzed on the nightstand.

"Meet me at Bleecker St Grounds at 1030. Bring the diary."

I felt a pit grow in my stomach. Finally, the bitch had summoned me.

I retrieved the diary from its prison, sat down at my desk, and opened the book to a random page. The entry was short and dated September 30, 1777:

I pressed Henry for more information about troop movements, but he refuses to divulge anything. It seems he does not trust me as much as I thought.

It made no sense to me. Who was Henry? I flipped through the worn pages, searching for something that would help me make sense of it all, but my throbbing head halted any further examination. I took the top half of Beatrice's note out of my desk drawer and placed it in between the pages.

That's when I noticed something else in the drawer, next to my ever-growing stack of tokens: a small green bit of something wrapped in plastic. It was the extra gummy that Steve had given me in the bar so many weeks ago. And, the perfect cure for my semi-hungover state.

I unwrapped the plastic and stared at the gummy. The last time I had eaten one of these, I had just imbibed several stiff drinks and it had magically whisked away the alcohol and returned me to my clear-headed state. But now I was several hours removed from my latest binge. Would it have the same effect?

I broke off roughly a quarter of the gummy, set it aside, and wrapped the remainder back up. No sense in wasting my only one if it didn't work. I popped the piece in my mouth and began to chew. The horrible taste of rotting fish was nauseating even the second time, but thankfully the whole ordeal was over in a few seconds. I waited for something to happen. Even if my headache dulled a little, it would be worth it, as I would need my full mental capacity to face Beatrice in case this meeting was anything like our first one.

Finally, after about five minutes, the pounding started to subside and I slowly stood up from my desk, the ill effects of my scotch consumption completely gone.

Incredible.

I walked over to my closet to dig out something big enough to hold the diary. Under a pile of old sweatshirts, I found my worn blue-and-gold backpack that had served me well in Ann Arbor. It had its fair share of holes and one of the straps was frayed within a few inches of life, but it would do the trick.

On my way to the subway, I shot off an email to my boss, explaining that I was coming down with something so I'd be working from home today. As I waited on the platform, my mind started racing. Would she try to get inside my mind again? Could she even? If the linkage between us was because of the apples we had both eaten, well, that was weeks ago and I hadn't dared to eat any of the leftover ones still in my freezer.

The train arrived and I grabbed a seat in the nearly empty car. I set my backpack down and pulled out Beatrice's note from the back of the diary. If she was still angry from our meeting at the party, her words held no trace of it. If anything, it sounded like she needed me to help her take the right course at her inflection point.

Then I read over the list of items in her note that she had fetched as part of her first Quest - 90/10 beef, a tillandsia, an apple popsicle, and a handful of blueberries - and my jaw dropped. They were the same items as my first Quest, except with a different blend of beef and a different flavored popsicle. What did it all mean?

I put the note away and tried to clear my mind for the encounter ahead, one that might change my life completely. I had relished this secret world that I had discovered, but now it seemed like I was at my own inflection point. Would I continue on with my Quest alone or would I take a chance and join forces with Beatrice? Would she even give me a choice?

The train arrived at the Bleecker Street stop. It was 10:25 and I was going to be late, so I dashed out of the car and up the stairs, breaking into a slight jog after I reached the street. As I drew closer, I felt as if my hand was being pulled toward the coffee shop like a fish on a hook being reeled in and I looked down at the silver ring on my finger.

I spotted her immediately, sipping a coffee on the brisk fall day in a high back chair just outside the shop, talking on the phone. My would-be mentor. The potential scorpion to my frog.

The force pulling my finger increased as I walked around to the seat across from her and sat down. Only then did I realize that she wasn't talking on the phone, but to a little boy in the seat next to her.

CHAPTER FIFTEEN

HELP WANTED

"We had won the war but lost half the Guild in the process."

"You're late," said Beatrice, ignoring the look of shock on my face. "I take it you have the book?"

I nodded, unzipped my backpack, and set the tome onto the table.

"Umm, yeah. You told me to bring it," I said.

"Oh. Right. Sorry, force of habit," she said, before turning to the little boy next to us. "Jack-Jack, Mommy and her friend have some things to discuss, so you can use your iPad now as a special treat."

Beatrice dug an iPad in a blue rubber case out of a tote bag and handed it to her son, who immediately began tapping away.

"I wouldn't normally bring him, but my sitter canceled last minute."

"Oh. No problem, I guess. Just, umm, didn't realize you had a kid."

"Yeah, well, we're both not what the other thought, it seems."

She ruffled Jack-Jack's hair, but he ignored her motherly affections, his eyes glued to the screen. I was still taken aback that this woman who had attacked me, who had invaded my mind and forced me to wear this ring, was actually a mother.

"Yeah."

An awkward silence fell over us and I took a moment to study this woman, who had caused me so much anguish but whom I had never actually met.

She had dirty blonde hair done up in a ponytail and was wearing a plaid pleated skirt with a cardigan that clung to her figure. Her green eyes were paler than they had appeared during our first encounter. If it hadn't been for the slight laugh lines around her mouth and the tiny crow's feet around her eyes (not to mention her son), I would have pegged her as a Catholic school girl on her way to a pep rally.

"So, should we get down to it?" she said. "You read the diary, I assume?"

I shook my head.

"No. After I read your note and you made me put on the ring, I locked the book away."

I wanted to unload on her, tell how I was going to spend every free waking moment I had trying to get this ring off, but for some reason, I held my tongue.

"Oh. Fine. You already know the truth. That much I saw in your head. And you already know the diary's true value."

"I do?"

"Yes. The ink. My note. You really didn't read any of it, did you?"

"No. Just the last entry about test subjects at Valley Forge. And the Compendium."

Beatrice took a sip of coffee out of the oversized mug and I saw it on her left index finger: the twin to the cuff on my right index finger with the same inscribed initials. I felt my right hand slowly drift toward her hand and I pulled it back, as a spark of anger ignited the rage inside me. She had brushed off what she had done as if it was normal, as if she had merely lent me some fancy jewelry for a night out.

"Ah. Well, you missed the par-"

"Why did you do it?" I shouted. The other patrons of the cafe turned towards us, but Beatrice maintained her composure and just smiled, which made me even angrier.

"Calm down," she whispered. It was so soft I almost thought for a second that her voice was back in my head. "You'll scare Jack-Jack."

"I don't give a fuck about your-"

"Don't," Beatrice said, holding up her left hand, and I again felt my right hand inch towards her. "I knew this was a bad idea, bringing him here. I thought maybe it would temper your anger toward me, seeing me here as a regular mom."

"The only thing that would do that is if you let me take this stupid thing off my finger."

She sighed.

"I can't. Well, I can. But it would be a waste."

"A waste of what?"

"The ink. Do you know how valuable it is? Did you stop to think what else it's capable of?"

I shook my head.

"Besides," she said, "it's a good way of keeping you in line. I'm sure you've felt it by now. Our rings are linked. Like there's an invisible string between them. I can tell when your ring is off. Every morning you try to remove it, only for the ink command to kick in again and you put it back on. You'll drive yourself insane if you keep trying that. Just do what I say and we'll get along swimmingly."

"And what if I don't? You'll kill me?"

"Please, Jen. Do I look like a killer? I'm just a simple stay-at-home mom trying to find enough hours in the day to get everything done."

I didn't buy the frazzled mom act for a second but antagonizing her more was not going to get me anywhere, so I took a deep breath and tried to just stay in the moment.

"So now what?" I asked. "You said in your note that you needed me. For what? To run experiments on, like back at the party with the apple pie?"

"No. You're too valuable to just be a lab rat. Although I'm sure there will come a time or two where you'll need to provide that service. Honestly, it's my own fault for not reaching out sooner. Polly told me about you months ago, but I had my hands full with … other things. We could have avoided all that unpleasantness at the party if I had."

"What are you talking about?"

"Polly's been one of my scouts for a few years. She keeps her ears and eyes open for any promising newbs and sends them my way. Did you think it was purely a coincidence that she had the call number for the diary?"

"I…" I stopped, my breath faltering. Had I just spent the last several months of my life as a puppet on the end of her strings?

"I don't know what to think. About anything anymore."

The tears started to pool in my eyes and before I could bring my hand up to wipe them, they spilled forth down my cheeks.

"Oh, keep it together girl."

Beatrice dug a pack of tissues out of her mom-bag and handed it to me. I turned away to wipe away the tears while Beatrice rolled her eyes.

"If you're done with your little crying fit, we have a business arrangement to solidify."

Beatrice pulled two stapled sheets of paper out of her bag and handed them to me. On the top of the first page, it said in printed letters: "Novice agreement."

It continued:

"This Novice Agreement (the 'Agreement') is made effective as of November 21, 2018 by and between Beatrice Taylor (the 'Alchemist') and Jen Jacobs (the 'Novice').

1. Description of Services

Novice will provide the following services to Alchemist (collectively, "the Services"): Raid assistance, Questing research, alchemic experimentation feedback and assistance, and additional miscellaneous services to be determined at a later date. Novice will make herself available to complete the Services upon request of Alchemist at times and places of Alchemist's choosing. Novice will use her best efforts to such comply with Alchemist's requests.

2. Payment

In exchange for Novice's performance of the Services, Alchemist agrees to pay Novice a monthly retainer of three bronze tokens, plus additional token dispensations for extraordinary performance at the sole discretion of Alchemist.

3. Term/Termination

The term of this Agreement shall be for one year from the effective date. At Alchemist's option, the term of the Agreement may be extended by one year provided that Alchemist gives Novice notice of such extension at least 30 days prior to the expiration of this Agreement.

Alchemist may terminate the Agreement by providing 30-days written notice of said termination to Novice.

4. Confidentiality

Novice shall keep the existence and contents of this Agreement and services provided hereunder confidential ('Confidential Information') and shall not..."

I stopped reading and looked up at Beatrice.

"Is this a joke?"

She shook her head.

"No. It's a necessity I've had to implement after a recent string of trainee failures. And as a show of good faith, I've bumped you up to the rank of Novice, with all the perks that entails. Normally I'd be starting you out dealing magic Adderall to the kids at NYU, but I'm cash rich at the moment so we can skip that."

Great, so I didn't have to be a magic drug mule. I just had to be at Beatrice's beck and call in exchange for some bronze tokens, and what was I supposed to do with these tokens? See how many I could stack on my desk before they toppled over?

"How generous of you," I said, my voice dripping in condescension. Beatrice frowned.

"I could just make you agree, you know. It wouldn't take much ink. But then you'd hate me even more. And that's not what I want. I've been dealt too many setbacks so far and I can't afford another one."

She took back the contract, pulled out a pen, and signed her name on the second page, and then handed it back to me.

"Look, go home, read through the diary and the contract. Think things through. I'm confident that you'll see that the path I'm offering you is the only way forward. Then meet me back here tonight at 10:30. This place has a speakeasy in the back that makes a mean martini."

"Fine," I said, glad to have at least the illusion of choice, if only for a few hours.

"Great. It's a date."

Beatrice tapped Jack-Jack on the shoulder and the kid broke out of his iPad daze and looked up at his mom.

"Sweetie, iPad time is over. Let's go down the street and check out the math museum."

"Just one more minute!" he whined in response. "I just want to finish this level!"

"Jack-Jack, I said no. Don't make me count to five."

Beatrice began slowly counting down from five, reaching one before switching to fractions, until at 0.5 the kid finally gave in.

I tried to suppress a laugh at this woman, who wielded power I couldn't even have fathomed, being outmaneuvered by a toddler.

"Say goodbye to Mommy's friend," said Beatrice as she started to push the stroller out of the cafe.

"Goodbye to Mommy's friend!" the little whelp said.

CHAPTER SIXTEEN

DECISION POINTS

"But recruitment would have to wait. This new country was in its infancy and I intended to have my say on how it should be run."

I sat at the cafe for about an hour before I worked up the strength to trudge home with the diary and my enslavement agreement. Despite the magnanimous way in which she presented it, there was no doubt in my mind what Beatrice was proposing.

I would be her lackey, her patsy, her guinea pig, her lap dog. And for what? A new kind of shiny worthless token? I already had one soul-crushing job where I was overworked and underappreciated. Why did I need another and one where I would be in the employ of someone who could bind me to her will with a bit of ink and paper?

But then I opened the diary again on my bed and started to read. The entries started almost as if they were recounting a history. An alternative history from the one I learned in school, where the first settlers of New York weren't seeking religious freedom or new trade goods, but something bigger.

Magic.

But what magic they had discovered remained hidden off the page. Or only in cryptic references to vaguely described locations that had probably been paved over by Robert Moses.

The narrative then abruptly shifted to Rita's musings on the Revolutionary War and her seemingly important role in it. Because after some quick Google research, Rita's letters, written apparently in the same ink that Beatrice now had, were responsible for the inexplicable buffoonery of one William Howe. Who upon receiving said letters no doubt filled with instructions written in the compulsion ink, committed military blunder after military blunder. And the sums of those blunders eventually allowed Washington to retreat to Valley Forge, and, well, the rest is history.

A secret history.

I closed the diary.

It was all so much to take in that my head began to spin and I collapsed backward onto the bed.

I reached for my phone. The digits were still burned into my memory after all these years: my mom's cell phone number. After she had died, I had called the number by mistake one day only to get sent straight to her voicemail. It shouldn't have gone through, I remember canceling it as part of the flurry of activity that had consumed me after the funeral. The sound of her voice had been too much to take, so I had hung up before her greeting could finish.

But I called back. I didn't know why it still worked, but hearing her voice, even for those few seconds, helped me in ways I couldn't explain. Then in college I started leaving messages. It was an accident the first time, as I had forgotten to hang up before the beep sounded. But the next time it was on purpose and I talked to my mother again for the first time in years, even if it was only one way. It felt like magic sometimes, like I was leaving her messages in Heaven.

Other times, I just felt pathetic, that I was pouring my heart out to a hard drive in some server farm in the middle of nowhere. Each time I called, I had wondered if this was going to be the time that the phone company caught on and shut it down, and my mother would be completely gone. Eventually I weaned myself off of that crutch, but a part of me wondered if she was still out there, waiting for me to call just one more time.

I must have fallen asleep before I could decide to call her, because next thing I knew, I was Beatrice again. In the cafe where we had just met. I was reading a newspaper, sipping coffee, and something in the paper made me smile, but I couldn't make out the words. Then a redheaded girl ran up to the table and sat down.

"Sorry I'm late! The subway was a complete disaster," the girl said.

"No worries. I take it you have the book?" I said in reply.

The beep boop of an incoming FaceTime call jostled me from the dream-memory and I sat up in bed, again covered in sweat. For a millisecond, I thought it was somehow my mom, but the number on the screen was Duncan's.

I looked over at the clock. It was one in the afternoon already, one a.m. the next day in Hong Kong. We didn't usually talk at this time, but maybe he was feeling guilty for having missed our last call. I clicked the green button and waited for Duncan's face to appear.

But it didn't.

Instead, a blurry dark image filled the screen and all I could hear was the unintelligible noise of what sounded like a party. He had pocket dialed me. Just what every girl dreamed of. I waited to say something, but the screen didn't change and then I heard the raucous muffled laughter of a woman followed by the similarly muffled tones of Duncan's voice.

"Duncan!" I screamed into the phone. Nothing happened. Several more shouts did nothing to get his attention, so I finally gave up and ended the call.

I wanted to believe that what I had heard was nothing out of the ordinary, that he was just out for a fun night with his co-workers, but instead all I felt was anger. Anger that he was not here when I needed someone to turn to, anger that he couldn't even make the effort to remember that he had forgotten to call me.

Well, I didn't need his counsel. Or my mother's, for that matter. I had done pretty well on my own, so there was no point in doubting myself now. I pulled out the contract, turned to the second page, and was about to sign on the anointed line, when a better idea popped into my head.

The inside of the coffee shop was practically empty, except for a sole barista behind the counter who was staring down at her phone. Behind her was an intimidating wall lined with cubbies full of bags of coffee.

"Hi," I said to the barista.

She didn't look up.

"Umm, where's the bar?" I asked.

"We're closed," she said, still not looking up.

OK then.

I stood there for a few minutes, to see if she would relent and reveal the secret entrance, but she kept on with her act and didn't say a word. I was about to risk the wrath of texting Beatrice, when suddenly the wall of coffee opened inward, and a gaggle of scantily dressed college girls burst through the opening, lifted up the counter, and brushed passed me.

The coffee wall remained ajar and the barista remained oblivious, so I crept forward and walked into the dark passage, which after several feet opened into a dimly-lit room.

The bar resembled more of a cellar than a lounge, with exposed brick along the walls painted black and individual light bulbs hung from wires attached to the low ceiling. I walked between the teal-upholstered leather booths on one side and the bar stools on the other, until finally reaching Beatrice at the end of the bar, an empty martini glass in front of her. I walked over and sat down next to her, and she glanced at her watch.

"10:29. Cutting it a bit close but fine."

She flagged down a bartender.

"Another martini please. Up, no vermouth, and very cold. And my friend here will have…"

"Gin, neat."

The bartender nodded and then retreated.

"So," said Beatrice, "did you think it over?"

"Yes," I said. "And I have a few changes to your deal." I took the contract out of my bag and placed it on the bar.

"Do you?" she said, raising an eyebrow.

"Yes. First, I want some real money, not just tokens. If I get fired from my job because I'm off on some crazy expedition for you, then I still want to be able to live."

"Fine, that's reasonable. In addition to the tokens, you'll get a $1000/month stipend."

$1000? That won't even cover my rent. I want $1800."

"$1500."

"Deal."

"OK, now that that's settled, let's-"

"I wasn't done."

"You weren't?"

A crinkle formed on Beatrice's nose and she took the olives from her empty glass and began chewing them slowly.

"No. The way I see it, this contract binds me to you indefinitely. I want a buyout option. If I want to quit after six months, you'll agree to release me if I pay back everything, the tokens and the cash."

The bartender finally returned with the drinks and Beatrice took hers, raised the glass to her lips, and took a long, drawn out sip, before setting the nearly empty glass down again.

"Two years," she said.

"What?"

"You'll give me two years. Then, we can reconsider the terms of your contract."

"That's too long, I don't want to-"

"No, it's not. I've been at this for 12 years, Jen, and I've only now just reached the crest, ready to make the final ascent to the top. So you can leave now, if you want, and waste the next decade of your life retreading my path up the mountain. Or, you can recognize the opportunity in front of you and grab it."

She finished her speech and got up.

"Another one, please," she said to the bartender before retreating into the back of the bar.

I sat in silence, contemplating her offer, and my thoughts drifted to the fragmented memories that had seeped into my dreams.

Beatrice had done this before - tried to train someone to help her - but what had happened to the girl from the dream?

Had she failed and been cast aside?

Or worse?

Maybe it was better to run now, while I still had the chance. I would just forget everything that had happened, that there wasn't a secret magic underpinning the world, that I didn't have a silver ring stuck on my finger for the rest of my life.

Or I could stick it out on my own. Learn everything from the ground up. If Beatrice could do it, then so could I. I could take my time, forge my own path, on my own terms.

I pictured late nights in my apartment trying to come up with my own concoctions, rainy afternoons spent in abandoned alleyways seeking out rats, weekends wasted in the bowels of a library trying to track down any reference to alchemy or to Rita or to prima materia.

It would be an adventure, sure, but one in which I was utterly alone.

The bartender brought Beatrice's third martini and I suddenly wished I knew enough alchemy to spike the drink with a poison that would kill her in just a sip.

But I didn't.

And I couldn't.

I stared off into space, angry at myself for even thinking about that path, when Beatrice finally returned and sat back down.

"OK," I said to her.

Beatrice turned to me.

"OK what?"

"We have a deal."

"Oh. Oh! Excellent. Let me just make a few edits to the contract and we'll be all set to execute."

She produced a pen from her own bag and began scratching out the provisions we'd changed, before sliding the document back to me.

"Just initial next to my changes and sign on the dotted line."

Without giving myself another chance to change my mind, I quickly jotted "JJ" next to Beatrice's "BT" and then signed on the second page.

"Fantastic. I'll make you a copy." She took the contract and put it in her bag and then raised her glass to mine. I clinked it and we both sipped.

"This is a momentous day for you, Jen. For both of us. I'm - we're - finally going to give the Guild a run for its money."

The Guild. Beatrice had mentioned it in her note to me, but I had completely forgotten about it.

"W-what's the Guild?"

"It's the biggest puppet master of them all. It runs the Council. It has been lurking in the shadows of New York before there even was a New York."

I suppressed a laugh. One minute into my new apprenticeship and apparently I had signed on to take down a hundreds-year-old secret society.

"You make it sound like they were the ones who bought the island from the Lenape."

Beatrice nodded.

"They were. Didn't you read the diary? Rita van Asch laid it all out for you. The Guild came to America to find a new source of magic, and as far as I know, they're still looking for it."

"But they did find something, Rita mentioned-"

"That's just the same trace of magic that you can find anywhere, if you know how to look for it. No, they were looking for pure magic."

"To do what though? Rule over everyone as our magical overlords?"

"Maybe, I don't know. Sometimes I feel like they don't know either. It's been so long, they might have forgotten."

"And the two of us are going to just bring down this Guild?" I asked.

"Don't be ridiculous," she said. "We're just going to steal from them."

"What are we stealing?"

"The Compendium."

"Oh. I thought everyone had a copy of that."

"No," Beatrice said. "Each family keeps a log of their discoveries, alchemic recipes, etc. You could call that a compendium with a lower-case 'c.' But the one we're after, THE Compendium, it's the sum total knowledge of the Guild. It's all their secrets, all their prima materia, everything. With even a fraction of that information, I could finally send a message to them that I'm here to stay."

She downed the rest of her martini and threw some cash down on the bar and got up.

"Where are you going?" I asked.

"I'm going to bed, Jen. I've got a toddler who will come bursting into my room without fail in about six hours and I need some sleep."

I followed her out of the bar and back through the wall to the coffee shop, which was now mobbed with people dressed to the nines. We pushed them aside and walked out to the patio where we had met for the first time only 12 hours earlier.

"Next time I see you, you need to have read that diary cover-to-cover, OK? I've sussed out all the secrets it's hiding but a fresh pair of eyes is always welcome."

"Will do," I said.

"Good. As long as you do what I say, we'll avoid all the unpleasantness of our first encounter."

She continued out of the patio and waved down a cab, before turning back to me.

"*Oh and Jen?*"

Her words sounded in my head, just like at the party, and I froze.

"*Don't try to fuck with me. Because if you do, the last thing you'll remember is reading the words 'kill yourself' on a random scrap of paper.*"

CHAPTER SEVENTEEN

BRIDESMAIDS

"I sat out the drafting of the Articles. We were away at war and I assumed that the Congress would absolutely make a mess of things. As usual, I was right."

"**S**o girls, what do you think?"

Lisa stood on a raised platform surrounded by mirrors, decked out in the eighth wedding dress of the afternoon. Stacy and I sat behind her on a plush couch, champagne flutes in hand and midway through our second bottle.

"Lis, you look stunning. I think this is definitely the one," said Stacy. She had said that about the last three, but who was counting?

"You think so? But what about the DeWitt? I think that one was very slimming."

"As if you need the help. But let me take a pic of this one and then we can compare."

"Good idea Stac!" I added. I was at my wits end with this outing and anything that sped it along was a win in my book.

Stacy got up from the couch and started taking pictures of Lisa from every conceivable angle, as I reached down into my bag to re-trieve the tiny piece of the gummy I had stashed away at the bottom. I hated to waste a piece, but if today was the day that Beatrice finally resurfaced, I wanted to be ready. And if it wasn't, then at least the late night at work I was going to have to put in to make up for skipping out early wouldn't be terrible. The taste of the gummy was slightly more palatable the third time around, and after a few moments, I felt the buzz of the champagne fade away.

A week had passed since I had become Beatrice's woman, and of course my new boss had gone silent again. It had given me time to do my homework though. I had finally made my way through Rita van Asch's diary, but hadn't gleaned anything more from it than during my first purview. All I knew was that Rita had the compulsion ink that Beatrice now had, and boy did that make me feel good inside, what with the death threat and all.

Every time my phone had buzzed the past week, my heart would start beating a mile a minute; I would warily look at the screen, waiting to see if it was a task from Beatrice that I couldn't possibly complete, which would be followed by the promised death note waiting in my mailbox or slipped under my door.

I tried to put Beatrice out of my mind, which was difficult because somehow she was still in my mind, and focus on the task at hand: getting a wedding dress purchased in as little time as possible. But that proved to be a tall order, as Stacy and Lisa spent the next half hour flipping back and forth through hundreds of pictures, while the saleslady came in every few minutes to see if we had made any progress.

"Shoot, you know what? We can't make this decision now anyway," said Stacy after finally putting her phone down.

"Well in that case," I said, "we might as well go-"

"You need to see how the dress looks with your veil!" she continued. "I'll go bring in some options."

"Oh good thinking Stac!" said Lisa. "While you do that, JJ, can you bring me the Vera? It should be the white one with the flowers over there." She pointed to the large pile of white dresses stacked on a chair in the corner and I grimaced.

"OK," I said. I walked over to the pile and saw that they all appeared to be white with flowers somewhere on the dress. The first one on top was too hefty to push aside, so I grabbed that one and carried it over to Lisa, who had stepped out of the monstrous gown she had been wearing.

"JJ, this is the other DeWitt, not the Vera. But that's fine. I wanted this one also." She took it from me and slid it on.

"Sorry, they all look the same to me," I said as I zipped it up. When I reached the top of the dress, I saw Lisa's eyes in the mirror and it looked like she was going to cry. Crap.

"Wh-why would you say th-"

"No, no, what I meant was, in the pile, they all looked the same. Now that you have it on, of course I can tell it apart. You look amazing!"

"Oh. Thanks," Lisa said in monotone. "I actually don't love this one. Let me go find the first DeWitt and you'll just hold this one for a second. Part of me wants to pick one of the DeWitts on the slim chance we meet Dalia after the lecture." She motioned for me to unzip, extricated herself from the new dress, and handed it to me.

"So, how's Duncan?" she asked as she considered the pile.

"Umm, good. He's good." It was so out of character for Lisa to ask about my life that I didn't offer anything further. We had maybe gone on one double date with Lisa and Brad in all the time we had been dating. The guys seemed to get along, as they were both in finance, but that only made the dinner more unbearable for me, as I had to listen to Lisa the whole time drone on about fashion and tangential topics related to fashion.

"He's been in Hong Kong for a month now, should be coming home soon," I offered. Lisa didn't answer, but soon returned with the first DeWitt and directed me to put the one I was holding down while she slid on the new one.

"Oh, I'm sorry JJ. That must be so hard for you."

"Yeah, it sucks. But we FaceTime every day, or at least try to."

"Still, to be apart for that long. Then when he's in town, you must feel a lot of pressure to make everything perfect. It's like you're always on *The Bachelor*."

"Ha, yeah, a little. But usually it's not lik-"

"Zip please."

I was going to explain how it wasn't like that between Duncan and me, that we always fell back into our casual rhythm, and that neither of us felt the need to make a spectacle out of our brief time together. But the zipper was giving me all sorts of issues and I didn't want to accidentally tear the delicate fabric. After some gentle urging, I finally navigated it to the top of the dress and then moved to the side so I could see how it looked.

Lisa did look stunning, I had to admit, and I was genuinely happy for her. It wasn't every day that one of your best friends got married, and deep down I was happy to still be included in her inner circle. She certainly had had plenty of opportunities to ditch me over the years, but she hadn't, and that had to count for something, right?

"Ooh, JJ, what is that on your finger?" Lisa suddenly turned around, grabbed my right wrist and held it up to her face. "Well, it's not an engagement ring, but I guess something is better than nothing. Let me see how it looks on my finger. I need to pick out a wedding band for the ceremony."

Before I could protest, Lisa started shimmying the ring off my finger and I heard the commanding words start to form in the back of my mind.

"NO!" I yelled, shaking free of Lisa's grasp and retreating back to the couch to push the ring back down to its resting place. The voice faded once again and I breathed a sigh of relief, but Lisa turned around fully and stared at me, a look of bewilderment in her eyes.

"JJ, what the hell is the matter with you?"

"N-nothing. It's just, this ring, it was my mom's. I didn't want you to … I don't want to lose it."

"I wasn't going to swallow it, Jen. Jesus Christ. You need to chill the eff out."

Lisa shook her head, stepped down from the platform, and sat down on the couch next to me. The contrast between us was ridiculous: me, in my work hoodie and her in a seven-thousand-dollar dress. And now I had made things even more awkward, but as much as I wanted to explain myself, what could I say?

"Hey, sorry Lis, it's just if I take the ring off, my sociopathic mentor's voice will start sounding in my head?"

Yeah, OK.

"JJ, is something wrong?" Lisa's tone changed abruptly from rage to caring and I looked down at the floor, embarrassed at my outburst.

"The last few months, it's like you've pulled yourself back. You never initiate, you zone out during dinner, you're really behind on your bachelorette planning tasks. I mean, at this point, we're going to have to take a boat to London if you don't get our flights booked ASAP. It's like you're just going through the motions."

"No, it's not like that, it–"

My phone suddenly buzzed and I pulled it out to see a text from Beatrice, now of all times.

"Where ru" was all it said.

"downtown," I wrote back quickly before slipping my phone back into my bag and hoping that her question wasn't a sign of things to come.

Unfortunately, it was, as my phone buzzed again a few seconds later and I sheepishly looked at Lisa.

"Sorry, Slack feed at work is blowing up," I offered before looking at the text.

"Need u to get to Raid Board ASAP."

Well, maybe it was nearby.

Another buzz.

"1391 St Nicholas Ave."

Shit. That was all the way uptown, practically in the Bronx.

"Go thru yellow door and up to floor 3 and turn left. At end of hallway."

Terrific.

"Im all the way downtown. might be awhile," I wrote back, trying to buy time.

A final buzz.

"well then youd better start running :)" was the response.

The smiley face almost made me throw my phone across the room. Was she kidding with this crap? I was supposed to just drop anything at a moment's notice and run off to some random place with barely an explanation?

"Do you need to leave?" Lisa suddenly cut in and I realized I had been staring at my phone for a minute without saying a word.

"Yes, I mean, I don't want to, but, it's my boss. I told him I had to a doctor's appointment, so I could duck out no questions asked, and now he's asking when I can get back to the office."

"It's fine. Just go."

She picked up Stacy's phone and started flipping through the dress pictures. I contemplated trying to explain myself further, but instead turned and walked silently out of the room just as Stacy was returning with her hands full of veils.

"JJ, where-"

I kept walking, not wanting to explain myself to her either.

"What happened?" Stacy asked Lisa from the doorway but I continued my exit into the main part of the boutique without looking back.

"Work emergency apparen-" was the last thing I heard before I sprinted out of the store and into the pouring rain.

Fan-fucking-tastic.

I pulled out the tiny umbrella I kept in my purse, only for it to be blown inside out immediately upon opening. The rain was coming down in sheets and it being the evening rush as well, there was no chance I could get a cab. So I broke into a jog towards the station that was several avenues away, weaving in between the throngs headed in the opposite direction, only to be greeted by a crowd of people seven deep trying to board an already overcrowded train and a countdown clock indicating that the next train was 17 minutes away.

I ran down the platform, looking for a shallower crowd to push my way through and after throwing a couple of elbows, I staggered into the train just as the doors closed for the final time. It took several stops before the car emptied enough for me to pull out my phone to text Beatrice that I would be there soon. A slew of texts greeted me on my screen.

"how far r u"

"whats tkaing so long"

"y arent u answering??"

"Sorry!" I wrote back.

"On subway. Very crowded. 7 stops away"

I waited for a response as the train exited onto the elevated tracks, which finally gave me time to read over her first text, my drenched clothing clinging to my skin.

What the heck was the Raid Board?

Beatrice hadn't bothered to mention it last week, but I knew what a raid was in a video game - a more complex task or quest that required multiple people working together - so maybe this was something similar. Why the Raid Board was in a physical location as opposed to just another section of the online Quest Board was a different story, but I guess I would soon find out.

The train slowed as it reached the last stop, and I bolted through the doors and down the stairs, the rain finally subsiding. I looked up the address on my phone and it was only two blocks north. No further word from Beatrice meant that I had maybe beat her there so I quickened my pace until the end was in sight.

It was only then that I realized where I was heading: an elementary school.

CHAPTER EIGHTEEN

LEEROY JENKINS

"It took longer than I thought for the Articles to collapse. I spent those years traveling the newly independent states looking for new recruits."

This had to be a joke.

Maybe it was Beatrice's attempt at hazing: make someone go to a random location and make a fool of themselves. But then I saw the yellow door just past the main entrance of the school. Prank or not, I needed to get to the third floor before Beatrice upbraided me further.

The door opened without issue into a landing with two sets of stairs: one with an arrow pointing up and one with an arrow pointing down. It triggered bad memories of my own elementary school in Brooklyn, where if you walked into the wrong stairwell, you would be barreled into by kids going the correct direction, and if you walked into the right staircase, you would be barreled into by kids who thought it was funny to walk up the down staircase.

Thankfully, the school appeared empty, so I made my way up to the third floor without incident and turned left as instructed, until I finally reached the end of the hallway to find … a bulletin board filled with Post-it Notes.

You would have thought there would be a cooler system for giving out requests to steal valuable items from highly-secured places than a small bulletin board with Post-it Notes. But nothing made sense in this messed-up world.

With Beatrice still nowhere in sight, I approached the Board, picked a random section, and then began scanning the notes.

"Wanted: silver pocket watch. Don't care where you get it, as long as it's stolen and at least 110 years old. Reward: 34 bronze tokens."

"Request: the 1954 Audrey Hepburn Barbie from the FAO Schwarz display case. The store is closed so you'll need to figure out where they put it now. I'll give you 70 iron tokens for your trouble or a bottle of rare (and I do mean rare) whiskey."

And on and on they went. The level of skill required to accomplish these Raids was overwhelming, especially for a still relatively newbie like me. Digging through dumpsters was one thing, but breaking into the Museum of Natural History to steal a stuffed penguin was something entirely else.

"Good, you're here."

I turned around and Beatrice was walking down the empty hallway toward me, dressed in a long white dress.

"Yeah, uh sorry about earlier. I had no service on the train."

"It's fine. You didn't actually need to be here to get the Raid, but I figured this was easier than setting up another meeting later."

"Oh."

So I had just killed myself getting here on time for absolutely nothing. It was like the time at work I rewrote the entire codebase for the Archer class, only to find out the next day that we were dropping it from the game.

"Did you get a chance to look at the Board?"

I nodded.

"It's just a bunch of really hard Quests. Like, incredibly hard."

"Yes and no. They're Raids, so you need at least two people. That's part of the reason I need you. I haven't been able to do a Raid since my last trainee left."

"So I'm not one of your first?"

"No, like I said, it's been slow going with my current pool of prospects. But you're probably the most promising since... ah, here it is." She grabbed a Post-it Note from the Board and pulled it off. "Didn't want someone beating us to this one."

"I can't believe there are this many," I said. I had no idea how many Questers were leveled up enough to even know about the Raid Board, or even how many there were at all, but this seemed crazy.

"Not really. This Board is for the entire East Coast."

"What? Isn't that kind of inconvenient for everyone?"

"Yes, but it just means that we are lucky that the Board is in New York City. They usually move it to other locations around town. One year I think they moved it to Wilmington, Delaware, but people flipped out. I wouldn't have minded that much, it would only have been an Acela ride away."

Beatrice handed me the note. Purple ink filled the small square and the handwriting was so sloppy, I could barely make out what it said.

"Some valuable information was recently tattooed onto the back of a woman who has no idea what it means. I need that information. Leave this note under the garbage can next to Belvedere Castle and await further instruction."

I read it over a few times before giving it back to Beatrice.

"I don't understand. We just need to look at this woman's tattoo? That's it?"

Beatrice frowned.

"No. That's not it. That tattoo is hiding something very important."

"What is it?" I asked.

"I don't know."

"Then how do you know it's important?"

"Because I got a tip an hour ago from a trusted source that this Raid was going to be posted here."

"And this 'trusted source,' as you put it, is worth listening to?"

"Yes. They're the reason I am where I am today. Well, that and my relentlessness."

"I don't understand. We're going to complete the Raid and then what? Keep a copy of the tattoo information for ourselves?"

"Maybe. Who knows? I told them that I was back in business and ready to move forward against the Guild and this was the first response I got back. But we can't do anything until we find this woman."

"It just seems like you're placing a lot of trust in this person and sounds like you've never even met them so-"

"Enough," said Beatrice with a huff. "If I wanted your opinion, then I would have asked for it. Just trust me that I know what I'm doing."

"OK," I said.

Clearly I'd touched a nerve and it wasn't worth crossing Beatrice over something like this. It wasn't like we were supposed to go kill someone. Maybe it would be as simple as tracking down this woman and asking to see her tattoo. Still, that seemed too easy to make a whole Raid out of.

"So this mysterious person also has an ax to grind with the Guild?"

"It would seem so. And I'll take all the help I can get when it comes to the Guild."

"Why is that?"

Beatrice pulled up the right side of her dress suddenly.

It took me a minute but I saw it, the faint line of a red scar going from her upper thigh all the way down past her knee.

"Because of this. Because I was minding my own business and the Guild tried to kill me."

"Oh. I-I'm sorry. I didn't realize."

She dropped her dress back down and stared at the note again.

"It's fine. It was years ago already. Doesn't really hurt anymore. Just a memory."

There was a sadness in her eyes with a twinge of fear that I hadn't seen before. Maybe she hadn't always been a borderline psychopath, maybe the Guild had driven her to become what she now was. That didn't excuse what she'd done to me, but it made her a bit more human.

"Has the Guild gone after you since?" I asked.

"Not directly. Listen, we need to leave. I don't want anyone to see us here. I'm on the Guild's radar but as far as I know, you're not, and I'd like to keep it that way."

She stuffed the note in her pocket and walked back down the hallway. I wanted to stay and study the Board some more. There was a whole assortment of magical items waiting to be found and it was all there for the taking, but that would have to wait for another day.

Beatrice didn't say a word until we were several blocks from the school and she had looked behind us 20 times to make sure we weren't being followed.

"I'll go drop the note in the park. Hopefully our requester will follow up by tomorrow morning, so let's rendezvous at 10 at the coffee shop."

"Umm OK. Can we meet a little earlier though? I ducked out of work early to go wedding dress shopping for my friend and I don't want to come in late."

"Oh. Fun. If you're a sadist. When's the big day?"

"Next June. But the bachelorette party is in February. We're going to some fashion lecture at the Met and then flying to London for Fashion Week."

"Wow, your friend sounds nuts. For my bachelorette, we went to the Bahamas and got hammered on the beach all day. But to each their own. Come to my apartment at 8:30 then. My sitter will take Jack-Jack for a walk and we'll have the place to ourselves. 1264 Madison Avenue, 31C."

The next morning, I arrived at Beatrice's building 20 minutes early and paced back and forth across the street until I saw a stroller emerge from the door pushed by a tall brunette who couldn't have been older than 18. When they were out of sight, I crossed the street and entered the palatial lobby. The doorman smiled at me as he dialed up to Beatrice's apartment before eventually waving me through.

The elevator creaked up to the 31st floor and I stepped into a small brightly painted hallway with two white doors. I knocked on the one labeled C and waited for Beatrice to appear. Except when the door swung open, it wasn't her that greeted me, but a man with reddish hair wearing only a towel wrapped around his waist. He looked vaguely familiar but I couldn't quite place him.

"Umm, hi," I said. "Is Beatrice here?"

The man smiled and I realized that I had seen him somewhere before.

"Sure, she's just getting ready. Come on in."

I walked passed him and into the living room and there was the couch I had sat on in the dream of Beatrice's memory.

And on the other side of the room, the kitchen I had been in.

"And you are?" the man asked.

"Oh. I'm Jen, I, uh-"

"Nice to meet you Jen. Didn't realize B had hired another tutor."

"Yeah, that's me." I lied. "And you are?"

"Garrett, B's husband." He extended his right hand, keeping the other strategically on the towel, and I tried not to stare as I returned the gesture.

It was then that Beatrice decided to finally make her entrance.

"Garrett, I told you I was getting the door," she said, a look of annoyance in her eyes. "Go put some clothes on."

Beatrice swatted away Garrett's hand and tried to shoo him out of the room, but he wouldn't budge.

"What? I'm not allowed to meet your new employee?" he said with an even wider grin on his face.

Men, ugh.

"No, and we're leaving. See you later."

Beatrice wrapped her arm around me and led me out of the apartment before Garrett could protest further. We rode the elevator down in silence and I smartly kept any mention of the dream to myself, not wanting to upset Beatrice any further. The weather was mild for the last day of November in New York, so instead of plopping down at a coffee shop, we walked into the park.

"So, your husband is-"

"An ass. Actually, that wasn't harsh enough. He's a pompous ass who thinks he's entitled to stick his-"

"Sorry, sorry, didn't mean to pour salt on a raw wound."

"It's OK. I'm far past caring."

This meeting was quickly turning into a disaster. I knew from the dream memory that Beatrice and her husband had some issues, but didn't expect her to be so upfront about it. It was like she was doing her best to convince me that she was a real person with real problems so I would sympathize with her.

"Umm, did you find out who the target is?" I said after we had crested a hill overlooking the Met.

"Yes," said Beatrice with a detached note in her voice. "Her name is Francesca Lewis. Goes by Frankie for some reason. Here." She handed me her phone and I looked down at a headshot of a woman who looked a little older than me, with strawberry red hair, too much mascara, a tattoo of two cursive words on her neck, and bronze skin from too many visits to the tanning salon.

"I take it that's not the tattoo we're looking for?" I asked, handing the phone back to Beatrice.

"No. The one we're looking for is on her back."

"Oh, got it. Kind of a weird Raid, isn't it?"

"They're all weird if you think about it," Beatrice said. "I just try to focus on the end goal. I've done so many of these and every time I think I've come one step closer, it ends up being another dead end. But maybe this time… Anyway, it doesn't do any good to hope that this will be the Raid that leads us to the Compendium."

"Why do you need it so badly? You have the ink. That was enough for Rita. She practically changed the course of history with it!"

Beatrice shook her head.

"It wasn't enough, not for her and not for me. Rita ran out of ink and had to leave the Compendium behind when she fled New York. And I only have so much ink left. I had to give most of it away, and I still haven't figured out all the prima materia in it. That's why the Compendium would be a game changer, the amount of alchemic knowledge in there…"

"I keep hearing those words: alchemy, prima materia. You don't mean turning lead into gold, do you?"

"No. Alchemy is just a fancy name someone came up with to describe the science of magic. And prima materia is anything that has any magic in it, even a tiny bit."

"Oh. I see. This is still new to me, it makes my head spin some-times."

"I'll make you a deal then. Prove yourself during this Raid and I'll give you a proper alchemy lesson."

"Sounds great," I said. "So what's next?"

CHAPTER NINETEEN

IDENTITY THEFT

"Henry's death shortly after the war presented a problem. No longer within the ambit of power, I needed to find a new patron. Luckily, I found two."

The instructor barked words of derision through her microphone as I-and 20 other women-pedaled furiously on our special bikes with our special shoes. Sweat coated my entire body, Rita's stupid ring was digging into the handle of the bike, and between the exhaustion from the workout and the overindulgent drinking I had done last night, it felt like every atom in my body was going to combust. And it had only been 10 minutes of the hour-long class.

"Come on Jane, you're the VIP. Get your ass moving!" Lanie the instructor barked at me.

No, I wasn't really Jane, and no, I shouldn't have been riding the front bike in front of a gaggle of women, and no, this wasn't how any of this was supposed to go down.

The plan should have been a simple one to execute. Beatrice had cyber- and regular-stalked Frankie to such an extent that we had her daily routine down to a science. She worked at a social media marketing firm in midtown, got lunch from the same salad place every day across the street, got coffee from the same third-wave coffee shop every day at 3:30, spun three times a week at a studio redundantly called Velo Bike, worked out in her building's gym the other days and frequented a number of different bars after work. One thing we hadn't learned though was where the actual tattoo was, it being the beginning of December and all. So it was decided that our best chance at completing the Raid was to sign up for the same spin class as Frankie and isolate her in the locker room afterward.

But, unfortunately, we both underestimated the power of spin.

Picture trying to buy tickets to Phish but replace the potheads with status-obsessed women whose worth increases ever so slightly depending on where their spin bike is located and who reorganize their lives so that they are in front of a computer on Monday at 11:59 a.m. If I was more entrepreneurial, I'd build a bot that automatically signed people up for the most desirable bikes. Then I would charge $10/class for access and make a killing. Maybe after my Zelda speedrunning comeback crashes and burns.

I had met Beatrice in the park on a Wednesday morning, so we had one more chance to catch Frankie that week. That was, if we could even get bikes. From Beatrice's research, we learned that Frankie only took classes with Lanie, who had over 90,000 Instagram followers and whose classes were booked up for the rest of the week.

Ugh. Maybe I should have written that bot.

We failed to get in off the waitlist for Thursday, which meant enduring the Russian roulette of the Monday noon sign-up. But as I told Beatrice a few minutes before go-time, our saving grace would be my fast finger and mouse movement, honed by years of speedrunning and coding.

Or so I thought. The clock struck noon and by 12:02, my defeat was sealed, as Lanie's classes were completely booked. Not even the back corner was available. I nervously called Beatrice back to explain my failure and was greeted with a barrage of screaming. It took me a moment to realize though that she was yelling at her kid, not me. But after that tirade ended and I calmly explained that I had failed to sign us up for any class for the entire week, the line went completely silent. After repeating Beatrice's name several times to see if she was still there, she finally responded:

"Fix it."

Great, so nice to finally have a manager who leads by example.

My first back-up plan failed fast. I went down to Velo Bike an hour before Lanie's 8 a.m. class to sweet talk our way in. It was snowing and cold and windy outside, but inside the spin studio, the bright green walls and lilac-scented air freshener painted a picture of spring.

I brushed the gray slush off my jacket and strode up to a receptionist wearing a matching bright green tank top. Even if we only got one spot in the class, I could still just hang out in the locker room until the end of the class. Or so I had hoped.

But the spinning gods had aligned against me in more ways than one.

First, the receptionist tritely explained that the waiting list was three figures deep, and owing to the equally three-figure cancellation fee, there was a better chance of someone discovering the Fountain of Youth than Beatrice getting into the class, let alone both of us.

I still had my back-up to the back-up plan though: sneaking into the locker room and ambushing Frankie. But that plan too went up in flames, when I realized that the locker room was inconveniently locked and the only way to gain access was through green key cards that all the regulars had.

Crap. Well, maybe I would get lucky and Frankie would just waltz into the studio without an overcoat and I would easily spot the tattoo. So I plopped myself down on one of the comfy green chairs and waited. And waited. And waited. The minutes seemed to drag on forever and I resisted the urge to stare at the time on my phone every five seconds. But finally, at 7:40, in walked Francesca "Frankie" Lewis.

She was sporting a full-length parka with a fur-lined hood and her red hair was done up in a high ponytail. I wanted to make up an excuse to go say hi to her, but quickly nixed that idea. Better to remain inconspicuous until it was absolutely necessary to initiate contact. Frankie waved to the receptionist, unlocked the locker room with her card, and then strode out of sight, leaving me to play the waiting game again.

Another hour passed, until finally the 8 a.m. spinners began streaming back out of the locker room. Finally, it was Frankie's turn, but much to my consternation, she re-appeared wearing that same stupid parka, leaving any possibility of tattoo interception lost to me. I stared at her, hoping that my mind would come up with a crazy plan to complete the Raid, but all I could do was watch as she left the studio and walked into the squall outside.

I was about to crazily chase after her when I finally caught a break, as a gaggle of girls had emerged from the locker room, chattering so loudly that I couldn't help but overhear.

"Jane, honey, you deserve better than him."

"He's not worth it."

"I can't believe Charlotte did-"

"Shh, don't say it, Maria."

The nexus of this conversation was a short, brown-haired woman walking in the middle of the cluster. Her face was red, most likely from the workout but I could also see tears streaming from her eyes. Even a breakup was not enough to stop someone from going to this spin class it seemed.

"I just want to go home and curl up in a ball until tomorrow's class," said Jane.

"Absolutely not," said one of the other girls. "And I don't know why you feel the need to go five days a week. You look amazing! We are taking you out tonight to make you forget all about-"

"Travis."

"Yeah, Travis. See, I've almost forgotten it already. Ladies, we'll reconvene at Muldoon's at 7:30."

The group continued offering words of encouragement to Jane as they too disappeared into the storm outside but a germ of an idea had formed in my head, and I texted Beatrice that tomorrow morning I would have a spot in Lanie's class waiting for her.

They say that to know someone's true name is to hold power over them. That made sense in the case of a dragon or some other mythical creature, but not for your average twenty-something woman living in Manhattan.

This was different though.

I knew her name, I knew her sorrow, and I knew I had to succeed in my task.

Jane was still alone when I walked into Muldoon's and was sobbing silently to herself, no drink in sight. The bartender stood a few feet back, unsure if he should do something, so I pulled up a stool next to the downtrodden woman and waited for my opening. She continued staring off into space, not acknowledging my presence, until I motioned for the bartender.

"A rum and coke for my friend here and a Laphroaig 10 on the rocks for me please."

"You got it," said the bartender, who seemed happy that someone was taking responsibility for Jane. He returned shortly with the drinks, but the woman remained unresponsive.

"Rough day?" I said, putting on my best sympathy face.

Finally, Jane noticed me. She looked about ten times worse from when I saw her this morning, and that was after an hour-long workout. Her eyeliner had dribbled down the sides of her cheeks, her eyes were bloodshot, and the less said about her hair, the better.

"W-what? Oh, sorry. Y-yeah."

"That's for you," I said, pointing to the rum and coke. "You look like you could use a drink. Or 20."

Jane stared at the glass in front of her and then back at me.

"Do I know you from somewhere?"

"No, was just stopping in for a drink, noticed you were sitting here alone, and thought you could use some company."

"T-thanks."

Jane turned away from me and resumed her catatonic staring contest, before suddenly grabbing the rum and coke and chugging the whole thing in one sip.

"Wow," I said. "You really needed that."

The lifelessness had faded a little from her eyes, and Jane swiveled 90 degrees toward me on her stool.

"And I need another. Finish that drink and I'm buying the next one, umm, what did you say your name was again?"

"I didn't. It's Jade."

There was no sense in giving her my real name. Plus, I liked the thought of having a separate Quester identity for clandestine missions like these.

"Hi Jade, I'm Jane. I just found out my boyfriend has been sleeping with my best friend for the past year."

"Yikes! And I thought I was having a bad day." I gulped down my whiskey and set it aside. If we ended up getting plastered here, where Jane's friends could show up any minute, I wouldn't be able to stay with her all night to make sure she didn't make it to spin tomorrow morning.

"You really don't need to buy me a drink, but if you insist, let's go somewhere with a little better vibe. This place reminds me of a bad college dive." I put down a couple of bills on the bar and began ushering Jane out the door.

"U–umm OK. But I think some of my friends were coming here soon. Let me just--" Jane pulled out her phone and began texting the social circle from earlier.

"You mean the same friends who also are friends with this bitch who just betrayed you?"

Jane stopped texting and looked at me, as I continued moving her towards the exit.

"You're right. I don't need them. Let's go get drunk."

"That's the spirit! Let's do it!" I said.

And we did.

I woke up the next morning on an uncomfortable couch to a fire siren beeping in my ear.

It was six a.m. and my six p.m.-yesterday self thought it had been a good idea to pick the loudest, most piercing ringtone as an alarm. What my darling past self failed to realize, however, was that even after consuming most of the remaining hangover gummy, drinking almost two bottles of whiskey was not going to leave me in the best physical state to go spinning. Plus that alarm was so frakking loud, I thought the apartment was actually on fire.

I mashed my palm several times over the phone screen to stop the bleating and sat up slowly. The first conclusion I came to was that I was not in my apartment. The second conclusion was that I was not lying next to a random guy on said uncomfortable couch. The third conclusion, which came to me after the rest of the night snapped back into focus, was that I had actually done it. I was in Jane's apartment, ready to convince her that I should go to spin class instead of her.

The place was silent, which was good, because the last thing I wanted to see was a chipper Jane making us coffee in her workout clothes before jetting off to class. I pushed myself off of the couch and crept along the creaky floor toward the bedroom.

The door was wide open and inside lay Jane, spread-eagle in the middle of a king-size bed, fast asleep wearing the same clothes from last night. I took a minute to survey the room. Pictures adorned the walls at various intervals. A short, brown-haired guy had his arms around Jane, their smiling faces gradually aging as I moved further into the room. They must have been high school sweethearts, I figured. In another picture, a girl with curly red hair and freckles was toasting a coconut drink with Jane on a beach somewhere, and I had a bad feeling that this girl was the infamous Charlotte. Jane's old life was on display all around me, but there was nothing I could do for her right now. Except go to the spinning class so she wouldn't be charged the cancellation fee.

I walked up to the bed and sat down on the edge.

"Hey girl, you alright?"

She didn't respond. I pushed her gently on the shoulder, but still nothing. My pulse quickened for a second as I watched to see if Jane was still breathing. The slow rise and fall of her chest answered that question, and I let out a small sigh of relief.

"Umm, Jane? It's me, uh, Jade. Time to get up."

And time for me to get the hell out of there.

I sat there for longer than I should have, and if Jane had actually woken up to see me sitting over her, she probably would have screamed bloody murder. But she didn't. So I did what any respectable guy did after a one-night stand: I stole her green spin ID and left a note.

"Hey Jane,

I hope you're feeling better. Haven't gotten that drunk in ages but it was fun. If you need to talk, you have my number.

XOXO,

Jade

PS: Oh and don't worry about making it to spin. I know you were worried last night about not being able to make it, so I'll go for you so you won't get hit with the no-show fee."

I left the note on top of her phone and pulled the Velo Bike card out of the sleeve on the phone case. When I set the phone back down, it sprang to life, revealing a string of texts from Jane's actual friends.

"Jane u alright? Went to Muldoon's but u weren't there"

"Eff Travis and eff Charlotte. Those two deserve each other. Pls txt me, me and Maria went to find you last night at the bar but you were gone."

Similar texts lined the rest of the screen and for the first time since I came up with this crazy plan, I stopped for a second to think about what I had done.

I had taken advantage of this woman, made her ignore her real friends, made her think that they didn't care about her, and for what? So I could chase down a different woman and lie to her too? Any moral reckoning would have to wait though, because Jane started to stir. I tiptoed out of the bedroom, out of the apartment, and out of Jane's life as quickly as I had entered it.

CHAPTER TWENTY

YELLOW
JERSEY

"Everyone knew that Madison's plan would set the foundation for the debate at the Convention. With my ink stores replenished, he and I began a fruitful correspondence."

By the time I got off the subway, my guilty conscience from using Jane as a pawn occupied an equal space in my mind as the prospect of me having to stop at a random garbage can and puke my guts out.

I should have expected as much, I wasn't 19 anymore, when I was able to rebound from a hard night of drinking with Lisa and Stacy and still make my nine a.m. lab. Plus, I had used up the final bits of Steve's gummy last night so the entirety of the second bottle of whiskey was still wreaking havoc on my liver and my head.

And really, was what I had done so bad? So what if it was me who helped Jane mourn her breakup and not her friends? The results were the same, right? I had given her a fun night of distraction, and now her real friends could help her through the next part.

What was more concerning to me now though was the complete silence from Beatrice. I checked my phone four times as I walked to Velo Bike, but there was no message from her. Things were going to get interesting in a hurry if I actually had to participate in this spin class.

The bright green paint covering the outside of the Velo Bike spin studio hurt to look at the second time around and the interior was a madhouse again, with all manner of woman milling about, chatting about things I couldn't even begin to understand. I weaved my way through the cacophony to the reception couches and waited. It was 7:20, still time for Beatrice to show up and for this Raid to not become a total dumpster fire.

I texted her again.

"At spin. Where ru."

Another ten minutes passed and I tried once more.

"Not really in any condition to spin. Plus will need both of us to get the tattoo. U close?"

I put my phone away and tried to ignore the throbbing pain in my head. Time was running out. Maybe if I hurried into the locker room, I could catch Frankie before class and not even have to spin, so I got up and walked to the front desk. There was a different chipper girl there than the one from yesterday, and this one was decked out in green Velo Bike gear from head to toe.

"Checking in for Lanie's class?" she said. "I don't think I've seen you here before. What's your name?"

"I'm Jane Hutchinson. I usually go to Todd's seven p.m. class," I lied. "I like to end the day on a high note, you know?"

"Oh totally. That's a good class, too. Hutchinson, Hutchinson, oh."

Check-in Girl stared at her computer screen while I pretended not to be concerned. I already felt like I was going to vomit from last night alone and the girl's pregnant pause made the bile start to rise even more.

"Ah, here we go. Good news! You've been promoted to the head of the class!" She beamed at me as if I was supposed to know what that meant, and waited for me to shriek in excitement.

"Oh, umm, err, that's amazing! Remind me again what that means. I've never been promoted before."

"It only means that you get the bike in the front row, dead center, of course! We always leave that one open for the random VIP of the class and that's you! Plus you get to wear the yellow jersey and our special green spin shoes."

Crap. Not only was I in no shape to spin on a good day, but now I was going to be on display for everyone to see. And how was I supposed to get a look at Frankie's tattoo from the front bike? What a disaster this was turning out to be. My stomach agreed and I scanned around the foyer for a garbage can.

"Oh awesome! Can you excuse me for one second?"

I didn't give her time to answer, as I made a beeline for the can right behind a huge pack of girls.

They parted like the Red Sea and I reached it in time, only to be hit with a bout of dry heaving that seemed to go on forever. I hunched over the green (of course) can until it finally subsided. But now it was 7:50 and all thought of ambushing Frankie in the locker room had gone up in flames.

Then someone tapped me on the shoulder and I slowly lifted my head up.

"Are you OK?"

The foyer was empty, except for the check-in girl and the one person who decided to be a normal person and see if I was alright. It was Frankie. Just my luck.

"Y-yeah, I'm OK. Must have been something I ate last night."

Frankie was taller than I expected, and from my crouched position over the lid of the garbage can, she seemed to tower over me. Her bright red hair was tied back in a familiar high ponytail and she was sporting a purple Lalamango tank top. Which meant...

I pushed myself up from the garbage can only for my arms to give out halfway.

"Ugh. Maybe I'm not. Could use some water. Is there any at the front desk?"

Frankie nodded. "Yeah, let me get you one."

She turned and I quickly grabbed my phone out of the back of my yoga pants. I didn't even have time to look at what I was pointing at before I hit the camera button a dozen times. A rapid-fire of clicks sounded in the near-empty foyer and I hoped like heck she didn't hear them. Only when I tucked the phone away did I see that it had all been in vain. Where the tattoo should have been was instead covered by a big, square bandage.

Before I could wallow in my failure, Frankie returned with a room-temperature bottle of Velo Bike-branded water. I grabbed it greedily, twisting off the cap and gulping down the water, which ran down my workout clothes. I must have looked pathetic.

"Sorry, I just, uh, really needed that."

"It's OK. I've been there. Well, not here. But elsewhere. Anyway, you sure you're alright?"

I nodded and took another swig, this time swirling the water around in my mouth and then spitting it into the can. I needed to prolong this interaction somehow, needed to give myself another chance to talk to her. Then a crazy idea crystallized in my head. One that would hopefully reveal the tattoo but also get me (really, Jane) banned for life from this place. Which was fine because this was the last spin class I ever hoped to do.

"Yeah, I'll be fine. Can't miss this class. I'm the VIP today." Frankie laughed.

"Honey, you're in no condition to spin. Let's get you cleaned up and then I'll call you a cab."

"No, no, I'm fine. Honestly." I pushed myself up from the garbage can and finally got back on my own two feet, but Frankie looked at me and frowned.

"Suit yourself. I'll see you in there then." I got another look at the bandage as she walked away. I was so close to actually pulling off this crazy Raid (and all by myself to boot), a thin layer of fabric separating me from glorious victory.

The check-in girl handed me the VIP jersey and green spin shoes and I grabbed them before buzzing myself into the locker room using the pass I had "borrowed" from Jane. The music blared through the locker room door, indicating that the class had already started. Great. I quickly changed and walked slowly to the door and pushed it open.

Memories of seventh-grade gym class flooded my mind, as 20 women swiveled their heads in unison to watch me walk awkwardly toward the glittery green VIP bike. Lanie, in the middle of some ridiculous set of arm gyrations, glared at me while barking out encouragement into the tiny microphone attached to her ear. I ignored her and tried to locate Frankie in the crowd, which wasn't difficult because she was right behind me, in the second row. She nodded at me slightly and I continued onward with my walk of shame, finally reaching my bike.

"Let's give a warm VB welcome to Jane, our VIP of the class, ladies!" cried Lanie into the microphone.

"Welcome Jane!" the spinbots replied.

"Now I understand Jane here was feeling a bit under the weather just now but that's nothing a little spinning won't fix, right ladies?"

"Right!"

"Excellent, now let's Velo!"

The next hour seemed to stretch on for ages, as I struggled to both maintain the pace and copy Lanie's ridiculous "dance" moves. When the final cool-down whistle went off, I was barely able to lift my right leg over the seat to dismount, and it was a miracle I hadn't vomited. Which was good, for more than one reason.

"Wow. I didn't think you would make it all the way through," said Frankie, who was looking at me with a mixture of respect and disbelief. The rest of the class had petered out, leaving us alone.

"Haha, well, you know what they say. The body does what the mind commands. And all my mind was saying during that torture was 'just keep going, just keep going.'"

We started walking toward the locker room, me a step behind her, and I was eager to dispense with this stupid yellow jersey once and for all. But not before I executed the final part of my plan.

"Oh, one of your straps on your spin shoes came undone, Frankie," I said. Her name slipped out of my mouth just as I realized that she hadn't actually told me what it was.

"Huh?" said Frankie. She looked down for a second to see that her straps weren't in fact undone and that's when I vomited all over her back.

CHAPTER TWENTY-ONE

MANAGING UP

"But that wasn't enough. I couldn't be in the room where it was going to happen, cursed again by my gender, but I could be in the room where something else happened."

I'm sure there was another way I could have done it. The best games programmed multiple solutions to the same problems and the real world was no different.

I could have accidentally spilled some water on her. That would have been much simpler. Or I could have ripped the bandage off and memorized the numbers quickly before she decked me. But my crazy plan had gotten me this far and my brain was already completely fried from the night before and the insane workout I had just finished, so I used the tools immediately available to me, and somehow, it had worked.

"I'm so so sorry!" I said, wiping the remnants of the vomit from my mouth. "Don't move, I'll go get something to clean you up."

Frankie turned around and stared at me with a look of disgust and helplessness, but didn't say anything. That was a surprise. I had expected that she would at least start screaming and I was prepared to deal with anyone who ventured out of the locker room to see what was going on. But her silence made things much simpler, I'd admit.

I ran to the front and started pulling wet wipes out over and over from the dispenser, until I had enough to clean an elephant, then hurried back over to Frankie, who was now crouched down on her knees for some reason.

I began wiping around the edges of the bandage, and I debated whether to first tell Frankie that I was going to take it off, or just give it a good ol' yank and apologize later. I decided on the latter, and after patting the bandage with several wipes, it actually slid off nicely. Finally, the tattoo would be mine.

It was bigger than I expected, with ornate ivy forming a ring around a set of cursive numbers. What a weird idea for a tattoo. But then again, maybe it hadn't been Frankie's idea in the first place. She was just a pawn in some unknown game, a piece being moved across the board without her even knowing it. But then again, so was I.

If Frankie realized what was going on, she didn't say and so I initiated the final phase of my plan: the collection.

I whipped out my phone, opened up a blank email, and typed in the numbers from the tattoo:

404442735627

It was harder than I thought, not just because of the archaic script but also because I seemed not to be able to remember each number long enough for my brain to tell my finger which key to press on the phone. Probably a side effect of the hangover. After another minute, during which Frankie still didn't say anything, I finally got all the numbers down and hit send. My eyes hurt from the exercise for some reason, so I decided to get a backup just in case I accidentally transposed a digit.

"Shoot, your tank top is just completely ruined, let me take a pic so I can buy you a new one, OK?"

Frankie nodded in silence and with several clicks, I got the goods.

I stood back from the crouching Frankie to bask in my accomplishment, only to snap out of it. I was still behind enemy lines and needed an extraction plan. Of course I could just run away, leaving Frankie there alone on the floor. It would be pretty simple - she didn't know my name, this spin studio didn't know my name - it would be like I'd never been here.

I couldn't though. I had been horrible enough for 24 hours and the least I could do was help her into the locker room. And that wasn't saying much.

"You want some help getting up?" I asked, walking around in front of her.

"F-fine," Frankie stammered, her ability to speak finally coming back to her. I reached out my hand and she reluctantly took, but refused to look me in the eye. It was a struggle pulling her up, as she had almost a foot on me, but somehow I managed it. Back on her feet, Frankie started walking to the locker room and I trailed behind her.

"I think I have an extra shirt in my-"

"Stop!" she cried.

"OK, but I just wanted to hel-"

"You've done enough. Just get the hell out of my sight."

I don't know why, but her words hurt more than they should have. After all, I was the one using her, stealing something from her, why should I care if she was angry at me?

"Oh-h, OK. But your tank top..."

"Forget it, just forget this whole thing."

The locker room was empty except the two of us, the next group having yet to arrive, so I quickly changed out of the stupid yellow jersey and green shoes, and threw them along with Jane's locker room card into an empty locker.

I glanced over at Frankie, who began taking off her vomit-stained tank top. As she pulled it up over her head, she ran her hand over the now-exposed tattoo and winced from the pain. I froze and as she turned her head towards me, I could feel the venom in her eyes as she realized what I had done. I'm sure she would have done something terrible to me, but a moment later I regained my senses and bolted out the door.

The inside of the coffee shop was packed as I waited for Beatrice. It was four days later and I was sipping a hot tea, still recovering from the Raid. The Raid I had single-handedly pulled off, no thanks to my employer. I didn't know if she was even going to show up this morning, as her radio silence had continued.

"Wth is going on. Meet me at Bleecker St Grounds at 9 tomorrow so i can give you the info from the tattoo," I had texted last night.

There was no way I was going to hand over the goods without at least an explanation of why she had ditched me, but that text hadn't merited a response either. I had nothing else going on this weekend except catching up on work, with Duncan not due back until mid-next week anyway, so I decided to head over to the coffee shop on the small chance Beatrice decided to show her face.

The intervening days had not been pleasant. There was the lingering hangover, the rawness in my throat, and the weight of the guilt from toying with two women. Plus Lisa had made me call the airline every morning at 7:30 to try to get our seats upgraded for London, which had been an utter failure so far. I hadn't heard from either Jane or Frankie since our encounters and the sense of relief I should have felt was just not there. It had all seemed like a good plan in the moment, and besides Frankie's tank top, what lasting damage had

I actually done? But I couldn't dismiss things that easily and Beatrice's prolonged absence wasn't helping.

By 10 o'clock, Beatrice still hadn't shown up and I felt nothing from the ring indicating she was getting closer, so I decided to call it. The snow from earlier in the week had mostly been plowed away, but the sidewalks were still covered in gray slush and I stood outside the coffee shop contemplating whether I should just head to the office to finish up the dialogue selection interface I had neglected earlier in the week. I kicked some slush in frustration and hit a passing car that thankfully kept going. I should have been learning more about alchemy, not wondering why I had been left to dither in the wind.

I was about to start the long walk to work when I saw something across the street that caught my eye.

A bulletin board.

Jumping over a huge slush puddle, I made my way over to it but was immediately disappointed to find it full of flyers about community events. But there was a perfectly good bulletin board stocked with Raids uptown. Maybe picking a new Raid would be exactly the kind of thing to get Beatrice to acknowledge my existence.

The yellow door was surprisingly unlocked again when I reached the school. I made my way without incident to the third floor and down that same hallway where I could see the Raid Board waiting for me at the end.

The Board was unattended and I took my time to read every single Raid before finding the one that was the most outlandish and difficult and that would freak Beatrice out if she thought I had taken it.

"There's a signed Mickey Mantle baseball at Yankee Tavern behind the bar in a glass case. The key to the case is buried under the warning track in left field at the stadium. Bring me both for one silver token."

I snapped a picture and texted it to Beatrice with a note:

"Here's our next Raid. Can we meet soon to discuss???"

If that didn't get her attention, then I was all out of ideas. Well, except for waiting for her outside her apartment. But I didn't want to turn into a stalker. Besides, she needed me, or so she'd opined, so eventually she would seek me out.

"Hi," said a voice behind me.

I froze before slowly turning around to find a young girl standing in the previously empty hallway. She looked to be about 16 and was wearing a jean jacket adorned with scores of pins. Her dark brown hair fell down to her shoulders and she sported a wry smile, the kind that said, "hey, I know you're not supposed to be here." Maybe there was a basketball game or something in the gym and she was here to cheer on her little brother.

"Umm, hello, sorry. Got turned around. What floor is the game on again?"

The girl's smile vanished in an instant.

"There's no game today. What are you doing here? I'm going to get the security guard!"

"I, umm, well, I went to this school when I-"

Her smile returned and she let out a laugh.

"Relax. I'm just messing with you. You were looking at the Raid Board. It's not a crime."

I breathed a sigh of relief, but only for a second. This girl reminded me too much of Polly, and that didn't make me feel any better.

"Oh, haha. Yeah, just looking for a new Raid. It's hard to choose."

The girl walked up to the Board and stood beside me, considering the Post-it Notes.

"Hmm. Yeah, I see what you mean. Not a good one in the batch."

"What do you mean?" I asked.

"Personally, my friends and I wouldn't do one for anything less than 90 bronze. This one," she pointed to the Raid requesting the stolen pocket watch that I had seen last time I was here, "looks OK, but pretty boring. Would have been better if it was asking for a particular 110-year old pocket. Just because something is old doesn't mean it's special."

"Oh, yeah. I'm Jade, by the way."

I held out my right hand, and the girl looked at me for a second, as if she was deciding whether to believe that Jade was my real name or if shaking hands was something only people over 35 did. But she eventually extended hers in return, which was decked out in various rings stacked on her fingers.

"Nice to meet you Jade. I'm Ty."

The handshake lasted a second too long and I slowly pulled away before things got more awkward.

"I like your rings," I said, trying to change the subject.

"Thanks! I like, umm, your locket."

"Thank you," I said, rubbing it with my fingers, before tucking it under my sweater. "It was my mom's."

"Well, I'll let you get back to your Raid selection," Ty said. "You were here first, so it's only polite, and my mom is always going on about etiquette."

"No, no. I was waiting to hear back from my friend about something. You go ahead."

"OK. Suit yourself. But don't get mad at me if I take the one you wanted."

She moved closer to the Board and I took a few steps back, not wanting to look over her shoulder, but I secretly wanted to know which one she was going to pick.

My phone buzzed and I pulled it out of my bag.

It was Beatrice. Finally.

"ru out of your mind," the text read.

Well, mission accomplished.

"So u dont want that one? Should i get another while i'm here?"

This time, I didn't have to wait a week for the next response.

"No. Come meet me at my apartment downtown in an hour."

"But u live on the upper east side," I wrote back.

"Not that apartment. the other one. 227 Bowery Apt 4a."

It must have been nice having enough cash lying around to own two apartments in Manhattan. I barely had enough money to rent half of a crummy walk-up. But in any event, my plan had worked and I had finally gotten Beatrice's attention. Now I just needed to extricate myself from this meeting of the Breakfast Club.

"Well, it was nice meeting you. Gotta head back downtown."

"Bye," she said without turning around.

Teenagers.

I knocked on the door of apartment 4a 90 minutes later, the D train deciding to stop between stations for no good reason. After a few seconds, the door creaked open, and there she was, with a sour look on her face.

"You're late," was all Beatrice said, before disappearing back into the apartment.

The tension from my ring felt like it was going to pull me through the door and I quickly followed her inside.

The apartment opened into a small foyer, with the kitchen and living room to the left and the bedroom straight ahead.

I froze.

I had been here too. In that same dream. The shards of the memory were slowly coalescing back into one piece and I remembered Beatrice fleeing her apartment, picking a random guy in her phone, and ending up here by the next morning. Had she smashed the mirror too or was that part of my own creation?

"So, you finished the Raid?" said Beatrice from the living room, where she had taken a seat on a small gray futon.

I walked past a large bookcase and sat down next to her.

"Yeah. What happened? I got the spot for you and you didn-"

"Life happened Jen. I can't just drop everything at the drop of a hat and waltz into a spin class at 8 in the morning. That's what you're here for. And if you had gotten the spots in the class when you were supposed to, I could have made arrangements ahead of time. But it seems like my presence was not needed anyway, so why are you so upset?"

"Because I … because it was pure luck. And you abandoned me."

"Oh please. You sound like I left you stranded in the Iraqi desert. If anything, you earned yourself major brownie points for improvising on the fly. I'm impressed. And, willing to let this attention-getting stunt of yours go."

"OK," I said, not buying her excuse but not really caring at this point what actually happened. "So now what?"

"Now it's time for your alchemy lesson."

Beatrice got up from the couch and walked over to the bookcase. She ran both her hands along the books before grabbing a different one with each hand and pulling. I stared in disbelief as Beatrice pushed the bookcase into the wall and then disappeared through the newly revealed opening, before popping her head back out a few seconds later.

"You coming?"

CHAPTER TWENTY-TWO

EQUIVALENT
EXCHANGE

"His name is William. He is unassuming yet powerful. A man of few words yet influential nonetheless. The perfect conduit to push things past the tipping point."

As a kid, I would fantasize about a secret room in our small apartment. I imagined that if you pulled out the correct brick from the living room wall, there would be a switch that would make the wall behind the fireplace rotate. Then, if you crawled through the opening, there would be a long, candlelit hallway leading to a set of stairs. At the bottom of the stairs would be a room where my mom would work late into the night on clandestine missions.

But no matter how many times I tried to find it, the key to that secret room remained hidden, and no matter how many times I tried to pretend otherwise, my mom was just an ordinary accountant, not a superhero or super-spy in hiding.

Stepping into the secret room behind the bookcase now, I couldn't help but feel some excitement that my childhood dream was at least partially coming true. The room was dark, only a sliver of daylight peeking through from above a bookcase to my right. Across from me was a long tabletop that went from wall to wall, held up by small sets of drawers, with two stools tucked underneath. Every other inch of free space was covered by shelves and bookcases filled to the brim with everything you could think of.

"Wow," I said. "This room is–"

"Incredible," said Beatrice. "I know."

I walked over to one of the bookcases, where one shelf held scores of small mason jars, each filled with liquid and a floating mass, and sporting pieces of masking tape with handwritten notes.

"Pigeon liver, 6/12/14," said one.

"Rat spleen, 11/9/11," said another.

I stepped away from the jars and resisted the urge to vomit (again), but then recalled what Steve had told me at the bar those many months ago about the utility of vermin organs. I just never thought anyone would take it to such an extreme as Beatrice apparently had.

"Yeah, best not to look carefully at that shelf," she said. "Sometimes it still makes me a bit squeamish and I'm the one who actually cut open all those animals."

Beatrice pulled out the stools from underneath the table and sat down.

"So, before we begin, let's see the goods from the Raid."

"Sure," I said, sitting down on the other stool. I brought up the email I had written to myself and handed my phone to Beatrice, who stared at the screen, a look of confusion on her face.

"What is this?"

"I don't know. I hadn't looked at it since the Raid. The tattoo was a ring of ivy on her back and these numbers were in the center."

"Oh. Well, this could be anything. It's 12 digits of nothing."

Beatrice handed my phone back to me and sighed.

"Sorry," I said. "It's not like I could have asked Frankie. Not that she would have told me anyway, after I threw up all over her."

"Wait, what?" said Beatrice, a look of shock on her face. "Start from the beginning please."

I recounted my two days of spin trials in excruciating detail and Beatrice nodded along, as if this was a perfectly normal day at the office and I was presenting at a status meeting.

"Well, that was an interesting way of getting things done."

"Thanks. I think," I said. "So what are we going to do now? Drop off the tattoo numbers and get our reward?"

"Of course not. We've got plenty of time before the Requester thinks we should be done and I'm not handing over the information until I know what it is we've found."

"That makes sense, I guess. But if we can't figure it out?"

"We will. I have plenty of stuff in here that will give us some … inspiration if you will. Now, since you've proven yourself above and beyond the call of duty, it's time to live up to my end of the bargain."

She walked over to one of the book-laden shelves and pulled down a small notebook with a worn blue cover.

"What's that?" I asked.

"This, Jen, is my compendium. At least one part of it anyway. I'll give you the basics of alchemy but this you can study on your own later. Here."

She handed me the notebook and I carefully opened to the first page, which was dated March 26, 2008.

"Finished reading diary and found silver ring taped to last page. Initials RvA inscribed on the band. Considering whether to put it on."

I held up my hand and looked at the handcuff on my right index finger, ignoring its urge to move toward its twin.

"You found this in Rita's diary?"

"No," said Beatrice, holding up her own hand. "It was this one. Yours I found later. The rings are a good starting point though because they're an example of one of the main classes of alchemy: linkage. You actually know a lot about it already, don't you?"

I thought for a second and then it was as if a light went off in my head.

"Vervorium - it links places. The apples - they link minds."

Beatrice smiled.

"Yes, very good. The apples contain celestonite if you want to be specific. And the rings are linked together with auragen. You apply a bit of it to each object you want to link and it's like attaching an invisible string. At least that's the theory. I've never been able to get a pure sample of it."

"Oh."

"Yeah, would be good to have some. I can think of all sorts of uses for it. But let's keep going. There's memory serum and truth serum and they sound exactly like what they're called - one will wipe a memory clean out of your head and the other will make you tell the truth. You would think they would be very useful in all sorts of situations, but I've used them pretty much only on Garrett."

I nodded silently, having a slight inclination as to why Beatrice had needed to use those serums on Garrett, but I didn't want to let on that I had more of her memories floating around in my head.

"Next is another big class: buffs. Sounds like you know about those too. Polly's dad is smarter than I give him credit for."

"You know Steve?" I asked.

"Not directly, no. It's too bad you used up the one he gave you, I would have liked to analyze it. Bet I could make a much better version."

"His was decent," I offered.

"Oh sure. But it didn't really help you so much during the Raid. Actually, come to think of it, I guess it did. If you weren't so hungover, you might not have vomited all over that poor girl. Heh."

Beatrice got up and walked over to the closet at the other end of the room, where a set of drawers was set inside. She opened the middle drawer and fished around for a second, before returning to the table and placing four little gummy squares of different colors on top.

"These are my specialty. Enhancement buffs. This one here," she said, pointing to the green one, "is like a magic Adderall. Gives you laser focus. Very popular with the college set. This next one," she pointed to the lilac gummy, "is a five-minute speed booster. Not just physical, but mental too. You'll run faster than you've ever run before and at the same time work through your multivariable calculus syllabus in your head. Don't eat these two at the same time though, unless you have someone looking after you."

I stared at the gummies, thinking of the possibilities they presented. Super focus, super speed, super smarts. It was like getting stat points from *Dungeons and Dragons*. Despite Beatrice's warning, I immediately wanted to pop both in my mouth and see what would happen.

"This third one," Beatrice continued, "It's like the buff you got from Steve, except much better. It's like a hangover cure, caffeine pill, and the feeling you get when you've slept for 12 hours all rolled into one. The last one gives you a burst of strength. Good for people who keep getting into fights. Though I always tell the buyer to make sure they end things quickly. It doesn't last very long."

"Wow. These are incredible," I said. I imagined taking all four at once and turning into a veritable Superwoman. Or at least a really powerful Batman.

"I know. I have more I'm working on but it's tough finding ways to test them out."

"Oh, wow. Do you have an imperfect phoenix down stashed away in here?"

I didn't mean to let my inner geek flag fly, but with everything else I'd seen today, maybe it was possible.

"What's a phoenix down?" she asked.

"Oh. It's umm, you know that video game *Final Fantasy*?"

Beatrice shook her head and looked at me warily.

"Well, when a character dies, another member of the party can use a phoenix down to bring the dead character back to life."

"Ah. Well, we're not living in a video game, so I don't have anything like that for you here."

She collected the buffs from the table in a single swooping motion and handed them to me.

"Here. You've earned these along with your token stipend and your cash."

"Thanks," I said, placing the four carefully in my bag and trying to remember which color did which.

"Now that last buff is a good segue into the final category for today. I'll skip the compulsion ink because you already know about that too."

A flicker of anger sparked within me at the mention of the ink but I managed to quickly suppress it. I was beginning to come around to my new boss, what with the secret laboratory and magical enhancers. As long as she didn't try to use the ink on me again, this arrangement I'd stumbled into could actually be the best thing that had ever happened to me.

Beatrice held out her right hand and my eyes were immediately drawn to the large rock on her ring finger.

"Wow, that's some ring."

Beatrice frowned.

"Oh that. Yeah, sure. But look above it."

I did and saw a smaller purple stone set in a silver band.

"It's amethyst. Not especially valuable. Except this stone has a special property."

She opened one of the drawers of the desk and pulled out a rock the size of a grapefruit, held it out for me, and I took it.

"It's a rock. Heavy."

"Yes. Just wanted you to confirm for yourself. Watch."

Beatrice took back the rock with her right hand, slowly closed her eyes, and started mumbling softly to herself. The amethyst stone began to softly glow before the rock suddenly shattered into a dozen pieces.

"What, what happened?"

"Did you see it?" Beatrice asked.

"See what? You crush the rock with your bare hands? Yes, how could I miss that?"

"Not that. The stone."

"Oh. Yes, it glowed a bit. But I don't underst … oh. Wait. The stone, it's like the strength buff, except … except you tapped it somehow."

"Exactly. The stone is a well of strength. Unlike the buff, it can be continuously tapped as needed."

"Wow. So then why do you bother with the strength buffs?"

"Three reasons," Beatrice said, and I noticed the little beads of sweat that had formed on her temples. "First, the stone's well is not limitless. I have no clue how much was in it when I got it, how much of it I've used so far, and how much is left. The buffs I can make more of, but the stone, the stone is practically priceless. Second, the amount of strength I can draw from the stone is much greater than the buffs. And third," she wiped the sweat from her brow, "even tapping the strength I did just now takes a toll on my body. If I kept tapping it, I would probably pass out."

"Oh. Still, must be reassuring to have that in reserve if you need it."

"Yes, it is. OK, final lesson. But I've got no demonstration for you, so you'll just have to trust me."

She walked out of the room and returned shortly with what looked like a small dagger sheathed in leather. Its grip looked smooth like ivory and the metal guard had an otherworldly sparkle to it.

"What is that?" I asked as Beatrice unsheathed the mystery weapon. The blade had a sheen that somehow topped the guard and I stared at its smooth surface wondering what magic was imbued within.

"This," said Beatrice, "is the creme de la creme of my alchemy arsenal. The Medoblad." She resheathed it with ease and set it down on the table next to us.

"Got it. Interesting name."

"Do you know what it does?"

"Well, actually, I got to pick the names of some of the weapons in our game a few months ago. Which basically meant translating weapon names into different languages and combining them with other random words. So blad is Dutch for blade. And medo ... no. You're not saying ..."

"Yes, I am. Continue."

"Medo is Greek for 'to rule over' and is the root for Medusa. But I don't understand. I already looked at the blade and nothing happened."

"It doesn't work like that. Besides, who would want to wield a knife that turned you to stone if you looked at it? No, that only happens when you stab someone with it. Ordinarily, I'd have a rat lying around here to show you how it works, but I'm fresh out at the moment. You can just use your imagination though."

I sat back in my chair and tried to wrap my head around it. A knife that turned you to stone. The sight of Steve's green scar was horrible enough, but this, this was another level. Taken with everything else stuff Beatrice had shown me today, it made my pulse start to race.

"Well, I think that's enough for today," said Beatrice. "We still need to tease out what these numbers mean. Go somewhere to clear your head. Maybe take a bit of the lilac buff. I'll do the same. Then let's meet tomorrow at 11 at BSG to compare notes. Sound good?"

She smiled at me as if we were working on a group project in college, as if she hadn't just unveiled an inventory of deadly magic and I struggled to maintain a calm and collected mask.

"Sure. That works. Umm, do you have anything to drink? My throat's a little dry."

"Yeah. The fridge is well-stocked with ginger ale, my favorite. Help yourself."

I got up from the stool and left the dark room, the collected sweat dripping down the small of my back. She didn't follow as I walked to the small kitchen, where, as promised, there was a fridge loaded with cans of ginger ale and nothing else. I took out a can, and, my curiosity getting the best of me, slowly opened the freezer to find it full of frozen green apples.

CHAPTER TWENTY-THREE

COOL RUNNINGS

"William's wife suddenly became too ill to travel, the poor thing, and I just happened to be there, waiting for him, when he arrived in Philadelphia. His rooms are much nicer than my own."

I began to run.

Not too fast at first. I was still somehow sore from spinning, despite it being five days later, and my body was threatening open rebellion after it realized my intentions.

The West Side Highway path was practically empty, it being December and Sunday morning and all. Only the most fanatical people would think it was a good idea to run in these conditions and normally I wouldn't be one of them. But after a fruitless afternoon spent tearing those 12 numbers apart while at the same time trying to forget the freezer of mind-reading apples, I decided to take Beatrice's advice and clear my head.

The wind swept up suddenly, blowing back my hair, and the icy breeze off the water made my insides turn, but I pressed onward up to the Whitney and turned into the grid. I slowed to a walk and pulled out the lilac buff, which had been tucked in the small pocket of my workout pants, along with a piece of paper with the numbers from the tattoo.

I hesitated.

Curing a hangover had been a neat little parlor trick and even the apples seemed quaint compared to what Beatrice said this buff would do. How would it feel, I wondered. Would anyone notice me or would I be an unrecognizable blur? And what about my mind? I held the buff up to my nose and breathed in. A sweet aroma of citrus hit my nostrils and that gave me the last sliver of confidence I needed to step over the Rubicon.

The taste of the buff matched its smell: it was like chewing an orange slice after a soccer game, almost refreshing and nothing like Steve's buff. I quickly swallowed it, started a five-minute timer on my sports watch, and resumed my previous pace.

A block or two passed and I felt the same. Maybe Beatrice's alchemy skills weren't all she made them out to be.

I kept jogging and started to cross Eighth Avenue, when, all of a sudden, a biker going the wrong way appeared out of the corner of my eye. I turned and locked eyes with him and it was then that the entire world, except for me, slowed to a crawl.

I considered the biker. He was only a foot away and his face wore a mask of fear, but I had nothing to worry about. At his current speed, it was as if he was ten blocks away and how could I not move a few feet forward to let him pass behind me?

The biker dealt with, I ran out of the crosswalk and into the oncoming traffic. The cars inched forward as I deftly weaved in between them. If they noticed me, I wasn't sure, but after a block, I grew tired of that game and jogged back onto the sidewalk and into the West Village.

I then set my mind to work on the numbers. They appeared in my vision, as if they had materialized into the real world. My mind moved them around in a circle, jumbled them out of order, reversed them, and then put them back in order. It was a neat trick but not all that useful to the problem at hand.

I pushed the numbers onto the various storefronts as I passed them. It was too long by two digits to be a phone number, but maybe the first two were a country code? Also how long were foreign phone numbers supposed to be? This wasn't a good use of my expanded brain power, so I moved on.

Next I decided to multiply each individual digit of the sequence together to see what happened. But all that got me was a large and meaningless number.

Maybe it was a set of IP addresses. I could check those later though.

Or a substitution cipher. That was a possibility. I blinked and each digit turned into its corresponding letter. Except the second digit was a zero. And what about all the letters after I? That couldn't be right. There were too many ways to separate the digits. And I could do that on paper at home later anyway.

I looked down at my watch. Only three minutes had passed and I had run across the West Village, down through NYU, and was now about to enter SoHo.

Insanity.

And I still felt like I could run all the way back up to the tip of the island and not be worse for wear.

The SoHo shops were of a different character but still offered me no clues as to the numbers' meaning. I decided to head down to Battery Park and then hope that I still had enough juice left to make it back up to the coffee shop. I passed an art gallery displaying an entirely white canvas except for the word "Baaaaah" in sloppy red ink, a store with columns of yogurt cups on rotating columns, and then finally a random dessert shop which had a line out the door for some reason.

Just as SoHo was beginning to melt away into Chinatown, I spotted an old hand-drawn map of Manhattan in a heavy wooden frame suspended precipitously from a piece of wire. It was one of those maps that was so old that its approximation of the dimensions of the island was quite laughable. 20 feet past the map I still could not get the neatly laid-out grid out of my head. As I progressed to the bottom of the island, the gridlines suddenly overlayed themselves in my vision. Numbers floated at every intersection, decreasing slightly each time.

I stopped running.

Could the numbers be a location? A latitude and a longitude?

I turned around and began running back uptown, the numbers on the grid slowly ticking up. I needed to slow down, to find a map so I could confirm this theory. But the world still moved in its nearly frozen state around me and I looked at my watch, which showed 30 seconds remaining. An eternity in my current condition.

Another 20 seconds had elapsed by the time I got to the coffee shop. Thankfully, there was still one chair and table out front despite the weather and I inched forward, trying to mimic a normal speed. I stood with my back facing in front of the chair and watched the seconds slowly tick down to zero, before closing my eyes and collapsing.

"Jen."

The word almost roused me from my slumber, but I was content to remain in this dream version of the coffee shop. The sun was warm and my drink was cold. I looked down at the newspaper I was holding and read the story above the fold.

"Kate O'Laughlin, 19, found dead facedown in dorm room," the headline on the page read. I folded the paper and put it on the table, as the chipper redhead I had already seen in the prior replay of this memory around ran up the street and sat down across from me.

"JEN."

The name sounded familiar, but I couldn't quite place where I knew it from. The redhead in front of me's name was Laura, that much I knew.

"Sorry I'm la-"

A hand smacked me hard in the face and I opened my eyes.

Beatrice stood above me. No, wasn't I Beatrice? And where did Laura go?

"W-hat's going on?"

Beatrice frowned.

"What's going on is I found you here in front of the coffee shop, your head tilted back and drool dripping down your mouth."

"Oh," I said. I looked at her. She was wearing a full-length jacket with a fur-adorned hood, a stark contrast to my own outfit. A cold chill suddenly swept through me and my teeth began to chatter.

"Come on, let's get you inside."

Beatrice extended her hand and I took it but nearly fell forward into her. She steadied me with her other hand, before hooking her arm around mine and guiding me into the shop. After setting me down at a table, she returned a few minutes later with a steaming mug, which I slowly brought up to my lips.

"So, it looks like you've had an interesting morning. Please tell me you didn't take the focus and speed buffs at the same time."

"No," I said softly. "Just the latter. It ran out just as I got here. But I think..."

I tried to recall what had happened during my run, but it was like someone had hit fast forward times 10 in my mind, whole scenes skipping by in an instant.

"You figured out what the numbers mean but now you can't re-member. It's my fault. I should have told you. Your brain at normal speed can't process what your brain at superspeed was experiencing. It's all a big blur, isn't it?"

"Y-yeah. Exactly. I can make out bits and pieces. I think I ran through most of lower Manhattan. It was incredible. Like I was the Flash. There were lots of stores and ... "

"Take your time. Keep thinking. Maybe a detail will crystallize and that will be the trigger."

"OK, I'll try."

I tried again. I remembered there was a biker, and he had run into me? Well, almost. But then I was blocks away in SoHo and there had been a window and…

"A map," I said.

"What?" asked Beatrice.

"I saw a map. In a window. It was … it was old. Wait a minute."

I pulled out my phone and brought up the twelve numbers.

"I think it's a place," I said. "A set of coordinates. Maybe a lati-tude and a longitude. The first six digits are one and the second six are the other."

Beatrice's eyes widened.

"You may have something here. Try putting them into your phone and see what happens."

"OK. Hold on."

A map of the world soon stared back at me, and I entered the two sets of digits carefully. With a tap of my finger, the digits went off into the ether. Then they came back with a big red X.

"*Error. Specify N or S, E or W,*" the screen read.

"Crap," I said. "We need to specify which quadrant. So that means the numbers could stand for four places, not one."

"Well, maybe it will be obvious which one is the right one after we go through all four."

I nodded and began inputting the four combinations. First, N and E, which brought back a mountain in Kyrgyzstan. Then S and E, which landed in a random spot in the Indian Ocean. Then, moving to the Western Hemisphere, I typed in S and W, which was just off the coast of central Chile, before finally putting in N and W and crossing my fingers that the location was somewhere even remotely close to New York.

I looked down at the screen.

It was Queens.

"It could still be the wrong one," I told Beatrice as we left the subway platform an hour later. She didn't seem to care and was practically running down the sidewalk. "It's almost too much of a coincidence that the location is in the city," I added.

"Maybe, but it's doesn't hurt to check. Besides, do you want to fly halfway around the world to climb up a mountain or jump in the ocean?" she said, and I struggled to catch up, my legs still on fire from this morning's earlier activities.

We were in an industrial area of Long Island City, the gentrification line holding steady, at least for the time being, further north. Large warehouses lined the streets and even on Sunday, trucks were loading and unloading, crowding the pot-marked sidewalks and forcing us out onto the street several times to maneuver around.

Finally, we reached our quarry: a two-story brick building, covered in colorful graffiti. Garage doors dotted the exterior, sporting more artistic renditions, like a menacing eagle face and a head sliced open to reveal the artist's tag.

Beatrice had cut her frantic pace to a crawl and held out her phone like it was a homing beacon. We passed several more garage doors before finally reaching a regular wooden door. A spray-painted street number was tagged above and various writing dotted the surface of the door, including the words "Pull hard to close."

Beatrice frowned and tried to open the door. Unsurprisingly, it was locked.

"Are you sure this is the place?" I asked.

She nodded.

"Yep. A direct hit on the coordinates."

"Oh. Was hoping maybe it was actually that door a little further down. One that we could actually open."

I waited for her snippy retort but instead Beatrice had closed her eyes and was mumbling something slowly to herself. An incantation of some kind? She hadn't mentioned anything about being able to cast a magic "spell," but maybe she didn't trust me enough to reveal all her secrets yet.

It was then that I saw her amethyst ring start to glow. This wasn't the pale flicker from before, when she broke the rock in her apartment. No, this was bright and nearly blinding and I tried to step back when I realized what was about to happen, but it wasn't soon enough.

Her fist collided with the wooden door and I brought my arms up to shield my eyes from the spray of wood I was expecting. But after feeling nothing but a gust of wind, I slowly lowered them and looked at the scene before me.

The door knob had fallen off but the actual door was still in one piece. Not even a crack or a dent or even a splinter of wood was visible where Beatrice had made contact. I slowly looked down and it was abundantly clear what had borne the full force of the punch.

CHAPTER TWENTY-FOUR

DROPPING
THE BALL

"There is not much for me to do during the day, so I frequent the various establishments and collect the gossip coming out of the Convention. My ideas on the unitary executive were agreed to almost immediately but now the delegates are squabbling over how to structure the Congress. As if it was important in the slightest."

The crystal orb shimmered in the night sky, its many facets reflecting the world down below. It hovered there for a few seconds before a burst of thunder erupted from the ground, causing the orb to slowly descend. The rumbling intensified as it plummeted to the earth, whipping the crowd into a frenzy. People were laughing, crying, and screaming, until finally it was too much for me to bear, and I closed my eyes so I would not have to witness the last few moments.

No, this wasn't the end of days brought on by a meteor falling to earth. It was 30 seconds to midnight and Duncan and I were about to share our first ever New Year's kiss.

I listened as the Times Square crowd a thousand miles away counted down in unison on the giant TV at the party. Lisa and Brad stood nearby in their own almost embrace and on the other side of the room, Stacy and her date had not even bothered to wait the extra seconds and were going at each other on the couch.

I opened my eyes to find Duncan staring at me and he pulled me closer as the last vestiges of the most momentous year of my life faded away into yesteryear.

"Five, four, three…"

I shut my eyes again and waited for the last second to finally pass. This kiss would stand for something more than just an ordinary kiss, I thought. It would be the start of a new beginning for Duncan and me, a consecration of our relationship that would soon hopefully be expressed in the form of a different kind of orb on my finger.

"Happy New Year!" the partygoers and TV crowd shouted and suddenly I felt Duncan's lips on mine and then … then they were gone again.

I opened my eyes and Duncan was still there, holding me close to him, but his gaze had wandered behind me and I turned to see Stacy grinding her body on top of her date as if the rest of the room was empty.

"Look at those two," he said with a smirk. "Do you think they even care?"

I rolled my eyes and extricated myself from Duncan's arms.

"No, but I don't see why we should either."

He pulled me back toward him and put his hands back around my waist.

"You know, we could be doing the-"

"Don't think so," I said. "After that wet noodle of a kiss, you could forgive me for not wanting the rest."

"Oh come on Jen. It's New Year's Eve, not our wedding."

"*Our* wedding? Seems like you're skipping ahead, mister."

I held my ringless hand up to his face before pushing his arms away again and walking out to the balcony. The crash of the waves on the beach below was soothing and I waited for Duncan to come out and apologize for completely ruining the moment. But when I turned to look back into the party, he was over at the bar, yucking it up with the bartender.

I gazed out at the ocean and tried to suppress the tears forming in my eyes. Why was I getting so worked up over an absentee boyfriend who a month earlier I was convinced was just keeping me around as his New York side chick to his actual girlfriend half a world away?

But a lot can change in a month.

A month ago I watched as my mentor lay unconscious at the foot of the door that would not open.

And a month ago I listened as a newly-returned Duncan had professed his undying love for me out of nowhere and how he couldn't imagine spending his life with someone else and how he wanted me to move with him to Hong Kong so that we could finally take our relationship to the next level.

I handled these new developments as best I could, which was to say, not well.

Beatrice was still breathing, that much I had confirmed. But after several minutes, she hadn't come out of her stupor and I worried that a passerby would see us and call the police. We didn't exactly fit the mold of the neighborhood, plus there was the attempted breaking and entering. So I did what anyone would have done in that situation: I called an Uber.

When the car arrived 10 minutes later, the driver rolled down his window and looked at me standing over Beatrice's unconscious body, and I thought for a second he was going to keep driving. But thankfully, he didn't and instead got out of the car and helped me moved Beatrice into the backseat. We rode in silence back into Manhattan and I debated which of her apartments we should be going to. In the end, I decided that it would be best to deposit her at home, where hopefully she could sleep the whole thing off under the watchful eye of her husband, rather than him wondering where she was all day.

When we arrived, I asked the doorman to call Garrett down to the lobby so he could help bring her upstairs, and he appeared with Jack-Jack in tow, who immediately began whaling "Mommy, Mommy!" My face turned beet red and I tried, unconvincingly, to explain that we had been out at a champagne brunch to celebrate the end of another tutoring semester and things had gotten very messy very quickly and I was so sorry I had let her drink so much and on and on. When I finished my story, Garrett didn't say a word, instead motioning for the doorman to help him carry Beatrice to the elevator and I stood there, wondering if I should follow them up, until they were gone.

Beatrice had not been happy with my decision.

"BSG tomorrow, 830," the text two days later read.

I tossed and turned the whole night, wondering what she was going to do to me. Would she just fire me outright? Make me test out her unperfected buffs?

But it was the fact that she didn't acknowledge what I had done that was the most unnerving. Instead, she told me that she had completed the Raid by delivering the information to the Requester and that maybe whoever it was would figure out how to actually open the door. In the meantime, I was to go back there and put a piece of tape between the door and the frame and check it every day, so we could see if anyone had managed to open it.

I obliged without a fight. Not that in my mind I had done anything wrong. We hadn't exactly talked through contingency plans if something horrible happened. Had she expected me to take her to the other apartment and keep a bedside vigil until she woke up? I didn't want to press the issue though. The door had been a literal dead-end and I was anxious to work on something new.

But that something never came. Instead, I dutifully taped the door and returned every morning before work to see if it had been disturbed.

Spoiler alert: it hadn't.

Luckily I had something else to distract me from the drudgery my secret life had become. Well, someone. Duncan had come back for a month-long stint over the holidays, his longest layover in New York in the time that we had been dating.

It was during his first night back that he dropped the bombshell on me: that he wanted me to move to Hong Kong, to live together, and to, eventually, get married. Yes, this was the same Duncan who during that ill-fated party in the Hamptons had disparaged me.

Of course, it had all been in his mind and he had no clue that I had heard. And the missed calls over these past two months hadn't exactly inspired confidence that this relationship was heading someplace other than a mutual parting of ways.

So yes, I viewed his newfound proclamation of love with skepticism. How could I not? But I didn't say no. I wanted to take this month slowly, I had said. To get back in the rhythm of being an us. A few days later he suggested that we go away to Miami for New Year's, not just the two of us, but Lisa and Brad too. He even lined up a friend of a friend for Stacy to hang with. The full court press was on and as much as I didn't want to admit it, it had worked so far.

The door slid open and Duncan finally joined me on the balcony.

"Hey," he said. "Look, I didn't mean to … it's just…"

Duncan waffled and looked down at the ground, then at me, as if waiting for me to let him off the hook.

"What?" I asked. "I'm not going to finish your thought for you."

"I'm sorry. I had forgotten it was our first actual New Year's together, like actually together in the same physical location. Not me calling you at noon and you calling me at noon. That's part of the reason I want you to come with me to Hong Kong. So we can just be a couple together."

"I want that too," I said, sliding over to him. "To be a normal couple. To have someone to come home to. But I don't know if I can just pack up and leave my life."

"I know. But you wouldn't be leaving your life. You'd just be starting a new chapter. Besides, the way you talk about your job, I would have thought you'd jump at the chance for a fresh start. I have tons of connections in the Hong Kong startup scene, you'd get-"

"It's not just that," I said. Leaving New York meant leaving the Quests, the Raids, the magic I had discovered. Not to mention the Novice agreement. Maybe there was another version of it all, in Hong Kong. And I'd be free from Beatrice. What was she going to do, follow me?

"I just need some time. To figure things out. That's all. I hope that's OK."

Duncan nodded, not saying anything, just continuing to stare out at the ocean.

"That's it? A nod?"

"No," he said and pulled me toward him to finally give me a proper New Year's kiss.

Several minutes passed until I finally drew back from him, my face flush and my breath short.

"Should we…?" he said with a wry smile.

I hit him playfully and shook my head.

"It's not even 12:30! Besides, first I want to commemorate this occasion. Our first New Year's."

I pulled out my phone and handed it to him. We turned our backs to the water and smiled.

"OK," I said, taking the phone back.

"OK what?"

"Now we, you know…"

He grabbed my hand without another word and didn't let go for a long time.

The January sun reflected off the water outside the window, finally rousing me from my sleep. Duncan was already awake next to me, holding my phone for some reason,

"Umm, Dunc," I said, rolling over in bed to face him. "What are you doing?"

"I, uh, just wanted to see the picture from last night but then I scrolled back a bit and … what are these?"

He handed me my phone and I looked down to see the picture of Frankie's tattoo. Crap.

"Oh, umm, that's a friend's tattoo. Took a picture to show to someone at work who's thinking of getting one."

"Ah. But does your friend have three very similar tattoos? Because you have three pictures here and the numbers in each tattoo are different."

"No, it's just the one…"

I scrolled through the pictures for the first time. It hadn't seemed necessary to look at them, because I had written down the numbers and those had led us to the unopenable door. But Duncan was right.

Each tattoo had a slightly different set of 12 digits and the three new strings of numbers were different from the numbers I had written down, but not by much. What the hell was going on?

"Oh, now I remember," I lied. "These other two are mock-ups that my coworker made based off of the original. Not sure why she wants to tattoo random numbers on her back, but to each her own!"

Duncan looked at me quizzically, before getting out of bed and walking to the bathroom, and I hoped he wouldn't press the issue when he returned. This was the last way I wanted him to find out about my secret double life, if I ever told him at all. But that was a debate for another day. Right now though, I had to tell Beatrice. Maybe that would put things back to normal, as normal as our relationship was.

I wrote a short text to her about finding a new clue about the tattoo and was about to hit send when I stopped myself. Why was I so willing to just hand over this information? After how she had been treating me? After I had been the one to complete the Raid on my own and figured out what the tattoo meant? Besides, I didn't have anything now but a set of weird pictures and three new locations a thousand miles away to investigate, and she would probably appreciate me not bothering her until I'd actually confirmed that I had a lead.

My eyes drifted over to my carry-on, where Beatrice's compendium was tucked away, still unread. I should have been more diligent in reading it, but there were only so many moments I had to myself on this trip, and it wasn't the type of book you could let someone catch you reading.

Maybe I could sneak a peek while Duncan was in the shower.

No.

I needed a break from that life and resolved to put all thoughts of tattoos and secret numbers and sociopathic bosses out of my head for the rest of the trip.

"Hey," said Duncan, reappearing in the bedroom fully dressed and holding a piece of paper, which he handed to me.

"What's this?" I said, looking down at a printed out flight itinerary between Hong Kong and Paris.

"I was going to keep it a surprise, but after talking to Lisa last night, now seemed like a good time to tell you. I'm coming to Paris and you going to meet me there after the bachelorette."

"Oh. OH. Wow, Dunc, that's … that's amazing!"

"I know. Figured it was better than spending a cold week in New York."

"Yeah, exactly! Now I'll have something to look forward to on that trip."

Duncan frowned.

"You sound like it's going to be a chore."

"No, I mean. Of course I'm excited," I lied again, "but you know how Lisa is. I don't know how much of my sanity I'll have left after that week."

"Ah. Well, try to enjoy yourself. Just a little?"

"I'll try. But can't make any promises."

"Fine. But promise me this. When I see you in Paris, you'll have an answer for me?"

I stared at Duncan, not believing what I had just heard. Did he just give me an ultimatum?

"I'm sorry, what?"

"What? You'll have had three months to think it over by then. How much more time do you need?"

"Oh, three months. You're right. That is long enough to decide whether I'm going to abandon my entire life and move halfway around the world."

"Your entire life? Right, I see."

"No, what I meant was…"

"It's fine. Forget it. Forget I said anything."

He took the itinerary out of my hands and stormed out of the room.

"Where are you going?" I yelled.

"To the airport," he shouted back. "You clearly need the space. Take it. Take the whole fucking continent."

I ran out to the living room only to hear the door slam shut.

He was gone.

CHAPTER TWENTY-FIVE

HISTORY HAS
ITS EYES ON YOU

"I heard an interesting account about Washington's evacuation during the Battle of Brooklyn. It seems like there are others at work on this continent besides the Guild and its former members. I need to be more cautious going forward."

I thought about running after him.

It would have been like a scene out of a movie. One that would probably have gotten cut, because, well, who would care about the out-of-town boyfriend who made a dumb ultimatum when there was a secret world of magic to get back to?

Well, for starters, me. And probably no one else.

The plane ride back was excruciating. I went back and forth a hundred times on what to say to Duncan, whether I should pour my feelings out in an email, try to somehow make a plane-to-plane video call, or just let things simmer for a bit until cooler heads could prevail. Of course, I took the easy way out and chose the third option. It would take Duncan a few days to get over the jet lag anyway, and I'm sure he would be too slammed at work to even think about it for a bit. I wanted to put it out of my mind, too, to escape back over the threshold of my new life.

So that was why, on a cold January morning a week later, I found myself on the Weehawken Cliffs, debating whether or not to knock over a bust of Alexander Hamilton.

The bronze bust rested on a column, which was surrounded by a short fence, an empty flagpole behind it. The face of the man was smirking, as the sculptor had wanted to portray him as a man who hadn't cared that he had gotten killed in a ridiculous duel with the Vice President of the United States. I walked to the back of the fenced-in area to find a boulder with words inscribed into the surface.

"Upon this stone rested the head of the patriot soldier, statesman, and jurist Alexander Hamilton after the duel with Aaron Burr."

I knew from my reading on the way over that the stone's claim was an unconfirmed myth, but so much of what I had thought was myth was not, so maybe there was something to this rock after all?

Four holes drilled into the stone formed a rectangle of sorts around the words, remnants of a long since stolen plaque that sported the same words now carved into the stone. If anything was hidden here, those holes were the best place, save for some secret compartment under the bust, and I wasn't ready to venture into destruction of property just yet. I made a lap around the premises and, satisfied that no one was around, climbed over the fence and stepped down next to the stone. It only took a few seconds to confirm that each of the holes was empty, except for wind-swept dirt that now adorned my fingers. I quickly climbed back over the fence and left the fallen Founder to his thoughts.

————————

Fortunately, the bust was a short walk from the ferry terminal and in no time I was looking back at the cliffs from the water and wondering if this whole sojourn was going to be a complete waste of time. The ferry soon docked, and I walked over to the subway to head uptown to the next set of coordinates.

My train car was empty so I pulled out Beatrice's little notebook and finally began to read. Her handwriting was sparse and neat and all the entries were dated, which made it easy to decipher. I quickly flipped to the back to see the last page dated 2010, which meant that this was potentially only a small sliver of Beatrice's knowledge. I turned back to the second entry, the one right after Beatrice had found her Rita ring.

"Put on ring. Nothing happened. Took off ring."

That was the extent of the note. Great. At least I already knew why nothing had happened when she had put on the ring. She hadn't yet found my Rita ring and whoever had it at that point wasn't wearing it. I read on to the next entry.

"Plan: identify locations mentioned in diary and visit to see if any prima materia left."

That seemed sensible, except that the intervening hundreds of years had probably reduced whatever magic was there to nothing.

"Identified pond mentioned in March 1777 entry. Located in Crotona Park in Bronx. Collected various flora in vicinity for testing."

So she had done the hard work of correlating the vague descriptions in the diary to their present-day locations. Smart. I read on.

"Incomplete May 1777 entry makes reference to rat. Hypothesis: vermin accumulate traces of magic. Will need to devise method to extract."

I didn't want to imagine how many rats, pigeons, and other creatures Beatrice had killed in her experimentation. But it was fascinating to read how she had sussed all of this out seemingly by herself. The screech of the train brakes shook me out of my reading stupor, and I put the book away and braced for reentry into the cold.

The second location was another relic of history - the former site of the Polo Grounds. Or, rather, the lone remaining stairway from that once-hallowed stadium, which led up to a small park. I walked to the designated spot and was greeted with another inscription.

"*The John T. Brush Stairway, Presented By The New York Giants.*"

This was turning into a ridiculous scavenger hunt crafted by an overly enthusiastic history teacher. I walked back down and underneath the portion of the stairs where the plaque was. The ground looked undisturbed, which I took as a good sign that someone hadn't beaten me here. Or a bad sign that there was nothing here to begin with.

I knelt down and started digging up the dirt with my hands. The cold soil came up in chunks and after a little while, I had made a perfectly good mess of the ground and myself. Still, I had nothing to show for it. Maybe whatever was supposed to be here was deeper than I'd managed to go.

I heard the footsteps of people above on the stairway and stepped away from the makeshift hole. If this was the right location, it would require a proper shovel and the cover of night. I bent down to smooth everything back to its original state and headed downtown to the final location.

"*First extraction a success, but a bit messy. Will test content of liver and preserve spleen for later.*"

The entry made me almost vomit on the subway, imagining what Beatrice had done, but I kept reading.

"*Liver dissolved and distilled. Unsure whether to mix with material recovered from pond or test on its own.*"

I hadn't thought of the difference between sources of prima materia. In my mind, it was like this one big well of magic that you could use in different ways. But maybe it wasn't that simple.

"Mixed liver essence with ink and wrote test command on paper: 'jump once.' Nothing happened."

So she had gone straight to the big stuff. I would have done the same thing too, although I was relieved that it wasn't as easy as mixing any prima materia with any regular thing and expecting a magical result.

I didn't have time to ponder further as the train arrived at my final destination for the day: Long Island City, not far from the door.

It had begun to snow as I descended from the platform and I pulled the top of my jacket close to my face. The last set of coordinates was in a small park surrounded by on-roads to the Queensboro Bridge. I walked along a cobblestone path that ran between the multiple lanes of traffic, columns of jagged rocks lining the way. The aesthetic was appropriate and, I hoped, a good sign that I was nearing the end of this journey.

I crossed over to the park and spotted my destination: a Dutch millstone from the 1600s that prior to the park's creation was buried in a traffic island. I wondered what else this city had buried and forgotten.

A small sign stood next to the millstone:

"In 1642, Dutch citizens were issued licenses to settle around a stream (or 'kill' in Dutch) that fed into Newtown Creek, which divides Queens from Brooklyn, and so the area became known as Dutch Kills. This millstone was used to make flour."

My eyes widened. Everything was starting to fit into place, and it couldn't have been a coincidence that I had been led here, to one of the oldest artifacts in the city, to where the first alchemists had settled after arriving from Europe.

But like the other two locations, this one was also empty. The center of the millstone, which would have been a great place to stash something, was filled in with concrete, and again I resisted the small urge to destroy an object of historical significance.

Dejected, I walked back up to the subway and pondered my next move on the way back into Manhattan, glad that I had not told Beatrice anything about this. I could only imagine what she would be saying right now if she was here, after a day spent running down dead leads.

But this couldn't be a dead end. Clearly there was something more to the tattoo ink - a second kind of ink that Beatrice didn't want to tell me about. That didn't make sense though. If she knew about this second ink, she would have told me to take the photos instead of just writing down the numbers by hand.

The day's travels had taken a bit out of me, so I leaned my head against the plastic subway seat just for a second and closed my eyes.

But when I opened my eyes again, I was back in that tiny bathroom, staring at the reflection of Beatrice in the unbroken mirror.

My eyes were weary with the weight of a thousand problems, my lips were tinged with sadness, and I let out a low sigh.

I turned on the tap and let the rust-colored water turn clear before splashing some on my face, my head pounding from the prior night's activities.

Three poundings on the front door shook me from my hungover stupor. I blinked and was standing in front of the door, flicking up the peephole to see a young woman outside.

I unlocked and unlatched the door, and the pounding stopped.

"Just a second," I said, opening the door slowly.

A girl stood outside, every part of her a mess.

"Kate, what are you doing her-"

The girl pushed past me without saying a word and deposited herself on the couch in the living room.

I blinked again, and I was setting a glass of water on the table next to the girl named Kate, who still hadn't responded.

I shouted Kate's name a few times before picking up the glass and throwing its contents on the catatonic girl. Kate regarded the situation with a detached look in her eyes before suddenly diving towards a pocketbook that was also on the table and pulling something out: an ivory-handled knife.

Kate held the knife blade point at me, her hand shaking uncontrollably. I felt my heart start to pound but tried to remain calm.

"More. I need more."

"More what, Kate? You know, you could have just called. Now why don't you just give me that-"

"The buffs. I need more."

"Oh."

I blinked a third time and I was in the secret room behind the bookcase, digging through the bottom drawer of an armoire. I pulled out a container and brought it over to the desk, where a note written in black ink was drying in the dim light of the room. I took out two envelopes and wrote "Kate O'Laughlin, 5H" on the front of one of them before opening the container and stuffing a small piece of something wrapped in plastic into the envelope and sealing it. I then turned to the letter, folding it neatly and stuffing it in the second envelope and writing a second name and address on the front.

I returned to the living room with the second envelope and handed it to Kate.

"Here," I said, handing Kate the envelope, who stared at it with a puzzled look on her face.

"What's this?"

"Your next task. Make sure this letter gets delivered, and I'll make sure you're taken care of by the evening."

The girl considered the envelope, the stoic look on her face never wavering, before stuffing it in her pocket and walking out the door.

"Well, time to start over again," I said to myself.

The train suddenly stopped short and I was jolted out of the memory. Unlike the previous times, the details of what I had seen were crystal clear, and I struggled to slot this latest piece of the puzzle into the right place.

I recognized the Medoblad in the memory and wondered if Kate had known its true power when she had threatened Beatrice. And what was in the envelope that Beatrice was going to give her later that night? A buff to wipe her memory or…

The realization hit me like the swing of a bat to the gut: the newspaper headline that Beatrice had been reading at the coffee shop was about Kate.

I started inhaling huge gulps of air but still felt like I couldn't breathe.

She had killed her.

And her threat to kill me if I crossed her wasn't an idle one. She would follow through, I was sure of it.

The train began to slowly inch forward and my mind spun in a million directions. If Beatrice had wanted to kill me, she would have already done so, I reassured myself. But it was just as likely that she still needed me to help open the door, and then she would dispose of me. One thing was clear though: I needed to figure out the secret behind the three tattoo locations before I faced her again. Except I was fresh out of ideas and I had no one to turn to.

"Times Square 42nd St," the conductor shouted over the loud-speaker.

Well, not no one.

FORCE
OF WISDOM

"The Convention plods on in the suffocating heat. Luckily, recruitment efforts are going well. Soon, we will have a full complement of Guild members again."

The sidewalks were white when I finally exited the subway. I didn't even know if she would be at the corner, but I was already here so it was worth looking before I messaged her. And somehow my luck finally hit because there she was, with that same stupid box and those same stupid shells that had first dragged me into this mess in the first place.

Polly Janssen.

A family of five all sporting fanny packs was in the middle of having their money stolen by the little punk, and I watched her seamlessly move the ball between the shells just like before. The father was about to tap the left shell when I interrupted.

"I think you want the middle one," I said, and a look of shock registered on Polly's face when she saw me.

The father stared at me as if I was crazy and withdrew his hand.

"Look, if I'm wrong, I'll take the loss," I said.

"Oh-OK," he said with an accent I couldn't quite place, and he moved his hand over to the middle shell and tapped it.

Polly glared at me as she turned over the shell to reveal the ball, and I smiled. She handed the man some money, and he and his family walked away.

"So," I said. "It's been a while."

"It has, hasn't it, 'Jade?'" Polly said with a sneer. "Or should I say, Jen?"

"Beatrice told you about me, did she?"

"Yep. Where is she? Or is she out with the family and too busy to give me a message herself?"

"Not exactly. I'm here on my own accord."

"Oh. Come to yell at me then? Or maybe I should be the one yelling at you, after all the trouble you got me in with my dad."

"Ah. Yeah. Sorry about that."

"It's fine. I'm good at lying. Anyway, what do you want Jen? I assume it's something you don't want to tell *her* about, since you're ambushing me and all."

"Sort of. We're not exactly on speaking terms at the moment."

"What'd you do? Screw up a Raid?"

"In a way. I need your help. Is there somewhere we can talk? Privately?"

"Sure. I know a place."

Sweat dripped down my brow as I waited in the steam-filled room. It had been 20 minutes and there was no sign of Polly. This was getting ridiculous. When I asked if she knew a place, I thought we would just go to the supermarket where she first wrote the call numbers of Rita's diary on the freezer case. But instead, she had stashed her box in a nearby parking lot and then beckoned me into the subway. We rode in silence, exited at Union Square, and then walked in silence to the East Village until we arrived at a Russian bathhouse.

"This is the place?" I said. "They're not even going to let you in."

"Don't worry about me," said Polly. "Just go in and I'll meet you in the steam room in a little bit."

"Fine."

I had done as she asked and was awkwardly waiting in a towel, hoping some overweight 70-year-old man didn't come in first.

The door swung open and I saw a figure walk in. The steam was thick so I couldn't make out who it was, only that the person looked to be tall with blond hair.

A bead of sweat trickled into my eye, and I wiped it away with my hand. But when I opened my eyes again, there was Polly, in a bathing suit.

"Hi," she said.

"Hey," I replied. "Did you walk in with someone else?"

"Nope, just me."

She walked up to the top level of the small room, sat down next to me, and let out a big sigh.

"Nothing better than a steam," she said.

"Aren't you a little young for this?"

"No. Besides, it's the one place I know we won't be overheard. So, what's so important that you needed to talk to me and not our mutual friend?"

"It's a long story."

I told her everything, from the showdown with Beatrice at the party, to becoming her novice, to the spin class shenanigans, and, finally, the door and the three hidden locations. It was cathartic in a way I hadn't expected. I had been keeping all of this inside for months, with no one to share it with except a woman who I was half-convinced was going to kill me at some point. I had left out that last part - the truth I had learned about Kate.

"Sounds like you've been busy," said Polly after I had finished. "But I still don't get why you want my help. You know I work for her, right?"

"I do. But you're not going to tell her about this."

"Oh, I'm not? You've got me all figured out?"

"Not exactly. But I'm guessing your dad would be furious to know that you, a Janssen, were working for a grinder like Beatrice."

"Are you threatening me?"

"No, no, of course not," I said with a smile. "Just putting every-thing on the table."

"Fine. I'll help you. Just this once."

"Thanks."

"It's called crypto-ink."

"I'm sorry?"

"The tattoo. You were right, there is a second type of ink. Although I've never heard of someone using it for a tattoo. Smart. Would be harder to get all the hidden information."

"So you don't think I got it all? That there's a fourth set of numbers in the tattoo."

"I don't know. Each new layer requires that much more...wait a minute."

Polly stood up and walked down to the door, which was covered in condensation.

"So you started in New Jersey, right?"

"Yeah, in Weehawken."

She made a little circle on the left side of the door.

"Right, and then you went up to Harlem."

Polly drew a diagonal line up from the first dot, stopping slightly off center about three-quarters of the way up the door.

"And finally, you came down to Long Island City."

The girl added another diagonal line going down to the right side of the door, forming two sides of a triangle. She completed the shape, connecting the first and third dots and then took a few steps back.

"Clever idea," Polly said. "Hide the three corners in the tattoo, but omit the actual location."

"Wait, so the real location…"

Polly nodded.

I walked down to the door and drew a line from each corner to its opposite leg. They intersected in the middle, at a location that was probably somewhere in Manhattan.

"Holy crap," I said, standing back from the rudimentary map. I looked over at Polly, noticing for the first time that she was sporting a silver ring on her right hand that she hadn't been wearing earlier.

The door suddenly swung open, and it was only then that I felt my finger tug toward it.

"My thoughts exactly," said Beatrice from the doorway.

The three of us sat in silence around a small table in the empty bar behind the coffee shop. It was an hour before opening and the bouncer, after some prodding from Beatrice, had let Polly in. I held my water glass close to my chest, as if that would stop someone with an arsenal of alchemy at her fingertips from slipping in a drop of poison.

"So," I said, looking at the two of them.

"So," said Beatrice.

"Yep."

I looked down at my glass, debating whether to take a sip or at least pretend to.

"Well, this is enthralling," said Polly. "Is there a reason I still need to be here? I already figured out the location and you were going to…"

"Zip it," Beatrice said to Polly with a scowl. "Jen, was there some reason you decided to keep all this to yourself and then go and ask Polly for help? I already told you she worked for me. What did you think was going to happen?"

"Kate O'Laughlin," I said, wondering if the Medoblad was still in Beatrice's bag, which was resting unattended under the table.

Beatrice took a long sip of her water. There was a note of sadness in the eyes that I couldn't believe, after what I had seen.

"Those stupid apples. More trouble than they're worth."

"That's it?" I raised my voice slightly. "You killed her!"

If this revelation was news to Polly, she didn't show it. Another sociopath in the making apparently.

"How much did you see?" Beatrice asked.

"Enough to know that I don't want anything to do with you."

Beatrice let out a long sigh.

"You know, the first time I did it, I couldn't sleep for months afterward. I told myself that it had to be done, that Doug wasn't going to leave me alone. But with Kate, it was easier. She came after me first, did you see that part?"

I nodded.

"So then what's the issue? I told you last time we were here that I would kill you if you fucked with me. Kate fucked with me, so I dealt with her. If the Guild has no qualms about killing people that get in their way, then why should I?"

She reached under the table and I recoiled, expecting the worst.

"Relax," said Beatrice. "If I wanted to kill you, you'd already be dead."

Beatrice plunked her hand down with a thud and pushed something toward me. It was the Medoblad.

"What…what are you doing?"

"What does it look like? Giving you a show of trust. Like I said, I don't need this to kill you. Also if I used it, then I'd be stuck with an incredibly heavy stone statue of you and what am I going to do with that? Put it in my living room?"

"No, but why are you giving this to me? After what happened before…"

I picked up the knife. Its handle was smooth, the material definitely ivory, and it was surprisingly light, even with the leather scabbard.

"You don't look like a crazed adderallic at the moment. Plus we need to start taking precautions, and I'm highly doubtful of your ability to properly defend yourself."

"What are you talking about?" Polly chimed in finally.

"Not you. What are you even still doing here?" said Beatrice.

"I was asking myself the very same question. But there is the little matter of my payment…"

"Oh. Fine. Here."

Beatrice retrieved a small box from her bag and put it in Polly's hands.

"Now you can go."

"You're welcome, by the way," Polly said as she got up and walked toward the coffee shop, and I wasn't sure if she was talking to me or both of us. Given that she betrayed me to Beatrice before I had even had the chance to blackmail her, I didn't exactly feel like thanking her.

"What did you give her?" I asked, once Polly was completely out of sight.

"That? Oh, a smidge of the ink. Just enough to get her into trouble, I'm sure."

"Aren't you worried about what she could do with it?"

I could think of a lot of things I would do with that ink and the idea that more people were running around the city with it gave me the chills.

"I probably should be, but we have bigger problems to worry about."

The ease with which we had returned to our regular banter worried me. Did she not care that I had gone behind her back? It was unnerving, but I needed to keep up a normal front, as difficult as that was, now that I knew what Beatrice was truly capable of.

"Such as?"

"The Guild. I think they're following me."

"Shit. How do you know?"

"I just have a feeling, ever since I turned in the location of the door. It's partially why I haven't been in touch. That and you brought me to the wrong apartment."

"What do you mean the wrong apartment?" I asked.

"Did you think it was a particularly good idea to bring me, passed out, back to my Madison Avenue apartment, so that my husband and son could see me like that?

"Oh. I'm … I'm sorry."

"It's fine, I'm over it. Never thought I would have to use the memory serum on my own kid. Garrett, I've given it to him so many times that I think he's developing a tolerance to it, but Jack-Jack …"

Beatrice took a swig of her drink and I pretended not to see her eyes tearing up.

"Anyway, you should be careful," she said. "I don't know if they know about you, but we should assume that they do. Try not to take the same routes you normally do. Switch the time of your coffee break. Anything to break up your routine."

"But why now? We can't even open the door."

"Exactly. So the next logical step for me would be to reach out to my source and ask for help. And that's when they would strike."

"But don't you get these tips all the time? Why do they care about this one?"

"No, it's not like that. I get one maybe once a year, if I'm lucky. And I've never failed before. But thanks to Polly, it looks like I'm not about to start. Now, let's see these pictures."

I reluctantly handed Beatrice my phone, and she put it beside hers, which she used to insert the three sets of coordinates into some sort of map app. The three points appeared on the screen and Beatrice connected them all to form a triangle, just like Polly had done on the steam room door. Then, Beatrice drew lines from each point to the opposite side and zoomed in on the intersection.

"Well," said Beatrice. "I wasn't expecting that."

"What?" I asked, peering down at the map, which showed the intersection forming right over a museum.

"You up for robbing the Met?"

CHAPTER TWENTY-SEVEN

THREADS
OF FATE

"Finally the proceedings have finished. William played his role to a T but the hard work continues. If my Constitution is to pass, it will need a rousing defense."

The office was pitch black except for the reddish glow from my screens. An assortment of empty energy drink cans littered the floor around my chair and on either side of my monitors, there were ever-growing towers of coffee cups.

It was crunch time, in more ways than one.

The newest demo of our game was due to the backers by the end of February, which meant I had spent all of January getting as many quests (the video-game kind) up-and-running so we wouldn't have an angry mob at our doorstep. And that had meant multiple back-to-back all-nighters, where I was oftentimes completely alone in the office, my other co-workers deciding that 10 PM was a good time to call it quits.

Lisa's multi-continent bachelorette party was also fast approaching, which meant my assigned responsibilities were all exploding at the same time. I still hadn't been able to get us upgraded to business class, still hadn't been able to get us a reservation at some fancy Indian restaurant in Westminster that used to be a Victorian-era library, and still hadn't heard back from some tiny boutique where Lisa's favorite designer was having a pop-up show. At least we already had tickets to the New York Fashion Week lecture, which was oh-so-conveniently located at the Met.

And, I had a Konami Code up my sleeve that I hadn't yet activated: Duncan, who could get the flight and restaurant reservations done with a 30-second phone call. But ever since our fight on New Year's, I had pulled back reflexively. We still kept up with our regular FaceTime calls, but there was an obvious tension each time we spoke, as if we were both just trying to maintain the status quo.

Our Paris rendezvous was just after the bachelorette, which meant coming up with the answer to his question, and I still didn't have it. It should have been an easy decision, after Beatrice's murderous admission. I would be insane not to try to get as far away from her as possible, and Duncan's offer was the best cover I was ever going to receive. Would she really insist I blow up my own life to honor my contract? But part of me didn't want to say yes to Duncan just to run away from Beatrice. Part of me wanted to keep going down the rabbit hole, and that same part didn't want to be stuck all alone halfway around the world with someone who I still wasn't convinced loved me.

And then of course there was still the Raid, which meant figuring out how to steal something from the Metropolitan Museum of Art, of all places. When I hadn't been coding into the wee hours of the morning, figuring out that puzzle out had been my other dedicated focus.

Beatrice had decided against going to the Museum just to figure what was hidden there, as she was certain that she was still being followed. Fortunately, the Met had made a bunch of virtual tours available online, but unfortunately, they didn't cover the whole Museum. And, there was the added complication that we didn't know which floor the latitude and longitude was "pointing" to. We had narrowed it down to either something in the Egyptian wing or a series of rooms on the second floor that housed a bunch of random objects not tied to any particular exhibition or collection. The latter seemed like the obvious choice, but the Museum's website was woefully out of date for that collection's current objects.

We also needed an escape plan, which Beatrice had taken on herself to formulate, and I assumed she was whipping up some sort of alchemic-timed explosion that would go off in the opposite end of the Museum and distract all the guards and the other people attending the lecture.

Oh, that was the other thing: we were going to pull all this off on the first night of Lisa's bachelorette party during the fashion lecture at the Museum. To say I wasn't thrilled about this particular aspect of the plan would be an understatement to the highest degree. The thought of Lisa, Stacy, and Lisa's other friends in near orbit of Beatrice had been giving me indigestion for weeks now

It was my fault, really. I was the one who had mentioned the lecture in the first place. But that had been months ago, and I didn't think Beatrice was the sort to pay attention to an offhand comment of no significance.

I had begged and pleaded with her to figure out an alternative, but on this point Beatrice would not bend. I still extracted a concession though: I could go to London and Paris free and clear. And if we succeeded in our mission at the lecture, Beatrice had agreed to handle the aftermath on her own if she didn't want to wait for me to get back.

As the days counted down to the lecture, I kept envisioning the million ways my entire life was all going to blow in my face at once. It was almost a relief when we were only three days away, and I would hopefully soon be on my way to London and away from it all.

The cursor on my screen hadn't moved down a line in about an hour and I figured 3 a.m. was as good as any time to pack it in for the night. I felt myself nodding off, my eyes closing for just a second, before I beat down sleep's siren call and snapped back to attention. But in that moment, somehow, a green apple had appeared on my keyboard, a string of random letters and numbers flying across my screen.

I looked down at my hands to see if I was awake or trapped in another memory before a familiar voice sounded in the empty office.

"Burning the midnight oil again?" said Beatrice, peering over the top of my monitors.

"What are you, how long have you been here?"

Beatrice let out a chuckle before walking around the long shared desk to take up the seat next to me.

"About ten minutes. You were out for about five before I put the apple down on your keyboard. I was going to wake you but it seemed like you needed the rest."

"You're so thoughtful," I said, rubbing my eyes before pointing to the apple. "What is that doing here?"

"It's for Thursday night. I wasn't sure if you had any of your own left over from my Quest so I wanted to give it to you ahead of time."

"I don't have any left," I lied, "but why do I need this?"

"So we can communicate while we're at the Met without your friends or anyone else knowing. Put it in your purse and start eating it halfway through the lecture and I'll do the same. I don't want anyone seeing us within five feet of each other."

"What about right now? I thought you were supposed to be keep- ing your distance."

"I was. But I snuck out the service entrance of my apartment and have spent the last four hours crisscrossing the city. If anyone followed me in here, then at least there's two of us to fend them off."

I grabbed the apple and put it inside my work backpack. "You do remember what happened the last time we ate these, don't you? Aren't you worried about more of your memories seeping into my mind?"

"No. Last time was different. As long as you don't do something crazy, this is just going to be like using a walkie-talkie."

"Fine. Did you finish whatever you were making to draw out the Met's armies? Make them blind to all else that moves?

"What the hell are you talking about?" said Beatrice.

"A diversion. You were supposed to be handling that part of the op."

"Oh. Yes, it's ready."

"OK, great. What is it?"

Beatrice shook her head.

"I'll tell you after you eat the apple."

"Umm, fine. But I feel like we should maybe think this through some more? We're talking about the Met here, not some two-bit pawn shop we're robbing. And we don't even know what we're supposed to steal."

"Just trust me, OK? Besides, we have the combined magic of alchemy and GPS tracking, do we not? They won't know what hit them."

I wanted to push her for more details but before I could, she got up from the chair and retreated back into the darkness from whence she came.

"Ladies and gentlemen, without further ado, the impeccable Dalia De Wyck!"

The audience burst into applause, as a woman with short jet black hair, an even shorter black dress, and knee-high boots strode out from behind the curtain, her image mirrored on a big screen hanging from the middle of the stage. She adjusted the tortoise shell glasses on her nose, cleared her throat, and began to speak.

"Thank you so much Cassie for that great introduction. You know, I remember coming up in the business as a bright-eyed young woman, like all of you, dreaming of a chance to sit front row at all the big runway shows. Hell, I would have killed just for the opportunity to stand on the sidewalk outside of Bryant Park and watch all the icons and the luminaries and the celebrities walk out of their fancy cars and into those white tents all those many moons ago. How many moons, I'm not saying…"

The audience burst into laughter at the line, worst of all Lisa, who I thought was going to pass out from all her fake guffawing. I wanted to tell her that no one would know if she didn't laugh at the joke, least of all this Dalia person, as we were so far back that we were almost outside, but I kept my mouth shut as Dalia continued. Her image towered over us from the big screen, and I noticed that what I previously thought was a simple black dress was actually covered in an intricate embroidery of black thread, the shape of which I struggled to make out. It looked like it could be a tree or a bush or a school of fish, I couldn't be sure.

I glanced at my watch. Five minutes of the hour-long lecture had elapsed, although it had felt like a lifetime already. And we still had an entire cocktail hour where Lisa was going to try to talk to Dalia before the attendees would be given free rein of the Museum.

The green apple, which I had cut into slices just before I left my apartment, was stashed away in the clutch on my lap. The remaining buffs Beatrice had given me were in there too. At Beatrice's urging and against my protestations, I had also brought the Medoblad. Bringing a knife into a museum, let alone a magic knife that turned people to stone hadn't seemed like a good idea, especially when we were trying to remain inconspicuous, but Beatrice was quite confident that the knife would sail through security. Or maybe *I* was the diversion that Beatrice would use to retrieve whatever it was we were looking for.

I had spent the rest of the lead-up to the lecture figuring out how to get the knife in undetected and had devised a pretty clever plan. I had slid the blade under my Spanx just above my waist and after slipping on the new dress that Lisa had picked out for me, I fastened a recently acquired belt with a disgustingly garish and, most importantly, metal buckle that was sighted right over where the knife was.

When we arrived at the Museum, the line to get in was already down the block, and I waited nervously with Lisa, Stacy, and the nine other girls as we had slowly inched toward the front. By the time we had made it up the stone stairs, my nerves were so frayed that I actually considered just turning around and flying straight to Hong Kong.

Finally, it had been my turn to go through the metal detector, which had immediately starting blaring. But thankfully, the guard spent only three seconds waving the beeping hand wand over my belt buckle before waving me in and I breathed a sigh of relief. One step down, only 400 to go, I thought.

"... I would not have believed you if you told me that someday I would not only be sitting front row but would also be invited to give the inaugural Tia Lansplan Memorial Lecture, especially after working so closely with her for so many years. Her wit, wisdom, and warmth will be severely missed. Now, I'm sure that a lot of you here today are wondering..."

I zoned out as the impeccable Ms. De Wyck blathered on about the seven things necessary for a successful career in the fashion world and how even she would have had such a tougher road today, but that didn't mean it was impossible, blah blah blah. The waiting was excruciating and at this point, I just wanted to eat the apple so Beatrice could start bossing me around rather than having to keep listening to this drivel.

"And so rather than naming my line after myself, as so many do, I wasn't talking about you, Lars."

The crowd burst into laughter again at the expense of whoever Lars was.

"I instead named it after my grandmother, Thera DeWitt. She lost everything when her childhood home, a house that had been in her family for hundreds of years, burnt to the ground one night."

My watch started blinking zeros and it was finally time. I reached a hand inside my clutch, pulled out a couple of the slices, and began to chew, waiting for the link between my mind and Beatrice's to open.

"But that didn't stop her. She rebuilt her house, rebuilt her family, and rebuilt her life. And, in a way, she built my life. I remember early in my career, working late nights for months on end, and whenever I felt the urge to quit, to just walk away from it all, I would remember the stories she told me and what she had been through and it kept me going."

I couldn't concentrate for the rest of the lecture, as any second I was expecting Beatrice's voice to start whispering in my head. Finally, Dalia got to number seven on her list, and the room erupted into a final round of applause and a standing ovation that I was forced to participate in.

Suddenly, I felt a throbbing in my head, as if someone had clamped a vice around my temples and was beginning to tighten it.

"*Leave the auditorium and go to the bathroom,*" said a voice that I could barely hear over the still-going applause.

"What?" I said out loud.

"*The bathroom, go now!*" said Beatrice in my head. "*And don't try to look for me.*"

"OK," I thought back as I slid out of the row passed Lisa, who had an annoyed look on her face.

"Sorry, just want to get to the bathroom before it becomes a mob scene," I said to her. I didn't wait for a reply or look back, and thanks to our terrible seats, a few seconds later I had cleared the auditorium and entered the foyer, which had been elaborately decorated with gowns from Dalia's line and pictures of her with various celebrities.

"OK, I'm out of the auditorium. Where's the bathroom?" I thought.

"*To your right,*" said Beatrice's voice, which, now that I was out of the raucous cacophony, sounded like it was coming from right next to me.

"Why can I hear you so well?" I asked her.

"*Been trying to improve the effectiveness of the apples. I have a small plot of land upstate where I hid the tree.*"

"What? If you had your own apples this whole time, why did you post that Quest to go to the orchard?"

"*Focus, Jen. And you already know the answer. Because I can't go back there and I didn't want to waste my own apples on an experiment.*"

"Fine. I'm in the bathroom" I said.

"*Good. Go into the third stall and open the toilet tank. There's an envelope taped at the top for you.*"

I walked over to the stall, which thankfully was empty, and locked myself inside. The porcelain lid on the tank was heavy, and I slid it off its moorings to see the promised envelope. I pulled it free and pushed the lid closed again before sitting down on the seat.

"What is this?" I asked.

"*Notes. For your friends. Go out to the reception and give one to Lisa and the other to Stacy and then meet me in the Egyptian wing.*"

"What? Why do I need to-"

I opened the envelope and pulled out two folded sheets. I slowly unfurled one, only to see the familiar dark black ink scrawled across the paper.

WORDS WITH FRIENDS

"The good thing about egotistical men is that they are so easy to control. I delivered so many papers to Hamilton and what did he go and do? He used them all! By my count, Madison wrote 29, John Jay five, and Hamilton wrote 10 on his own, taking all of mine for a staggering total of 51."

"Don't. Read. Them,"** said Beatrice, her voice booming in my head. *"Put them back in the envelope and go deliver them."*

I complied but my hand was gripping the papers so hard I thought I would tear the notes in two.

"What do they say?" I shouted in my mind.

"You don't want to know," said Beatrice.

"Yes, I think I do, seeing as they involve my friends."

"Friends you don't even like, friends who you think keep you around because they pity you."

How did she know th-

"We don't have time to play this game, Jen. You saw my memories, I saw yours, remember? Your friends are the diversion you asked about earlier. And anyway, we have a contract. I've fulfilled my end and now it's time for you to fulfill yours."

"I never thought that meant, that you would make me…"

"You can make your excuses and your apologies later. But now you will do what I ask."

"Why does it have to be them? There are hundreds of people here. Any one of them would do!"

"No, they won't. The ink needs a name to work. It can't just be a random person. And I wasn't about to bring the ink here to write a note on the fly. So I'll leave you to it now and trust that you'll get the job done."

The throbbing subsided and I was alone again with just my thoughts and the notes. I stared at the envelope, wondering what commands Beatrice had written for Lisa and Stacy. Would the notes just make them start yelling uncontrollably so they would be escorted out? Or something far far worse, like a death note?

No, she wouldn't go that far. It wasn't necessary and would probably cause even more of a scene.

I could just run away. Maybe if I got far enough, the apples would stop working and she wouldn't be able to find me.

I held up my hand and felt the ring tug my finger gently forward.

I could resign myself to wearing this stupid thing for the rest of my life if it meant stopping Beatrice from ruining tonight. I would go to the airport now, fly to London, meet Duncan in Paris, go straight to Hong Kong, and then never return. I would find the Quest Board in Hong Kong and then grind my way up so that if I ever felt this ring tug on my finger again, I would be ready for her.

My hand trembled as I lifted the seat and I held the envelope over the open toilet. All I had to do was let go. Let go and run. Run and never look back.

No.

I couldn't.

It was too late.

The plan was already in my head. If I ran, as soon as Beatrice came back into my mind and I didn't answer, she'd know what I was going to do. I doubted if I could even get out of the Museum

I put the envelope in my clutch and opened the stall to see Stacy washing her hands at the sink. She spotted me in the mirror and turned around.

"Oh hi JJ!" she said. "That was a great talk, don't you think?"

I walked over to the sink next to her and started to wash my hands, the pounding of my heart so loud it sounded like someone had pulled it from my chest and held it up to my ears.

"Oh, umm, yeah. It was, uh, interesting. But I'm looking forward to getting to walk around the Museum a little bit. Haven't been here in ages."

"Well, don't take too long. Lisa wants an early night tonight, so we don't miss our flight at 6 tomorrow morning."

"Right," I said. I walked over to the hand dryer and debated whether to give Stacy the note now. It didn't sound like there was anyone else in the bathroom, which would make things simpler, but with the reception about to begin, she might start going crazy in front of everyone.

I looked over and Stacy was still at the sink, fixing her hair.

I wasn't going to get a better shot. It had to be now.

I opened my clutch and pulled out both notes. Looking at the ink through the paper, I could see the one that had Stacy's name at the beginning and slid the other one away. I walked back over to Stacy and held out the note.

"What's this?" she said, giving me a funny look.

"Oh, it's just a little note I wrote. Was feeling sentimental thinking about how much we've changed since you guys walked by my dorm room that day."

"JJ, that's so sweet! I'll save this for the plane ride tomorrow morning. I really need to get back out there. Lisa's going to try to talk to Dali-"

"Would you mind reading it now? I just, I don't want you to forget."

"Oh. OK," she said, unfolding the note.

I bit my lip as Stacy began to read. The note looked short and in a few seconds, Stacy looked back up at me with a confused expression on her face.

"JJ, what-"

Stacy's eyes suddenly turned glassy as the command activated and without another word, she sprinted out of the bathroom.

"Stac, where are you going?" I yelled after her, but she was gone.

"The first note is away," I said loudly in my head and felt the familiar pressure return.

"*Good,*" said Beatrice. "*Now go give the other one quickly. We won't have a big enough window if you don't.*"

"OK," I said and she was gone again.

I put Stacy out of my mind and walked out of the bathroom.

The reception was bustling with women in incredibly high heels and dressed to the nines, who were still making their way out of the lecture. If Stacy had caused a scene, it must have been a minor one, because everyone was acting normal. A server passed by with a tray of champagne flutes and I grabbed one in stride, taking a long sip as I continued to scan the room for any sign of Lisa, but didn't see her. I walked over to a set of blown-up photographs I had seen earlier, which were mounted on easels and relatively unattended.

An older looking woman stood stoically in front of a young girl in pigtails on a random city street. I didn't need to read the caption to figure out that it was Thera DeWitt and a young Dalia, as the woman and her granddaughter, as she was now, bore many of the same features.

I heard a small commotion as the actual Dalia entered the foyer on the far side of the room.

She had changed out of the boots and was now sporting a pair of incredibly high platform heels and a jewel-studded handbag. A gaggle of women had already made their way over to pay homage to her, so I left the photos and walked to the periphery of the gathering, note in hand, hoping to see Lisa. I spotted her after a few seconds, slowly pushing her way toward Dalia. If she got to Dalia before I got to her, I would lose my chance, so I started politely elbowing my way through the outer circle of the group until I reached her.

"Lis, there you are. Been looking all over for you. Listen, can I talk to you for a sec?"

"One minute, JJ, just want to try to say hello to Dalia."

She lurched forward further into the crowd, but I grabbed her by the arm and held her back.

"JJ, what the fuck are you-"

I held the note in front of her face and watched as the hard expression softened into the glossy mask that Stacy had also worn. All fight drained out of Lisa, and she took the note from my hand without a word, before sprinting away and almost knocking over a waitress carrying a full tray of champagne.

A sudden wave of despondency came over me, and I brought my hand up to my eyes to block the tears that were forming, but it was too late. I had sacrificed my two friends on the Questing altar and for what? A pat on the back from a murderer? There would be time enough to wrestle with what I'd done, but all I wanted to do now was get the hell out of this museum.

"It's done," I said in my head.

"*Excellent!*" said Beatrice. "*I'm already in the Egyptian wing at the spot. There's nothing here, so it must be in the second-floor collection. Meet me there."*

"OK," I said. The room was filled to the brim now, and I slowly forced my way against the stream of people until I reached the stairs leading up to the second floor landing overlooking the foyer. I walked as fast as my heels would allow, passing an assortment of silver plates and amphoras. The next room was filled with statues of Buddha but thankfully no one else. But as I made my way up a small staircase that led to the next room, I saw in the distance someone running toward me.

I quickly walked back down the stairs and crouched down behind them. The footsteps got louder and I held my breath, waiting for one of my friends to appear. But instead, I heard the crackle of a radio as someone made their way down.

"Requesting backup in Abstract gallery and in Arms and Armor. Multiple alarms triggered in each gallery," said a voice over the radio.

"Copy," said the security guard as he walked into the room and out the way I had come in. I emerged from my hiding place and continued on, my pace quickening.

"Security is heading toward Lisa and Stacy," I said. "Just hid from a guard and heard over the radio."

"Then we don't have much time left. Hurry," said Beatrice.

The stairs led up into a room with two lion statues astride an opening in the shape of a half-moon on the opposite wall. I passed through the doorway and suddenly found myself in what appeared to be a re-creation of a Chinese courtyard. I ran through a rock garden and onto a stone terrace that lined the perimeter of the room. My heels echoed so loudly on the stones, I thought the security guard was going to do a 180 and come after me, but thankfully I reached the doorway leading out without incident.

"Where are you?" asked Beatrice in my head.

"Just walked through a weird courtyard and am now in a room filled with objects in glass cases," I said.

"Me too," said Beatrice, who appeared from around the back of a case with shelves of different colored jugs wearing a short red dress and black heels. "You look terrible."

"Fuck you," I said without thinking. "You couldn't have come up with a different plan? One that didn't involve my friends getting arrested?"

Beatrice took her phone out of the small purse slung over her shoulder, looked at it, and frowned.

"Great, no GPS. And yes, I did come up with a different plan. Several, actually. But all involving multiple moving parts and too much uncertainty. Seems like I was right anyway. We are where we need to be, and our escape should be relatively easy thanks to Lisa and Stacy."

"I don't care! About any of it!" I tried to rein in my shouts, but it was like a dam had burst and all my anger had come pouring out.

"*Keep your voice down, for fuck's sake! You want to ruin everything after your friends are already expended?*" Beatrice said in my head.

"No!" I answered in my mind. "But that doesn't mean-"

"*Enough,*" she said. "*We'll sort everything out later, your friends, the bachelorette, Duncan's ultimatum. Let's just get what we came for and get out of here.*"

"How do you kn-"

"*You're not very good at compartmentalizing your thoughts, Jen. A lesson for another day if you still want to stick around. But right now, we need to look through these cases and see if we can figure out what's hidden here.*"

"Fine," I said.

I pulled out my phone and saw the same "No GPS" indication. This would make things nearly impossible, given the number of items on display. There were pewter mugs, crystal candlesticks, decorative plates, small busts of historical figures, and on and on. It was too much.

Who knew which of these mundane objects was really something fantastical, hiding in plain sight? Maybe the silver pitcher in front of me was actually a magic pitcher that turned water into wine. Or maybe it was just a silver pitcher, stashed here in obscurity, to be forgotten until the Museum closed.

"*Any luck?*" said Beatrice.

"No, it's just a bunch of old junk. Whoever hid something here was smart though. It's like the room where they hid the Ark at the end of *Raiders*. One of these stupid cups could be the Holy Grail for all we know."

I touched one of the glass cases, dragging my fingers along the surface.

"There has to be something here we're missing," I said. "It's like a twisted game of *Let's Make a Deal*, except instead of three doors, it's a thousand."

"*Clearly,*" said Beatrice. "*With insight like that, I don't know how we haven't already opened the right door.*"

Wait, that was it!

"Find a door knob!" I shouted in my mind.

"*What?*" said Beatrice.

"The door in Long Island City. You knocked the knob off when you punched it. But maybe that knob wasn't the real one…"

"*Oh. OH! Of course!*"

We ran down the rows of cases in unison, trying to find the door knob in a haystack. Even knowing what we were looking for wasn't enough, as the shelves and cases and items seemed endless.

"Found it!" called Beatrice from several rows over and I dashed to the end of my row and looped back around to find her standing in front of a shelf lined with spoons and three brown door knobs.

"There's three of them," I said, leaning my head close to the glass.

"Another brilliant deduction," said Beatrice, sarcasm dripping in her voice. "I'm glad I brought you tonight."

"Shut it, OK?" I snapped and Beatrice went quiet.

The door knobs were lined up in a neat row, the dark brown mottled with white streaks. A tiny card affixed to the glass read "door knobs, circa 1850."

"Smash and grab job, huh?" I said, rapping on the glass with my knuckle.

"Slightly more complicated than that," Beatrice said, fiddling with her amethyst ring. "Not sure I won't smash the door knobs too if I use this." She slid off that ring and put it on to her left pinky finger before sliding off her rock of an engagement ring too.

"You're going to cut through the glass with that?" I asked. "I thought that only worked in the movies."

"No, I'm taking these off so I can get a better grip on the Medoblad. You have it, right?"

"Yep. Snuck it through security in my Sp-"

"Just give it to me, please."

"Fine," I said, unbuckling my belt so I could pull up my dress.

"What the hell are you doing?" Beatrice said, turning away.

"I told you, I hid the knife in my Spanx under the belt buckle. I thought it was a pretty neat-"

"The Medoblad isn't made of metal. It wouldn't have set off the detector."

"Oh," I said. I pulled the knife free and handed it to Beatrice, who flipped it around and gripped the leather sheath.

"OK, no more talking from here on out. Put your belt back on and get ready to leave. You remember the exit route?"

"Yes," I said. "But what about Lisa and Stacy?"

"What about them? I'm sure they'll let them out of whatever holding cell they're in by the morning. The command should have worn off as soon as they finished their tasks."

"And if it hasn't?" I said.

"Well, then they might go insane from the command echoing in their ears all night. But that likely didn't happen. Anyway, don't contact me until you get back. And if the trip gets canceled, wait a week before reaching out. Unless you need bail money for your friends."

"How generous of you. That's the thing I love about this job, all the unexpected perks."

Beatrice rolled her eyes at me and shook her head before taking a small piece of plastic out of her bag. She unwrapped what I assumed was one of her strength buffs, popped it in her mouth, and began to chew.

"Stand back."

She tapped the ivory handle against the glass in front of the knobs three times before drawing her arm back and, in one smooth motion, smashing the knife handle against the case. Beatrice withdrew her now-bloodied hand out of the newly formed opening and handed the knife back to me, which I quickly stuffed back under my Spanx before putting on my belt again.

"Shit," she said. *"Too much force."* She reached her hand back into the opening and carefully retrieved the door knobs one by one, placing them in her bag.

"Hmm, thought there would be an ala-"

The blaring interrupted the thought, and I slowly backed away from Beatrice, before turning and walking out of the maze of cases.

"See you on the other side," she said. *"And Jen?"*

"What?" I said, reaching the staircase at the end of the gallery.

"If you don't come back from Paris, I'll still find you. Eventually."

A LIGHT
IN THE DARK

"Delaware has ratified and I am confident we will reach nine by the end of next year. There is now the matter of what to do with the last Guild seat."

Somehow I made it down the stairs, through the Egyptian section, and out a side door with no one the wiser. I quickly caught a cab that had just crossed the park, and we sped away from the Museum.

The Raid was finally over, but any thoughts of escaping from Beatrice's clutches had been squashed in an instant. If I somehow still made it to Paris, what was I going to say to Duncan?

"Hey, sorry I don't want to be with you, my secret evil alchemy mentor has me locked down in a two-year contract, but I'll touch base with you when it's over?"

Maybe I just wouldn't go at all. The one silver lining of this disaster of a night was that the rest of the bachelorette was likely canceled. I pulled out my phone and was greeted with a wall of text messages from the other girls at the lecture.

"Anyone seen Lisa?"

"Weheres lisa."

"Cant find Stacy or Jen either"

"No one picking up their phones."

"Just talked to security. Lisa knocked down several suits of armor! They've taken her to local precinct"

"Wtf she wasn't even that drunk"

"Stacy's there too. She took an abstract painting off wall"

"I don't understand. I was with lisa in the foyer. she was fine"

"What about jen."

"Nothing"

"Where's jen"

"havent seen her but security didnt mention her"

"Shit shit shit"

"Someone call the airline ill go over to see if i can get them out"

I put down my phone and tried to convince myself it would all be fine. People got drunk all the time at famous museums and knocked over priceless artwork, right? That wouldn't even merit a mention on the bottom of *Page Six*. And maybe they wouldn't remember that I was the one who gave them the notes.

But I couldn't lie to myself, couldn't try to brush away what I'd done, and I buried my face in my hands and began to sob.

"*goto do…*"

The thought crackled in my head like static and I looked up to see if it had come from the driver's phone or someone standing outside the car.

"*Go … door.*"

This time I recognized it as Beatrice's voice, but I could barely pick out the thought from my own.

"Beatrice?" I shouted in my head.

"Lost him for now but…"

"Lost who? What are you talking about?"

"Spotted … Guild. Need to ge…"

"Beatrice? Beatrice!"

She didn't respond. I started to text her but then immediately stopped. If she could have texted me, she would have.

"Excuse me?" I said to the driver. "Sorry, going to be a different destination."

I had the cab drop me off several blocks away from the door in Long Island City. If the Guild was following us, I didn't want to lead them right to the door. But none of it made sense.

"Beatrice?" I said in my head. "I'm close to the door."

"Good. Meet me there."

"I don't understand. Why would you go to the door now, if they're following you?"

"I was always going to go now."

"Oh. Why didn't you tell me?"

"Was trying to let you go. Didn't need to get you more involved."

"But…"

"But then I saw him. From the balcony overlooking the foyer. Gilbert."

"Who's Gilbert?"

"A member of the Guild. He's the one who sent the enforcer after me. Thought we had a truce."

"Did he see you?"

"Don't think so. But didn't want to come here underequipped, since I gave the Medoblad back to you.

"Oh. Got it."

I turned the corner and saw Beatrice already standing next to the door, confirming that the piece of tape I had placed there weeks ago was still there. She was holding the door knobs and considering the empty socket in the door where one of the knobs would hopefully fit.

"Hi," she said.

"Hi. So, you're just going to put one of these in and magically the door will now open?"

"Pretty much. But to where, I'm not sure."

"What do you mean?"

"These aren't just door knobs, Jen. They're the key to a portal. They're made of vervorium."

My eyes widened.

"What? So, wait, the door will open to somewhere else?"

"Yes. That's why I couldn't open the door before with the knob that was already here. The question is, which one is the right one?"

She took one of the door knobs, fitted it into the socket, and slowly turned it as she pushed on the door. It didn't move.

"Hmm, not that one. Let's try the second one."

Beatrice removed the first knob and replaced it with the second one and again turned the knob and pushed.

This time, however, the door slowly slid open, just a crack, and all I could see behind it was darkness.

Beatrice peered into the opening and pushed the door inward another few inches, before gingerly moving her arm across the threshold and then withdrawing it.

"Hmm. Doesn't feel like my arm went anywhere."

"Same thing happened with my finger when I played Polly's shell game. It was like I was sticking my finger in an empty tube."

"Well, we'll just have to take the plunge and see what happens. Ready?"

I nodded.

"Yes."

"Then let's go."

Beatrice opened the door all the way, stepped into the darkness, and vanished from view.

I waited for her to re-emerge and tell me it was all clear but she didn't and I stood on the precipice alone, deciding whether to move forward into the unknown or run back to try to pick up the pieces of my other life.

The decision, just as when I agreed to be Beatrice's novice, was an easy one. I had run from so many things in my life and knew that if I ran from this, I would never get the chance to come back.

I held my breath, closed my eyes, and stepped through the doorway.

I couldn't breathe.

That was the first thing I noticed.

I also couldn't see and couldn't tell if my eyes were opened or closed.

It was as if someone had blindfolded me, spun me around, and tossed me into a tank of water. Up and down had no meaning and my hands and legs searched for purchase on a solid surface but just thrashed in the ether.

Then, off in the distance, a small flicker appeared. I held my hand up to it but it was far away and I still couldn't see anything else. The light grew larger, as if my body was being pushed toward it by some unseen force, until finally I saw it.

A doorway.

I tumbled forward onto a hard wooden floor and gulped in a huge breath. Beatrice was standing above me, fist cocked as if she was ready to knock my head off.

"Sorry, you took so long to come through that I thought Gilbert had gotten you."

She opened her fist and I grabbed her hand to pull myself up, taking in our new surroundings.

The room was dark but for the light coming from Beatrice's phone flashlight, which was on the floor. It was a small room, maybe seven steps across in length. Pairs of boarded-up windows framed doors on all four walls. Beatrice let go of my hand and pushed the door we had come through closed with a shove. A familiar brown door knob with white mottling was in the socket on this side as well, but two of the three other sockets were empty.

"Where are we?" I asked. Beatrice ignored me and pulled the door knob, grasping it free from the socket, before handing it to me.

"Hold onto this. Now we can go back through later without someone else coming through from the other side. And we're in Minneford Lighthouse in the middle of Long Island Sound."

"W-what? Really?"

I opened the map on my phone and the cursor zoomed in on a barely-there island not far from the Throgs Neck Bridge.

"Yes, I was disappointed too. But maybe one of these doors leads to somewhere cooler."

I walked over to the door with a knob and tried to open it, but it wouldn't budge.

"That one's no good. Can't even free the knob; it's rusted over," said Beatrice. "Hopefully on the other side too."

"Oh. What is this place?"

"If I had to guess, some sort of waypoint. A way to travel to and from multiple locations."

"Incredible," I said.

"Yes and no," said Beatrice. "Why would someone go to all this trouble to hide a gateway from an abandoned warehouse to an abandoned lighthouse? There has to be something else through one of these other doors."

She fit both remaining knobs in the empty sockets and motioned me over to one door while she tried the other.

"Won't open," I said and removed the knob. I looked over to see Beatrice pushing her door open a tiny crack before closing it shut.

"I'll take that one back," she said and I handed it to her. "Don't want to mix them up."

"Good thinking. So, we going to go through this one?"

Beatrice considered the door for a moment, a somber look on her face.

"I suppose. But that trip through the first door nearly made me vomit. Hopefully it won't be so bad the second time."

She opened the door again, this time all the way.

"Come right through after me."

"OK," I said as Beatrice stepped across the doorway and disappeared into the darkness once again.

I walked quickly to the doorway and joined her.

I was falling this time. My stomach lurched as if I was plummeting down the tracks on a roller coaster, the familiar darkness enveloping me. I waited for the light to appear but I just kept falling and falling. Seconds, minutes, hours crept by. How many, I didn't know. There was no anchor point in this void, no horizon off in the distance. I tried to call out to Beatrice but if words actually came out, I wasn't sure.

Finally, though, a shimmer of a speck of light appeared above me, gradually getting larger and I realized I wasn't falling down, I was soaring up towards it.

———

The ground was hard and cold when I fell through the doorway and Beatrice was again waiting, her phone flashlight providing the only light.

"That was … unpleasant," I said, getting to my feet. "Where are we now?"

"Don't know," said Beatrice, closing the door and trying, but failing, to remove the door knob. "No service, no GPS, but from the looks of it, somewhere underground."

She shone the light in a circle, revealing carved out walls of stone and a path of jagged rocks leading down a dark corridor. The door was set into one of the walls but the path leading away from the corridor was blocked with a mass of rock.

"Looks like we're in an abandoned mine," I said. "Do you think we traveled farther this time? It felt like an eternity in there."

"Maybe, but let's keep moving," said Beatrice. "This place is giving me the creeps."

She pointed her phone in front of us to illuminate the path and we began to walk. The air was cold and damp, and I cursed myself for not bringing a shawl to the lecture. We must have looked ridiculous, two women in cocktail attire walking down an abandoned mine shaft in high heels. The path took a slight curve to the left and abruptly ended in a small chamber, not much bigger than the interior of the lighthouse. Beatrice slowly moved the flashlight over the left wall to reveal several sconces carved into the surface.

I walked over to the nearest one, my heels kicking up water pooled on the ground, and peered inside to find a red stone the size of a tennis ball resting in the interior. Its surface was smooth like marble and as I slowly withdrew it, the stone suddenly began emitting a soft glow that illuminated part of the chamber.

"Wow," I said. "How did it light up?"

Beatrice shrugged but reached her hand into another sconce on the opposite wall to pull out a similar stone, which also lit up at her touch.

"Maybe from the warmth of our bodies? Haven't seen something like this before."

She put her stone back in the sconce and it cast a dull light out into the chamber. I did the same, and the combined glow of the stones revealed a larger sconce in the back wall. This one didn't have a stone inside. Instead, a large leather-bound book was propped up next to a wooden box.

We ran to the back wall at the same time and nearly collided. Beatrice slowly removed the book from its resting place and opened to the first page, a look of excitement spreading across her face, before we were greeted with familiar handwriting written in green ink:

Rita van Asch, 1787

Beatrice flipped through the pages to reveal dated entries just like the 1777 diary we already had.

"Ugh," she said, slamming her fist against the wall. "For a second, just a second, I thought that we had hit on the mother lode, that this was where the Guild had hidden its Compendium. Instead, it's just another diary."

"Maybe there's still something valuable in there?" I offered. I was disappointed too. We had made it all this way, messed up so many lives, traveled so far, only to be rewarded with another dusty book to read and a stupid wooden box.

"Maybe," Beatrice said, putting the book back down in the sconce before picking up the box. It was simple: no ornate flourishes or intricate designs, just six pieces of wood stuck together with a metal latch on the front.

"You take the book, and I'll carry the box," Beatrice said. "I also want to take one of these light stones, could be usef-"

Beatrice began to cough uncontrollably and a second later, I did as well. We both turned in horror to the entrance of the chamber to see smoke flowing out of a small metal object. I grasped my chest as I stumbled forward onto the cold, wet ground and tried to bring my hand up to cover my face, but the smoke was overpowering and I fell into a third black void.

CHAPTER THIRTY

TIME'S SCAR

Smoke lingered in the air as I slowly came to, but its sting forced my eyes shut. I felt the Medoblad pushing up against my stomach and I opened my eyelids a crack to try to take in my surroundings. In front of me was a figure prone on the ground, but it wasn't a mop of blond hair that I saw. It was one of fiery red.

"Frankie?" I croaked before a coughing fit seized me again. The figure didn't move and it was then that I noticed that her hands were tied behind her back and her ankles bound together.

I rolled over on my side to see Beatrice passed out on the ground to my left.

"Bea-Beatrice!" I said with my hand over my mouth. I rolled over again until I was right next to her and shook her shoulder with my other hand. She thrashed back and forth several times before she too slowly opened her eyes and looked at me.

"W-what's going on? What happened?"

I shook my head.

"I don't know, must have been some sort of gas grenade, knocked us out. And, look there. It's Frankie, the woman with the tattoo. But she's tied up and unconscious."

There was a panic in Beatrice's eyes that I had never seen before, but she quickly suppressed it and groped around for her bag at her side. She withdrew her hand and was holding something maroon wrapped in plastic.

The vitality buff.

Beatrice fumbled with the wrapping for almost 30 seconds before finally freeing the buff and handing it to me.

"Here, take half."

I pushed her hand away and shook my head.

"No need. I brought the one you gave me."

"Oh. Good. Take it now." She popped the buff in her mouth and began to chew as I reached for my own in my bag. Within seconds, Beatrice was on her feet, the smoke seemingly having no effect on her. I found the maroon buff in my own bag and started chewing. It tasted like wet socks wrapped in week-old fish, but as soon as I swallowed, my eyes jolted open, and I pushed myself up from the wet ground with ease.

"It's gone," said Beatrice, who was standing at the back sconce, her elbow over her mouth.

"What?" I said, careful to not breathe in too much of the smoke. "The diary?"

"No, that's still here, but the box isn't. Shit. Should have opened it right away. Stay here with the girl, I'm going to go check up ahead."

"What if whoever attacked us is still there?"

"Then I'll handle them," said Beatrice, making a fist with her right hand.

"OK."

Beatrice walked passed me and disappeared into the smoke, while I bent down to check on Frankie. Her eyes were still closed, and I could see the slow rise and fall of her chest, along with raw red skin on her wrists. Whoever had done this to her had kept her tied up for longer than this evening and I shuddered at the thought.

I heard a yell up ahead and left Frankie to investigate, grabbing one of the red stones from the wall to light the way. The smoke eventually dissipated as I made my way back up the path. Turning the corner, I saw Beatrice holding her phone flashlight over a large wall of debris that completely blocked the way back to the door.

"Shit!" she yelled. "We're trapped. God damn it!"

Beatrice kicked the air in anger and began pacing back and forth.

"How are we going to get out of here?" I said.

"Stand back," said Beatrice.

"What?"

"STAND. BACK," she commanded and I complied as she set her phone on the ground and closed her eyes.

A light began to glow on her right hand. At first it was barely as bright as a firefly, but as it intensified, the light became almost blinding and I shielded my eyes. Soon though, it wasn't just the amethyst ring that was glowing but Beatrice's entire body, which radiated with the same light from the ring.

"What are you doing?" I yelled, but Beatrice didn't break her concentration. The last time she had drawn power from the ring, it had knocked her out for at least an hour, but this time she was going far beyond that.

Another minute passed, and Beatrice's body shimmered with a purple halo of power.

Suddenly, she opened her eyes and surged forward toward the rock. The first punch blasted a small chunk of the debris free and she brought her fist back again before smashing it into the rock again. Then it was her left fist that connected with the rock, then the right again, a small opening slowly forming on the right side of the debris. Beatrice continued to hammer away until, finally, her right hand punched through the rock and hit the air on the other side. She widened the opening with a couple more punches before stumbling through to the other side.

The purple light suddenly vanished and I rushed forward through the gap in the wall to find Beatrice unconscious on the ground.

"Beatrice! Are you OK?"

She didn't respond, but from the light of the red stone, I saw the door just a few feet ahead.

"Hold on, I'm going to get Frankie!"

I bent down and fished through Beatrice's bag, hoping that she had brought her full complement of buffs, but withdrew only a single lilac buff.

I unwrapped the speed buff and took my strength buff out of my bag and began to chew both of them. A surge of power rippled through my body, followed by the familiar feeling of time slowing, and in a second I was through the wall and back in the chamber, huddled over the still-unconscious Frankie. I wrapped my right arm around her and lifted her upward, and it was as if I was holding a bag of feathers. The strength coursing through me felt incredible, but I knew I only had moments to spare, which, thanks to the speed buff, were stretched out a little longer.

I carried Frankie up the path and through the gap, setting her down next to the crumpled mass that was Beatrice, and hurried to the door, hoping that whoever had done this had not had the foresight to remove the knob from the other side.

The knob turned slowly in my hand and, miraculously, I pulled the door open. I could feel my well of strength fading, and I ran back to the unconscious women, picked them both up with one last raw burst of power, and threw them into the black void beyond the door.

I was about to walk through when I had the nagging feeling that I was forgetting something.

Of course.

I ran back through the debris and, in a flash, was standing in front of that stupid diary. If we were actually going to make it out of this pit alive, at least we should get something for our troubles. I took the book from the sconce and seconds later was staring at the void through the doorway again. I closed my eyes and greeted the darkness like an old friend.

I opened my eyes to see a blaze of red and orange all around me. Was this the void? I squinted and as my eyes adjusted, the true horror of the situation revealed itself.

It wasn't the void at all.

I was back in the lighthouse, which was now an inferno of heat and ash.

Beatrice and Frankie were right in front of me on the ground, unmoving, and I called out to them, but neither responded.

"Beatrice, wake up!" I said to her in my mind. She didn't answer.

"WAKE UP!" I cried out again, but all I heard from her head was static.

Chunks of wood from the ceiling began to rain down on top of us as the fire continued to rage. My body suddenly collapsed, the strength from the buff completely gone, and I fell forward onto the ground, barely able to move.

My mind was still racing at a million miles a minute, and so I began to play out dozens of possible scenarios.

I could crawl past them, push myself up, put the door knob back on, open the door, and then pull both of them through. That would only take 10 minutes, at which point, the ceiling would have collapsed on top of us seven minutes earlier.

I could only save one of them. That would take five minutes, still two minutes too long.

I could save myself. Not going back for them would leave me with plenty of time to spare, but also with a lifetime of guilt.

Then I saw the ring on Beatrice's hand and a new idea snapped into focus. There was still a chance it wouldn't work, but I had to try. It was the only way. I reached out my hand to grab Beatrice's ankle and then hurled myself into her mind.

I floated through the abyss.

It felt like the void between the doors, except where the void had been all darkness, here there were swirling lights all me. They looked like little galaxies, light years away, and when I reached out to touch one, it moved out of reach by just a hair.

"Beatrice!" I called out and one of the lights blinked. It blinked again as I called out her name a second time and then a third. Suddenly, I felt myself being pulled toward the light like a bungee jumper snapping back up just before hitting the water. The light grew bigger and blinding and I closed my eyes as it enveloped me.

When I opened them again, it was dark, except for a small sliver of light peeking through a door. I looked around and found myself in a tiny closet next to a small girl.

"Hi," I said.

The girl turned and looked at me and I nearly fell backward. Even though she was eight or nine, the girl was a spitting image of Beatrice.

"Hi Jen," she said.

"What's going on? Why are we in this closet?"

"Don't know why you're here. I'm hiding from Burt."

"Who's Burt?"

"My mother's asshole boyfriend. Typical abusive drunk. Beat my mom real good over the years. Me a couple times too."

"Oh. I'm so sorry!"

Young Beatrice just shrugged her shoulders.

"It's OK. I killed him the summer after college. Hit him with a metal pipe when he wasn't looking."

"W-what?" I said. "But you're just a little girl, how did you-"

"It's still me, Jen. Sometimes I fall back into this memory though. I guess you can't really escape your past, no matter how hard you try."

"I thought you said Doug was the first person you killed."

"No. He was just the first person I regretted killing. But enough about me. Why are you here?"

"You don't remember? The Met, the lighthouse, the cave?"

"Oh. Right. What happened?"

"We were trapped in the cave and then you, you smashed through the rock using your ring, but then…"

"Got it. And so now what? I've been unconscious for so long you thought I was dead?"

"No. I used a strength buff to carry you and Frankie back through to the lighthouse. But whoever trapped us set the lighthouse on fire for good measure and I'm all out of strength. Can barely move. Do you have any strength left to lend me? So I can get us out of here?"

Beatrice peaked through the sliver of the closet door before huddling down in the corner, her knees tucked against her chest, tears trickling down her face.

"I'll never get out of here," she motioned to the closet. "But why are you trying to save me anyway? I mean, I threatened to kill you, what, two hours ago? This is your chance to get rid of me. Maybe I deserve it, for all that I've done."

"What? No, I'm not leaving you here to burn to death. Or Frankie. Please, Beatrice, you have to tap the ring just a little more. I've worked through all the scenarios in my head. There is no other way."

I reached out my hand to the girl. She considered it for a long moment before taking it and pulling herself to her feet.

"I'll help you. If I can. We're so far down in my mind, I don't know if I can reach her from here."

"Reach who?"

"You have to get out of here now. He's coming."

Beatrice suddenly pushed me backward, but instead of hitting the closet wall, I was soaring back upward, through the galaxies of memories, and across the link to my own mind.

The fire rampaged me as I opened my eyes again, my hand still gripping Beatrice's ankle. In front of me, Beatrice still lay unconscious and I wondered if the whole thing had been a hallucination. But then a soft purple glow appeared around her hand and it slowly surrounded Beatrice's entire body before spreading across to me, and as soon as it did, I felt a familiar surge of power. Except it wasn't like the buff I had eaten before. It was like my body was being filled with a river of strength and I wanted it all.

I opened myself up fully to draw whatever power the ring had left to give me, but after only a second, which in my heightened state seemed to drag on forever, the glow vanished. I let go of Beatrice and stood up slowly, still holding the diary under my other arm, and reassessed the scene.

The door to Long Island City was still intact but the fire had already engulfed the wall. Would the door still work if it was on fire?

I didn't want to find out. I blinked and was at the door, my preternatural speed on its last legs. I fished the door knob out of my purse and turned back to the unconscious women, a new set of choices playing out in front of me, but somehow, they were even worse than before.

I clutched the diary against my stomach, only to feel the Medoblad press back against it, and my eyes widened as my mind raced ahead and finished the thought.

No.

It couldn't be the only way.

There had to be another solution.

Maybe Beatrice had another buff in her bag in a hidden pocket or something. Maybe I could break the amethyst ring and swallow the pieces to draw out the last bits of strength. But, as if rebelling from my conscious self, my mind played out the scenario over and over again. After watching it play out for the tenth time, I screamed and the visions stopped.

The flames were now only inches from the doorframe on either side, but that still gave me enough time to do what needed to be done, and I reached one hand behind me to open the door a crack. My hand refused to let go of the knob, and I stood frozen for just a second as I came to terms with what I was about to do.

I thought back to that stupid Quest to make an apple pie and wondered if I had just picked the Quest right below it, would I be here now?

I thought about my friends coming to in the drunk tank, wondering why they weren't getting ready to go to the airport.

I thought about Duncan and what I was going to say to him.

And then finally, I thought about the two women in front of me, one who had wronged me in so many ways and one who had only walked into the wrong tattoo parlor at the wrong time on the wrong day. I had tried so hard to save us all, pushed my mind and body to their limits, but it wasn't enough. I felt a different fire begin to spark inside of me, a fire of pure rage at the ones who had forced me onto this path.

The Guild.

Enough stalling, I thought to myself.

It was time.

Tears welled in my eyes as I ripped the Medoblad free from my dress and decided which woman to turn to stone.

CHAPTER THIRTY-ONE

SHADOWS
OF THE PAST

*"My mind is nearly full. After this task is done, I must consider what
I need to take with me into the next century."*

Once upon a time I was a normal girl living in a normal
world with normal friends, a normal job, and in love with
a normal boyfriend.

Now I only really had one of those things. The normal friends,
who had spent two nights in prison. The normal job, which I still had,
for now. The normal boyfriend, who had already flown all the way to
Paris only to find out I wasn't coming.

Once upon a time, I also stole a tattoo, slowed time, traveled
through a magic door, and turned a woman into a statue.

I sighed and took a sip of my tea as I waited on the patio on a chilly February morning for her to arrive.

Finally, after I nearly reached the bottom of the mug, a chipper blonde approached the cafe and took the seat across from me.

"Sorry I'm late!" said Beatrice, her face flush. "Subway was a disaster."

"No worries," I said. "I take it you have the book?"

"Yep," she said, pulling out the diary that had cost us so much.

"And?"

"It's … well, it's a fascinating upheaval of what we thought we knew about the Constitutional Convention. But in terms of alchemy, it's a complete bust."

"You cannot be serious," I said. "There's nothing in there? Not even a wisp of some new recipe? Why the hell was it hidden then?"

"I'm … umm… I'm not sure. Maybe whoever hid the box just wanted to stash this in the mine too."

I shook my head and nearly laughed at the role reversal. Ever since Beatrice had woken up from her near coma the next afternoon, she had been walking on eggshells around me. But that was exactly what I didn't want. After the bachelorette fallout, what I needed more than anything was a friend. I felt my eyes begin to tear, which was becoming a common occurrence these days, and brought my hand up quickly to cover the evidence.

"Are you really still upset about that girl? You didn't even know her. And anyway, we barely got out alive as it w-"

"I'm not like you!" I nearly shouted. "I've never killed anyone before. And you didn't see the stone sprout from where I had plunged the Medoblad into Frankie's shoulder. You didn't see it work its way over her entire body until she was nothing but, nothing but…"

I collapsed onto the table and began to sob uncontrollably. It was all too much to bear. I could make new friends, sure, and find a new boyfriend. But there was no getting over this.

I felt Beatrice's hand touch my arm and I looked up at the woman I had chosen to save.

"She's a statue, Jen, but she's not dead. You have to realize that. If it weren't for you, she would be though. So stop beating yourself up over things you have no control over."

"OK," I said with a whimper before clearing my throat and trying to regain my composure. "How is the research going?"

Beatrice looked down at the table, her eyes refusing to meet mine.

"Haven't found much there either unfortunately. The Medusa legend doesn't really touch on reversing the curse. Even killing her didn't undo it. The best I found was a mention of two veins in her neck: blood from one would curse you and blood from the other would purify you. But we're dealing with a knife, so not sure how that helps us."

"That's not a knife. It's a nightmare machine. I wish I had left it in the lighthouse."

"Good thing you didn't," said Beatrice. "We'll need all the help we can get now that the Guild has it out for us."

"How do you know it was them?" I asked.

"It wasn't just a coincidence that Gilbert followed us to the Met, and then we're attacked and left for dead. He planned this whole thing, from the start. To get whatever was in the box."

"Why didn't he just do it himself?"

"The Guild isn't like you and me," said Beatrice. "They've spent generations getting people to do their dirty work, all the while sitting atop a trove of the most powerful alchemic items on the continent. Even as far back as Rita."

Beatrice opened the diary to a random entry and began to scan the handwriting as she spoke.

"It's a miracle Gilbert even managed to do as much as he did to us. Guess they are still out of enforcers."

It was bad enough I had to deal with one sociopath with only two magical items, but a whole guild of them? I sighed and reached for the tea, only to have my ringed finger jerk forward slowly toward Beatrice.

"Get this fucking thing off of me!" I yelled.

"OK," said Beatrice.

"Excuse me?"

"I said, OK. It's the absolute least I could do, after what you did for me."

"Oh. Fine. But don't think you're even close to making us square."

Beatrice pulled out a piece of paper, a quill, and a vial of pitch-black ink. She unscrewed the vial and began stirring the ink with the quill.

"I don't."

"Good. What are you going to write?"

I walked over to the other side of the table so I could see the note. As much as Beatrice was playing the part of the grateful victim, I still didn't put it past her to just do away with me now and not have to be in my debt.

"Should only take a few words, just need to phrase them carefully so it doesn't accidentally give you another lingering command."

"How about just, 'Jen, take off the ring'? Seems like that would do the tr-"

A gust of wind blew the pages of the diary to the end and my finger suddenly lurched forward.

But not toward Beatrice's ring.

Instead, it stopped on the blank last page of the diary. The ring began to press my hand down into the worn paper as if it was being drawn to a giant magnet hidden in the book and I yelped in pain.

"W-what's happening?" I cried out.

"I don't know!" said Beatrice, who slowly stood up and backed away from the book.

I felt the metal of the ring grow warm around my finger and

watched as glowing glyphs on the band appeared. The ring continued to heat up, and I thought it was going to burn my finger off, the pain was so intense. But then the glyphs faded as the ring simply melted into a pool of molten liquid on the page, and I slowly lifted my now-free hand away.

The ring (or what used to be the ring) wasn't finished though. The silvery liquid spread out onto the entirety of the page, forming into neat handwriting that I immediately recognized as Rita's.

"*December 31, 1787,*" the top of the page said.

"Beatrice, you have to see this!" I said and she took a few steps closer to the diary, still not convinced that her own ring wasn't going to flying onto the page.

"It's … it was ink!" she said. "All that effort and we had what we were looking for already."

"No. I don't think that's right," I said. "Is it possible-could my ring have been linked to more than one thing? So it wouldn't have just melted onto any old page. It had to be this one."

"But why?" Beatrice said.

"Of course," I said.

"What?"

"To conceal the diary's true secret. In case it ended up in the wrong hands."

I started to read the final entry, Beatrice peering over my shoulder.

"*Today I hid the last remaining gold token of the original 12 we minted. I have no use for it now, but I foresee a day when the seats of the Guild will be occupied by foes or scoundrels or ne'er do wells, and I will have need of a trump card.*"

The words continued down the page and I tried to keep reading, but the ink began to shimmer. I wanted to look away, but my eyes remained fixed on those letters. Then, without warning, I fell forward into the page. But instead of smacking my head on the diary, I felt myself falling through space, my body incorporeal. It reminded me of the space inside Beatrice's mind, except there was nothing but emptiness around me.

It was then that I spotted it.

A single solitary memory, so tiny that if it were a star in the night sky, it would be a speck thousands of light years away.

The speck grew larger after a time, and I braced my mind for what was to come as it finally enveloped my being.

The end of the year comes and another begins and I wonder how long this can continue.

I always seem to get philosophical on December 31.

I suppose it is because the passing of time should always have meaning, even for someone like me, but it gets harder and harder with each successive turn of the calendar.

Today I have a task to complete, though, one that I will need to forget by tomorrow.

I put on my overcoat, making sure the letter is still there, and immediately pull up the hood. This will all be for naught if I am spotted as soon as I step foot onto the street.

It is days like this one that I am glad I had the foresight to install the tunnel. It was expensive and I did not fancy killing the laborers who built it, but it has served me well over the years.

I pull back Volume II of *Land Owners, Great Britain* and the bookcase creeps forward just a tad. The stairway is dark and the corridor darker but I know my way. When I reach the end, the second set of stairs ascends sharply, and I find the catch on the bookcase's twin and push it outward.

The townhouse is empty, as it should be. I purchased it a lifetime ago, and it has gotten very little use since. There is a door in the back that leads to a small garden. It is unkempt now, which is a pity, but I remember when all manner of flora were planted back there. In the kitchen is another door that leads to a winding alley and it is the one I take today.

I make my way onto Pearl Street and then head west along Wall Street before reaching William Street, which finally takes me to Hanover Square. The route is circuitous by design, and I convince myself that I have not been followed. I weave through the crowds to 11 Hanover Square. The bank is new, having been housed in Walton House until earlier this year. I much prefer the new location as it does not allow William Walton easy access to snoop around.

The lobby is empty and I summon a young clerk from behind the counter.

"Good morning, ma'am," he says. "What can I assist you with?"

"I wish to deposit something in a safety deposit box," I tell him.

"Certainly, ma'am. Does your husband already have an account with us?"

"He does not. Did not, I should say, as he is no longer among the living."

"Oh, my apologies, ma'am."

"It's quite alright. Now, I am assuming there is a good deal of paperwork to fill out?"

"Yes, ma'am. You will need to open an account, which will need to be approved, of course, by the board, and after that you will be able to lease a box in our vault. There are many different si-"

"I am afraid that is not satisfactory nor convenient to my needs. I would like to deposit something today, not next year."

"I am terribly sorry, ma'am, but we have protocols you see. Protocols I am duty bound to follow. So if you do not mind, we can just-"

"But I do mind," I say. "Let me suggest an alternative option."

I pull the letter from my jacket pocket, unfold it, and walk over to the counter and pull out my quill and vial of ink.

"Pardon me, what did you say your name was?" I ask the clerk.

"It's Stewart, but I don't understand what…"

"Thank you."

I append Stewart's name to the beginning of the letter and hand it to him. His eyes glaze over as he reads the commands and I suspect that the rest of this errand will go smoothly.

Stewart escorts me wordlessly into the bowels of the bank, stopping in one room before leading me down a set of stairs, and then along a corridor until we reach a large iron door. It is locked but Stewart has the key. The door swings open and Stewart walks inside to light the oil lamp before retreating to just outside the door. He hands me another key and I enter the room.

It is lined with wooden rectangular boxes sitting on opposing shelves, all numbered with gold lettering. I light another lamp midway into the room before stopping at box number 42, which matches the number on the key. It fits snugly in the lock and I open the lid to reveal an empty red velvet interior. I retrieve the tiny package wrapped in paper from my coat pocket, place it in the box, and then lock it again.

Stewart escorts me back to the lobby before returning to behind the counter. By the time he resumes his post, I have left the bank, and he has forgotten everything from the past 30 minutes. As an extra precaution, in three months' time, he will, for no reason that he can comprehend, quit his job, move to Boston, and drown himself in the Charles River.

I return to the empty townhouse and retrieve a simple wooden box from upstairs into which I place the key. I walk out into the garden with the box. There is a rusty garden hoe just by the door and I use it to dig a hole in the back right corner of the garden. I place the box in the dirt, cover it back up, and then finally return through the corridor to my house.

The day is still young, but I am exhausted, and there is still the matter of forgetting what I have just done. I walk upstairs to my desk, take out my other vial of ink, and begin to write.

"Wake up!"

The paper felt rough against my forehead, and my nose hurt from being pressed into the diary. I opened my eyes and slowly sat up to see Beatrice with a manic look in her eyes.

"Wh-hat happened?" I said. "How long have I been out?"

"11 seconds," said Beatrice. "I was trying to move you off of the page so I could read it, but it was like you were a stat... err, it was like your head was stuck to the diary."

"Oh."

My mind was still hazy, trying to reorient myself. Wasn't I just upstairs at my desk writing in my diary?

No, that wasn't right. It wasn't my diary, was it?

It was hers.

Rita's

But in my head there now sat a memory of a cold December morning of me - again, not me, but Rita - hiding a gold token in a safe deposit box. I could replay the events of that morning over again, like they had occurred yesterday, and I could recall her thoughts and opinions as if they were my own.

Beatrice suddenly closed the diary in a huff.

"The writing is just gibberish after the first sentence. I can't make heads or tales of it."

"What are you talking about?" I said, opening the page a peek to see black ink smeared in patterns down to the very bottom.

"No, that's not right. It wasn't like … it was a memory! Her memory, Rita's. It's in my head now. I can see what she saw, remember what she thought. I know where the token is."

Beatrice looked at me with a wide-eyed expression as if I had just escaped from the psych ward.

"Where?" she said.

"It's in a … wait. Do you have our contract with you?"

She nodded and took it out of her bag.

"Rip it up," I said.

"What?"

"Rip it up. I'm done being your novice. We're equals now, as far as I'm concerned. And if you want to know where the token is, then you'll do as I tell you."

"Fine," Beatrice said, tearing the papers in two before stacking the halves and tearing them again. "Satisfied?"

"Yes."

I recounted the memory in exquisite detail, the scenes playing out in my head as if they were a movie, until finally I reached the end and let out a sigh.

"Incredible," said Beatrice. "I never thought that these rings, that there was a way to…amazing. So now what?"

"Now," I said, "now it's time for us to take on the Guild."

FINISH WHAT
YOU START

The first Quest was easy.

I retrieved the handful of blackberries, a tillandsia, a grape popsicle, and four pounds of 75/25 ground beef from Chelsea Market, and left it in the windowsill of 194 West 9th Street.

The wooden token that I found taped to the back of a fire hydrant across the street from Yankee Stadium I burned, but not before extracting two fingerprints first. They led me to the requester, a girl in her twenties by the name of Beatrice Stallard.

I followed her progression closely over the next several years, as she seemed like she had a good head on her shoulders. Smart but also creative. Willing to take risks. So many of our ilk had gotten lazy and entitled that it was refreshing to see someone take on the Quests with zeal.

Then I started hearing whispers on the streets about new alchemic creations.

I dismissed it at first. People had always been searching for hang-over cures and the like, and if someone had decided that that was the market they were going to corner, well, I had bigger fish to fry. But the rumblings continued. A substance that made you strong as an ox with just one bite. Another that made your mind sharper than Einstein and quicker than a Jeopardy champion. That had been more troubling.

I eventually traced the source back to her and set up a meeting. Well, more like tracked her for a few days and then quietly approached her when her guard was down. She was cagey when I asked her for the source of her prima materia for what she called the "strength buff." A stupid name for sure, reducing the majesty and might of magic and alchemy to something out of a video game. I didn't even bother to check the location she told me, as I immediately knew she was lying. Also, it was all the way at the northern tip of the island and that place brings back bad memories.

But I knew from after that meeting that Beatrice would have to be dealt with, one way or the other. The Guild is powerful, sure, but it likes playing with a stacked deck. The relative stability the orga-nization has enjoyed for the past hundred years allowed it to quietly and methodically move pieces across the board to finally set up our endgame: the reintroduction of magic into the wider world with the Guild acting as the steadying hand for the tumult that would follow.

And Beatrice threatened to upend all of that before our work was finished.

Fortunately, an opportunity had presented itself in the form of one Douglas Kettner.

A disaffected millennial who had discovered the Quests, as so many do, during a late-night Internet search for meaning and purpose in this lonely modern world, Doug had become Beatrice's trainee. And a potential entry point to use her for our purposes.

I observed them for several months and it soon became clear to me that I was mistaken. Not only was Doug infatuated with Beatrice, but that he lacked the necessary constitution to make an effective tool.

It would have taken some time, but I would have beaten him into shape as a dog trainer educates his charge.

Except Beatrice had other plans and that is why I found Mr. Kettner sitting at a table in one of the 6 ½ Avenue atriums, on the verge of death. I had known what she was up to weeks before, the prima materia required to make her death kiss a far cry from the pigeon spleens and rat entrails staples used by your run-of-the-mill alchemists.

And so I applied the antidote with relative ease and after a few minutes, Doug's eyes fluttered open and he stared at me with a puzzled expression.

"Who … who are you?" he said.

"You can call me," I said with a smile, "Gilbert."

STRANGE
TIDINGS

*"I have lingered on for longer than I would have liked. But it was
necessary in view of the recent conflagration."*
— RITA VAN ASCH, JUNE 1, 1814

The cold water splashed up from the river as the boat crested
a wave, and I staggered backward into the helm to avoid
its path.

"Hey!" said Beatrice, who was driving said boat. "Just sit down in
the back and stay out of the way, OK?"

"Sorry," I said, walking gingerly down the stairs to a small couch
at the stern. "Was just trying to see how far away we were."

It was not yet 5 on a Sunday morning in March and the East
River was quiet, no other boats in sight.

"Another 20 minutes. I'm trying to go slow enough to not attract attention but fast enough that we don't look like a bunch of idiots who rented a boat and don't know what they're doing. Also I'd like to get back before Garrett realized I never came home last night."

"Got it. But, umm, *do* we know what we're doing?"

"I do," said Beatrice. "The one benefit of being married to a jackass whose parents summered in Newport. Everything revolved around boats. Although I've never driven a pure motorboat before, but the principles seem to be the same."

"How comforting," I mumbled.

"What?" shouted Beatrice as she gradually increased the speed of the boat.

"Nothing, just wondering if she'll still be there."

"She will. The Guild had no use for her alive so why would they have use for her now?"

"I guess," I said, trying not to think about Frankie and her tattoo.

That tattoo, which on its surface was just a series of digits, ended up holding so many secrets and causing so much suffering.

It had led me to a door in Long Island City, a bust of Alexander Hamilton, the remains of the Polo Grounds, a Dutch millstone, the Met, and finally, back to that door, which was really a gateway to the lighthouse where we were now headed.

"Still," I continued. "The lighthouse *did* burn down. They're not just going to forget about it."

"Stop stressing about it," said Beatrice. "Besides, I did some digging. The North Shore towns have been squabbling for weeks now. Everyone loved that stupid building when it was the historic Minneford Lighthouse, but now that it's a pile of rubble, suddenly no one wants to take responsibility for cleaning up the debris."

"Oh, that makes me feel a little better," I said. "But the sooner we get Frankie somewhere safe, the sooner we can find a cure."

Her disappearance had been all over the local news and blogs for weeks, and her friends had plastered social media with "Have you seen this woman?" posts. Of course, there was nothing linking the two of us to Frankie, so I was confident that the police weren't going to show up at my door one night. But it was only a matter of time before someone did actually come to the tiny island and clear out the remains. And when they did, they would find an incredibly lifelike statue of Francesca "Frankie" Lewis and everything would hit the fan.

"Let's not get ahead of ourselves," said Beatrice.

"OK fine," I said, with a tinge of annoyance in my voice. As the days had passed, the old Beatrice was beginning to reassert herself, the role reversal that occurred after I had saved her life slowly fading. I wanted to think of us as equals now, but I was beginning to suspect that Beatrice resented the fact that she was now in my debt.

The first rays of the morning sun crept up over the horizon as our goal finally came into view: Minneford Island and the ruins of its eponymous lighthouse.

Beatrice slowed the boat to a crawl as we approached before cutting the engine altogether and walking to the bow, where I soon joined her.

"Hmm," said Beatrice. "There's no dock."

"Should there be?" I asked. "It's not like the lighthouse was being used."

"No, but there must have been one at some point. Very strange. Anyway, we'll just need to be careful disembarking. Don't want to fall on those slippery rocks, now do we?"

Her comment sounded like a veiled threat, and I considered whether her plan all along was to pretend to be grateful for me saving her life and then lure me out here so she could chuck me overboard. But I pushed those thoughts aside as the product of a night spent sleeping on a boat moored in the East River.

Beatrice walked back to the helm and started the boat up again and I grabbed onto the lines to avoid falling into the water, as if confirming my suspicions.

"Sorry!" she called. "Still getting the hang of the boat."

I shimmied my way back from the front and retook my seat in the stern as Beatrice inched us up alongside the island before finally stopping the boat a few feet from the rocky shore. The entire atoll was no larger than a tennis court and where the once proud lighthouse had once stood now only a pile of burnt debris remained. And somewhere, underneath it all, was Frankie.

The gangplank barely bridged the gap between the boat and the moss-covered rocks that lined the outer edge of the island, and I scrambled up to the edge of the former lighthouse on my hands.

The aftermath of our last visit here was evident. Blackened beams lay scattered about and pieces of glass from what must have been the lantern room made sifting through the debris treacherous. But there was work to be done, so I reached into my pocket to pull out a strength buff. I set my watch and choked down the wretched taste and waited for that familiar surge of power.

The first beam I hurled into the water like a javelin. The second one I broke in two and then in two again. I felt shards of glass scrape against my hands and arms as I worked, but I didn't care. Until the buff wore off, I was a demigoddess, and the cuts and bruises of mortal women were far below my concern. Whether Beatrice ended up helping me at all, I wasn't sure, but when the seconds finally ticked down to zero, there was only one small pile of refuse left.

I felt the strength leave my body and I collapsed onto the ground. Blood covered my shirt, hands, and fingers, and it took all of my will to reach my hand into my pocket to pull out a different buff, this one maroon. I closed my eyes, even that small task taking most of my remaining strength, and began fumbling with the plastic wrapping.

"Let me help you with that at least," said Beatrice. I opened my eyes and she was crouched down next to me, no worse for wear, and I unclenched my fist to offer her the vitality buff. She freed the buff from the plastic and put it back in my hand, which she lifted up to my mouth.

A strange sense of nostalgia flared up within me, as if I was a 10-year old sick in bed with the flu and my mother was next to me feeding me chicken soup. I suddenly became very aware of her locket around my neck. It had been a birthday present on my 11th birthday and I had stuffed the thing away in my closet in a teenage rage, angry that my mother hadn't bought me the little purse I had wanted. There it had stayed until the day after her funeral, when I had tearfully retrieved it and put it around my neck. I had rarely taken it off since, the most notable time being when I used it as bait to kill that stupid rat in the alley.

My reminiscing must have gone on too long, because the next thing I knew, Beatrice grabbed my hand again and forced the buff into my mouth.

"Next time maybe wait for me to help?" she said as I felt the energy return to my body. "You didn't even give me time to eat the strength buff. It was like you were some sort of possessed madwoman. But why didn't you finish?"

I slowly pushed myself up from the ground and looked over at the one undisturbed pile.

"Because," I said, "because I can't face her yet."

Beatrice looked at me quizzically.

"Then don't. You've done enough. Go back to the boat and I'll take it from here."

I awoke to the sound of a foghorn, and the faint rays of the morning sun reflecting off the water made me quickly close my eyes again.

Shielding my face, I slowly opened them again. A large wake trailed behind our boat and an immense yacht a hundred yards off our stern was slowly making its way toward the horizon. We were otherwise the only craft on the wide expanse of water, the closest shore barely visible.

I slowly got to my feet and walked to the helm, where Beatrice stood, her hands gripping the wheel so tightly they were almost white.

"Wh-where are we? How long was I out?"

"Welcome back to the land of the living," said Beatrice. "Not sure. Took me longer than expected to finish up at the lighthouse." She motioned to a large black tarp that was laid out over something on the bow of the boat.

"Is that-"

"Yep. Do you want to go look?" she asked.

"I ... no."

"OK, suit yourself, but I'll need your help getting her off the boat, so you'll have to do it at some point."

"Fine. But where are we? This doesn't look like the East River."
Beatrice chuckled.

"It's not. Did you think we were taking her back to Manhattan? I mean, we probably wouldn't get a second glance carrying Frankie down Houston, but I am not lugging her up five flights of stairs."

"Oh. Then where are we going?"

"There," said Beatrice, pointing out to a spot nowhere in particular ahead of us.

"I don't see anything. Please tell me you're not planning on dumping her over the side of the boat."

"No, but not gonna lie, I did think about it for a minute. We've been too distracted trying to find a cure that we haven't made any progress on the Guild front."

"I'm not giving up," I said.

"I know you're not. It's adorable, in an incredibly annoying way.

But let me concentrate. We'll be coming up on our destination soon."

The coastline came into full view and I saw a string of small barrier islands off of the south shore of Long Island on the electronic map next to the wheel. The little triangle on the screen that was our boat inched toward them and I wondered if we really were just going to dump Frankie on a beach somewhere and hope no one found her.

We sailed around a wooded island and Beatrice cut the engine speed down to a crawl as I spotted a half-moon sea wall made of rocks that was conspicuously absent from the boat's map. Just beyond the wall was a dock leading up to a small house on stilts.

"What is that?" I asked.

"That," said Beatrice with a smile, "is our new headquarters."

THE SPACE BETWEEN

*"War split the Guild once before, but this time I resolved,
no matter what, to keep it together."*

For a hideout secreted away on a random uncharted island, the place turned out to be a dump. The dock was missing too many wooden boards for comfort, the front door barely opened, and the less said about the smell inside the better.

"What?" said Beatrice, after I walked back out of the house after stepping foot inside for exactly four seconds. "Do you know how much the nice private islands were going for? This was the best I could do without looting one of Garrett's trust funds."

"It's … fine," I said. "But what was wrong with your Bowery apartment? That at least had a cool secret doorway. And the added benefit of being, you know, easily accessible."

"Oh. I cleared that place out weeks ago. It was only a matter of time before the Guild found it. Can't tell you how many speed buffs I wasted packing that place up."

"Why didn't you tell me? I would have helped."

Beatrice shook her head.

"Thanks, but I needed to do it myself. Plus you were still moping around about Frankie so you wouldn't have been very useful anyway."

I wanted to defend myself but she was right. I had been next to useless in the weeks after the lighthouse disaster. Even the sense of accomplishment from our discovery of the memory ring had only lasted a day or two, and I had withdrawn from almost every aspect of my life. That had included avoiding Lisa and Stacy, who had spent two nights in jail after their acts of vandalism at the Met. I hadn't seen them since I had handed them the compulsion-ink notes, pretending to buried in 100-hour weeks at the office with barely a minute to brush my teeth.

And I also had avoided Duncan, who had flown to Paris a few days early to take in the sights only to immediately fly back to Hong Kong 12 hours later when I texted him that I was no longer going. We were technically still "together," at least until next Monday when he was due back in town to review our latest game build with his boss. Part of me was happy that I hadn't had to decide after all whether to move to Hong Kong. Now all that was left to do was have a really awkward dinner and get dumped. Hooray.

I held my breath and reentered the house.

The interior was dark, which made sense because the room was empty, the windows were all caked with layers of grime, and it was barely morning. It reminded me of the day I left my old apartment for the last time, after everything had been taken off to a storage locker, a few days before I left for college. I squinted to make out the dimensions of the room. For a Manhattan studio, it would have been luxurious but the lone room still felt small without anything inside.

I opened the door at the back expecting to find a second room, but on the other side was only water.

"The place needs some work," I said, closing the door. "And a light."

"Obviously," said Beatrice. "But I had to come here first before I could move all my stuff in."

"That's going to take a lot of trips on that boat. Unless Garrett's parents have a yacht somewhere you can borrow?"

Beatrice smiled.

"Nope. But we don't need a boat."

"What do you mean?"

Beatrice reached into her back pocket and pulled out a small circular object. A brown door knob to be precise.

"Oh no. No no no," I said, the feeling of helplessness as I drifted untethered through the dark void flooding back into my mind. I had traveled through the vervorium doorways enough in one night for a lifetime and there was no way I was going to do that ever again.

"Your choice," said Beatrice. "You can leave the boat at the docks by the River Club. Just make sure no one sees you and I'm sure it'll be fine."

Before I could protest further, she walked back out the front door, leaving me alone in the dark. A wave of fear washed over me and I crouched down to the ground, as if that would help me avoid it.

I had tried so hard to hide from the aftermath of that fateful night at the Met and the lighthouse, to pretend like my life wasn't in shambles. But denying my new reality only left me feeling like I was trapped in the space between the vervorium gateways, where up and down had no meaning, where time passed in an instant and dragged on for an eternity.

I had felt that emptiness before, when my mom had died, and it had taken me a long time to climb out of that pit and return to the world. But I had done it, one step at a time. And now I would do the same thing all over again.

Beatrice was fussing with the tarp-wrapped statue on the boat when I emerged from the house a few minutes later.

"Good, you've come to your senses. Let's get this inside and then we can get out of here."

"Her," I said.

"Right, her," said Beatrice.

I walked along the creaky dock and back onto the boat. With our remaining strength buffs, we easily carried the statue into the house before each taking another vitality buff. The tarp still wrapped around her, we placed Frankie in one of the back corners of the house, and, the task done, I collapsed onto the cold wooden floor. It was just a shade before 8 a.m., but even with the restorative effects of the vitality buff, I felt like I had just spent the last week hauling coal out of a dank mine.

I heard Beatrice walk over to the front door and begin fiddling with the existing door knob. So, we were really doing this. I wondered where the door would now lead, how it would feel to again travel dozens of miles in an instant. But I had no time to dwell on the intricacies of the folding of the fabric of the space-time continuum, as Beatrice cleared her throat in a pronounced manner and I pushed myself up to my feet.

"See you on the other side," she said, as she pulled open the front door, revealing a familiar black abyss instead of the path back out to the boat. Beatrice stepped across the threshold without hesitation and then vanished.

I looked back one more time at the woman frozen in stone before I closed my eyes and embraced the darkness.

The fifth time I walked through the vervorium portal was different than the previous times. Instead of wondering if I would ever escape that hellish dimension, I simply gave myself to the emptiness and waited for the light to return.

So I was beyond surprised when no sooner had I entered the gateway, that I found myself stepping out of a door into a nondescript corporate office, the Manhattan skyline beckoning outside one of the windows.

"Good, that was quicker than I thought it would take," said Beatrice, who shuffled past me and shut the door I had come through, which I saw sported one of the door knobs we had stolen from the Met. "Did the trip go by quickly for you too?"

"Yeah," I said. "We're … we're back in the city?"

"Yep," said Beatrice, smiling. "The 47th floor of the Chrysler Building to be exact. Welcome to the other half of our new HQ."

The office was a single room with gray carpeting, fluorescent lighting, an old refrigerator, and boxes upon boxes stacked along one of the walls and Beatrice's familiar workbench set against the other.

"This is everything from your apartment?" I asked.

Beatrice nodded.

"Just about. Had to put some of the other stuff in storage until we got the back office operational, but now that that's done, we can finally get properly situated."

"You don't mean…"

"I do. Grab a box and get cracking. I need to head back to my apartment and deal with my familial responsibilities for the rest of the day. It shouldn't take you more than a few hours to ferry everything through the door, especially after she gets here to help."

"Who?"

The front door of the office suddenly opened and a tall blonde girl sporting an incredibly skimpy dress, platform heels, and way too much black liner waltzed in.

"Ah, good, you're right on time," said Beatrice to the mystery girl.

I stared at our new guest and my mind wandered back to something I thought I only had imagined in a haze of steam.

"Polly?" I asked, in disbelief.

The girl smirked.

"No, I'm Eva," she said with a coarse voice as she grasped the small green stone that hung around her neck. Her visage shimmered, and the tall would-be model blinked out of existence and in her place was 12-year old Polly Janssen. She was wearing the same dress, which looked ridiculous on her, and the platform heels brought her height up almost to mine. I looked over to Beatrice to see if she was surprised at what we had just witnessed, but her expression had turned to one of annoyance.

"Were you out all night again? I'm not just going to give you a free buff because you thin-"

"God, you sound like my dad," said Polly. "I'm here, aren't I?"

"Wait, wait," I said, interrupting the weird mother/daughter dynamic that was starting to develop. "Are we just going to ignore the fact that she just transformed from a 20-year old into a pre-teen who looks like she spent all night watching a makeup tutorial video?"

Both Polly and Beatrice rolled their eyes in unison.

"It's a glamour, dummy," said Polly, who walked over to the workbench and plopped herself down on top of it. "And you're one to talk about makeup."

"A what?"

"You saw it already, that day in the Russian baths."

"Wait, what? I thought that was my eyes playing tricks on me."

"They were," said Beatrice. "And your ears. It's one of the older uses of alchemy. When activated, the glamour projects a false image of the person. Your brain thinks you're looking at a 20-year old wannabe model who sounds like she did way too much coke last night, but in reality, it's just Polly."

"For your information, I didn't do an-"

"Don't care, you're not my kid. Anyway, I'll let you two started. Let me know when you're done."

Before I could say anything further, Beatrice strode out the door.

But I was done being her underling and wasn't about to spend my Sunday moving boxes through that damned portal. So I followed her out into the hallway to give her a piece of my mind.

"Hey!" I said to Beatrice, who had walked to the far side of the elevator bank. "You ripped up our agreement, remember? I'm not just going to do your grunt work because you have a Sunday brunch to attend."

She looked back at me with tired eyes and sighed.

"It's not grunt work, Jen. We need to get back up and running if we are going to locate that gold token. And since you were too busy feeling sorry for yourself for the last few weeks, I already did most of the hard work. So if you want to pull your fair share, moving those boxes would be a good place to start."

The elevator opened with a ding and I let her go back to her domestic life. I would hold my tongue, for now. And, much as I was loathe to admit that Beatrice was right, I had not been holding up my end of the partnership. That needed to change if she was ever going to see me as an equal.

Eva was there when I walked back into the office and I stood there, staring at the illusion. My eyes could detect no trace of the 12-year old scamp hiding behind the magic, but I wondered how far the glamour extended to my other senses.

"Take a picture, it'll last longer," said Eva, before a coughing fit came over her.

"If I did, who would I see?"

The girl considered my question for a few seconds before nodding to herself.

"Me," she said, matter-of-factly.

"Not helpful," I said. "How do I even know that you're the glamour and Polly is the real person? Maybe it's been the reverse this whole time."

Eva smiled.

"That would be something, wouldn't it?" she said as she removed her necklace and the vision of Eva abruptly disappeared and there was Polly again. "You want to try it out?"

I took the necklace from Polly and looked at the green stone. It was tiny, no bigger than a raisin, but its color was dark and deep, like the redwood forest I hiked with my mom when I was 11. I wondered how something so small could hold so much magic. I started to put it on but then stopped myself.

"No thanks," I said, handing the necklace back to her.

"Suit yourself," said Polly, who slipped the delicate chain around her neck and tucked it into her dress. "And to answer your question, the glamour holds, even against technology. Course, it doesn't extend to my clothes, so I'm stuck in these ridiculous heels until we finish."

For the first time in a while, I was the one who smirked.

"Just don't walk out onto the dock, and you'll be fine."

"The loading dock downstairs?" asked Polly.

"You're joking, right? Beatrice didn't tell you *where* we were moving this stuff?"

"No, why? Is it far?"

"Yes. And also, no."

"What the hell does that me-"

My phone suddenly starting blaring in my pocket, like a mini air-raid siren. I pulled it free to see a big, blinking red pop-up window covering the whole screen.

"*JadePhoenix42: you have been summoned to appear at the next meeting of the Questing Council. 10:37 PM. March 5, 2019. 334 West 36th Street, Suite 4312.*"

CHAPTER THIRTY-FOUR

COUNCIL OF FOOLS

"But this was a different sort of conflict. Old wounds on all sides had been left to fester for too long."

"We're fucked."

I stood with Beatrice at the back of our new coffee hangout: a massive food market in the Garment District, like a bodega on 17 rounds of steroids. Even at 10 p.m., the place was mobbed, with tourists filtering in from further north in Times Square to fill plastic containers with the multitude of food laid out in big buffet trays.

"Why do you say that?" I asked her.

"Because," she said, "in all my years of Questing, I've never heard of anyone being summoned to the Council. I didn't even think it did anything!"

"Maybe they just want to commend us on all our hard work," I offered half-heartedly.

Beatrice glared at me before taking a sip of the decaf coffee she had loaded with several packets of sugar. We were a block away from the Council meeting, which was seemingly housed at the same address as a denim manufacturer. It may have been the last one left standing in the city. I guess that's why it was a good place to hide a clandestine meeting of the governing board of a secret magical society.

"You brought the Medoblad?"

I nodded, tapping my purse. It had been the first time since that night in the lighthouse that I had held the wretched thing, but I understood the necessity of arming ourselves appropriately as we entered the lion's den. Not that I thought we would actually use it. Speed would be a far better ally than the blade. Or our own glamour, if we had one.

"How come you never told me about glamour alchemy?" I said, as Beatrice refilled her coffee cup for the sixth time.

"I didn't want to overwhelm you with too much at once," Beatrice said. "Plus I've never been able to get my hands on one, so it seemed pointless to tell you about it. Come on, we're going to be late."

"OK."

We walked out of the market into the cold night. Beatrice chugged the rest of her coffee as we slowly made our way down 7th Avenue until we reached 36th Street and hung a right. Colorful bolts of fabric lined the windows on the block and my thoughts drifted to Lisa, who would have loved spending entire weekend afternoons browsing through the various shops in the district. At the moment, I wasn't sure if I was more nervous for the Council meeting or for that eventual confrontation.

"You think they know about the Met? The lighthouse? The cave?" I said quietly, as we approached our destination.

"I've got no fucking clue," said Beatrice. "But if I had to guess, Gilbert's had a few weeks to stew over failing to kill us, so he pressed the Council to confiscate all of our stuff. Which is hopefully beyond their reach at the moment."

After the Council summons had arrived yesterday morning, Beatrice had returned to the office five minutes later, her face beet red. Between the three of us, we had ferried every single box through the portal and stowed them safely in the island house. Polly had vomited immediately upon exiting the door the first time and had nearly refused to go back through. Again, Beatrice had pointed to the boat moored out front, and the girl had quickly sucked it up and made the return trip. But I gathered from our parting late morning that it would be a long time before Polly would agree to do another favor.

We reached the factory and I peered through the big glass windows that lined the front of the building. The hulking metal machinery stood quiet and if there were any signs of the Council inside, I didn't see them.

I walked over the sidewalk cellar door and tried to pull the front door open, but it wouldn't budge. Then I noticed a small intercom to the left with seven rows of buttons, each corresponding to a different office in the building. Unsurprisingly, none of the office names said "Questing Council" and none of them listed a Suite 4312.

"Now what?" I said to Beatrice, who was silently considering her clenched right fist in front of the windows. "You're not thinking of-"

"No," she said, walking away from the glass. "I've used the ring too much already. Besides, we're smarter than that. Maybe if we just knocked."

I nodded and banged on the door three times. No one answered and I knocked again. Still nothing.

"Try one of the buzzers," said Beatrice.

I complied, working my way down the intercom after a few-second pause in between. Each buzz was greeted with silence, except the last one, where I was hit with a string of expletives before the intercom abruptly cut off.

I looked over the intercom directory again to see if there was some sort of message hidden amongst the office names. Was finding the Council meeting the whole purpose of our summons? And if we passed, we would be granted a great reward for our ingenuity?

"Suite 4312, what if it's not an office number, but a sequence?" I said, a surge of excitement in my voice. Without waiting for Beatrice to respond, I pressed the intercom buttons again in quick succession, but in the order of the suite number.

No sooner had I hit button 2 than a soft beep chimed from the intercom, followed by a clinking sound next to my feet. It was the sidewalk cellar door, which, much to my astonishment, began opening on its own, revealing a set of stairs down into the dark.

"Well, that's not foreboding at all," said Beatrice, who crouched down next to the newly revealed set of stairs. "Can't see much, but doesn't look like a bloodthirsty mob is waiting for us at the bottom." She stood up and descended into the basement and I followed.

We were in a long, narrow hallway, the only light coming from a single bulb hanging from the ceiling at the end. It took only a minute to reach the terminus, where a large wooden door with an ornate metal door knocker in the middle waited for us. I looked at Beatrice, who shrugged her shoulders and then rapped the metal against the door several times. At the fourth knock, the door slowly opened inward a few inches, the sounds of ambient chatter spilling forth.

I pushed the heavy door forward and walked through, only to be greeted by a hundred people seated in neat rows of chairs facing a long front table all turn their heads in unison to stare at me.

"The next meeting of the Council will be held on April 10, same time, at the MacDougal Street location."

A heavyset man with graying hair and spectacles banged a gavel on the front table and the throngs of people began slowly exiting, only as we had just sat down in the back row. Two women were seated abreast of him: one who looked like she could be his wife and another who I could have sworn was a finalist on some terrible reality show a few years back and maybe now sold kitschy motivational artwork on Instagram.

"How are we this late?" I whispered to Beatrice. "We weren't fumbling with the door that long."

"Dunno," she said. "Maybe they just wanted to ID us for later. Let's get out of here while we can make a stealthy exit."

Beatrice got up quickly from her chair and I followed, but no sooner had we done so did the man at the table's gaze lock in on us with his beady eyes.

"You two, stay," he said, pointing his gavel at us, and we slunk back down in our seats and waited as the room slowly emptied.

I watched the attendees filter out through at least four other doors scattered around the large room and realized that despite my 13 months in the Questing world, up until this point I only had known a handful of people who had taken the same crazy plunge as me. And one of them was heading right toward us.

"Hi Jade," said the girl with a smile. She was wearing that same jean jacket decorated with dozens of pieces of flair, but her hands were missing the stacks of rings from our first encounter at the Raid Board.

"Hi," I said, as Beatrice turned to stare at me with daggers.

"Who's your friend?"

"Molly," said Beatrice, cutting in before I could answer. "Molly Vestrit. And you are?"

"Ty Anzio. Nice to meet you," said the girl. "How'd that Raid work out for you, Jade?"

Ty sat down in the chair in front of us and swiveled around, blocking my view of the front dais.

"Umm," I said, my mind racing back to that brief encounter at the elementary school. "I ended up not taking it, too much going on at work that week."

"Ah," she said. "I hear they're moving the Board next week. You missed a rousing debate over the possible new locations. The crowd wants another school, this time on the Lower East Side, but those three up there have other ideas."

"Well, that's all very interesting," said Beatrice, "but we reall-"

"Skylarose101 and JadePhoenix42, come forward."

I turned and looked at Beatrice.

"Skylarose101? Really?"

"What?" she said. "It was a long time ago."

We shuffled out of the row, away from Ty, who had a big smirk on her face.

"Oooh, what did you two do?"

"None of your business," said Beatrice curtly as she walked to the front of the room.

"Your friend is nice," said Ty, shaking her head. "Well, if you guys ever need help, here's my card." She reached into her jacket pocket, pulled out a black rectangle with gold writing on it, and handed it to me.

"I didn't know 16-year olds today carried business cards. Or knew what they were," I said. "But thanks. Hopefully we're not in-"

"Let's go!" said Beatrice from the front of the room.

"Sorry about her," I said, turning back to Ty, but she was gone.

I quickly joined Beatrice in the center of the first row. The table stood only a few feet in front of us, which meant that the horrible body odor from the rotund man in the middle had nowhere to go before it reached us. I winced at the smell and Beatrice elbowed me in the ribs before giving me a dirty look.

"Ahem," said the man. "Let's get down to business. You two know why you are here?"

"No clue," said Beatrice.

"No, sir," I said, as if I was addressing my old boss at the library.

"Gerald, get on with it, already," said the reality TV starlet. "Just read it to them so we can get out of here. I have a million things I need to be doing."

Gerald's maybe-wife glared at the younger woman.

"Hold your tongue, Sara. This is important! It's not every day that the Guild asks us t-"

"They've asked us to read a piece of paper, you dolt. It's not a test for a Guild seat. So just-"

"Enough, both of you!" said Gerald, banging his gavel before shuffling some papers around on the table. "Now, where was I? So. You two have been summoned here today so that we, as the esteemed Council member to my left was so inartfully saying, can deliver a message from the Guild."

My eyes widened and I turned to gauge Beatrice's reaction, but she just kept staring ahead at the three Council members, unfazed.

"Skylarose101 and JadePhoenix42," Gerald said, reading off a brown piece of parchment, "you are hereby charged by the Board of the Dutch West India Company, doing business as the Worshipful Company of Alchemists, i.e. the Guild, with the kidnapping of a Guild asset and theft of Guild property. Return the kidnapped asset and stolen property listed in Schedule A within one week of this summons, or you will be indefinitely banned from participating in any Quests or Raids, along with forfeiture of all tokens. Call 679-241-5125 for drop-off location when ready."

Gerald put down the parchment, picked up an envelope, and held it out in front of him. Beatrice quickly rose from her chair and snapped it from his hands before tearing it open savagely and pulling out a piece of computer paper with small black text printed on it.

I peered over her shoulder and quickly read the words, and my heart started palpitating.

"Schedule A," it said in printed black letters at the top. Below that were two underlined column headers, each with a single line underneath.

"Guild Asset," said the first, and below that was printed "Francesca Lewis."

"Guild Property," said the second, and below that was printed "One wooden box, 2 feet by 2 feet by 2 feet, with a metal latch."

My eyes met Beatrice's and she slowly shook her head.

"Like I said," said Beatrice. "We're fucked."

FRIENDS FOREVER

"Our enemies abroad were distracted by Napoleon's antics, but our enemies at home were not so encumbered. And so they made their move."

"We've already been over that plan, no."

Beatrice paced back and forth across the small office on the 47th floor as the sun crept toward its zenith outside the window. I had been there since 7 a.m. after a night spent staring at the ceiling without any sleep, after spending the previous day typing the same four lines of code over and over again at work.

Luckily Beatrice's supply of vitality buffs was deep and I had sprung back to life immediately after I washed the awful-tasting gummy down with some coffee. I suspected, though, that the next week would be filled with a similar combination of sleepless nights and buff-fueled benders.

"The Schedule doesn't say anything about the condition of the Guild asset," I said for what seemed like the tenth time. "So all we need to do is just-"

"No, no, no," said Beatrice, walking over to the workbench, where Rita van Asch's diaries were propped open. "You don't understand how the Guild works. We show up with statue Frankie and they're more likely to break it into pieces and bludgeon us than thank us. And that doesn't even address the box, which we obviously don't have."

"But they already have the box. At least Gilbert does, right? And he's in the Guild, so why do they think that we have it?"

"I told you, I don't know."

"I still don't understand why we don't just use the speed buffs to help us sort through this," I said. "It worked twice before, so-"

"No," said Beatrice. "We don't have enough of the picture. All that will do is confirm in half a second what we already know, which is nothing. Not until we get the other ring back."

"Fine," I said. "Can I go then? At least until you hear back from Polly? I would still like to make it into the office today, and tonight's not exactly going to be a walk in the park."

After almost a month of silence, of course today was finally the day I heard from Lisa, asking to meet her and Stacy for dinner tonight. I had been dreading this moment ever since the morning after the Met lecture, going over in my head a hundred times what I was going to say. But it was Beatrice who eventually put my mind at ease, when one night in the library a few weeks ago she had slid a small vial across our small table. Her memory serum. Well, a new version of it.

"You can go if you want," said Beatrice, her nose buried in one of the diaries. "But don't you want to test out the serum first? It wasn't really meant for older memories. The modifications I made should fix that, but I can't say for sure."

"And how would I do that?" I said. "Are you offering up yourself as a test subject?"

"Yes."

"Oh," I said. "OK then. What do you want to forget?"

Beatrice slowly closed the diary, pulled out her phone, and brought up a picture, before handing it to me.

"Him," she said.

"Who is that?" I said, looking at the image of a man with grey hair standing behind a podium at some lecture.

"He's the husband of Garrett's old boss. Was, I should say. He died a few months ago."

"Oh, I'm sorry. Did you know him well?"

"Not really. I slept with him once to get back at Garrett, who was fucking his boss at the time. Long story."

"Got it," I said, not wanting to press further on what was obviously a sensitive subject. But Beatrice kept going.

"He and Garrett's boss got divorced soon after. I didn't care at the time, as Amelia was a real bitch. But then I found out he slowly drank himself to death. Maybe he would have done it anyway, I don't know, but I don't need any more things weighing on my conscious. Especially now."

She turned away from me and wiped her eyes and I stood there, not knowing if I should comfort her or pretend that she wasn't crying. Eventually, she collected herself and took a can of ginger ale out of the fridge.

"You have the serum?" Beatrice said.

"Yeah," I replied, removing it from my bag. "But you never told me how-"

"Good," she said. "Then let's do this."

———————

"So," I said.

"Yeah," said Stacy, who looked at Lisa, waiting for her to start the inquisition. But Lisa refused to take the baton, and instead just stared off into the ether.

"Why don't I get us drinks?" I said, and got up quickly before either of them could respond. The tiny basement restaurant was packed to the seams and understaffed to boot, so I wedged myself between two groups of finance bros and ordered two rum and cokes and a whiskey.

I pulled out the tiny vial while I waited and gently uncorked it. It smelled sweet, a marked change from Beatrice's other concoctions, but I had seen how much power even a few drops held.

The bartender brought over the drinks and I handed her a stack of twenties. I pulled the glasses close to me, the vial concealed in the palm of my hand, and slowly added three drops of the serum to all but one of the brown drinks.

"Hey," said a voice.

I looked up and the bartender was nearly on top of me.

"Oh, it's, umm," I said, fumbling for a plausible explanation. "It's CBD oil."

"Obviously," she said, "but we charge extra for that. Make sure I don't see that again."

"Sorry!" I called as I grabbed the drinks and retreated to the back. I set the glasses down on the table and slid into the booth, my heart pounding. Lisa still had the same forlorn look on her face and I wondered how much she and Stacy actually remembered from that night.

"Cheers," I said, raising my own glass awkwardly. They responded in turn and clinked my glass, before each taking the smallest of sips.

Shit.

"Come on," I said. "The more sober we are, the more painful this is going to be."

I polished off my whiskey in a single gulp and hoped that Lisa and Stacy would follow. The silence that ensued was so painful that I nearly got up to run away, but after the longest minute of my life, both Lisa and Stacy took a second short swig of their drinks.

It was showtime.

"Look, I'm sorry I've been MIA for so long and I'm sorry I didn't come bail you out after the lecture. I didn't even really know what had happened. You both kind of just ran off suddenly and then Duncan was calling me from and then I dropped my phone and then–"

"Are you fucking serious?" said Lisa, her eyes filled with fury. "That's the best you've got? 'My phone died, sorry?' Did you think we just … you know what, forget it."

"Forget what?" I said, but part of me knew the answer already.

"Everything," said Stacy, chiming in. "We're done with you, Je–"

Stacy's face suddenly froze mid-word, her eyes unblinking. Lisa too sat there with the same slack-jawed look, as if something deep in her brain had overridden her conscious thought to tell me off. Because that's what was happening.

The same thing had happened earlier that day during the test run with Beatrice. Except that was more controlled, more thought-through. She had pictured in her mind the man she was trying to forget. Not just a particular memory, but his entire being. If they met downstairs in ten minutes, she would not recall who he was. If Garrett mentioned his old boss's husband, she would shrug and say "Hmm, don't remember him."

And it had worked. I didn't want to believe it at first, but it had worked.

So I knew in an instant that the serum had been triggered, not during Lisa and Stacy's recollection of the night of the lecture, but at their adamant and explicit desire that they wanted to forget me.

It had taken only a minute for the life to flood back into Beatrice's face. And so I counted down the seconds until my two best friends returned to the waking world without a memory of who I was. What would they think, I wondered, when they saw pictures of the three of us or when someone mentioned me in passing? And wasn't a part of me being erased too? If our memories together were now only in my mind, how could I prove to anyone (and to myself) that they had been real and not just the delusion of a lonely 18-year old looking for a place to belong?

Lisa blinked. And then Stacy did too. They both gave me a look as if they were trying to remember where it was they had seen me once before, but couldn't quite place me.

"I'm sorry," said Lisa. "But could we get another round of drinks? This one tastes a bit off."

I nodded, fighting back the tears that were slowly welling in my eyes, grabbed the two glasses, and started to walk away.

"Hey," said Stacy, and I looked back.

"Take this one too," she said, pointing to my own empty glass. "It was here when we sat down."

I stood there, unmoving, as the full reality of what I had done finally snapped into place.

"Hello?" said Lisa, waving her hand to get my attention, before turning back to Stacy. "I swear, the service in this city has been going downhill for years now."

I grabbed my glass without another word and walked out of their lives.

CHAPTER THIRTY-SIX

WHAT'S PAST
IS PROLOGUE

*"They forgot one thing though. Never do in the open what can be better
accomplished in the shadows."*

It is raining. How fitting. But time is short and my window to leave the island is closing. So today will have to be the day. I wrap the Compendium in cloth several times over before placing it in the familiar worn wooden box with several metal weights, and grab my umbrella. It is a short walk to the stables and my horse is saddled and ready to go. Luckily for me, he has seen too many winters for the British to find him useful but he still suits my purposes and I hope the hands will still take care of him after I leave the island.

I secure the box to the saddle and the animal winces as I lead him into the cold and the wet but he will have bear it now and he will have to bear it later, just as I will and just as the boxes have always done. We ride north, out of the city and through the abandoned farms, until at last I see the fort looming on the hill. A dozen memories flood into my mind about this place. It has been nearly two lifetimes since we came ashore at the edge of that forest for the first time, when we bought this island from the Lenape.

I hope I am the only one left among the living who remembers that day.

As the teeming mass of Redcoats come into view, I have second thoughts about approaching on land but quickly cast them aside. I do not mind manual labor, as my blooming garden each summer can attest to, but only on my terms and at a time of my choosing. It is a privilege I believe I am entitled to after all these years. Still, rowing up the length of the island and back by myself would be fraught with peril, and I would rather rely on my wit and my charm than my ability to outmaneuver the British in open water.

I dismount and pull out some sugar chunks from the saddlebag. The horse does not like the mud sticking to his hooves but he happily takes the sweet reward. I tie him to a tree and walk into the lion's den.

Two soldiers approach, their faces red to match their jackets, and I pity them, but only for a minute.

"Halt," says the first one.

"What are you doing here?" says the second.

I dispense with the formalities and summon the word to my tongue.

"*Peitho.*"

I felt something grasping my shoulders and I struggled to stay in the moment. The power that had been at my command was unlike anything I had experienced before. It wasn't borrowed or siphoned or tapped, it was raw and it was mine. But the pulling persisted until I was wrenched out of Rita's memory.

For a second, I saw her from the back, standing there on the dirt road. Her tied-up brown hair rustled slowly in the wind and I wanted to hold out just a second longer so I could finally see this woman whose essence had seeped into my mind.

But when I opened my eyes again, all I saw was the dusty, old book in front of me and the dim light of the lone lamp in our island headquarters. I turned around in the chair and saw Beatrice standing behind me, her brow glistening with sweat, and unsure if she should come closer.

"Wh-what happened?" I said. "The memory, it wasn't…" I looked back at Rita's 1777 diary to find the ink that had appeared on the page from Polly's ring smeared into an indecipherable blob like last time. Which meant one thing: the memory was gone.

"Why did you pull me out of it?" I said, trying to stand up, but my legs gave way and I stumbled back into the chair.

"Take it easy," Beatrice said. "Here." She offered me the familiar maroon buff but I refused her. We were both beginning to rely too heavily on them and I worried that I was treading Kate's path all over again.

"I'm fine. It's just . . . I didn't get far enough. She was heading north"

I recounted Rita's memory to Beatrice and her face fell when I reached the end.

"Oh," she said. "I wanted to let you go further, but this time it was different. With the other diary, you kind of were just asleep on the page. That's how it started out this time, at least. Then, your hands started moving, making these really weird gestures and then you started talking."

"*Peitho*," I said without thinking and Beatrice drew back, but nothing happened.

"She did something, to the soldiers. On her own. They were dead, but not dead, if that makes sense."

"Not really. I've never heard of anyone using alchemy like that, like the magic was inherent to them. This is why more than ever we need to get that Compendium."

"Agreed," I said. Our latest harebrained idea had been to find Rita's Compendium, which would, and this was all wishful thinking, include the antidote for the stone curse I had inflicted on Frankie. Rita's last diary entry from 1777 had stated briefly that she had "hid Compendium in the usual place" before she had left New York to join her husband at Valley Forge.

Reading that passage over again now, with the knowledge of the memory rings, had been a revelation, and Beatrice had practically run to Polly's apartment to take back the ring after her own ring hadn't worked. But I convinced her to play it cool, to not let Polly in on the fact that the ring was more than just a band of silver, lest she demand something in return. Fortunately, by the time I had stumbled back teary-eyed to the 47th floor last night after my disastrous dinner, the ring was there. And when it had dissolved into a pool of silver ink and then into the familiar handwriting this morning, it seemed like things were starting to go our way.

"I wish I could have seen just a little bit more, seen who she gave the Compendium to. Maybe it's still sitting in a library somewhere, just like her diary."

"I know, but I didn't want to let you keep going and have it be her who woke up."

"You think that's what the rings are? Some sort of distributed consciousness that will bring Rita back to life?"

"Maybe," said Beatrice. "I don't know. That's why I wanted to let Polly try the memory this time. Probably better that she didn't. The girl already knows too much. But I'm glad we don't have another diary. I don't want to find out that I was right."

"So now what?" I asked. "We're quickly running out of leads."

"I wouldn't call it a lead. What were the chances that Rita knew about the Medoblad, knew how to reverse its effects, and just happened to write it down in neat handwriting for us to discover 200 years later? I mean, I found the thing in a cave on a Greek island you've never heard of."

"It was worth a shot," I said. "Even if it didn't have the cure, it would still have been a good chip to barter with. Seeing as how Rita's gold token is probably lost in the ether as well."

"I know, I know," said Beatrice. "Maybe City Hall will surprise us and find the property records we requested."

"Yeah, in like 100 years. Right around the time the sea rises and sinks all of Manhattan."

"Wait a minute," Beatrice said with a note of excitement. "You said Rita was heading north, to the place where the Dutch bought Manhattan from the Lenape."

"Yes, she hoped she was the only one alive who remembered that day. I figured it was just a meeting place where she was giving the Compendium to someone. You don't think…"

"I've been up there. Took Jack-Jack to run around for an afternoon a few summers ago. It's probably the last piece of mostly untouched land in Manhattan. And there's a rock with a plaque on it that claims to be the spot where the sale to the Dutch was made."

"Then maybe the Compendium is buried under that rock," I said, although I knew it couldn't be that simple.

Nothing ever was in this messed-up world I inhabited.

FORBIDDEN FOREST

"By the time they reach Hartford, it will already be too late. I will make sure of that. Even if I have to continue on in my current state a little while longer."

"Why did we come here at night again?" I asked as we walked down from the elevated tracks of the 1 train. It was nearly midnight. Another day gone, another day closer to our doom.

"Because," said Beatrice, "do you want to be the bottom-of-the-hour story on the local news? 'Two women arrested for digging up historic rock.' No thanks."

"Good point."

We walked west and then south before reaching an odd sight: a pair of magnificent stone staircases set between two buildings that led up to the rest of Inwood.

"This city," Beatrice muttered, as she began her climb. I followed, taking deep breaths on the flat landings interspersed throughout and ticking off the steps as I went. By the time I made it the top, my count had reached 110 and I was drenched with sweat, despite the cold night air.

"I hope that's the most exercise we have to do tonight," I said, as we continued onward toward the park.

"Not likely," said Beatrice. "And don't think we're going to take the easy way out either. No buffs, no ring, if we can help it."

"Fine," I said. The streets were deserted and I felt like we were invaders from across the sea, come to plunder this land's treasure. We had taped shovels to the inside of our long winter coats, but the adhesive was failing and so I brought my arm tight against the side of my body.

Finally, we reached the edge of the park. I considered the threshold we were about to cross. It was as if the forest beyond had finally said "no more" to the city and used the last of its strength to throw up a barrier against further human encroachment. Still, we stepped into the park with little fanfare and continued onward.

"How are you doing?" Beatrice said, after a few minutes.

"I'm fine," I said. "I feel like this shovel is about to fall out of my coat, but otherwi-"

"No, not right now. I meant, how are you dealing with the aftermath of accidentally erasing yourself from your friends' lives?"

"Oh," I said. "I … I don't know. I haven't exactly had the chance to process it. Maybe when this is all over and I can finally catch my breath, but for now I've forced myself to just keep looking forward."

"I guess that makes sense. But make sure you look back eventually," she said.

I nodded but didn't respond, and Beatrice took the hint to drop it. After all we had been through, these random moments of kindness from her still surprised me. Even though I had saved her life, even though I had proven myself, there was always a nagging thought that this would be the encounter that would set Beatrice off. But I pushed such speculation to the back of my mind, along with the blank stares on Lisa and Stacy's faces, and tried to focus on the task at hand.

We passed an empty baseball field before the path curled into the trees, around the edge of a field that abutted the marshy water of an inlet from the Harlem River, and we closed in our quarry.

The rock had been unceremoniously plopped in the middle of the path and we approached it gingerly. A lone streetlamp cast a dim glow across the plaque affixed to the boulder, just enough to make out the words.

"According to legend, on this site of the principal Manhattan Indian village, Peter Minuit in 1626, purchased Manhattan Island for trinkets and beads then worth about 60 guilders.

This boulder also marks the spot where a tulip tree grew to a height of 165 feet and a girth of 20 feet. It was, until its death in 1938 at the age of 280 years, the last living link with the Reckgawanc Indians who lived here."

I finished reading and opened my coat. The shovel fell free onto the dirt and I stooped down slowly to pick it up, feeling a familiar pang of unease. After all, this was now the second historic rock in a month that I was attempting to unearth. And, given the size of the thing, moving it without any alchemic assistance looked to be a tall order. Beatrice, too, appeared to have misgivings, as she was still considering the text of the plaque.

"Should we get on with the digging?" she asked. "Maybe if we started here," she scratched a circle in the dirt a few feet away from the rock, "we could tunnel under the rock without having to move it."

I stared at the dirt, my mind trying to recall that day when I, no, when Rita must have stood on this spot. Despite the incomplete memory, something felt off about what we were attempting to do. It was then that it started to rain. A cold rain, like the one I remembered from that late December morning.

"No," I said. "This isn't right."

"What do you mean?" said Beatrice, who had unsheathed her shovel from her own coat and was testing the stiffness of the dirt.

"She didn't hide it here."

"Don't be ridiculous, of course she did, you said that-"

"I know what I said. I know what I remember, too, and this doesn't fit. She didn't pack a shovel."

"So?" said Beatrice. "Maybe you didn't see that part."

"It's not like that," I said. "Even if I didn't remember packing up the shovel, I remember walking to the stable carrying the box in one hand and holding an umbrella in the other. What was she going to dig with? Her hands?"

"Maybe," Beatrice said. "Or maybe someone was going to help her. You didn't get to the end, remember?"

"Oh, I do," I said, the irritation in my voice growing. "But I remember enough. I didn't hide … she didn't hide the box here." I read the words of the plaque again and a smile suddenly bloomed on my face. "And this proves it."

"What?"

"There was a tulip tree here. A tall one if this plaque is to be believed. So how did Rita, without a shovel, dig through the roots and hide the box? Does she sound like the kind of woman who would get down on her hands and knees and start digging like a gopher?"

"No, but-"

"*I do not mind manual labor*," I said, and I could almost hear her voice coming out of my mouth. "*But only on my terms and at a time of my choosing.*"

"Stop!" cried Beatrice.

"She came through here, the two soldiers must have escorted her. With them as cover, no one would question her. Much simpler than rowing a boat all the way up the East River and then the Harlem River. She wouldn't have stopped to dig a hole that any idiot could have uncovered later that day, even if the tree hadn't been planted yet. No, not Rita. She hid the box someplace that would leave no trace that she had been there, that no one would stumble upon accidentally."

I turned away from the rock and everything suddenly clicked into place.

"There," I said, pointing toward the water at the edge of the field.

Beatrice followed my gaze and when she saw what I was looking at, her face fell.

"You're joking, right? The great Rita van Asch hid her most important treasure in the muck of this swamp?"

"Exactly."

The stone sunk into the brackish water, its otherworldly red glow piercing through the muck. I crouched down, the cold marsh soaking my pants for the third time and the cold rain continuing to drench the rest of me, and scanned the radius of light to see if the box was there.

It wasn't.

I stood up, cringing as the trickle of remaining sludge dripped down my legs, and fished the stone out of the water again with my shovel.

"Any luck?" called Beatrice from the shore.

"Nope," I replied as I waded even further into the morass, the red rock beating back the darkness like the Phial of Galadriel. It was a stroke of luck that I had even managed to hold onto the stone during that awful night in the cave, but at the time it seemed like a useless consolation prize for surviving Gilbert's attempt to kill us. Who needed a magic glowing rock when you had one of the most powerful flashlights ever created included as a throw-in feature on your phone? But the last marsh in Manhattan had bested our technology and so alchemy had answered the call.

"How much longer are you going to trudge around in there? I told you that there wasn't a snowball's chance that the box was still there. She probably came back after the war was over and fished it out."

"Then why did the memory ring still exist? No, it's still here, we just need t-"

My foot knocked into something hard on the swamp floor and I nearly tumbled face first into the water. I traced the contours of the object with my foot before dropping the stone. This time, its light illuminated the lid of a familiar wooden box and I nearly jumped in the air with joy.

"I found it!" I yelled to Beatrice and her face lit up as she ran to the edge of the water.

"Are you sure?" she asked.

"Sure enough that I think you need to come into the water and help me."

Beatrice winced as she entered the mire but soon was standing next to me over our submerged prize. I dug my shovel into the ground below the box and tried to wedge it free, but it protested.

"The weights must still be in there," I said, recalling the metal that Rita had placed inside. "We're going to have to pick it up ourselves."

Beatrice nodded and together we reached into the water, grabbed an end of the box, and pulled upward. It was as heavy as I remembered, but with our combined strength, we wrested it free from its watery prison and slowly carried it to shore.

The rain beat down upon us as we considered the box. Its similarity to the one that we had found and then lost that night in the cave was eerie, almost as if it hadn't been sitting at the bottom of the marsh for who knows how long.

"Shall we?" said Beatrice.

I nodded and lifted the lid, which, surprisingly, opened without a fuss. And, inside, just as Rita had placed it, was an object wrapped in cloth, along with the metal weights.

"I don't believe it!" I said, shaking my head.

"Well, don't believe it just yet," Beatrice said, as she retrieved the object and peeled back the wrapping to reveal a brown leather tome.

"That's just how it looked, incredible!" I said. The weights, too, looked exactly as they had in the memory, and I removed them carefully from the bottom of the box and dumped them on the wet grass.

I closed the box, laying the linen on top, and Beatrice put the Compendium down on the lid. It hadn't aged in the slightest from the day it was hidden, its cover still the same shade of brown. I wondered if it was the box or the linen shroud or something else entirely that had protected the book from the ravages of time.

We huddled close together to block the rain from soaking our newly found treasure and I pulled back the cover to reveal the first page.

Which was blank.

I turned the page to find a second blank page, and then again to find a third, a fourth, and so on. The book must have been hundreds of pages long, but I had a sinking feeling in my stomach that I could sit here for hours flipping through it and not find a hint of writing.

"What. The. Hell," Beatrice said. "It's completely empty!"

She shook her head and repeated the fruitless exercise, before closing it and throwing her hands up in disgust.

"I knew it couldn't be that simple," I said. "I knew it, I knew it, I knew!"

I stared at the book and wanted to light the damned thing on fire before dropkicking it into the swamp.

"Calm the fuck down," said Beatrice. "Let's just get out of here and we can regroup at the office. Maybe there's something we're missing."

"Fine," I said, as I ran my fingers down the edges of the pages, which ran together as if the book had never been opened. It was then that I felt it: a small bump, barely perceptible among the scores of vacant sheets. I searched for it again, to make sure my mind wasn't playing tricks on me, and found it a second time.

"What is it?" asked Beatrice.

"There's something in here, just need to…"

I opened the book near the spot and slowly turned the pages until I found them. A trio of them was stuck together, but my fingers worked them apart quickly. The first page was blank, along with the second, but the third had several lines of handwritten letters at the bottom, in a familiar script.

"The discovery of *Raphus cucullatus* in 1598 by the VOC was a revelation, but like most discoveries of the last several centuries, it quickly succumbed to the savage appetites of a populace hungry for new magic. Untold dodo bird specimens were wasted by virile men hoping to be imbued with the power of ancient times. It was not until the wife of a board member secreted away a pinch of the ground-up beak for her ailing daughter that the bird's true potential was realized. The restorative properties were soon demonstrated to be almost unparalleled, capable even of reversing the effects of Relics now lost to us."

I looked up from the page and my eyes met Beatrice's, who nodded silently. We were cold, tired, and soaked to our cores, and to top it off, we now had to locate the remnants of a bird 400 years extinct in just four days. Not to mention that we still didn't know where the other wooden box was.

Even with alchemy fueling our bodies and our minds, it all seemed too much to bear. A growing part of me just wanted to give up, to let the Guild kick us out, and then I could go back and pick up the deteriorating pieces of my old life. But as I learned long ago, for every action, there is an equal and opposite reaction. And as I struggled to pick up the wooden box, I saw that opposing force running toward us from the tulip tree rock.

CHAPTER THIRTY-EIGHT

NONSTOP

"The Convention was a rousing success and the Federalist secessionists are now a laughingstock. But to be certain of their demise, and of their patron's, I must pursue one final course of action before my days are over."

We fled along the water.

Not with the quickness of the speed buffs, which were stupidly in a box in our island headquarters, but with the urgency of a gazelle trying to outrun a hungry lion. The hooded figure pursued us with equal zeal, and I braved a half-second glance back to see him slowly gaining.

Beatrice ran a few paces ahead while I lagged behind, thanks to the wooden box.

"I can't keep this up!" I shouted to Beatrice, my forearms burning from the strain. "It's too heavy!"

Beatrice suddenly stopped short and I nearly collided with her from behind. I could see the edge of the park and the city streets just up ahead. She turned and there was something small and smoking in her hand.

"Keep going," she said and I saw the fire in her eyes. "I'll catch up to you."

"O-OK," was all I could muster as I left her there, alone. I reached the street and started retracing our route from earlier. Beatrice would be fine, I tried to convince myself. She had no shortage of weapons in her arsenal, and apparently had a few that I still didn't know about. And if she really got into trouble, she could always use whatever strength was left in the ring. I, on the other hand, had nothing of the sort, unless my mom's locket had somehow been gifted with alchemic powers when I had fed it to that rat all those months ago.

The streets were eerily quiet, devoid of people and cars, and I realized with a sinking feeling that we were trapped here until the next train arrived. I ran along 215th Street until I saw two flickering lights appear in the distance.

The stairs. Which meant that the subway platform was only a few blocks further. I crossed the street and was about to descend to the lower depths of Inwood when I heard a shout from behind me.

I turned and saw Beatrice sprinting toward me, her face red with exertion.

"Go, go!" she cried, grabbing the box from me. "We don't have much time." She rushed passed me and disappeared down the stairs. I followed, my arms relieved to be free of the burden but my legs now protesting as I tried taking the steps two at a time.

"What did you do?" I yelled ahead.

"Threw a special firecracker at him," she said. "Hopefully it set him on fire. Keep moving."

I reached the landing halfway to the bottom and heard the whistle of an approaching train. It was an unbelievable stroke of luck, but one that was immediately eclipsed by my very next step. I felt my foot barely scrape the edge of the stair before my body tumbled downward.

The next landing quickly rose up to meet me and I held out my hands to brace myself for the impact. I heard a crunch erupt from my right wrist as I hit the pavement and cried out in pain. Beatrice was almost at the bottom, but had stopped and was now gripping the banister, looking past me with a look of horror on her face. I slowly swiveled my head around to see the figure, smoke billowing from his still burning cloak, standing at the top of the stairs.

I summoned what little strength I had left and tried pushing myself up with my left hand, but the night's exertion had completely drained my reserves and I slumped back down. The train whistled again in the distance and I watched as Beatrice turned toward the platform and then back at me and our pursuer above.

"Help. Me," I croaked, before trying and failing again to get to my feet. The seven seconds it took for Beatrice to make her decision ticked off like they were days, but when I saw her set the box down and leap up the steps toward me, all remaining doubts I had about her were erased. As she slung my limp arm around her shoulder and hoisted me up, a crack erupted above us.

"What … what was that?" I said with a whimper.

"Don't know," said Beatrice. "But we need to get the hell out of here. Now!"

Somehow she braced me against her body and dragged me down the rest of the stairs, grabbing the box on the way. We reached the bottom and I finally steadied myself. The subway tracks loomed in front of us and I finally saw the train chugging slowly down the elevated platform to the north.

"Can you make it the rest of the way?" asked Beatrice, who had broken into a jog. "If we're not on that train…"

I put one foot in front of the other, ignoring the throbbing pain in my hand and the protests of my body and the terror flooding my mind, and nodded.

The ceiling was ugly, that much I had concluded from my 30 minutes of ceaseless staring. The carpet was also ugly, a dull gray that had maybe once been brown before the years of uncleaned dirt and grime had ossified on top, but it was oddly comforting. I don't know if I had slept in the hours since we had stumbled into the office, as the pain in my wrist made it hard to keep track of anything else but its constant presence.

It had eventually died down to a dull hum that ignited whenever I tried to lift my arm, and so I had waited patiently on the carpet until Beatrice returned from the other side of the door. A vitality buff would be welcome, but I doubted it would do anything more than get me to my feet and what I needed now, more than anything, was nothing. I just wanted to be able to close my eyes and let everything fade away. But the events of the evening kept playing over and over again in my mind, like a tape stuck on loop in an old VCR.

Somehow, we had made it up the platform steps before the already waiting train had closed its doors. Our pursuer, by some stroke of luck, had not, and so we had sat silently in the almost-empty subway car with the almost-empty Compendium until the conductor sleepily called out "Times Square, 42nd Street." From there, it was a short but paranoid walk east to the Chrysler Building, where we were greeted with a raised eyebrow by the security guard until Beatrice had flashed him our badges and he nodded.

We had stood vigilant by the door, waiting for the hooded figure to burst through, but after an hour of perfect silence, we nodded to each other and I had collapsed into my current position.

It would be another hour before Beatrice would finally emerged from the black expanse beyond the door. She looked alert but exhausted, and I wondered how many buffs she had eaten.

"Here," she said, crouching down beside me and placing a small vial next to me.

"Wh-what's this?" I asked. "Haven't seen this before."

"It's a vitality serum. It wouldn't congeal into a gummy for some reason, so it's less portable but far more potent. Don't know if it will actually fix your wrist but maybe it will dull the pain for a while."

"Thanks," I said.

"Don't thank me yet, you haven't drank it."

"No, I mean, for earlier."

"Oh," said Beatrice. "I hope you didn't think I was just going to lea-"

"I didn't. But, still, thank you."

I waited for Beatrice to launch into a speech about how now we were even or that we were something closer than partners, more like sisters, but she just stood over me with a dispassionate expression on her face.

"What? What can I say, except, you're welcome?"

"No, that's enough," I said, pushing myself up to a sitting position with my good hand and picking up the vial. The liquid was brownish-gray, which was fitting, and I swirled it around for a few seconds before Beatrice took it back to unstopper it for me. Downing it in one big swig, I waited for the familiar rejuvenation to wash over me.

What happened next was something else entirely. It started in my stomach, a warm soothing feeling like the one you felt when drinking a mug of hot cocoa after a cold day out in the snow. But then that warmth exploded into a deluge of heat that washed over my entire body like an unexpected wave during low tide. The heat and the pressure kept increasing, as if the liquid wanted to force its way out of every pore of my body. I gritted my teeth and fell back onto the floor, trying to hold back a scream. But it was too much to take and I let out a loud, guttural cry as I reached my breaking point.

And then, it was gone.

The heat, the pain in my wrist, the constant tiredness and anxiety after too many late nights and too many days filled with endless worry, gone. I tested my wrist by trying to push myself back up and found that while I didn't feel any pain, neither did I have the strength to support my weight.

"Huh," I said, trying and failing again.

"What?" asked Beatrice.

"My wrist, I don't think the serum fixed it."

I rotated it back and forth, still feeling no pain but doubted I could lift even a pencil with it.

"Well why would it? It's not a healing potion."

"But I thought maybe th-"

The door suddenly swung open and we both looked over with panicked faces, but it was only Eva standing at the threshold.

"Wh-what are you doing here?" asked Beatrice, running over to the girl and pushing her inside.

"I need something," said Eva in a voice barely above a whisper. She walked over to the lone chair at the workbench and sat down, a forlorn look on her face.

"And you have a perfectly good method of contacting me without risking someone following you up here," Beatrice said. "Which in this instance would have been fucking prudent to use, seeing as how we were just attacked by the Guild."

Eva looked out the window, before the glamour vanished and was replaced by a scared little girl.

"Oh," said Polly. "Didn't realize."

"No, you didn't," said Beatrice sternly. "Hence why following the communication protocol before barging in here unannounced would have saved you a trip down here. Go home and get some sleep and I'll touch base with you soon."

"But-"

"Go."

Polly rose from the chair, rubbing the green stone as she did. The tall blonde who took her place glared down at Beatrice, before walking out the door without another word.

"What that really necessary?" I said. "She looked lik-"

"You too, Jen," said Beatrice.

"What?"

"Go home. I'm going to do the same. Can't remember the last time I slept there alone."

"Where's your son? And your husband?"

The question left my lips before I realized that maybe she didn't want to answer.

"They're somewhere safe. Well, at least Jack-Jack is. Don't really care where Garrett went."

"You don't know?" I asked.

"No. I sent them both away a few hours after the Council meeting. The benefits of being over-prepared, I guess."

She quickly wiped away a tear and looked out the window.

"So what time should we meet back here? Noon?"

Beatrice shook her head.

"9 a.m. On Monday."

"What? That only gives us two more days and we sti-"

"I can't keep doing this," said Beatrice. "I know you probably think I'm some sort of inhuman robot that can just plow ahead, no matter the circumstances, but even I have a breaking point and I don't want to reach it."

"But we're no further along than we were a few days ago. We might even have moved backwards, seeing as how our only lead is to find a fucking extinct dodo bird!"

"I found one already," said Beatrice. "It's in the Natural History Museum."

"Oh," I said, before I burst out laughing.

"What's so funny?" said Beatrice, looking at me like I had just lost my mind, but I couldn't stop.

"It's just … of course it is. We needed to find a way to open the door in Long Island City and there was a pile of old door knobs just sitting there at the Met. Now, we need to heal a mythical curse and there's a long-dead bird on display at the museum across town."

"You think it's a trap? But that doesn't make any sense, how would they know that-"

"I don't know what to think. What I do know is that I'm going to take you up on your suggestion that I get some sleep."

I lied.

ROUNDABOUT

"Fortunately, I sent the other end of the portal south months ago."

"Hi, it's Larissa Jacobs, I can't get to the phone right now, probably because I'm on shift, but if you leave a brief message, I'll get back to you as soon as I can. Bye!"

I hung up the phone before the beep sounded and it took every remaining ounce of strength not to cry. Not that anyone would have noticed, as the car was mostly empty. I had already ridden the train all the way to the end at Pelham Bay Park before we turned around at the terminus and slowly rumbled along the elevated track back toward Manhattan.

Why had I decided, after all these years, that this was the moment that I wanted to hear my mom's voice again?

It wasn't as though if I left her a message, she would call back in a few hours and tell me everything was going to be OK. Even when she was alive, that would sometimes take days. I didn't understand it then, why she worked double shifts so often that there were weeks where we saw each other for a few minutes at most. To be honest, I still really didn't understand it. But that message was one of the only things I had left of her, besides some photos and the locket.

The train screeched to a halt at Hunts Point and I pushed aside old voices and memories as Ty Anzio entered the car. We ignored each other for a solid 40 minutes while the train resumed its southward trek. She was dressed in grey sweats, the hood of her sweatshirt pulled tightly around her hair. It would be another half hour until our official meeting time and when I saw her doze off in her seat, I took the cue and I closed my eyes, trying to rest my overtaxed mind. But such efforts were useless and instead my thoughts drifted back to the black business card with the gold writing that had led me here.

The Chrysler Building elevator hadn't even reached the 20th floor before I had pulled the card out of my bag and began typing the number into my phone.

"It's Jade, from the Raid Board and the Council meeting. I need help," I had texted, as I exited into the empty lobby. It had been nearly 8, when the earliest of the worker bees would be trudging in with sleepy eyes holding cups of coffee purchased from the cart outside. But then I had realized that it was actually Saturday. One less email to send then, I had thought, as I had been calling out "sick" from work since the day after the Council meeting, and would continue to do so until this whole business was behind us.

"It's early," the reply had said. And then, "what do you need?"

"Something to cure a wound with an otherworldly glow."

The lie was a good one and I thought of Steve and that scar on his stomach all those months ago. How had he actually gotten that scar, I wondered.

A silence of minutes had ensued until finally, the response came.

"Be in the third car on the 6 train, at Brooklyn Bridge, at 10:30. Don't acknowledge me before then."

That's where I had sat and that's where I awoke when the conductor finally called out "Brooklyn Bridge/City Hall, next and final stop on this train." I looked over at the middle door to see Ty standing against the metal poles and I slowly got up and joined her as the train ended its long journey. Stepping out onto the platform, I felt Ty's hand immediately pull me back into the car and before I could protest, the doors closed.

The train rolled out of the station and I started to ask Ty what we were doing here, but she held her hand up. We continued on into a dark tunnel, only to emerge a few minutes later in the most magnificent subway station I had ever seen. Tiles decorated the walls up to the arched ceilings, where honest-to-goodness skylights and chandeliers were interspersed throughout.

I took in the sights, the train banking slowly around the curved tracks when suddenly, the door in front of us opened.

"This is where we get off," said Ty, who hopped out onto the platform without a fuss.

I looked at her as the train car finished its turn through the curve and she shook her head at my hesitation, as if I was her mom and had just embarrassed her in front of her friends.

"Come on," I muttered to myself, before counting to three, closing my eyes, and jumping out of the train.

That proved to be a mistake.

I felt my feet hit the platform at a horrid angle and down I went, my hands instinctively reaching out to brace my fall before I remembered the sorry state of my wrist and pulled them back. My shoulder hit first and then my head, and I yelled out in pain.

"Shh," said Ty, who ran over to me and helped me to my feet. "Don't want the conductor to hear us and stop the train."

"Sorry," I said, getting my bearings. My head throbbed and my shoulder twitched, but I ignored both and followed Ty to a nearby stairwell. We walked halfway up until the platform was completely out of sight at which point I collapsed against the wall.

"Couldn't we have met at a coffee shop?" I asked.

"Nope," said Ty, who sat down across from me with her legs criss-crossed like she was attending a middle school assembly. "Not with a Guild tracker on your tail."

"What the hell is that?"

I started frantically turning out my pockets looking for a silver ring or some other object that wasn't supposed to be there, but Ty waved off my search.

"What it sounds like. A person hired by the Guild to follow you around. And from the one they've got following you, looks like you are at the center of the Guild's radar."

"Great," I muttered.

"Luckily for you, he doesn't know about that malfunctioning door, so he's still riding a car behind, waiting for you to get off."

"Oh, thanks, I guess."

"You're welcome. Everyone always forgets about this place. There are private tours a couple of times a month, but you'd be surprised how many people riding the 6 through the turnaround don't even notice that there's this entire station, hiding in plain sight."

"I could believe that," I said. "Same way people don't realize magic is real."

"Yeah, exactly!" Ty said, clapping her thighs before staring at me more intently. "You look like shit, by the way. Did you actually get stabbed with a Relic or were you just out all night partying?"

"Neither," I said, making a mental note of her Relic reference.

"Was out all night, but not to drink. And the cure I need isn't for me, it's for a friend."

"I see," said Ty. "That blonde you were with the other night? Molly?"

"Yep," I said, continuing the lie. "So, can you help me?"

"Ummm, obviously. That's why we're here. I happen to know a guy who trades in the sort of thing you're looking for."

"He has ground-up dodo bird beaks?" I said, as Ty raised her eyebrows. "I mean," I stammered, cursing myself for giving away the farm, "someone once told me that it was the ultimate curative."

"That's the rumor, at least," said Ty. "But I hope you didn't think you were just going to waltz into the Natural History Museum and take theirs."

"I wasn't," I lied, "but why not?"

"Because it's a fake. The real one was stolen years ago. Now the only one left that anyone knows about is at Oxford, but good luck getting through their security."

"Oh, so then what does your guy have?"

"You'll see. Just make sure you arrive right when he opens tomorrow night. He's very particular about punctuality."

"Tomorrow night? I don't think my friend has that kind of time."

"I don't know what to tell you, Jade, but the Market isn't even open today, so looks like you don't have a choice. Besides, it gives you some time to enjoy this beautiful forgotten piece of New York's history."

Ty pushed herself up to her feet and stretched her hands over her head, and turned to walk up the steps and out of the station.

"Wait!" I shouted to her. "What about the Guild tracker? He's eventually going to find me again, right?"

Ty smiled, before pulling something shiny out from the front pocket of her sweatshirt.

"Not if you're wearing this."

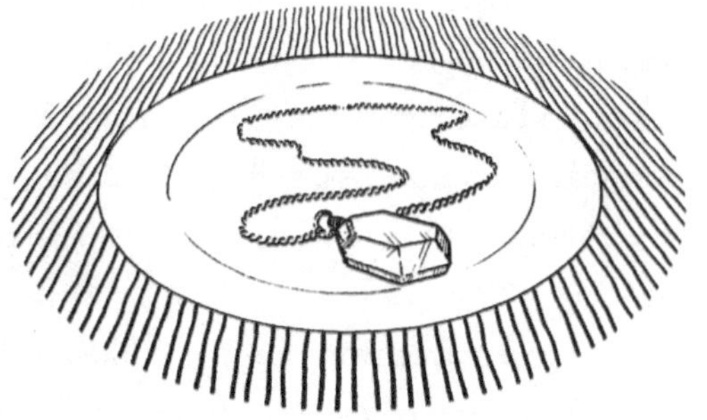

CHAPTER FORTY

A GLAMOUROUS LIFE

*"The journey through the blackness took a toll on me. I do not know if I will be able
to go back that way in my current state, but I must press on to the south."*

The redhead with the sparkling green eyes, brown freckles, and the deep, raspy voice walked into the lobby of the posh Upper East Side hotel, plopped down the no-annual-fee credit card made of cheap plastic, and then took the elevator up to her suite overlooking Central Park for the night. She tapped her room key against the sensor, walked through the spacious sitting room and into the marble bathroom, where a floor-to-ceiling mirror proudly reflected her smiling features.

But then the smile wavered, slightly, and the woman brought her hand up slowly to the small green stone hanging around her neck over a silver locket. She squeezed it gently between her thumb and index figure, and then vanished.

In her place, was me.

I looked at myself in the mirror for a brief second, before squeezing the stone again and closing my eyes. When I opened them, the reflection of the redhead once more stared back. I gazed at the glamour in the mirror for nearly ten minutes, trying to spot some trace of me underneath the alchemy, but the illusion was impenetrable, just as Ty said it would be.

I had grabbed the necklace from her hand like a child being offered a piece of candy after a day spent eating nothing but broccoli. She had explained how to activate it and then watched as I placed it slowly around my neck and pinched the stone. The sensation was like nothing I had ever felt before, as if someone had dumped a never-emptying bucket of water on me.

"Hello, my name is Jade," I had said with someone else's voice, extending someone else's hand, and Ty had rolled her eyes, before shaking it. "Nice to meet you."

I had repeated the vocal exercise until I could utter more than those simple phrases without the cognitive dissonance threatening to overwhelm my already overtaxed mind.

"Don't overdo it," she had warned me.

"What do you mean?" I had asked, still marveling at my new appearance.

"Spend too much time as the glamour and you begin to lose sense of yourself. At least, that's what my mom told me when she gave it to me. I've only used that one sparingly. There was something thrilling about walking around as a fully-fledged woman, but maybe it won't affect you as much, since you're old."

"Hey, I'm only 28!" I had said. "And I'll only use it when I'm out in public."

"Even so, try to take a break every so often. And don't get caught up in your own reflection."

I had ignored Ty's advice and instead had spent the entire day as "Jade." After getting used to the feeling of having an invisible sheet of fluid draped around my entire body, the experience was oddly freeing.

Jade didn't have two friends whose memories she had accidentally erased. She didn't have a long-distance boyfriend who was about to dump her. She didn't have a soul-crushing job or a partner who at any moment could betray her to save herself. Most of all, Jade didn't have a Guild summons hanging around her neck like an anchor.

As I had meandered through the Village before finally making my way uptown, I had seriously contemplated getting on a train at Penn Station and not coming back. But then the dull throbbing in my wrist had snapped me back to reality, and I had ducked into Macy's and deactivated the glamour in a dressing room. I had sat there for almost an hour in front of the mirror, resisting the urge to transform back into Jade, until finally a saleswoman had banged on the door and demanded that I come out. A tweak of the stone and Jade had returned. I had resisted the mirror's final siren song and walked out, but now found myself unable to break free from the current lure.

It was then that Ty's last warning finally reverberated in my mind and I pulled myself away from the bathroom mirror, walked into the bedroom and collapsed backward onto the bed. My phone buzzed after a few minutes, and I pulled it out to see a response from Beatrice to my warning earlier in the day that we were being followed.

"K" was all it read and I tossed the phone aside in exasperation.

Fine, I thought. She can take care of herself.

I closed my green eyes and moved my injured hand slowly up to the green stone. It was only for a split second, but I could swear I felt the glamour tighten around me, as if Jade didn't want to disappear. Except that was ridiculous. As much as I had lived as Jade when I played *Warriors of Olympus*, or when I began the Quests, there was no Jade. It had always been just me.

But before I could send her back into the stone, my hand suddenly fell slack against my stomach and my mind drifted away into the abyss of sleep.

The market stirred with a raucous energy, even though it was Sunday night. Everywhere I looked, crates of fruits or vegetables were being pushed on hand trucks and forklifts with such velocity that several times I nearly found myself knocked to the ground. The woman who had sold me my pass into the market had regarded me with suspicion and now I understood why.

This was not a quaint farmer's market where you could leisurely browse for organic fruits and vegetables while sipping an oat milk latte. No, this was one of the way stations responsible for feeding millions of New Yorkers and 99% of them probably had no idea that it even existed. Just as the City Hall station had, the market reminded me of magic and alchemy, this important, fundamental truth of the world that remained just out of sight.

I picked up my pace as I searched the rows for the aisle number that Ty had given me. Somehow half an hour had already passed since I had entered Hunts Point, and yet I still hadn't even made it halfway across the massive expanse. The speed buff hidden deep in my bag would have made all this running unnecessary, but Beatrice had made me promise when she had restocked me before I left the office yesterday morning to only use the buffs in an absolute emergency going forward.

Finally, with only a few minutes to spare, I reached the designated aisle and pulled the glamour free from under my sweater, activating it without breaking stride. The now-familiar weight settled around me, but I ignored it and pressed on, until I saw a sign with large black letters taped above several columns of wooden crates.

"Mackinaw Brothers Produce," it said and peaches peeked out through the slats of the dozen columns of crates stacked end to end and I looked at my watch to see the clock strike 10:04 p.m.

"Hello?" I called out in Jade's voice, but no one answered. "Anyone here?"

I walked the length of the crates several times looking for the vendor, but to no avail. Had this whole thing been some sort of practical joke by Ty? Or worse, had she lured me into the bowels of this urban monstrosity so I would be easy prey for the Guild tracker?

Fortunately for me, the answer was neither, as one stack of the crates suddenly lurched forward to reveal a small gap and a small man with grey hair and half-moon spectacles peeked his head out.

"You Jade?" he asked, his hunched back making it difficult for him to look at me through the glasses.

"Yes," I said.

"You're late," the man said.

I began to argue that there was no way for me to know that he was hiding behind the crates, but he waved away my protestations and beckoned me through. As my host pulled the crates back into place to seal us away from the rest of the market, I looked around the small interior.

At one end sat a small card table with a green shade lamp that dimly illuminated the space and two folding chairs on either side. On the backs of the crates hung rolled-up pieces of tarp. I wondered what sorts of objects were hidden beneath and whether there was something here that would free Frankie from her stone prison.

"So," said the man, sitting down slowly in the far chair, "now that we're alone, would you mind taking off that ridiculous disguise? It's hurting my eyes."

"Wh-what are you talking about?" I said, the weight of the glamour suddenly feeling even more constricting around my body.

"That glamour. Deactivate it, please. As much as I like it when a pretty woman comes to see me, I prefer to see who I'm actually dealing with."

I complied and then cringed as the old man looked me up and down before I crossed my arms against my chest and sat down across from him.

"Don't know why you're using that anyway, you're almost as pretty as she was."

"Is that supposed to be a compliment? Because I really don't need to-"

"Calm down, calm down. Didn't mean anything by it. Forget I said anything."

"Fine. Can we just get on with it then? I'm kind of in a hurry."

"No, you're not," the man said. "Those people out there, hauling produce around at all hours of the night? They're in a hurry."

"I didn't mean-"

"No, of course you didn't. Now, what is it you think that I can assist you with?"

"I need a curative. My friend, she ... she was hurt by a Relic."

The old man's eyebrows rose at the mention of Relic and he muttered softly to himself before slowly standing up and walking over to one of the rolled-up tarps. He began to untie the knot but then stopped and returned to the table.

"Your friend, what happened to her?"

The vision of that night flashed in my head, and for a moment I was back there, the fire raging all around me and Beatrice and Frankie unconscious on the lighthouse floor.

"She ... she was turned to stone."

The old man stared at me in silence and I waited for him to unfurl his wares and offer me a vial of silvery liquid that would undo the curse. But he just sat there, as if he too had been petrified.

"Sir?" I said after several more minutes had passed.

"Thinking," he said. "Shh."

"Sorry," I replied, looking at my watch. I had hoped to make it back to the hotel in time to get a decent night's sleep before reuniting with Beatrice, but at this rate, that wasn't going to happen.

Finally, he clapped his hands and stood up again.

"OK," he said.

"What?"

"I have something special for your friend."

"You do?" I practically shouted.

"Yes. It's a serum distilled from the needles of a golden porcupine. Very rare creature. Lives in one particular part of one particular jungle in Indonesia. Half of its needles are venomous and half are curative."

"Fascinating. Can I have it?"

"No, that's not how it works. Come back by 5 a.m. with your payment and you'll get your cure."

"You must be joking! My friend, she can't-"

The old man shook his head back and forth.

"This market has existed, in one form or another, since 1812. And since that time, we alchemists have plied our wares according to a simple set of rules, number one of which is payment before goods. So go bring me something of equal value and then you'll get the help you need. I'm sure your friend can manage in her state a little while longer, no?"

"What the hell does that mean, equal value? You didn't even name your price!"

I dug my hand into my bag to retrieve the Medoblad only to pull out a large but very ordinary chef's knife.

The man gave me a smirk before pulling the chain of the lamp down to extinguish the light as if he was packing it in for the night.

"Wait a minute," I cried. "We're not done here, I have something else!"

I pulled the chain and the light flickered on again, only to find myself surrounded by nothing but peaches.

CHAPTER FORTY-ONE

APPLE
OF MY EYE

*"The capital is burning. A city for a city. It has happened so many times
and likely will happen again and again."*

I awoke to find the tip of the Medoblad hovering inches above my
nose. It was held there by an irate Beatrice, whose eyes burned
with an anger I had yet to see her unleash on me.

"Stop, Beatrice, it's me!"

The words felt foreign as they left my mouth and I quickly moved
my freckled hand down to my chest, but Beatrice brought the blade
even closer and I stopped.

"It's me, Jen! This is just a glamour!"

Beatrice slowly retracted the knife and I scrambled to my feet and staggered backward to the window. I held the green stone out in front of me, the reflection of the mid-morning sun lending it an uncanny luster, before pinching it and letting the illusion fall away.

"Where did you get that?" Beatrice demanded after sheathing the Medoblad.

"Where did you get that?" I said, pointing to the purloined blade.

"I took it out of your bag when we got back from Inwood," she said. "Replaced it with a regular knife so you hopefully wouldn't notice."

"Why?"

"Because you're not the one the Guild is really after," said Beatrice. "And it seems like you've been hiding things from me. Polly give you that little necklace?"

"No, I got it from that girl Ty we met at the Council meeting. And, I'm not hiding anything. I was going to tell you everything in a few hours, but I found a cure. From a vendor in Hunt's Point Produce Market. Ty told me about him, after she told me that the Dodo bird in the Natural History Museum is a fake."

"Oh?" said Beatrice. "I thought you were going home to recuperate, not go rogue on me again and seek out another teenager you just met to help."

"And I thought you trusted me," I said. "After all we've been through. But when I got back here last night, I found the door knob gone, and so I took the only other thing of value I could find."

"Please tell me you didn't…"

I nodded and pulled the small vial out of my bag and offered it to Beatrice.

"Are there any left? Or did you steal them all?" she asked.

"The answer to both of your questions is yes."

"What the fuck does that mean, Jen?"

Beatrice ran to the freezer and opened the door to find it bereft of anything.

"I took all of your apples, yes," I said. "But I still have two left at home from my own haul from the orchard."

"Oh, aren't we lucky then? Two whole apples. Do you know how long it took me to gather all those apples?"

"Years, I'm sure. The sack was quite heavy, but he didn't seem very impressed at first. After all, we were in the middle of an Empire State-sized produce market. But after I gave him a demonstration of their power, his whole attitude changed and I knew I had him."

"So great, he gave you that vial and you just ran out of there?"

"No, of course not. I asked for a demonstration and he obliged. First, I made him heal my wrist. Only took the tiniest of drops."

I rotated my right hand back and forth and then lifted the workbench chair up over my head with ease, before setting it down with a big grin on my face.

"Congratulations," said Beatrice. "And I'm sure after that, you were convinced."

I shook my head.

"Still no. So I stabbed him."

"You did what?"

I smiled at Beatrice's reaction.

"Relax, he's fine. I pulled the knife on him quickly and he didn't react, not in words and not in thought. He just nodded and stuck out his hand."

"And you, Jen Jacobs, who a few months ago wouldn't have said one bad word about anyone, stuck a knife in the hand of a little old man?"

"I've changed, maybe not for the better. And how did you know he was an old man? I never said what he looked like."

"This 'vendor,' he have half-moon spectacles and a very pronounced slouch?"

I nodded and Beatrice stormed pass me to the back door and reattached the missing knob.

"Come on," she said.

"What? What are you doing?"

"What does it look like? Going to see if what that old bugger gave you really works."

"I told you it did! Wait, you know him, don't you?"

Beatrice nodded before holding up her right hand, which bore the small ring with the purple stone.

"He sold me this."

I entered the portal after Beatrice and emerged a few seconds later into the dark, creaky house only to find that I wasn't myself.

Beatrice looked back at me with a look of consternation on her face.

"Why did you activate it?" she shouted at me like a teacher lecturing a misbehaving student.

"I didn't!" I said in that now familiar voice. "I swear! This thing, sometimes, I feel like it has a mind of its own."

"OK OK, I believe you. Might as well keep it on. If this serum works, it's probably better that Frankie doesn't recognize you."

"Good point. We didn't exactly leave on the best of terms at our first meeting."

I walked to the back corner of the house where Frankie still lay under the tarp. Summoning all of my courage, I pulled back the covering and prepared myself for the worst.

It was even more horrible than I remembered.

Frankie lay prone on her back, still in her clothing from that night, which hadn't been affected by the Medoblad's alchemy. Her stone hands were positioned under her and her stone feet were close together as if they were still bound, but her face was frozen into a mask of calmness.

I didn't want to imagine what, if anything, she was thinking. Was her mind still awake within the stone, radiating anger at me for trapping her in there? Or was she merely sleeping, with no knowledge of what had happened to her? In either case, part of me was glad that I wouldn't have to face her directly.

I uncorked the vial, careful not to let any liquid slip out. One droplet had healed my wrist and two had cured the bloody wound I had created in the vendor's hand, and I hoped that the rest of the contents would be enough to undo the petrification I had unleashed.

"Ready?" asked Beatrice.

I nodded twice and poured all of the serum onto Frankie's cheek. It hit the stone and trickled down, the golden liquid pooling at the base of her neck. We waited with bated breath for what seemed like hours for something to happen, until finally, the serum dissolved into the stone.

"Look!" I cried and the pale hues of Frankie's skin began to blossom amongst the cold gray. The color spread until her entire head was free from the prison and I saw her eyes begin to move slightly back and forth before she finally opened them.

"Can you hear me?" asked Beatrice and Frankie's green eyes shifted toward her. She nudged her head up and then down ever so slightly but in that moment, it felt like an enormous weight had been lifted off of my shoulders.

"You're safe now," I said, in Jade's voice. "We're here to help you."

Frankie turned her gaze to me and I swore that she looked right through the glamour and saw me underneath.

"Let's help her up," I said to Beatrice and we each grabbed one of Frankie's arms, only to feel cold stone underneath her clothes.

"Something's not right," said Beatrice as we watched Frankie's face writhe in pain before she opened her mouth.

"The pearl in the triangle is gold."

Her voice was barely above a whisper and as soon as the last word left her lips, Frankie closed her eyes and the stone retook her.

"No!" I cried as the red strands of Frankie's hair turned gray and she became still once again. "It ... was ... supposed ... to ... work."

My fists pounded the wooden floorboards and I sobbed uncontrollably until Beatrice finally pulled me away from her.

"Get a hold of yourself! She's gone."

"That's not true! We just need more of that healing serum. Maybe we can trade the old ma-"

"Enough," said Beatrice, who threw the tarp back over Frankie. "It's one dead end after another. First we dredged up a hundreds-year-old book out of a swamp only to find the thing practically blank. Then you somehow pull that miracle serum out of your ass and it actually worked! But only for five fucking minutes, just long enough for dear 'ol Frankie to recite us a cryptic riddle. And you'll probably tear your hair out over the next two days trying to figure out what the hell 'the pearl in the triangle' means."

"It must be where the gold token is locat-"

"By all means try, but I'm done."

Beatrice stormed off to the portal and disappeared, leaving me alone with my failure.

The empty serum bottle lay next to the tarp and I picked it up to peer through the small opening. There was a drop or two collected at the bottom, which alone was probably worth more than all the money in my bank account. I re-stoppered the vial and tucked it into one of the still-full cardboard boxes that were strewn about the room.

My phone suddenly buzzed in my pocket and I pulled it out to expecting to find the daily reminder I had made for myself to call in "sick" to work, but instead, it was a text from Duncan.

"Dinner tonight at 8."

Shit. Was it Monday already? The last thing I wanted to do now was have a heart-to-heart with Duncan. What was I going to say?

Maybe his offer to move to Hong Kong was still on the table.

Only a month ago I had contemplated accepting it to escape from Beatrice, but now I found myself in need of it again.

"I'll be there," I responded before leaving Frankie to her endless sleep.

I found Beatrice staring out the window when I returned to the office, the glamour tucked in my pocket to avoid any accidental activation mid-transit.

"Look, I thought about what you sai-"

"In college, I used to think I'd have an office like this. High floor, big windows looking out over the city, the mere mortals below hurrying to and fro while I watched from up here, above it all. I thought that was power. But that was before the Quests though. Before someone gave me the call number to Rita's diary."

"And then what happened?" I asked.

"After I learned the truth? I realized I had been trying to climb up the wrong ladder. That the real power was wielded in the shadows, wielded by the ones who had mastered the secrets of alchemy, or had it handed it to them by their forebears. And I wanted desperately to ascend to their heights."

"We still can," I said.

"No, it's over. I have half a mind to walk back through that door and burn the whole house to the ground, drown myself in memory serum, and try to have as happy of a life as I can with my jackass husband and my kid before the Guild tracks me down."

"That doesn't sound like the woman I know. The woman I kn-"

Beatrice turned back from the window and glared at me with venomous eyes.

"Oh, give it a rest, Jen. You never really knew me. I may play the tough-ass bitch that takes what she wants, but deep down-"

"You're still that scared little girl hiding in the closet," I said and Beatrice gasped.

"How … how do you know about that?"

"And you're the woman who's had enough. You're the woman who went toe to toe with the Guild with nothing but perseverance and ingenuity on her side. You're a mom with a son to protect. And you're the only person I've got left in my life."

I tried to hold my stoic facade together until Beatrice decided whether I'd given the most inspirational speech she'd ever heard or the craziest. She closed the gap between us in two strides and wrapped her arms around me and I found myself comforting the woman who had threatened to kill me but had also saved me.

"So, now what?" Beatrice asked as she slowly pulled back and pretended that she hadn't just hugged me.

"I don't know," I said. "But I'm sure we'll figure something out."

CHAPTER FORTY-TWO

LIVE. LIE. REPEAT.

*"The British blockade is holding, but I have bought passage aboard a Dutch ship
bound for New Orleans. If the winds hold, we will make it there in time."*

"So, do you two know what you're having?" the waiter said as he set down our glasses of whiskey, one with ice and one neat.

"I'll have the caprese salad to start and then the sea bass for my main," I said, handing back the paper-thin menu.

"Same," said Duncan, as if he couldn't be bothered to give the meal anything more than the minimum amount of attention.

The waiter nodded and shuffled away, leaving us to our drinks and our awkward silence. I finally broke it by clinking my glass against the other one, which had remained on the table, before taking a sip of the cold spirit.

"Ahem," I said, bringing his attention back to the glass, which he reluctantly took a sip of.

"Look, Dunc, I'm sorry. About standing you up in Paris. About avoiding your calls the last month. About not giving this relationship the attention it deserved. About taking you for gran-"

"Enough," he said. "I didn't ask you here to dinner just to hear this pathetic groveling, Jen. I at least owed you the courtesy of a face-to-face breakup after all we've been through."

"I see. So it's really over."

"Did you really think otherwise?"

"No," I said. "I didn't. I'm not that dumb. I just thought that after what you had said in Miami that there was still a tiny chance tha-"

"Whatever chance of us staying together evaporated after you couldn't even be bothered to pick up the phone and call me. What was I supposed to think?"

"You're right. About everything. I should have called you right whe-"

Duncan's face suddenly froze and I felt a wave of relief wash over me. I didn't know how much longer I could keep up the groveling, but I was running out of ways to say I was sorry.

The scheme had been Beatrice's idea when I told her about the dinner. I was reluctant at first after the fiasco with Lisa and Stacy, but she had assured me that if I used her original short-term serum, I wouldn't run the risk of another colossal mind wipe. Still, I had reservations. What was the point of confirming my worst suspicions about Duncan if we were just going to break up anyway?

"Because," Beatrice had said. "You deserve the truth and this is the only way he'll give it to you."

So I had shown up 20 minutes early to dinner, ordered us both drinks at the bar, and slid the small ice cube containing a single drop of memory serum inside.

"Don't hold back," Beatrice had said. "Every suspicion you've ever had, every missed phone call, every half-baked excuse, call him out on it. If he doesn't give in at first, keep repeating until he does."

"OK," I had said. "But … I mean, he did say he wanted to marry me. There must be something there."

"Do you really think he wanted you to say yes?"

"I … I don't know."

"Then find out."

Those words echoed in my head while the serum removed all trace of our conversation from Duncan's memory. As his unblinking eyes stared off into space, I took advantage of his 60-second incapacitation to let free another drop of serum into the whiskey with the vial I had concealed in the palm of my hand.

"Ahem," I said, bringing Duncan's attention to the glass as he came to, and he, again, reluctantly took a small sip of the drugged whiskey.

I played out the conversation the exact same way, except instead of pretending to be resigned to the break-up, I tried a different tact.

"Did you really think otherwise?" Duncan said again.

"Yes," I said. "Because I believe in second chances and I know you do too. That's why I want to move to Hong Kong. To be with you. To try again."

Duncan smirked and then shook his head.

"Too little, too late. Because I'm moving back to New York. And now that we're no longer together, Jeff is giving me a more active role in overseeing our RPGLab investment. So I'll be there at tomorrow's run-thro-"

The serum kicked in again and I re-upped the dose before trying to quickly process what I'd just learned. So instead of exiting my life, Duncan was invading my city and my job.

"Ahem," I said for a third time and Duncan again took a small sip of the whiskey.

This time, I went on the offensive.

"Who was she?" I asked

"What are you talking about?"

"You drunk dialed me one night last fall. Well, it was night time for you, for me it was one in the afternoon. I picked up and heard you laughing with some woman. Who was she?"

Duncan shifted his eyes around the room before grabbing his glass to take another sip of whiskey, but I folded my hands over his and made him look me in the eyes.

"What? I don't know what you thought you heard Jen, but I was probably out at a bar with some potential clients. I don't think you realize how much of our deal flow is based on schmoozing. It's how we came across your company."

"I guess I was wrong."

I treaded water until the serum activated again. Then I repeated the last loop to see if Duncan would tell the same story a second time.

"When did you imagine this happened?" Duncan asked.

"November."

"So six months ago? If you thought I was cheating on you this whole time, why'd you wait this long to confront me? No, I think this whole thing is you trying to make me the bad guy so you can let yourself off the hook."

"You're right. I don't need to feel bad about not going to Paris because you've been cheating on me this whole time."

"You know, what Jen? Fuc-"

I replayed the conversation six more times, and although each time Duncan reacted slightly differently to my accusations, he never broke down completely and gave me a name. And without that, I was just a soon-to-be ex-girlfriend with a huge paranoid streak.

As I began the ninth go around, the waiter appeared in my peripheral vision, but I waved him away. The last thing I needed right now was for the steady state to be upset by two little cups of gazpacho.

But on second thought, maybe a little chaos was just what this time loop needed.

"Are you going to say anything or are you going to put this all on me?" Duncan finally said after a minute or two had passed without him having taken a sip of whiskey. "I'm not the one who fucked everything up."

"That's true. You're not the one who was sleeping around on the side this whole time. My bad…"

Duncan nearly did a spit take after I dropped that nuke and I worried for a second that the serum wouldn't take this time around, but I pressed on.

"His name is Garrett. He's married with a kid. I feel sorry for the wife, but if she can't please her husband, not my problem. You know?"

"No, I don't. Listen, if you just came here tonight to rub my face in your unfaithfulness then-"

"I didn't. Frankly, I had hoped we could both clear the air here tonight and part on equal footing, but if you're going to insist on claiming that you never strayed, then I guess I have no choice but to believe you."

"You can believe me because it's true."

I was running out of time before the serum kicked in again and still Duncan's cold-blooded front would not fall, so I went for the hail mary.

"Garrett said you would say that. Said you would hold out until the bitter end before admitting it. But I'll have to tell him later that he was wrong."

"You're something else, you know that? I don't know what the hell happened to you, but it's like you're a completely different person.

Seeing as how you're so eager to jump back into his bed, why don't you just get out of here?"

"I will, but give me a name, Dunc. I laid all my cards on the table. It's time you did the same."

"Fine. Her name is Laura. She works for one of our portfolio companies in Shanghai. And fuck you, by the way, and Garrett."

I smiled.

"There is no Garrett."

Duncan opened his mouth to say something but then the serum kicked in, returning the conversation to the beginning of the night once again. But I now had a game-changing arrow in my quiver. As my fake infidelity was wiped clean from Duncan's mind, I added another serum drop into his nearly-empty whiskey and waited to nock the arrow and let it fly.

Except that moment never came, because no sooner did Duncan come to than my phone did as well.

"911," the text from Greg read. That meant all hands on deck. Even if those hands had been out sick for the last week, I was still expected to get my butt into the office and help out any way I could.

I clinked my glass against his one more time and downed the rest of my whiskey, and he followed suit.

"Well, this has been great, Dunc, but I've got a work emergency to attend to. See you tomorrow."

"Wait, what? How do you know that?"

Duncan looked at me strangely, trying to process why his whiskey glass emptied so easily and why I knew he was going to be at the run-through. I kicked myself for being careless and started stumbling out an explanation but then realized I didn't need one.

"You know what," I said, "on second thought, forget I was here."

And he did.

———————

"**M**ake the call."

I held the phone to my ear as I waited for Beatrice to respond.

"Do you know what time it is?" she said in between yawns.

"It's 5:30 a.m. and I've been stuck staring at a computer monitor for the last seven hours and I just came off of half a speed buff trying to fix some crappy coding my co-workers saddled me with."

"Right, so why don't you make the call, since you were already up?"

"Because," I said, popping a quarter of my last vitality buff into my mouth, "like you said, you're a known quantity to the Guild."

"Fine. I'll call you back."

She hung up and I felt the revitalization wash over me again.

It had been a maddening all-nighter of pointless tedium up until a few hours ago. I had arrived at the office within 20 minutes of the 911 text only to be put to the extremely important task of checking to see if our code was properly commented. Which, of course, would be the absolute last thing that Jeff and Duncan would either care about or want to see.

I half, no, fully-suspected that the other devs had convinced my boss to call me in because they were annoyed that I'd been excused from fine-tuning the VC branch of the main build the last three weeks. And it certainly hadn't helped that on top of that, I'd been calling out "sick" all week.

But then at 3:30 I came across a potentially catastrophic error.

"Umm, guys?" I had said to the devs who were working on the other side of the room.

"Not now!" Greg had called back. "We're finishing something. 30 minutes til we compile the final build."

Shit.

The error was a relatively simple one to fix. Somewhere along the way, the run-through boss's signature move had been changed to an overpowered melee attack that would kill everyone in one hit, rather than a spell that slowly drained one player's hit points while at the same time spreading like a virus to the nearby players, as we had intended.

The only problem was that the original code for the spell was somehow missing from this build. So I had scrambled over to my regular workstation to look through the main codebase only to find it in deep hibernation because of my prolonged absence.

Cursing under my breath, I had trudged back over to the other computer and reluctantly pulled out the speed buff. Rewriting the code from scratch after biting off half of the lilac square had taken a few seconds in real-time, even with my overclocked brain offering up dozens of different options for every decision branch.

But then I had hit a roadblock when I reopened the game to play-test the fix. While my body and mind had gone into hyperdrive, the game was still running at normal speed and so my avatar slowly trudged across the screen as if he were stuck in molasses.

Fortunately, the solution had been obvious and after cranking up the game speed to 50x, my character's movements had soon matched my relative speed. I soon confirmed that my fix had worked and so I closed the play-test window with a satisfying click and waited for my mind and body to decelerate.

But staring at the code as the seconds ticked off at a glacial pace had made me antsy, so I couldn't resist combing through the codebase making tiny tweaks where I could. Nothing major that anyone would really notice at the run-through, but it would end up saving me a week's worth of work on the main build once I was in back in the office.

I had thought about telling one of the other devs how close we had come to screwing up the entire run-through but decided to hold my tongue for now. If anyone tried to give me crap in the next few weeks, I could point to the change control logs and show how I had saved everyone's ass.

My phone rang and I saw Beatrice's number appear on the screen.

"What happened?" I asked.

"Called the number and it went straight to voicemail. I hung up and then a minute later got a call back from a restricted number."

"Who was it?"

"Nobody, it was just a recorded message with an address and a time. 1218 Avenue of the Americas. 42nd floor. 2:30 p.m."

"2:30? But the run-through starts at 11."

"And that's my problem because?"

"Because I'm not going to be done by then. It's going to take at least three hours, maybe more, depending on how stable the current build is."

"Fascinating. I'll just call the Guild back and ask them if we could push the summons until 4. I'm sure it's fine, they're a very understanding organization."

"Not funny. I'm going to get fired if I duck out early."

"So? Duncan was probably going to get you fired soon anyway. At least now you can leave on your own terms."

"You know what? You're right. Why even stay for the run-through? I may as well march down to my boss's office and leave my resignation let-"

"I'm going back to sleep. See you at 2:20 outside the building."

A CERTAIN SET OF SKILLS

*"The voyage has given me time to think. Maybe too much time.
I always forget how sentimental I get before the end."*

So as you can see, we've got our party assembled here at the outskirts of Haven's Forge. This will be one of the five main cities that players will explore once they get past the first few hours of the game. What's different about *Hero's Bane* is that these cities are huge. We're talking millions of different NPCs you can talk to, which makes-"

John Hammond, our founder, droned on about the game's many radical departures from traditional MMORPGs, before introducing each of the devs and their respective handles who would be participating in the run-through.

"And you both know Jen. She's playing as a paladin, Laura_X-23."

I had my avatar do its class-specific dance on the screen at the front of the conference room and suppressed a smile as Duncan winced at the mention of my handle. He was probably convincing himself that it was only a coincidence, that it must be the name of some character from a dorky comic book that I'd read as a kid. Which was true, but I enjoyed seeing him stew.

"As our bold group of adventurers heads into the mountains that surround Haven's Forge, you'll get to see some of the-"

We fought our way up the mountain pass for the next hour before finally reaching the entrance to the dungeon, a set of stone doors carved into the mountainside.

"Normally it would take the player another four hours to locate the key, but we've had a bit of fun for the run-through. Jen, if you don't mind."

I nodded and typed "Friend" into the chat window, and the digital doors opened inward. Jeff and Duncan seemed unfazed by the easter egg we had spent weeks debating whether to include, and John tried to explain the reference before giving up and moving on.

The dungeon was immense and it was another hour and a half before the five of us had managed to get to the antechamber next to where the final boss of the run-through, Rakkah the Soul-Weaver awaited.

"Ok guys," said Greg, "I'll run in first, use Intimidating Shout to kinda scatter Rakkah's minions, and then Anthony you come in and drop your Shout too so we can keep them scattered and not fight too many of them. If things get hairy, Jen, you'll cast Divine Intervention on Frank, and then he can cast-"

"Greg," I said politely, not wanting to make my co-worker look like an idiot in front of Hammond, "if I do that, then Frank won't be able to cast *anything*."

"Oh. Right. Fine. Jen, just make sure you're healing us throughout so that-"

I tuned out the rest of the discussion and glanced at my watch. It was almost 1 and if we cleared out this boss in 15 minutes, even with the debrief after, I still would have about 40 minutes to head uptown to meet Beatrice.

Our plan seemed to be working fine. Rakkah waited off in the corner as he was programmed to do, letting his minions try to take us down. They were unsuccessful, as video game minions so often are, and once there were only a few left, the big boss rumbled forward on his four enormous legs and began casting his signature attack.

"Now, we've improved the lag compensation in the engine to handle even the most intense graphics, like our friend Rakkah here. So, Bill, could you please crank up the lag?"

One of the devs in the corner who wasn't playing nodded and my eyes went wide.

In my speed-addled state this morning, I had completely bypassed testing for lag, which would have taken too many real-time minutes to finish before the compile deadline. Plus I was almost positive that my one little change wouldn't be affected by lag anyway.

Spoiler alert: it was.

Rakkah's movements suddenly became stiff and blocky and my own avatar now moved across the screen as if I was suddenly playing on a dial-up connection.

"What's going on?" Greg typed in the chat that only the players could see. "This never happened before. Ever since we changed the attack to an insta-kill."

Shit.

It was now crystal clear that the error I had fixed was in fact put there by design to pass the lag simulation they knew Hammond was going to run. As the game continued to hang, the players all glanced at each and then at Hammond, imploring him to smooth over the situation. But Hammond just sat there watching the screen in silence, his perfectly choreographed script going up in flames.

That's when I took matters into my own hands and silently activated the locket around my avatar's virtual neck, which pulled our entire party into a shimmering portal just as Rakkah's attack landed on Greg.

"What … what happened?" typed Anthony into the group chat.

"I got our asses out of there is what," I responded.

We emerged from the portal into the middle of a bustling square in Haven's Forge full of NPCs milling about their business.

"Shit, I'm dying!" typed Greg. His health was slowly draining down to zero and I cast Holy Light on him to stem the tide. But the hit points that been replenished were quickly consumed by Rakkah's lingering spell and in a matter of seconds, Greg's avatar collapsed onto the ground.

Anthony was next, the spell having begun its viral spread to nearby players, and soon our entire party and the surrounding NPCs were all infected. We respawned on the spot, only to be reinfected by the NPCs, who couldn't die and therefore were free to spread the spell to us over and over again.

"Err, why don't we take our lunch break now while we sort this out?" Hammond finally interjected as he ushered Jeff and Duncan out of the room before they could say something.

The door closed behind the three of them and I slumped back in my chair. It would only be a matter of time before someone looked at the logs from this morning and saw that-

"I figured it out!" said Bill. "Someone changed Rakkah's attack back to the virus spell."

"Perfect," said Greg. "So we'll just change it back and then wait five hours until the whole fucking thing compiles again! Who changed it?"

I didn't wait for Bill to state the obvious, so I fell on my sword.

"I did. Last night. Thought it was a mistake, there were no comments in the code and I-"

"Fan-fucking-tastic, Jen," said Anthony. "Bad enough that you decided to call out sick while we've been busting our asses so we can impress your boyfriend, but in the five minutes you were here, you managed to completely screw up everything!"

"I didn't mean to … I … I can fix it."

"You will do no such thing," said Greg, who glared at me while taking up a seat next to Bill. "You've done enough. We'll take care of it, somehow."

The devs continued to squabble with each other while the minutes ticked away. Soon Hammond would be back with Jeff and Duncan, and my job, relationship, and partnership with Beatrice would be gone within the hour. It was almost a relief that Lisa and Stacy had no idea who I was, as it was one less set of people to disappoint.

"I know!" said Greg "We just reset and then-"

"No, that won't get rid of the virus," Bill responded. "You'll just die again. And again. And again."

My eyes perked up at the mention of virus. If they wouldn't let me touch the code base, then I would just force my way in.

I pulled out the untouched focus buff from my bag along with the remaining piece of the speed buff. The former was green and a putrid smell hit my nostrils as I tore it in half. Beatrice's earlier warning echoed in my head, but I ignored it and smushed the two halves together before popping the multi-colored concoction into my mouth.

The room slowed to a crawl and I went to work. But where before I had seen thousands of possibilities arrayed before me, here only one path presented itself and my mind had no choice but to follow it. The lines of code flew onto the screen from my fingertips like a virtuoso constructing her masterwork. My virus would hook itself into our procedural generation engine and flood the city with undead ghouls who by definition could not be infected with Rakkah's curse. This would provide the necessary buffer for our party to run away, like King Arthur away from the French.

In only a minute of real-time, the thousand-line virus was finished and I sent it off into the build to work its magic. After another 10 seconds, I could see the ghouls beginning to appear as red dots on the overworld map, my coworkers still obliviously arguing with each other.

I glanced at my watch. It was 1:40 and that meant that I could still make it uptown in time. So I scratched a message on a Post-It note, stuck it on top of Greg's keyboard, and walked out of the conference room just as Hammond was escorting Duncan and Jeff back in. They couldn't see me of course, the speed buff still working its alchemy. Later I would wish that I had doubled-over Duncan with a punch to the gut, but the focus buff had other ideas.

Such as how we were going to survive the summons.

We had plenty of individual pieces to bargain with, but on their own, they wouldn't be enough to stem the Guild's wrath. But just like with the virus, my brain pieced together a plan and it flowed effortlessly from my head into an essay-length text to Beatrice.

The mid-day sun hit my eyes and I recoiled from the light. Throngs of people were out and about on their lunch hours, and I weaved through them with ease until I reached the street and climbed into an empty cab.

"48th and Sixth," I yelled to the startled driver. It was then that the focus buff gave me one final parting gift and I scrambled to write down the pearl of wisdom before my brain conked out like an overclocked processor. But it slipped from my fingers as time resumed its normal flow around me and I collapsed into unconsciousness.

———————

"You brought everything?" I asked, my footsteps clacking against the floor of the marble lobby as I trailed behind Beatrice, who was carrying a large cardboard box.

"Yes," said Beatrice, "although I'm still not convinced this is the right play."

"Me neither, but when I was hopped up on the buffs, it all made sense. At least I think it did. The last 30 minutes are pretty foggy in my mind."

"Great," said Beatrice.

The cab driver was nonplussed to find me passed out when we had arrived, but fortunately, Beatrice had been waiting there to retrieve me. As she pulled me from the car, she had forced the remaining portion of the vitality buff into my mouth as instructed, but that had barely made a dent in the pounding headache I was currently experiencing.

"You able to find out whose office we're going to?" I asked as we gave fake IDs to the guard at the security desk, who lets us pass through the turnstile with a nod.

"Nope, nothing. Either for the 42nd floor or any of the five floors above and below it."

"Well, that's reassuring."

The elevator door opened and we walked inside. Beatrice's eyes darted around the empty cab until she spotted something in the back left corner.

"Stand under there and activate the glamour," she said.

"What?"

"The camera is up there. So stand under it so you won't be seen."

"Ah. Right. But why the glamour?"

"Because I'm trying to protect you, dummy," said Beatrice. "The Guild only knows your handle, not your face."

"Don't they though?" I asked, as I moved to the corner and rubbed the stone. "Those three at the Council meeting probably told them."

"The Guild doesn't care about the Council. Bunch of self-important idiots. They were lucky they got to help out at all."

"Oh. Gilbert then, he saw us in the cave that night," Jade's voice said.

"I'm not convinced that it was him. It's been bugging me this whole week, but I can't quite put my finger on it."

"I guess we'll find out soon enough."

The elevator doors slowly opened on the 42nd floor and we waited in trepidation to see what lay beyond.

It was a hallway.

It had beige walls, carpeting that was once the same shade of beige as the walls, and off in the distance, what appeared to be a beige-colored door.

"No welcome wagon?" I said, stepping out of the elevator.

"Guess not," said Beatrice.

I led the way toward the lone door at the end of the hallway, expecting at any moment that Gilbert or the hooded figure from Inwood or some other sinister character was going to come bursting through. But we traversed the hallway without incident, and I turned the knob slowly and opened the door outward to reveal the top of a dimly-lit staircase.

"Huh," said Beatrice, peering down the stairwell. "Now we know why there's no record of anyone on this floor. What a waste of prime Manhattan real estate."

I helped Beatrice carry the box down the stairs, where another beige door awaited us at the bottom. Beyond it was another beige hallway, this one only a few feet long capped by yet another door. We walked forward and Beatrice nodded at me.

My heart pounded in my chest like a boxer thumping a punching bag as I opened the door and stepped through the precipice into a sun-drenched room with floor-to-ceiling windows and a massive wooden table at the center.

A black-haired woman stood with her back to us at the far end of the table and after a few seconds, she slowly turned around.

"Good afternoon, ladies," said Dalia de Wyck.

BEHIND
THE CURTAIN

"Treaty negotiations are going smoothly. There should be an agreement within a fortnight. Or so I hear. It will take some time, however, for the news to reach anyone other than me."

"Y-you!" I stammered before Beatrice nudged me in the ribs.

"Shhh," she said as she set the box down on the table and waited for Dalia de Wyck to respond.

"Hmm," said Dalia, who was holding a crystal tumbler with some sort of brown liquid at the bottom. "Why are there only two of you?"

"I'm sorry," said Beatrice. "Are we in the right place?"

Dalia took a sip from the glass before taking a seat in the head chair.

"Can't hear you so well. This table is ridiculously large. I'm not sure why I ever bought it. Can you come up here and take a seat?"

I looked at Beatrice for her lead, but she just shrugged her shoulders slightly and picked up the box. The far side of the room sported a large flatscreen television mounted on the wall, an old-fashioned bar cart, and two more doors, which would complicate any escape route that way, and I doubted that the elevator the floor above us would answer our call.

So we walked the length of the table slowly and my thoughts raced in 40 different directions, none of them helpful, until we reached the second and third chairs away from Dalia and sat.

"Much better," she said. Her black hair streaked with strands of silver and brown, which fell down past her shoulders. She was wearing a bright red dress that had the same intricate embroidery as the dress from the Met lecture. Up close, I could see that it depicted a magnificent tree.

"Now, before we go any further, you," she turned her eyes at me, "seem to have an idea of who I am, but I think some formal introductions are in order. I am Dalia de Wyck, creative director of Thera DeWitt, but more importantly for our purposes, the 13th chairman of the Guild."

"Wait, *you're* the head of the Guild?" I said, incredulously.

Dalia smiled.

"You were expecting a wrinkled old geezer with a monocle? Or a maybe a slightly younger but taller man who dyes his hair gray to look more distinguished?"

"Well, no," I replied, "but–"

"You must be the famed Beatrice Taylor née Stallard," said Dalia, turning her attention away from me. "I've heard a lot about you. Mostly good. Although it's my understanding that you were the one responsible for the demise of Winston."

"That's because you sent him to kill me," she said calmly. "And I didn't mean to kill him."

Dalia raised an eyebrow.

"Oh? Well, in any event, you're mistaken. *I* didn't send him after you. That was all Gilbert's doing. I only heard about it afterward. We generally stay out of the murder business, whereas you seem quite drawn to it."

Another jab landed and I wondered when the dam would break and Beatrice would unleash her fury. But instead, Dalia shifted her focus back to me.

"And you, well, I'm afraid I don't really know who you are, other than Ms. Taylor's latest trainee."

"I'm Jade Peters," I said, gripping the leather armrests with my fingernails. "And I'm no trainee."

"If you say so," said Dalia. "But that leaves one person missing. Where is Francesca?"

"She's somewhere safe," said Beatrice.

"I see," said Dalia. "But where are my manners? Would you ladies care for a drink?" She gestured to the bar cart in the corner, which held crystal decanters of various shapes.

"No th-" I began before Beatrice cut me off.

"Thank you. We'll have whatever you're drinking."

"A fine choice," said Dalia, finishing her glass off. "Although I can assure you that the other bottles are not poisoned either."

She stood up from the table and returned with a decanter full of the same brown liquid that had been in her glass moments ago, along with two tumblers. Those Dalia filled, along with her own with what I assumed was whiskey and we each grabbed one with trepidation.

"To a fruitful discussion," said Dalia, raising her glass, which I now saw had a small bird etched into one of its facets. I pantomimed her gesture, as did Beatrice, and then took a sip of the liquor. It felt smooth, yet also hot against my throat, it tasted smoky but somehow also sweet, and it smelled like a thousand different memories that had come bursting out of my brain.

"What is this?" I asked, taking another sip.

"Something from the Guild's private collection," said Dalia. "At this point, we've lost track of the year it was made, but if I had to guess, it probably dates back to the early 1800s."

"And you just have it lying around here, like a bottle of supermarket whiskey?" Beatrice said incredulously.

"Of course not. I had it brought over from the Guild Hall specifically for the occasion. But let's get back to business, shall we? You were saying that Ms. Lewis is somewhere safe. When were you planning on releasing her to our custody?"

"First things first," said Beatrice. "Call off your dogs. Gilbert, the tracker, whoever else you have stalking us."

"I can assure you I don't know what you're talk-"

"And then you'll explain why you attacked us in the cave and again in the park."

Dalia stared at us as if her gaze could pierce into our minds, and my heart skipped a beat at the thought that she had acquired the apples from the old man at Hunt's Point. But after a few moments, she shook her head and let out a big sigh.

"I'm afraid you are sadly mistaken on all fronts," she said. "No one from the Guild attacked you, either in a cave or a park, and we certainly aren't 'tracking' you."

"Then why don't you tell us wh-"

Dalia held up her hand and Beatrice stopped.

"Let's just start from the beginning. You two took on a Raid last month to uncover information from a tattoo on Frankie's back, correct?"

"Yes," we said in unison.

"But what you didn't know was that you were working on behalf of our adversary, who has been trying for years to locate our Keeper."

"Frankie?" I asked.

Dalia nodded.

"And a Keeper is . . ." Beatrice chimed in.

"A protector of Guild secrets. The responsibility is passed down from parent to child, much like our Guild seats."

"So you're saying that whoever posted the Raid was trying to steal something from the Guild . . ." I said, the pieces slowly falling into place.

"Exactly. And they got you two to do their dirty work. We of course intercepted the first set of coordinates you turned in. But we didn't know if you had figured out the rest."

"So that's why Gilbert was at the Met that night," said Beatrice.

"What?" said Dalia, a tiny note of worry in her voice. "No, he wasn't. He was staking out the door in Long Island City."

"I saw him there. After we stole, err, took the door knobs," said Beatrice.

"I can assure you that wasn't him," said Dalia. "You two have a long history, perhaps you were just imagining things."

"Maybe," said Beatrice. "Or maybe you're just full of sh-"

"So," I interjected. "If Gilbert was watching the door, then he saw us enter it?"

"Yes," said Dalia. "He tried to follow but couldn't open it."

"That's because we removed the knob from the other side," said Beatrice.

"Ah," said Dalia. "That explains that mystery."

"But that doesn't explain who attacked us," I said. "If Gilbert couldn't get through the door, then how did someone attack us in the cave?"

"The lighthouse has four doors," said Beatrice. "Well, had four doors before someone burned it to the ground. They must have come through that door that still had a knob."

"So someone else has access to the waypoint," said Dalia, who finished her drink with a gulp.

"Is that what it was?" I asked.

"Yes," said Dalia. "Our Keeper is responsible for guarding the location of the waypoint and its keys. But apparently somewhere along the way, one of them strayed in their mission. Continue."

"We unlocked one of the doors with one of the knobs from the museum, passed through another portal, and ended up in a cave. Where we found this…"

I reached into the box, retrieved Rita's diary from inside, and slid it across the table. Dalia eyed it silently for a few seconds before cracking open the cover and flipping through the pages slowly.

"This diary, it has been missing for a long time."

She set it down in front of me and I picked it back up and flipped to the first page.

"Who was Rita van Asch?" I asked.

"She was the sixth chairman of the Guild. It was a particularly taxing time for the company. The Guild had splintered during the War for Independence and this," she patted the cover of the diary, "recounts some of Rita's efforts to rebuild our ranks in the war's aftermath."

"I see. Was this also hers?"

I put down the diary and pulled out the wooden box from the swamp, my eyes never leaving Dalia's. Her features strained to hold back the excitement in her eyes and she rose from her chair to walk to the box.

"And thank you for returning this. We've-"

"It's not what you think it is," I said.

"What do you mean?" said Dalia, as she opened the box and pulled out one page of parchment with a small paragraph of writing. "This is-"

"The only page that was in the box," said Beatrice. "Written in Rita's handwriting. We were hoping you could help us make sense of it."

Dalia poured over the front and back of the page as if the rest of the Compendium would magically unfold itself from within the paper.

"Where did you get this?" she said slowly.

"We think you well know where we got it," said Beatrice. "Seeing as how one of your thugs tried to attack us immediately after we found it."

"Again, I don't know what you're talking about. There's no one from the Guild following you or tracking you or whatever you may think is happening. You're attaching a level of importance to yourself, Ms. Taylor, that is not in tune with reality. So now that we've established that, why don't you tell me what the beak of an extinct bird has to do with our present situation."

"It's Frankie," I said slowly.

"What about her?"

"She's . . . I . . . I turned her to stone."

Dalia's hands suddenly strained against the table and I was afraid that she was somehow going to crack through the wood. But after a few moments, she eased back and sat down.

"You turned her to stone," said Dalia, repeating my words back to me as if I was a child telling an obvious lie about why the cookie jar was empty. "Explain."

I nodded and recounted the rest of our misadventure in the cave. Dalia's eyes perked up at the mention of the missing box but she let me continued uninterrupted and I described how we had been rendered unconscious and had woken up to find a bound Frankie lying on the cave floor, the box gone. I clamped down my emotions as I narrated our escape, neglecting to mention Beatrice's ring, and my decision in the fire to stab Frankie with the Medoblad, rather than let her burn to death. The ordeal finished, I picked up my glass and relieved it of the rest of its contents.

"A fine tale, to be sure," said Dalia. "But not the truth."

"What do you mean?" I asked, wondering if she had picked up on my strategic omissions.

"You expect me to believe that hoi polloi like you have one of the legendary Relics."

"We don't need you to believe anything," said Beatrice. "Because, yes, I am the Keeper of the Medoblad."

"The Keeper of the Medoblad?" Dalia let out a chuckle and I sensed this meeting was taking a course from which we would not be able to correct. "Did you happen to bring that Relic with you today?"

"Why would I do that?" asked Beatrice. "So you can just take it from me?"

"How convenient," said Dalia. "But yes, I would have. Regardless, if you actually possessed the Blad, like you claim, we wouldn't be in this mess to begin with."

"What do you me—"

"This audience has gone on long enough. You two have 24 hours to return Frankie to me, in whatever state she's currently in, along with the Medoblad. We'll settle your debt to the Guild then."

"You can have the girl," said Beatrice. "But you're daft if you think I'm giving you the Medoblad."

"I see," said Dalia. "So be it. But before you go, let me leave you with a history lesson. Have you heard of *Curtana, the Sword of Mercy?*"

"Can't say that I have," said Beatrice.

"The blade itself dates back to the time of Tristan. Yes, that Tristan. It's also one of the swords used in the coronation of a new British monarch. Well, it was, until it went missing in the early 1600s and had to be remade by the London Worshipful Company of Cutlers. I'll leave you to ponder who took it and whether you think you're capable of succeeding where the British royal family failed."

We stood up and Beatrice began putting the book and wooden box away when Dalia started shaking her head.

"What are you doing?"

"We're leaving," Beatrice replied curtly. "What does it lo-"

"No, I meant with those," Dalia said, pointing to the trove we had brought. "Those are Guild property. So you'll be leaving them here, if you don't mind."

Beatrice clutched the diary against her chest and I looked back and forth between the two of them, wanting more than anything to duck under the table. The battle of wills continued for another minute before Beatrice finally relented and put the book back down on the table.

"Fine," she said, stacking the diary on top of the wooden box.

"Ahem," said Dalia. "I believe you're forgetting something."

"What is that?" asked Beatrice.

"That ring, below your wedding band, it's ours too."

Beatrice opened her mouth to say something but thought better of it and silently removed her wedding band and then the last memory ring, which she plunked down on the table.

"Anything else?" said Beatrice, the anger in her voice rising. "Would you like my fir-"

I grabbed her hand and she stopped.

"Let's just get out of here," I whispered.

"It's been a pleasure, ladies," said Dalia. "We'll be in touch about tomorrow. You can see yourselves out."

STALKING HORSE

"More often than not, it is the small things that end up causing the biggest of impacts. For instance, I was recently the guest of the Villeré family, and before I departed, I made sure to unlock a particular window in the back of the home. Today, the young scion arrived at General Jackson's encampment, having escaped from the British out that same window. Jackson departed soon afterward to take the fight to the enemy."

"**W**ill you turn that stupid thing off?" Beatrice scowled at me as we walked into a coffee shop in Times Square and found the lone empty table near the back.

"What?" I said. "How do you expect me to change back when there's all these peo-"

"We're in the middle of a crowded hellhole within another crowded hellhole. No one is giving us a second glance."

"Fine," I said, rubbing the stone with one hand as I attempted to cover my head with the other. I felt the glamour melt away once again. "It was your idea in the first place to wear it."

"And your point is?"

"I don't why you're so–"

"Can we just sit here for a minute without launching into another therapy session?"

"Fine," I said. "I'll go get us some coffee."

I returned a few minutes later with two steaming cups of sludge doused with too much cream and sugar and set them down on the table. Beatrice eyed them with suspicion before taking a sip and nearly spitting it back out.

"What did you put in here?" she asked, her features recoiling. "It tastes like burnt trash."

I took a sampling myself and had nearly the same reaction. "With just a hint of tart. It must be because of that whiskey she gave us. Should have stuck with water."

"What we should have stuck with was the original plan, which was silence. Instead, you let her take almost everything of Rita's that we have."

"Exactly," I said. "You brought the page from the 1777 diary like I asked?"

"Yes," said Beatrice. "And kept it stowed in my pocket, also like you asked. But I don't see the . . . oh. Very clever. This page has the memory ink, which used to be the ring, which is still linked to both the other ring and the memory ink in the other diary, both of which Dalia now has on her person."

I smiled.

"But insane," she continued. "So now we're just going to follow Dalia around and hope something fruitful comes about? You're not exactly James Bond. What if she spots us?"

"She won't. Because thanks to you, she still has no idea what

I look like. And she won't spot you, because you're not coming with me."

"This just keeps getting better and better. Since you seem to have everything figured out to a T, what shall I do, oh wise one?"

"You're going to go find that gold token."

It was 3 a.m. and the lone waitress in the 24-hour diner on Madison Avenue where I was camped out was reluctantly refilling my mug with decaf coffee for the umpteenth time. I gave her a sheepish smile and promised her a big tip come morning and she walked away, muttering to herself. The coffee tasted like charred toast but it was oddly soothing in a weird sort of way. As I lifted the cup up to my mouth, I felt the familiar gentle pull of the parchment paper on my arm.

It had been a little too easy to trail Dalia with my makeshift compass. She had emerged from the hulking office building sometime around 5 and into a black sedan. This I had known when the diary page had started gently trying to pull itself free from under my sleeve. Fortunately, I had been waiting next to a bikeshare stand and quickly grabbed a red-painted bike and began my pursuit up Sixth Avenue.

Her car eventually stopped outside a tony boutique and I hung back a block as I saw Dalia open the door and walk into the store. Several minutes later, she had exited carrying several small bags and the car had resumed its journey northward until it turned west and stopped in front of an even tonier apartment building, just a stone's throw from the Met.

So began three hours of circling the building, waiting to see if Dalia would show herself again and lead me to someplace interesting. But by 10, I was beginning to suspect that she had called it in for the night and I had debated whether to continue my surveillance or go home and come back at 6.

I had chosen the former.

The foot traffic on the surrounding streets had petered out around midnight, which is when I had taken refuge in the diner. My dinner with Duncan and even the run-through had seemed like a lifetime ago and I had so far resisted the urge to open my work email, where no doubt news of my firing had been delivered. Maybe Duncan had mercifully ended our relationship electronically too and then I wouldn't have to deal with that part of my life at all.

This had all seemed like a great idea when I was in the throes of the buffs. My mind had neatly laid everything out in front of me and it had all made so much sense then. But now, as I reread what I had written, the words felt like they had been the product of someone else entirely and I was just following orders.

The whole exercise just seemed to be long on cleverness and desperation, but short on usefulness. If I picked up Dalia's trail again tomorrow morning, then what? She was going to lead me right to the cure to the stone curse? And I wasn't optimistic at Beatrice's chances of finding the gold token based only on my drug-induced hunch.

Something from the meeting also still gnawed at me. Why was Dalia so insistent that we didn't have the Medoblad? I set my brain to the puzzle, but found that it was in no mood for any further mental exertion, so I leaned my head back against the booth to rest just for a second.

And then it was morning and my arm began to twitch.

I jumped up from the booth, threw a bunch of uncounted bills on the table, and ran out the door into the pouring rain. The cold wind whipped through me, and I ran up the block to take refuge under an awning and gather my bearings. The bike dock was opposite me on the east side of Madison, so I dashed across traffic and quickly mounted my two-wheeled steed. Back on Dalia's block, I spotted the black car from yesterday and the chase was on again.

The rain beat down on me as I furiously tried to keep up with the sedan's crisscrossing path downtown. Finally, it turned west onto 51st Street and pulled into a parking garage mid-block. I stowed the bike and continued on foot, watching from afar as Dalia walked up the ramp from the garage with a big red umbrella. The tension on my arm threatened to cut off my circulation, but I trailed after her nevertheless.

She veered off the sidewalk and walked under a wooden trellis, which led to one of the most peculiar things I had seen during my years living in Manhattan. Up a short flight of stairs was a gorgeous little pocket park, with rows of trees and potted plants creating a veritable forest in the middle of midtown. At the back was an enormous waterfall cascading down a wall of stone, which looked ominous in the rain. My arm beckoned me further but I retreated back out and across the street, lest Dalia spot me.

I spent the next 20 minutes battling both the rain and the cheap umbrella I had purchased from one of the street vendors that always magically appeared as soon as the first drops began to fall. Finally, my arm jerked forward again. I waited for Dalia's red umbrella to appear from the park, but then my arm shifted in the opposite direction and then back again as a man with slicked-back hair in a blue blazer holding a green umbrella in one hand and carrying one of Dalia's bags in the other crossed under the trellis and began walking west.

Was this the famed Gilbert that had dogged our steps for so long? I quickly snapped a picture and sent it to Beatrice to confirm while my arm continued its schizophrenic movement. It was then that I realized what was happening: Dalia had split up the items she had taken from us.

I glanced across to the park and a foolish thought entered my head. That foolish thought became action as I crossed the street and entered the park. It was practically empty, the rain likely driving everyone indoors, but of Dalia and her red umbrella, I saw no sign. The tension on my paper compass faded to a dull twitch the further I went into the park and I doubled-back to the street. How had I missed her?

The man in the blue blazer, meanwhile, had not gotten very far, so I gave chase. He descended into the subway at Lexington and down the long escalator to the E/M platform. As I slowly followed behind him, two trains entered the station, one heading to Queens and one heading downtown. I tried to break through the barricade of the unmoving people in front of me, but they held firm, even as we stepped onto the platform.

As throngs of commuters jostled against me in their rush to get to either train, the glamour stone sprung free from under my shirt, along with my mother's locket, and I foolishly grabbed both of them with my bare hand, only to feel the ripple of Jade wash over me. But I didn't have time to worry about the consequences of my public transformation, as the doors-closing chimes rang in stereo. I held my arm out in front of me, felt it drift to the right, and quickly pushed myself into the train car and into a woman with blonde hair, who had entered a step ahead of me.

"So sorry," I said to the woman, who was locked arm-in-arm with an older man with a very pronounced slouch, but when she turned around, I froze dead in my tracks, as Eva's green eyes met mine.

CHAPTER FORTY-SIX

BACKDOOR

"The treaty has been signed. I could tell the British and they may give up their campaign and sail home. I could tell Jackson and he may throw himself at their mercy. Or I could tell no one."

"Watch where you're going," Eva said, a scowl on her face.

"S-sorry," I said again.

Eva considered me for a few seconds as I held my breath, wondering if she could see through the glamour somehow. But then she just shook her head and led the man further into the car. I retreated to the other end but peered through the crowd, trying to get a glimpse of the man in the blue blazer, but the train was packed with rush-hour commuters. Finally, after three more stops, the mass of people had diminished and my jaw dropped at what I saw.

The old man on Eva's arm was none other than her dad, Steve. It had only been a year since I met him that night in the church base-ment, but he looked as if he had aged 20. His hair was grayed at the roots, his eyes were sunken, and he sat with a pronounced hunch.

I turned away quickly and located the man with the blue blazer on the opposite bench. It couldn't be a coincidence that the three of them were here on the same train, in the same subway car, sitting a few feet away from each other. And I had a sinking feeling that this clandestine meet-up had something to do with me.

At 14th Street, the car emptied further before a new glut of people spilled inward, and I was jostled away from my spying post. When I recalibrated myself, I saw that the man was now sitting next to Eva, his eyes staring down at the floor. I brought my phone out for more reconnaissance only to see a text from Beatrice.

"its him," it read and I felt my pulse quicken.

"Hes sitting next to polly on subway. With her dad. Im in pursuit," I wrote back, but the message bounced.

I looked back at the man I now knew was Gilbert and I felt a chill ripple through me. It was as Beatrice had described him. Were it not for the trendy blue blazer he wore, there wouldn't be anything remarkable about him. But I had heard what he was capable of, how he had stalked, tracked, and tried to murder Beatrice for reasons that were still unclear to me. Not to mention attacking us a few weeks ago. If Polly was in league with him now, then we were truly screwed.

The train reached the next station and I quickly sent my message again and put my phone away before I could see if it went through. The same chaos of exit and entry repeated itself, and when things settled down again, I saw Gilbert's hand extending down under the subway bench. He still didn't meet Eva's gaze and neither did she look at him, but then she mouthed something softly and he nodded.

It took me a minute to realize what she had said, and when I did, it felt as if my stomach had fallen into a gaping hole.

I steeled my nerves and waited for the next stop. When the doors finally opened, I pushed through the incoming crowds, my phone in hand, and frantically texted Beatrice.

"Weve been betrayed."

"W̶e're fucked," said Beatrice when I met her half an hour later on a park bench in Washington Square Park. The morning rush was at its tail end, but it was still early for the NYU students, who had just emerged from their dorms and were crisscrossing the park on their way to class.

"You said that last week," I replied.

"Was it only last week? God, it seems like it was months ago. But it doesn't make it any less true. And just when I thought we had the upper hand on them."

"What do you mean?" I asked. "You mean…"

"Yes," said Beatrice, half-smiling. "I found it. The gold token that Rita hid in that bank deposit box all those years ago."

"You mean we found it," I corrected. "If it weren't for my brai-"

"I wasn't trying to take credit, Jen. Calm down."

"Sorry," I said. "It was a long night."

"Same here."

"So now what? Please tell me you took the door knob to the island out of the office."

Beatrice shook her head no.

"Maybe we can head them off," I said. "Gilbert didn't get off the train when I did. It might take him a while to go back uptown. We could sti-"

"Walk right into the Guild's trap? No. But we can get the drop on them if we hurry."

"How?"

"Follow me," she said.

We walked across the park with a quick gait and we were soon in front of the Washington Square Arch. I started to continue through the center but Beatrice veered to the left and I followed. She stopped in front of the western pier of the Arch and I saw it: a small door set in the middle, like something out of *Alice in Wonderland.*

Beatrice reached into her pocketbook, pulled out a key ring, and approached the door. It had two locks and a deadbolt, which she first removed from the door as easily as if it were attached with plastic tape. Next, she inserted a key into the top lock and turned it, before removing it and placing the key ring back in her bag. Finally, she reached under her sweater and pulled out something that hung around her neck.

It was another key. But unlike the first one, its color was a familiar dark brown with white streaks.

"What … what is that?" I asked as Beatrice grinned.

"This," she said, inserting the key into the lower lock and turning, "is our back door."

Beatrice removed the key and nudged the door open. A familiar black expanse peeked through the crack.

"Let's go," she said. "Before someone sees us."

"I don't … how?"

"No time, just trust me."

Beatrice slid into the space between and was gone. I glanced back and forth to see if anyone had noticed our trespass, but the city's anonymity had fallen over us like the morning fog, and I knew I could delay no longer. The darkness beckoned me from the doorway and I greeted it as if it were an old friend.

The journey was over in an instant but something felt different as I emerged into the dimly lit room with the wooden floor.

It wasn't just that the glamour had activated again during transit and that Jade's freckled hands had replaced my own.

No, it was the sharp pounding in my head and the fact that Beatrice was not already in the island headquarters to greet me.

And that I had apparently forgotten to turn off our lone lamp before I had left Frankie two days ago.

And that Frankie's stone figure was propped up against the wall, free of the tarp.

And that there was a familiar man standing near the open front door, a wooden box at his feet that hadn't been in the house before.

Towers of unpacked supplies and books were still stacked throughout the house, allowing me to observe the intruder.

It was Gilbert.

But he wasn't wearing the blue blazer or slacks he had been sporting an hour ago on the subway. Instead, he was dressed in a gray t-shirt and worn blue jeans. And his hair, it was no longer perfectly coiffed and slick, but dirty and unkempt. Finally, his face was sunken and wrinkled, as if he had somehow aged 10 years.

My next step on the creaking floor betrayed my presence and I reluctantly walked out from behind the boxes to see a startled Gilbert nearly fall backward into the door.

"What … what are you doing here?" I asked.

"Waiting for someone else," said Gilbert, collecting himself. "And you are?"

"Jade," I said, my stomach tying itself into a myriad series of knots.

"Jade, Jade, why does that name ring a bell?" he said, stroking his chin. "Oh, yes. JadePhoenix42. But you look nothing like you did that night. Why is that, I wonder?"

Gilbert suddenly reached back to grab the vervorium knob on the front door. My eyes followed his and I saw it: a little chunk missing. No doubt the knob on the other side had a similar piece removed.

"I wonder what would happen if I took this off while she was mid-transit? Would she just get stuck in there forever? Let's find out, shall we?"

He pushed the door shut and jerked the knob free from the rim and I faked a gasp.

"Clever of her, to repurpose the vervorium knobs to put her stash out of reach," Gilbert said. "I read about them in the Guild archives. Do you know where they hid the other door to the lighthouse? At the top of Belvedere Castle in Central Park. How much more cliched can you get?"

"So it *was* you who trapped us there. Dalia said-"

"Dalia doesn't know anything," he snapped. "Well, that's not quite true. She knows a great deal. But not about me. He made certain of that."

"I don't understand."

"No, I'm sure you don't. You're still a baby in all of this. But you hitched your cart to the wrong horse. You all should have died that night in the cave, but somehow you escaped. Which was actually quite beneficial."

"Wh-what are you talking about?"

If Gilbert heard the slight creak of the floor behind me, it didn't register on his face, and I wondered how long Beatrice would remain in hiding.

"I thought Frankie only carried the location of this box," he said, tapping it with his foot. "It never occurred to me that she would hold the key to it as well. So I was relieved when I found out that you all had escaped, so I could extract the key and claim the Relic inside for myself."

Gilbert picked up the box from the floor and I recognized it immediately: the box from the cave, the one we had been accused of stealing.

"But you had unexpectedly turned poor Frankie to stone. And so the key was lost to me yet again. Until now. Come out, I know you're there."

I turned around to see Beatrice appear from behind the boxes, the Medoblad drawn at her side.

"You," said Beatrice, her voice dripping with venom and disgust. "What happened to our truce? I knew I should have gone after you when I had the chance. That you weren't going to leave me alone. That-"

"I never had a truce with you," said Gilbert, who was suddenly clutching a small stone on a chain around his neck. "Trinity."

CHAPTER FORTY-SEVEN

SEEING DOUBLE

"The battle was a rout, Jackson is ascendant, and the Guild's enemies are on their last legs. Tomorrow will be a celebration worthy of a queen."

I blinked and Gilbert was gone.

Another man stood in his place. He was younger, by at least a score, but he had the same gaunt look in his face that Gilbert had worn.

I looked back at Beatrice and she had turned white as a ghost.

"No," she said. "It can't … you're dead."

"Yes, well, the thing about killing someone," said the man who had been Gilbert, "as I've learned recently, is that you need to make sure it actually takes. But now that you're here, we can-"

"I don't mean to interrupt," I said. "But who the fuck are you?"

"Tell her, Beatrice," said the man. "Tell her what you did."

"His name is Doug, and he was my first trainee."

The name rang in my head and I recalled my confrontation at the bar, when I had accused her of killing Kate.

"And..."

Doug gestured for her to continue.

"And I killed him. You. At least I thought I did."

"You would have, if someone hadn't intervened to reverse what your lipstick had done."

"Who?" asked Beatrice, who was now visibly shaking.

"Maybe I'll tell you, after we sort out our business here. Or as I watch the life slowly drain out of you."

"I don't fucking think so," said Beatrice and she charged past me, the Medoblad leading the way.

But Doug was faster, gracefully shifting his torso out of the path of the knife and in the same movement extending his elbow outward to hit Beatrice squarely in the gut. She staggered backward from the blow and fell to the ground, the Medoblad slipping free from her hand and landing at my feet.

I picked up the Relic and pointed it at Doug, but it felt like I was threatening him with a tree branch. Beatrice grunted and pushed herself up from the floor, clutching her stomach, while the soft glow of the amethyst stone in her ring began to spread up her arm.

"Don't," said Doug. "Wouldn't want you to waste any of more of her strength."

The purple light vanished in an instant and we stood in silence at the mercy of the man who had cheated death.

"Now, let's get to it, shall we?"

A crooked grin permeated Doug's face as he stooped down slowly to pick up the wooden box, all trace of his earlier calisthenics gone. Had he actually anticipated Beatrice's attack or was it a stroke of pure luck?

He placed the box back down a foot or so from Frankie, and then dug something out of his pants pocket.

A small vial of black ink.

"Where … where did you get that?" Beatrice asked, her voice trembling.

"Where do you think?" Doug snapped at her. "From Polly. After you refused to help her find a cure for her dad's condition, who do you think she turned to? She was only too eager to provide what we ne-"

"What happened to Steve?" I interrupted. "Last time I saw him…"

"He was barely holding it together," said Doug. "And that was before the scar's venom began to spread. Now, he probably has a few weeks left. Too bad Phineas sold his last vial of golden serum to some redhead. Oh wait, that was you."

The words landed with the same force as his blow to Beatrice's stomach and I felt my insides clench together.

"I was … we were trying to heal Frankie."

"And I see you succeeded! But don't worry, you'll get the opportunity to try again, right now in fact."

Doug reached into his pocket again and produced a pen and some paper, which he placed on top of the wooden box, before unstoppering the vial. His hands worked furiously and within a few seconds, he had filled the reservoir and reassembled the pen.

"How are you doing that?" asked Beatrice.

"Doing what? Moving so fast? You should know. After all, it's your buffs."

"Mine don't work like that. It's all or nothing."

Doug looked at her and shook his head.

"They didn't when we bought them from Phineas. But I've had a long time to study them and make improvements, despite your refusal to share your prima materia source, and so now they do. Funny how so many of your decisions are coming back to bite you in the ass, it's really quite amazing."

"Shut. Up," said Beatrice. "I'd do it all again, including killing you. But the Guild will probably do that for me, once they find out what you did."

"No, they won't, not after you open this box for me."

"And how are we going to do that?" I said. "You said it yourself, Frankie holds the key and she's not exactly in an unlocking mood at the moment."

"Truth be told, I had thought that your nighttime excursion to Inwood would have provided the answer, " said Doug. "The great and all-knowing Rita van Asch surely would know how to cure a Relic's curse! But then Trinity here threw a firecracker at me and you got away."

"I wish I had known it was you that night," said Beatrice. "I would have finished the job."

"And I would have killed you then and we wouldn't be having this lovely chat now. Which I'm going to pause for a moment so that you can read this."

I glanced down at the box and the piece of paper was gone, and only the uncapped pen remained. When had he written something with the ink? I looked back up at Doug only for the paper to suddenly appear in right in front of my eyes.

"Reverse the curse on Frankie," the words said and as I read them, the command suddenly floated above the paper like I was watching a 3D movie and hit me square in the face.

"Reverse the curse on Frankie," Doug's voice whispered in my head and I flinched. The words repeated again, except louder and more forceful, and my hands began to shake. This was worse than Beatrice's original command to me to put on the ring. That had been easy to comply with. But this, this was asking me to do the impossible.

From behind me, I heard Beatrice shout something, but Doug closed the gap between them in a flash and doubled her over with another elbow to the gut. But I couldn't worry about her right now.

I needed to reverse the curse on Frankie, like the voice said.

I closed my eyes and an avatar of Doug appeared in my mind. He was translucent, like a ghost, but his will was absolute.

"Reverse the curse on Frankie," he said.

I nodded and suddenly I was in a vast library, with shelves of books reaching to the ceiling.

The me in my head ran to and fro, fetching volumes from different shelves and arranging them on a big center table made of ornate wood. The books each opened on their own accord, and when they did, voices spilled out from them.

"Regardless, if you actually possessed the Blad, like you claim, we wouldn't be in this mess to begin with," said Dalia at our meeting yesterday.

"Its restorative properties were soon demonstrated to be almost unparalleled, capable even of reversing the effects of Relics now lost to us," said me, reading Rita's entry from the Compendium.

"Half of its needles are venomous and half are curative," said the old man with the half-moon spectacles named Phineas.

"… we're dealing with a knife, so not sure how that helps us," said Beatrice at the coffee shop a few weeks ago.

The voices swirled above the table, and I imagined them as pieces of a puzzle that wouldn't stay still long enough so I could grab them. And the bits and pieces of my memories were so disparate that I didn't see how they fit together at all. We didn't have the beak of a dodo bird, I had used up all but a few drops of the healing serum, and I couldn't make heads or tails of what Beatrice was talking about.

"Reverse the curse on Frankie," said Doug again and I so wanted to stab him with the Medoblad, if only to expel him from my mind. The blade suddenly appeared in my hand and the memory of that horrid night flew down from a shelf and set itself on the table with the rest. I grasped the imaginary Medoblad and walked toward Doug's apparition, but he uttered the words again and my mental self was forced back to the table.

Dalia's voice sounded again and that gnawing feeling from earlier returned. Why did she think the Medoblad was so important to curing Frankie? What was I missing?

I squeezed the Medoblad's ivory handle harder as my frustration and fury rose to a boiling point and it disappeared into a puff of smoke, the now-unsupported blade floating in mid-air for just a second before falling to the ground. But that didn't satiate my anger and I unleashed it further on the table, toppling the massive wooden beast on its side and sending all the books to the ground.

But Doug was unfazed and as the words of the command formed again on his lips again, I let out a guttural cry.

It was then that I heard it.

Beatrice's voice, from one of the books. I had listened to it moments ago, but not all of it.

"The Medusa legend doesn't really touch on reversing the curse."

I froze as the rest of her words spilled forth.

"Even killing her didn't undo it. The best I found was a mention of two veins in her neck: blood from one would curse you and blood from the other would purify you."

Two veins, two golden needles, two opposing forces: one to curse you and one to heal you.

The library scene dissolved as I opened my eyes, and I saw that the real Medoblad was still in my hand, the ivory handle intact.

I would soon change that.

Beatrice was slumped on the ground, and I walked over to her and propped her up against the wall.

"What are you doing?" Doug asked.

"What you told me to," I snapped at him before turning my attention to Beatrice. Her eyes were closed and her breathing was heavy, and I wasn't sure if she was still conscious.

"Hey. Hey! Snap out of it. I need some of the strength from your ring."

Beatrice's head rolled back and I was afraid that the ring and Doug's attacks had already taken too much of a toll on her. But then I remembered that barely empty vial of gold that I had tucked away in a box, and I hurried to the back of the house to retrieve it. Two drops of the shimmering liquid still remained at the bottom and I unstoppered the glass quickly before pulling open Beatrice's mouth and letting the serum trickle free.

The alchemy took only seconds to work and Beatrice slowly opened her eyes and looked at me.

"Activate the ring," I said, grasping her right hand.

"No … I … why?"

"Please."

She nodded and shut her eyes. The purple glow was dim but I felt the tiniest bit of raw strength travel from her hand to mine. I stood slowly, careful not to let our hands fall away, and stared at Doug.

"Reverse the curse on Frankie," I said as I shattered the handle of the Medoblad.

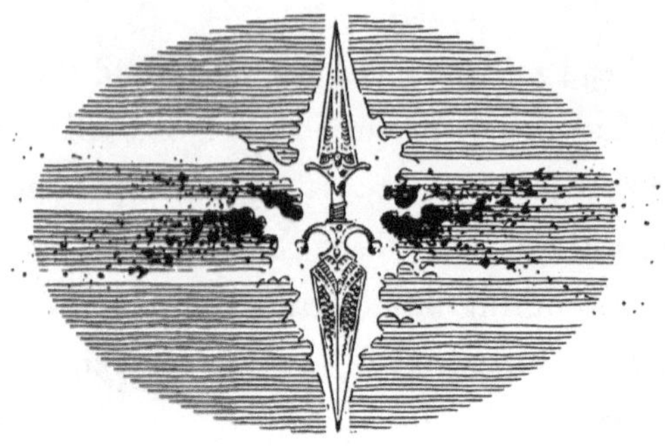

KEEPER

"I awoke this morning alone in an unfamiliar room. My mouth tasted of blood. They took everything from me. And then some. But this book remained, yesterday's entry completely blank."

My hand should have been bleeding.

Not from the broken pieces of ivory that had already fallen to the floor.

But from the twin blade that had been hidden beneath the handle.

Its edge was sharp, that much I could feel. But the healing blade of the Medoblad, the reverse of the curse, it wouldn't harm me.

Doug looked at me with a mixture of awe and fear, but I didn't care about him. All I cared about was one thing and one thing only.

I stood next to Frankie, and then, careful not to cut myself with the other end, slid the blade effortlessly into the same spot where I had unleashed the curse on her. What the healing serum had failed to do, the Medoblad was accomplishing in spades, and I watched as the stone fled from her body. When I finally saw Frankie's feet begin to twitch, I knew that the cure was complete and pulled the blade free. As I did, Doug's command in my head ceased and I turned to face him, but then I felt something grab me from behind.

"What have you done?" said Frankie, whose hand was now wrapped around my wrist.

"I … we saved you," I said, nearly dropping the blade to the ground.

She withdrew her grip and then slowly took in her surroundings, while Doug stood silently at the front of the house, and her eyes went wide when she finally saw him.

"How? He's the one who kidnapped me in the first place!"

"He's from the Guild," said Beatrice. "Thought he was doing his boss a favor by opening that box. But he's not too smart, that one."

"Shut up!" said Doug. "I'm going to-"

"He just wants what's inside the box," I interjected. "You're the Guild's Keeper, aren't you? You can open it and then we can all leave."

Frankie shook her head slowly.

"No, you have it all backward."

"What are you talking about?" I said.

"I'm not the Guild's Keeper. Far from it. For 200 years, my family has kept the cave and that box hidden from the Guild. Until someone found out that I had taken up the charge."

I brought my hand to the glamour stone and felt Jade fade away, and it took a few seconds for the glimmer of recognition to appear on her face.

"YOU!" Frankie shouted. "The girl from the gym, the one who tore off the bandage on my tattoo, you…"

"Didn't know what we had done," I said. "We thought it was just another Raid. We didn't realize what we were doing. And then Dalia said that the box was Guild property so-"

"You ignorant fools!"

"Why did you tell us where the last gold token was then?" said Beatrice, producing a small golden coin from her pocket. "When we healed you the other day, you told us where to find it."

"That token was lo-"

"Enough!" said Doug. "I don't care about any of this. You," he pointed at Frankie, "are going to open that box and I'm finally going to get my hands on that Relic."

"Over my dead body," said Frankie calmly. "I may have failed my family but I won't allow you to open the box. That key will die with me here and now and you'll never be able to-"

"I was expecting you to say that," said Doug. "But fortunately, our friends here have provided me with a convenient method of getting what I want out of you."

We stood helplessly as Doug crossed the house in an instant and Frankie could do nothing as he held up a second note written in black ink in front of her eyes. Before she could react, the command had already taken effect.

"I'm going to open the box for you," Frankie said in a monotone voice. She slowly walked forward a few steps to where Doug had placed it and picked it up, sending the ink vial and pen falling to the ground as she did.

Frankie lifted the box aloft with her palms and closed her eyes. Her body began to twitch and her lips began to tremble as violent spasms rippled through her limbs, but somehow she kept a hold of it. It was like I was watching an exorcism from a horror movie with Doug as the priest. The tremors continued to wash over Frankie until finally, her eyes reopened, and her pupils were surrounded by a silver aura.

"*Ephphatha*," she said and the box complied. A gust of air burst forth from the opened lid, spreading to every corner of the house, and

I felt a strange sensation around my neck as the glamour suddenly reactivated.

"And now I'm going to die," Frankie said in the same monotone as she collapsed onto the ground, the box tumbling from her hands.

"Well done," said Doug. "Well done. And now the Relic is mine, and Gilbert and Dalia and the Guild will-"

"What did you do to her?" Beatrice said, anger rising in her voice.

"What you must have known the ink was capable of," he replied.

"No!" I shouted. "I healed her. I saved her. And you-"

"Told her to open the box and die," said Doug, smirking. "She would have died anyway soon enough. Being a Keeper extracts a great toll on your body. I just sped up the process a bit."

He nudged Frankie in the ribs, as if double-checking that his command had taken effect, before picking up the now-unlocked box and retreating to the door.

I rushed to Frankie's side, my fingers frantically searching for a pulse in her neck, but the only thing I felt was the coldness of her skin. Without thinking, I plunged the healing end of the Medoblad into Frankie's shoulder over and over again, each jab becoming more frantic, as I waited for the blade's magic to restart Frankie's heart.

"Give it a rest," said Doug. "You should be more worried about yourself. Can't decide whether you would be more useful to me alive or dead, but I suppose I'll have time to figure that out once I kill Trinity back there."

Doug laughed and I looked back at Beatrice, who had barely blinked at the taunt.

"He kept me holed up in the Guild Hall for far too long, so I've had a lot of time to consider how I was going to do it, if I ever got the chance."

"Who?" I asked.

"Gilbert," said Doug. "He's had a special interest in you, T, for a long time. Was stalking you even while I was doing the same. So fortunately for me, he showed up in the atrium that night shortly after you left me there to die. He gave me the antidote and asked if I wanted to learn under a real mentor. Of course I said yes, but didn't realize until much later what I'd signed up for. It was only in the past few years that he let me out on my own. But only while wearing this."

Doug held up the glamour stone around his neck. It was green, like mine, but lacked Jade's luster.

"I wonder what it would feel like to wear that one," he said, pointing at my neck. I glanced down and saw a sight I'd never seen before: my mother's locket, ajar.

I looked back up at Doug, only to see him vanish again and reappear at Beatrice's side, holding her chin with his fingers, as if he was a lion surveying his prey.

"In case you were wondering, it's going to be slow and painful and I'm going to enjoy every single minute of it," Doug whispered in her ear, but Beatrice remained preternaturally still.

"Where's that arrogant spirit I know so well?" said Doug as he released his grip on Beatrice and shook his head. "I thought you would put up more of a fight, but now that you've finally met your match, you're nothing but a scared little girl. Figures."

Doug turned around and walked over to the wooden box, and I saw Beatrice clench her fists tightly. I searched for some sort of signal in her eyes, but she just stood there, staring at Doug, as he bent down to pick up his treasure. He slowly opened the lid, his face erupting into a vicious smile. But the glee was only temporary.

"No," he said, closing the lid and opening it again. "This isn't right. It's not-"

The purple blur hit Doug at full speed, pinning him against the wall and sending the wooden box careening across the room. When the dust settled, I saw Beatrice with her arms locked around him, her body completely surrounded by the purple aura.

"Hurry," said Beatrice. "Don't … know … how much longer … I can hold him."

Doug struggled to break free from her grasp, but Beatrice's strength was equal to his own, and I stood there, frozen with fear.

"Jen!" Beatrice yelled. "What the hell are you waiting for? Do it!"

I looked at her and suddenly I was back in the lighthouse again, a raging inferno all around me, two lives hanging in the balance.

Except I was no longer the morally righteous, foolishly naive woman I had been. The Quests and the Guild had seen to that. And Beatrice. And Doug. And even Duncan. They had all shaped me into a different sort of instrument. One that had no reservation of doing whatever it took to survive.

I pulled the blade free from Frankie's shoulder in one long arc before reversing my grip. It should have been slick with her blood, but the metal was perfectly pristine, shining brightly somehow in the dim room. I pressed the edge into my palm as I closed my fingers around it, took a deep breath, and then charged at the man and the woman who had upended my life.

It all happened in an instant.

Beatrice spun Doug around and then released him, his forward momentum impaling him on the outstretched blade. The recognition of his impending demise slowly dawned on his face as he looked down to see the Medoblad plunged into his stomach. Gray stone erupted from the wound and Doug frantically tried to pull the blade free, but the alchemy was quicker, and his hands stopped short only a few inches from the Medoblad. The rest of him followed suit, until he was nothing but an angry, snarling statue.

"Pull it out," said Beatrice, her body still flickering with power.

I complied, only to watch in horror as she smashed her palms through Doug from behind, his body shattering into a hundred pieces.

"Why did you do that?" I yelled. "It was over. We beat him. We didn't need to-"

"Yes, we did," said Beatrice, brushing the stone fragments from her hands. "I made the mistake of leaving him alive last time, I won't do it again."

"But-"

"It's done, Jen. Nothing to do now but move forward. In the box in the back, there's another vial of the vitality serum. Quickly now, before…"

The ring's power vanished in an instant and Beatrice fell forward, but I caught her with my free arm, and we toppled to the ground. I slid out from under her, careful not to let the Medoblad touch her, and flipped her over onto her back. The serum I found in a box with several jars of preserved rats and pigeons, and I quickly grabbed the vial and raced back to the unconscious Beatrice. Propping her head up on my legs, I removed the wax stopper and poured the brownish-gray liquid into her mouth.

Beatrice gritted her teeth as the serum began its savage work restoring her body. After a few minutes, she finally opened her eyes and stared straight up at me, a look of shock on her face.

"Jen," she whispered. "Your locket."

"I know," I said. "Somehow, it opened during the commotion."

"No, it's not that. It's … look inside."

I pulled the front open all the way to find a shiny golden circle with a small bird-like creature etched in the middle nestled in the interior of the locket. My fingers pried it free easily and when I looked down at my palm, I was holding a gold token.

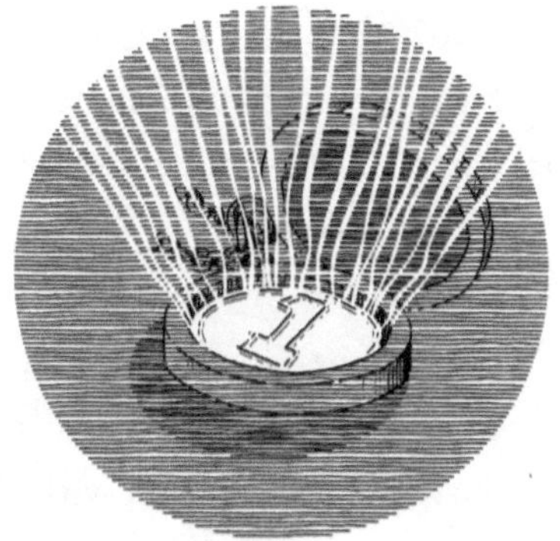

TWO OF A KIND

*"My memory is hazy but this much I know: I will make them pay for
what they have done, even if it takes a lifetime."*

We stared at each other with matching looks of bewilderment on our faces as Beatrice produced an identical token from her pocket.

"What ... how is that possible?" I said.

"Where did you get that locket?" Beatrice asked.

"It was my mom's. She gave it to me on my 11th birthday and I've worn it ever since she died. Where did you get that token?"

"Where you thought it was. The 19th-century townhouse on Pearl Street, with the triangle carved into the stone wall. The token was buried underneath."

"Ah," I said.

So much had happened since yesterday that I didn't feel like patting myself on the back for finding where the token from Rita's memory had been hidden. How it had made its way to that townhouse from deposit box number 42 was a mystery I didn't feel like solving. Besides, it was Frankie who we had to thank for finding it, and now because of Doug, we never would be able to.

My eyes drifted toward her unmoving body on the floor and I suppressed a sob. I could blame Doug for killing her and blame the Guild for sending us after her in the first place, and wipe my hands of everything. I could justify my absolution with that twisted pretzel logic and pretend that I had done nothing wrong. But that would be the first step onto the path that Beatrice had taken long ago, and as much as we had bonded over the weeks, I didn't want to end up like her.

I looked down at the token that had been hanging around my neck for half of my life and thought of my mom. Was the locket just some old piece of jewelry she had lying around or did she know what was hidden inside? I didn't want to think about what that meant.

The token, like the Medoblad, gave off an otherworldly shine. Unlike its wooden, iron, and bronze cousins, this one lacked the number one etched in the center. Instead, there was a beakless bird that looked like a cross between a pigeon and a hawk.

"What is this on the token? A dodo bird missing its beak?"

"No," said Beatrice. "It's an alerion."

"A what?"

"A mythical bird. Only two were said to exist at a time. Every 60 years, they lay two eggs, and then when the eggs hatch, the parent alerions down themselves. It's the Guild's sigil. Don't ask me why."

"Oh," I said. "So now what? Are we actually just going to walk into Dalia's office, plop the tokens down on her fancy table, and demand to join the Guild?"

"I don't know," said Beatrice. "Maybe?"

"Or maybe we should take that box and these tokens and get as far away from the Guild as we can," I offered.

"First things first. Let's just get out of here. We'll come back for Frankie later."

Beatrice reattached the knob to the front door and opened it slowly. But before she could step through, she was knocked backward by a man wearing a blue blazer.

It was Gilbert.

Beatrice retreated to the middle of the room and I stood next to her, clutching the Medoblad.

"Beatrice," he said cooly, his eyes surveying the room until they reached Frankie's body. "What happened here? Where's-"

"Doug?" said Beatrice. "Dead. Thankfully. Frankie too."

"I see," the real Gilbert said. "How…"

"Doug, with that," I pointed to the spilled command ink that had seeped into the wooden floor. "Right after she opened the box."

"So you did have it," he said.

"No, your crazed lackey took it, after he trapped us in the cave and left us to die," said Beatrice. "Why are you here? Come to finish what Doug failed to do? Because if you are, then I'm-"

Gilbert held up his hand.

"No, I'm not. I came to sue for peace. And to stop Doug. But it seems like you handled that on your own."

"Sue for peace? You're the ones who keep coming after me," said Beatrice.

"That was Doug," said Gilbert. "I gave him the glamour to use when he was out in public. Seeing as how he was supposed to be dead, which I seem to recall was your doing."

"Yes," Beatrice said. "Except you saved him for some reason. Thanks for doing that, by the way."

"Enough," I said. "We never asked to be involved in any of this.

But we're not just going to walk away now and pretend like nothing has happened. I'm afraid you're going to be stuck with us."

"How do you figure?" said Gilbert.

"Because," I said, holding my gold token aloft while Beatrice did the same. "We're joining the Guild."

"John, Ms. Jacobs's just walked in," said our HR manager Margaret to a speakerphone in the middle of the conference room table. She beckoned me to sit at the chair across from her and then turned her attention back to the phone.

"Ah, good. Sorry we have to do this over the phone Jen, but I got called away to London last minute. Anyway, I know you were supposed to have your annual review next week, but something's come up, so I wanted to do this now."

"Umm, OK," I said into the phone while trying to avoid Margaret's blank face.

"Now you've done great work for us in the past, and this year–"

"Look, is this about the run-through? Because I emailed the team afterward to say I was sorry for running out. But I did fix the bug and–"

"What?" interrupted John. "Oh. No, no. That was some inspired thinking. Really saved the day."

"Then what? The other devs are mad I was out sick last week?"

"No, it's not that either. If you'll just let me explain, then this will go more smoothly."

"OK," I said. The last thing I wanted to do was sit through a lecture from Hammond about God knows what, especially with tonight's summons looming.

A week had passed since that morning on the island and my life had almost returned to normal. Well, my new normal as a Guild recruit. Gilbert had stared at our tokens for what had seemed like 10 minutes before nodding.

"This is … unexpected," he had said. "But that's why we have bylaws. You'll be hearing from us soon."

And then, before we could do anything, he had grabbed the box and escaped back through the front door. We had foolishly given chase through the portal, but luckily Gilbert hadn't pulled off the knob on the other end, and so we had emerged into the Chrysler Building office a few moments later to find him gone.

"-took them a while to sort through everything, but when Anthony and Greg laid it all for me, I made the decision immediately."

"What?" I said. "Sorry, I didn't quite catch that."

"Does the night of March 26, 2018 ring a bell?" Hammond said, a note of irritation in his voice.

"I don't think so," I replied. "Should it?"

"Yes," he said. "Because on that night, our logs reported a massive power outage. Every computer in the office except one went out at the exact same time, only to be rebooted a few minutes later."

My eyes went wide. It was the night I had first discovered the Quest Board.

"And the only employee at the office that night was-"

"Me," I said. "But, nothing happened. I mean, I didn't-"

"Erase anything? No, fortunately not. But you did install a backdoor into your workstation during the outage and who knows how much of our code you've purloined."

"A backdoor? What the hell are you talking about it? I didn't-

"I'm sorry, Jen, but you're fired."

"What's wrong with you?" said Beatrice, as we got off the subway at 51st Street just after 1 a.m. "You haven't said a word all night."

"I got fired," I said, the glamour's weight feeling heavier than usual.

"Oh? What for?"

"For loading the Quest Board onto my computer at work."

"Wait, really?"

"Yes, but the company thinks I committed corporate espionage or something. I just can't believe–"

"Let it go, Jen. Or Jade, I guess. Are you really planning on wearing that thing for the rest of your life?"

"No, it's just that, Gilbert, he only knows me as Jade. I'd like to keep it that way for as long as I can. This is the Guild we're talking about."

We crossed under the familiar trellis into the pocket park, which was predictably deserted. But the gurgle of the waterfall at the back broke the relative quiet of the night, and we sat down at one of the tables near the freshly-packed dirt that was awaiting a spring planting.

"True," said Beatrice. "But we are about to be members of said Guild, so that should provide us with a measure of protection."

"After all we've been through, do you really believe that?"

"Not for a second. But we don't have a choice. I'm not just going to hand these tokens over to Dalia and hope she leaves us alone."

The park suddenly went quiet and I looked up at the waterfall to find it had stopped. I stood up from the table and walked through the dirt surrounding the now-still collecting pool, and nearly jumped out of my skin when I saw a dark figure walk out from the ivy wall that lined the back of the park.

"Hello, ladies," said Gilbert.

"Gilbert," said Beatrice.

"Why are we here?" I asked. "This doesn't look like the Guild Hall. Even Dalia's conference room would have been preferable."

"We are here because there are some preliminary matters to attend to before you can be sworn in as the newest members of the Guild."

"And what are those?" said Beatrice, glaring at Gilbert. "We have the gold tokens. We know that they confer Guild membership. What else is there? You going to dunk us in this pool here to see if we're witches?"

"Not quite," said Gilbert, who pulled a small vial from his pocket. "Under the Guild bylaws, the holder of a gold token is entitled to one of the 12 Guild seats. The seats usually operate in a hereditary manner, the gold token passed down from parent to child and so on. There have been a few occasions where hard-up families have sold their seats, but that hasn't happened in a century."

"Fascinating," said Beatrice, rolling her eyes, and I nudged her with my elbow.

"Anyway," said Gilbert, ignoring Beatrice's comment, "you two have presented the requisite tokens for membership, but there remains the issue that 11 of the 12 seats are currently spoken for. And earlier this evening, we called a full meeting of the Guild, at which 11 tokens were presented."

"What are you saying?" I said.

"Either you are engaging in some extreme sleight of hand with one of our members, or one of your tokens is a fake."

Before we could say anything to object, Gilbert unstoppered the vial and dumped half the contents into the pool. The surface of the water flashed bright red three times before returning to its normal opaqueness and Beatrice and I looked at each other, not knowing what to do.

"What … what was that?" asked Beatrice, clenching her fists, and I saw the outer edges of plastic wrapping.

"That," said Gilbert, "will tell us which of your tokens is true. Now, Beatrice, if you wouldn't mind, toss your token into the pool."

"Fine," she said, producing it from her pocket and flicking it into the air.

The token hit the water with a plop and sunk to the bottom.

I looked at her and she shrugged her shoulders, and we waited for something momentous to happen.

After a few moments, I saw it: a faint glow at the bottom of the pool. It grew brighter by the second, but the light that radiated from the token wasn't gold. It was green.

Then everything exploded.

The blast knocked me backward onto the dirt and a few seconds later I was hit with a frigid wall of water. Ignoring the ringing in my ears, I wiped the mud from my face and slowly sat up and looked over to see if Beatrice was all right.

Except, she was gone.

"Huh," said Gilbert, who was seemingly unharmed. "Wasn't expecting that. Well, I was. Just not that forceful."

He walked over and extended his hand to me, and I reluctantly took it, his clammy palm sending a shiver up my arm.

"Seems like your friend made off clean and left you here to take the fall," he said, coldly.

"I ... no. She didn't kno-"

"You don't have to answer for her. Not unless your token also tries to blow me up. Shall we?"

Somehow, there was still water remaining in the pool and we walked to the edge together, where Gilbert emptied the remainder of the vial. The water flashed red three times again and he gestured for me to surrender my token just as Beatrice had done. I silently complied and held my breath.

Nothing happened.

No glow, no exploding tsunami of water, not even a gurgle from the pool.

"OK, yours is good," said Gilbert, nonchalantly. "You can retrieve it."

"What? I don't understand. What was that liquid?"

"That? Just a little something to weed out fakes. Yours didn't react, so it's the real deal."

"Oh," I said, stepping over the lip of the retaining wall around the pool and into the cold water. The token gleamed up at me, like a coin in a wishing well, and I thrust my hand into the pool and quickly pulled it out.

"So, now what? Is there some sort of ceremony or something?"

Gilbert raised an eyebrow.

"Something like that. But are you sure you want to go through with this? Once you join the Guild, there is literally no turning back. It's for life. Now, if you were willing to part with the token, I could offer you a handsome sum of money."

Now it was my turn to be surprised.

"Define handsome."

"Enough money that you wouldn't have to work another day in your life if you didn't want to. You'd of course also have to agree to let us wipe your memory of the past year. But the money would more than make up for that, I think."

"I see."

The offer was tempting, for sure. I was unemployed, my oldest friends literally didn't remember me, my newest friend was now probably in permanent hiding, and my life had been threatened more times in the past year than I cared to think about. Gilbert was literally offering me a fresh start, the chance to chart whatever course I wanted.

But all the money in the world, I suspected, wouldn't buy me peace of mind, even if I couldn't remember the truth about magic or what Beatrice and I had been through. And what about Beatrice? Could I really just leave her to fend for herself? Walk away from everything and go sip scotch on a beach somewhere for the rest of my life?

I clutched the gold token in one hand and my mom's now-empty locket with the other.

"Keep your money," I said. "I'm in."

CHAIRMAN
OF THE BOARD

The south tower of the Guild's headquarters was situated such that Dalia de Wyck could just see the tops of the trees beginning to bloom at the edge of Central Park. Although her apartment further south provided a much more expansive view, there was something more satisfying about the view here. Perhaps it was because that while hundreds, if not thousands, of people could say that they had apartments that abutted Central Park, only Dalia could say that she overlooked the park from an actual fortress.

The tower's windows, along with the rest of the windows of the building, were coated with sheets of a particularly remarkable material. It had all the benefits of a two-way mirror, allowing Dalia to look out onto the street below and points westward, while blocking all passersby from peering into the seemingly abandoned Madison Avenue Armory.

The Guild's previous headquarters, an unassuming brownstone on East 68th Street, had outgrown its suitability after a developer bought up the rest of the block and tore everything down in the late 1950s. The Armory too had almost been torn down completely, but the Guild had managed to whip up a number of frenzied protests, which was enough to sway the Landmarks Preservation Commission to designate the remaining portion of the building as a landmark in October 1966. The Guild moved in later that month and had been there ever since.

Dalia walked away from the window and over to the magnificent wooden desk on the other side of the room, and sat down in the cushioned chair. Two identical wooden boxes rested on the middle of the desk's top surface, one of them empty and one of them full. She couldn't remember the last time she had seen the two vessels together, but that was by design.

A design that had worked too well, unfortunately, resulting in layers of setbacks that only now Dalia had just managed to undo.

Well, almost.

The door to the study opened and Gilbert walked in.

"We have a problem," he said.

"What? One of our new recruits had a fake token? I could have told you that without having to call roll. But you insisted that-"

"Yes, but it's more than that. The fake, it was laced with alkahest. Would have blown up the north tower and everyone in it if I hadn't screened it first."

"Oh," she said. "That is a problem. And yet, you waited until the morning to come tell me? I assume you have the bitch stashed somewhere so we can interrogate her?"

"Not exactly. She fled almost immediately."

"Of course," said Dalia. "Do you think that was one of her designs?"

"Beatrice? She's quite capable, but not of something like this. No, I think it's more likely the handiwork of-"

"Will you take off that ridiculous glamour?" said Dalia. "You know I can't stand looking at him."

"Fine, fine," said Gilbert, who pulled the stone out from underneath his shirt and squeezed it.

The visage of Gilbert crackled like the static on an old television set, and Ty stood in his place, dressed in a blue blazer and grey slacks.

"Happy now, Mother?" said her daughter.

"Yes. And honestly, I think it's nearly time to retire those glamours. The other one ended up doing a number on Doug, it would seem."

"That and you made me keep him confined to the Mooney House basement for several years," said Ty.

"Enough. It's over now. Next time you plan on taking on such an ambitious project, take a day or 30 and really think it all the way through."

"Deal," said Ty, whose eyes drifted to the silver ring on her desk. "Is that..."

"Yes, it is. From 1815 if I'm not mistaken. But the diary will know for sure."

Dalia rose from the chair and scanned the volumes on the third shelf of the massive bookcase behind the desk, before finding the one she was searching for. She placed the book down on the desk and opened to an empty page about two-thirds of the way through. The ring began to wobble before shooting forward onto the page. After a few seconds, it dissolved slowly into a circle of silver liquid, and then began rearranging itself into neatly-written words that filled the sheet.

Dalia lowered her head toward the page and sank into the past.

"Mother?" said Ty, when she re-emerged from the memory and slowly sat back up, her head pounding. "Are you all right?"

"Yes, I'm fine. It's just ... I'd forgotten how it feels. It's a strange experience, reading about what I did back then. It's almost like Rita *was* a completely different person, that these just are the missives of a woman long dead. But the memory in that ring, that is as raw as if it happened to me yesterday. And it was something I really didn't want to relive ever again."

Dalia opened the lid of the box that had been locked for so long, before tilting it on its side, and watched as hundreds of silver rings spilled onto the desk.

"Incredible," said Ty. "It's all there. The Compendium."

"Not quite," said Dalia. There remains the matter of the physical book itself."

"I'm sure Beatrice has it. She did have the one entry you left unhidden."

"I agree," said Dalia. "But luckily our newest Guild member is perfectly positioned to help us recover it from her former partner. And once we do, it is only a matter of time before the full might of the Guild resonates across the continent."

"Wait, how did you know she didn't take the money and run?"

"I didn't," said Dalia, smiling. "But there's enough of Larissa in her daughter that I was confident that she wouldn't run from her birthright. Even if she doesn't know it yet."

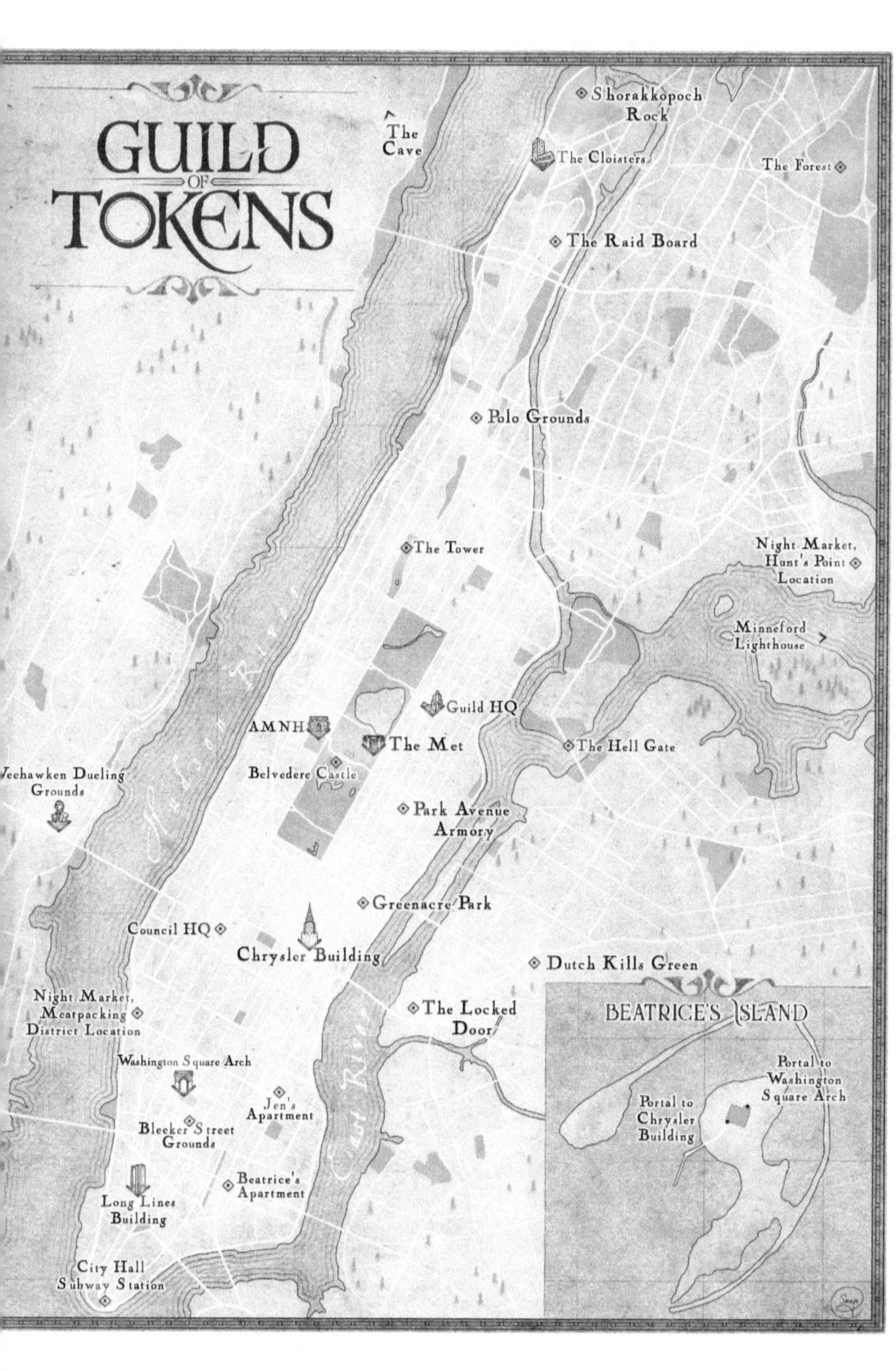

GUILD OF TOKENS
The Cave
Shorakkopoch Rock
The Cloisters
The Forest
The Raid Board
Polo Grounds
Night Market, Hunt's Point Location
The Tower
Minneford Lighthouse
Guild HQ
AMNH
The Met
The Hell Gate
Belvedere Castle
Weehawken Dueling Grounds
Park Avenue Armory
Greenacre Park
Council HQ
Chrysler Building
Dutch Kills Green
Night Market, Meatpacking District Location
The Locked Door
BEATRICE'S ISLAND
Washington Square Arch
Portal to Washington Square Arch
Jen's Apartment
Portal to Chrysler Building
Bleeker Street Grounds
Beatrice's Apartment
Long Lines Building
City Hall Subway Station
Hudson River
East River

TRAINEE

INTRODUCTION TO TRAINEE
Trainee takes place two years prior to the
events of *Guild of Tokens*.

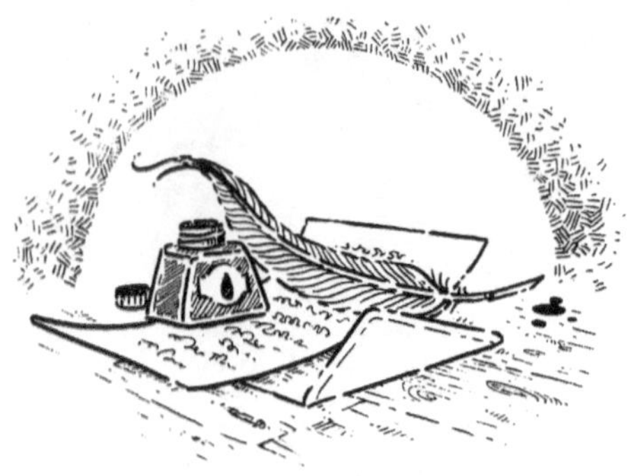

The girl was late.

Ordinarily, Beatrice Taylor would not have cared.

She wasn't a stickler for people following her Quests to a T, and could deal with a bit of improvisation if the Quester got the job done.

"Results-oriented" would be on her resume if she still had a normal job.

But this morning was different.

This morning, her usual sitter texted her at 6:15 saying that she had been up half the night sick.

And, the last-minute replacement looked more suited for changing tires than changing a diaper.

Beatrice sighed and took another sip of her coffee. She watched the throngs of people on Bleecker Street pass by and she envied the carefree mornings they were probably enjoying. She wished she could return to those days, when all she had to worry about was where she was going to meet her friends for brunch or when Garrett was finally going to propose. But that had been a lifetime ago, before the baby, before Garrett had started sleeping with his analyst, and before she had discovered the Quests.

"I'm so sorry I'm late!" A chipper brunette wearing a pink backpack sprinted up to Beatrice's table in front of the coffee shop, and took the empty seat across from her.

"It's fine. I take it you have the book?" Beatrice studied her latest trainee, who had clearly run the last few blocks, as her face was flush and her breathing heavy. Good, she thought. She liked it when her trainees were afraid of displeasing her.

The jury was still out on Kate, a sophomore at NYU from Nebraska. The girl fit the new profile perfectly: enthusiastic, hard-working, a desire to please, and most importantly, no strong attachments to family.

"Yep!" Kate dumped her backpack on the table and began rifling through it, finally withdrawing a leather-bound book.

"Excellent. How is the old professor? Still a disgusting lecher? I hope he didn't leer at you too much. You're just his type."

Kate's eyes widened.

"Wait, how did you know that he had… Oh. This was just a test. Again."

Beatrice smiled. At least this one was perceptive.

"Of course. You think you're ready for the big time already? Did you read the book?"

"I did. Was up all night. Then tried to take a quick cat nap but slept through my alarm. That's why I was la-"

"Then you know that this wasn't something I would leave to the likes of you if I didn't already know I could get it back."

The trainee's face turned sour, her achievement quickly undermined by a few choice words. But Beatrice preferred it this way. Last time she had let a trainee get a big head, things had gotten ugly, and with a baby to take care of, Beatrice didn't really have the time anymore to keep starting from the beginning.

"Oh don't be so sensitive. You did well regardless. Here's your reward."

Beatrice set the stack of iron tokens on the table and took the book. Kate stared at the tokens for several seconds before finally grabbing them and stuffing them in her backpack.

"Thanks."

The girl's earlier perkiness had faded in short order. Kids these days. They wanted a pat on the back, a trophy, and to be enthusiastically congratulated for doing what was expected of them. Kate should be grateful that she was even getting this chance to be her trainee. Did the girl know how hard Beatrice had worked to get to where she was? Of course not. But she had to play with the hand she was dealt, even if it meant a little extra coddling here and there.

"And because you were up all night, here's something extra."

Beatrice withdrew a small green square wrapped in plastic from her pocketbook and slid it across the table.

"What's this?"

"A little something to help you next time you need to finish a paper. It lasts only a couple of hours, so don't waste it, but it's one of my better buffs, if I do say so myself."

The girl stared at her blankly.

"You don't know what a buff is?"

Kate shook her head.

"OK, fine. Think of it as a magic version of the Adderall you've been dealing in your dorm for me. Which it is."

"Oh. OH. Wow, thanks!"

"You're welcome. Don't waste it though. I don't hand those out to everyone for free you know."

"I won't. So, what's my next assignment? Do you have the next volume of the diary? I have so many questions!"

"Easy there, tiger. I'll be in touch. Go get some sleep. You're beginning to sound like a chipmunk."

The girl nodded, grabbed her stuff, and left the coffee shop. If there was one thing Beatrice had impressed upon her trainees, it was that she didn't much care for small talk. She wasn't there to be their friend or their mother. Speaking of, little Jack Jack would be waking up soon. Beatrice sighed again, finished the last dregs of her coffee and headed back uptown to her "normal" life.

The apartment was finally quiet and the wine was flowing. Tonight's selection was a pinot grigio that Garrett had brought back from his trip to Rome last year. Beatrice was relaxing on the couch in the middle of her second glass and Garrett, as usual, was late. But she didn't particularly care. It gave her time to catch up on how her latest batches of Questers were faring.

She logged on to the Quest Board and flipped over to the inbox, expecting to see a bunch of messages asking where the Questers could pick up their tokens. But it was empty. She frowned. Maybe she had just been unlucky. It happened from time to time. She would post her standard set of Quests and the luck of the draw would bring her an utterly incompetent set of noobs who shouldn't have even been told about the Quests in the first place. It was so frustrating, but also necessary, if Beatrice wanted to keep her pipeline fresh, to have a replacement for Kate far enough along if the need arose.

Maybe it was the wine, but tonight she was in no mood to let these idiot Questers continue on for weeks attempting to complete the simplest of tasks. She opened another page on the Board, clicked on her active Quests, and cancelled them all. Then she brought up the new Quest page and reposted the same ones she had just cancelled.

"I need a handful of blueberries, a tillandsia, an orange popsicle, and three pounds of 80/20 ground beef from Chelsea Market. Leave in the windowsill of 194 W. 9th Street. Thanks! Reward: One wood"

This was the standard opener, a modification of the first Quest she had ever done. None of the items alone or in combination did anything, she had later discovered, but it was a good exercise in attention to detail. She couldn't count how many times she had received the wrong mix of beef or a flower that was not a tillasandia. Also, the building on W. 9th Street had been abandoned for many years, so it was a good drop location.

"One Central Park pigeon. Preferably dead. Well, actually, definitely dead. Reward: one iron."

Pigeons and rats were the bread and butter of a good alchemist. The spleen of a freshly killed pigeon was an excellent source of prima materia and you could never have too much of that. Beatrice made a mental reminder to check her stock of preservatives at the downtown apartment. There was nothing worse than going through the laborious (and messy) process of extracting organs only to find that there was nothing to keep them in, and any off putting smell would most certainly result in the old lady across the fifth floor landing calling the super, or worse, the police.

"Three leaves from a khat plant. Dried. Reward: Eight wood."

Those outside the Questing world knew that chewing khat leaves produced an Adderall-like high. Amateurs. Those within the Questing world, at least the ones that Beatrice had come across, did not have the creativity to come up with any new transmutations. So that had let her and her chemical engineering degree run rampant, combining all manner of ordinary matter with prima materia to get fantastical results, giving her a nice slice of the market.

Two markets, actually. One version of her offerings she diluted down and sold to regular college kids and 20-somethings as black market hangover cures, Adderall substitutes, and other mind-enhancing offerings. It brought in a steady stream of real money that gave Beatrice a degree of independence and also let her rent the downtown apartment with Garrett none the wiser.

The other version she sold to Questers for tokens. It was a much better method of accumulating wealth than what she used to do, when she herself was a newbie Quester. Sure, she liked going on raids and piecing together what the Questing 1% were up to, but she worried that her continued success would make her a target eventually, and she wasn't ready to go toe-to-toe with the Guild or the Council. Yet.

The last Quest went live just as the door to the apartment opened, and Beatrice quickly closed her laptop and turned to greet Garrett. It was 10:45.

"Honey, you're home," she said, mustering a phony smile. "I was beginning to think you were spending the night in the office again." Garrett dropped his briefcase unceremoniously by the front door and walked into the living room.

"Sorry I'm late," he said, giving her a quick peck on the cheek and taking a seat on the couch next to her. "This new deal is killing us. Hopefully it'll calm down after we close."

She looked at her husband. His red hair was slightly out of place, his shirt was wrinkled, and his eyes were bloodshot. The rigors of the private equity grind, she thought. Or maybe the aftermath of a quickie at his analyst's apartment in DUMBO. Beatrice preferred not to know.

She had her secrets too, her own past transgressions that she had never owned up to. And it wasn't like she was trying to snoop around, but Garrett had stopped trying to hide what he was doing a while ago. Plus, his analyst was a step up from herself looks wise and ten years younger to boot. If he was going to cheat, and Beatrice long ago accepted that he was, then she would have preferred that his dalliances were with girls who were on the same level as her.

"But then you'll just move on to the next deal," she said. Beatrice knew that in addition to the cheating, this was what she had signed up for when she agreed to marry Garrett, even though it had taken him seven years to actually pop the question. These late nights bought her a big apartment on Madison Avenue with a view of the Park, a week in the south of France, and the freedom of not having to have a day job. Sure, she had her tutoring business to keep up appearances before she had Jack Jack. She would work with a couple of rich kids once or twice a month, blow the money on cabs and coffee, and spend the rest of her time devoted to the Quests.

"Anyway, I hope you don't mind, I cracked open the bottle early, wasn't sure if you were even making it home tonight. Want some?"

Garrett shook his head.

"Not tonight, B. I need to get some sleep. Have a 7 AM call with Taipei." He got up from the couch and walked down the hall into their bedroom, leaving Beatrice alone again with the wine and her thoughts.

The subway car was crowded. Beatrice hated riding the subway, and normally she wouldn't be caught dead riding it during the morning rush. But that wouldn't do for today's errand, as Beatrice had decided to bring Kate along to get her some on-the-ground training. She also wanted to see how the girl's skills measured up first-hand, to see how she was progressing.

They had met up near the W. 4th Street station, and it was two transfers in before the crowds thinned enough before Beatrice felt comfortable talking shop out in public.

"Today's raid should be simple," she said. "We get there, buy the requested items, and get the hell out of there before we run into anyone else."

"Why's it called a raid?" Kate asked. The girl's chipper demeanor had returned, and Beatrice suppressed the urge to roll her eyes before answering.

"Because it's meant for a group. The task is harder, but the reward greater. Also the members of the Council must have all played Everquest back in the day and they think they're being cute."

"What's Everquest? Some sort of match-3 puzzle?"

"Never mind. How is your research coming?"

She had sent Kate deep into the bowels of one of the NYU libraries, ostensibly for a paper for her American history class, but actually to transcribe a set of rare 18th century manuscripts. Beatrice had tried multiple times to get access to the same collection without any luck, but Kate's request had been granted within days. It was one of the reasons she now liked using college students as her trainees: no one took them that seriously. Plus they helped push her wares without her having to hang out in Washington Square Park all day.

"Good! I've been indexing the Valley Forge journals. The library's records are pretty terrible, so it's slow going, but after that's done I'll cross-reference those with the entries in Rita's diary and hopefully that should give us some insight into what-"

"Excellent progress," Beatrice said, cutting off the girl before she could start blabbing too much about the project. She wasn't the paranoid type, but she never liked discussing things of a sensitive nature out in public, in case this was the day that someone was actually stalking her again.

"When you've gotten a bit further, we can discuss in private."

"Oh, sure," said Kate, clearly disappointed that she wasn't going to get the chance to impress Beatrice with her meticulous research. "By the way, I took that buff you gave me the other day to help finish the research. Got the rest done in 20 minutes, then did a bunch of my friends' papers, then some random freshman's problem set, and then it was only 1 AM, so I-"

"Glad you liked it. Packs a punch, doesn't it?" Beatrice made a note to dilute the next batch she made. It wasn't supposed to cause such a strong reaction, but maybe Beatrice had misjudged how intense Kate was.

"Definitely. Umm, say, you wouldn't happen to have any more of those, would you?"

Red flag, red flag, thought Beatrice. The last thing she needed was her trainee to go on a bender and end up being fished out of the East River naked.

"You're in luck," Beatrice said, reaching into her bag and pulling out one of the "regular" buffs. "It's my last one. Waiting for some new raw materials to make another batch, so don't waste it."

She handed it to Kate who eyed it greedily before stuffing it in her own pocketbook. Beatrice regretted her generosity immediately, but the regular-strength version was only a hair better than a regular Adderall, so the girl wouldn't get in too much trouble. At least she hoped.

The train screeched to a halt at the elevated station, and Beatrice beckoned Kate to follow her. They climbed down the stairs in silence as Beatrice checked her watch. 1:10. They were going to be late, and late meant not only a squandered opportunity but a ding to her reputation on the Raid Board. She had come close to failing a raid, once, but repressed that memory. No need for unnecessary negativity.

"Come on, it's not much further," she said to Kate as she quickened her pace.

"Where are we going anyway?" asked Kate, who matched her brisk strides.

"The Requester wants us to procure certain items from an estate sale," Beatrice said.

"That's it? Couldn't they have gone themselves?"

"Sure, but when you're flush with tokens, why would you stoop to such labor yourself when you can sit back in your comfy chair and let others do the dirty work for you?"

When she first received access to the Raid Board, Beatrice was beyond ecstatic. Her years of fetch Quests would finally be over, and she pictured grander Quests uncovering ancient magical objects and the like. But her enthusiasm was tempered during that first visit to the Board, when all but a few of the raids were just more elaborate fetch Quests. Plus, she hadn't realized that the raids required more than one person.

That was when she had begun her trainee program, and it had mostly been an unmitigated disaster thus far. The hours Beatrice spent seeding the Quest Board in search of potential partners had been too many to count, and all she had gotten for her efforts was a handful of abject failures.

Her first attempt she could chalk up to inexperience. He was a dorky engineer, the kind that had littered her undergrad classes and who had quickly become infatuated with her to the point of obsession. Not that Beatrice was the second coming of Helen of Troy, but she had the rare combination of attractiveness and approachability that made all manner of nerd think they had a shot with her.

After that unfortunate ending, she had made a rule: women only. But her next attempts suffered from the wrong power dynamic - they were older women who came to the Quests later in life and didn't like taking orders from someone 20 years their junior. Most ended up going out on their own, which saved Beatrice from any real unpleasantries. Now she hoped she had identified the perfect candidate pool for future prospects, but the jury was still out on that.

"We're here," said Beatrice. They had stopped in front of a five-story walk-up with a rusty fire escape, the kind that littered the streets of Bed-Stuy. She hit the buzzer for 5A, and a few seconds later, the outer door clicked open.

The lobby was deserted, and so Beatrice ventured cautiously toward the stairs, stopping at the bottom.

"What are you doing?" asked Kate.

"Listening. Shhh."

If anyone had gotten there ahead of them, they weren't making a lot of noise. Beatrice retreated and walked towards the mailboxes at the back of the lobby, and began rummaging through her purse.

"Why aren't we going up?"

"Because I need to give you something first," said Beatrice, reaching her hand into her bag. "I said that our employer probably was just using their money to hire us instead of getting their lazy ass down here, but there's also a chance that someone else knows what's for sale here, so we need to be adequately prepared for that probability."

She removed the knife and unsheathed it from its leather scabbard. The smooth metal of the blade reflected the dirty fluorescent light in the vestibule, emitting a glossy sheen. She grasped the ivory handle and made a few quick stabs in the air before resheathing it.

"Here," said Beatrice, handing the knife to Kate, whose eyes widened.

"W-what, why are you giving that to me?" It was clear from the girl's suddenly pale face that she had never handled a weapon before, and Beatrice didn't have to use her imagination to picture what would happen if the girl tried to use the knife. Especially that particular knife.

"You know what, on second thought, why don't you let me hold onto that?"

Beatrice took the knife back and placed it in her pocketbook.

"If the raid goes south, just try to stay out of the way," she offered.

"Umm, OK," said Kate. "Aren't we just going upstairs, buying some random item, and then leaving? It's not like we're breaking into the Met or something."

"You'd be surprised at how often a mundane exercise turns into an extraordinary one, especially if the Guild decides to get involved," said Beatrice, her eyes drifting down to the almost-faded scar under her jeans that ran the length of her right thigh. "Let's go."

They walked up the short flights of stairs in silence. Beatrice grasped the strap of her pocketbook tightly, as if that would help calm her nerves. It didn't, but the amethyst ring that was normally slotted below her engagement ring would have. Except, in a bone-headed move, she had left it downtown. Not that she expected to need it today, as it would be an absurd waste to use it during such a routine task. But wearing it provided a manner of reassurance that she was now lacking. Well, what's done was done, and the knife would have to be enough today.

The door to 5A was slightly ajar when they arrived on the final landing. Because they're expecting us, thought Beatrice. Not because that fop Gilbert was lying in wait inside. Well, she thought, only one way to find out.

Beatrice pushed the door open and stepped in slowly. The room was empty. No, that was a bad word. It was bare. Where the furniture had once sat, only dents on the pale green carpet remained. The walls too were barren, except for rectangle-shaped squares of white where paintings or pictures had once hung. She was too late.

"Hello," said a soft, raspy voice behind her, causing Beatrice to nearly jump out of her skin. She lowered her hand into her pocketbook, ready to brandish the knife at whoever had spoken, and slowly turned around.

A little old man who looked like a mole rat with glasses and an ugly sweater sat in a worn, leather chair right next to the door. Why she had missed him at first glance, she wasn't sure. But he wasn't Gilbert and he didn't seem very threatening, so she let go of the knife and lowered her guard slightly.

"Hi, umm. We're here for the estate sale?" Beatrice said. She could see Kate peering in from the hallway and waved her inside.

"What? Oh right. My sister's things." The old man pulled a piece of paper out of one of the pockets in his sweater and held it close to his face. "Yes, there's an estate sale here today at 1:30. But it's over."

"But it's only 1:33, sir. How is the sale already over?" asked Kate. "We didn't see anyone leaving on our way up."

"Hmm?" the old man peered through the thick lenses of his glasses at Beatrice, then at Kate. "There's two of you? You're a looker, aren't you?" he said, pointing at Kate. "And you're not so bad either. Must be my lucky day."

Kate blushed at the comment, and Beatrice grimaced.

"Anyways, what was I saying? Oh right. Someone came this morning and offered to take the whole lot off my hands. Offered next to nothing but I took it just the same. Heh." The old man's chuckling gave way to a hacking cough, and Beatrice turned away in disgust.

"Serves Doreen right. Wasn't even giving me the money. Nope. All going to some stupid charity for cats or something. She didn't even have a cat!"

"I see," said Beatrice. This whole outing was turning into an outright disaster and she was furious at herself for ruining her perfect raid record because she hadn't thought of going to the estate sale before it started. It was a mistake a seasoned Quester like her should never have made.

"It sounds like she was very difficult to get along with," said Kate. "My mom was like that, always complaining about this thing or that thing. She probably set the record for angry letters to the editor in our town paper."

Beatrice glared at her. What was she doing? Trying to make the old man even more annoyed?

"Oh yes. That was Doreen to a T. She had a talent for it though.

Always seemed to get what she wanted. Like getting me to schlep up here from Baltimore to take care of her stuff. At my age. As if I had all the time and money in the world. Which I don't. But then I got that letter and, bam, suddenly I'm on the next bus."

Beatrice's face lit up and she turned to look at Kate, who smiled. The girl was full of surprises, apparently.

"Do you happen to have that letter still?" asked Kate.

The old man nodded.

"As a matter of fact, I do. It's in my bag over there in the kitchen. Be a dear and bring it over, would you?"

The girl dashed over to the kitchen and returned with a folded piece of paper.

"Mind if I take a look at that?" said Beatrice.

"Knock yourself out," said the old man.

Beatrice unfolded the crinkly yellow paper. The text was barely legible but her eyes were for some reason drawn to the words, which were written in deep black ink.

"Morton,

I'm dying. Get up here and take care of my stuff after I go.

-Doreen"

Beatrice ran a finger over the words. The ink felt almost like finger paint, like she could scrape it right off the paper with the right tools.

"Your sister wasn't much for words, was she?"

Morton shook his head.

"Nope. Can't say I'm sad she's gone, she was as rotten as a person could be, but part of me misses her phone calls."

"When they came and took out her stuff earlier, did you happen to see the pens or the ink she used to write this?"

Beatrice held the letter in front of Morton, whose eyes suddenly became fixed to the paper, as if he were in a daze, and she quickly withdrew it from his sight.

"No. They took everything. Well, except the bed. Couldn't get it out the door for some reason. And this chair obviously. I wasn't about to let them pull it out from under me. Not sure if they're coming back, but I hope they don't. I need somewhere to sleep tonight and this chair is qui-"

Beatrice sprinted to the little bedroom, hoping beyond hope that the Guild had not been as thorough as it appeared. The windowless room was as empty as the other one, save for a queen mattress on a box spring. It took up more than half the room and featured all manner of stain and discoloration, but at this particular moment, Beatrice couldn't care less, as she flipped up the mattress in one fluid motion to reveal...

Nothing.

Except the top of the box spring. She flipped that up too and was rewarded with a view of the parquet floor underneath. No secret stash, not even an empty box or a note saying "Haha, beat you to it." She had failed. For a second time.

Beatrice let go of the box spring and sat on top of it, the dirty mattress now leaning against her back. This should have been a simple raid, an easy win. But no. The Guild had bested her again. She felt all the fury and rage build up inside her - this failed raid, Garrett's latest dalliance, her chronic lack of sleep. What was the point of all of this? Was she going to have to keep grinding forever, the Guild forever taunting her from slightly out of reach?

"Hey. Look at that."

Kate walked into the room and Beatrice quickly brought her hand up to her eyes to wipe away the tears. She couldn't let her trainee see her this emotional over a stupid raid.

"What?" asked Beatrice.

"There's a bulge in the box spring. Right next to you."

Beatrice looked to her left. Sure enough, there it was. How had she missed it? She ran her hand over the protruding fabric and could feel the outline of several small objects. A quick slice with the ivory handle of the knife sheared the fabric of the box spring, and she pulled it back to reveal a ziploc bag resting on top of a wooden slat. A ziploc bag containing two fountain pens and a small bottle of ink. She took the bottle out of the bag and shook it next to her ear. The sloshing of liquid inside filled her heart with a joy almost equal to hearing Jack Jack's wailing cry in the hospital that first time.

"Is that it then?" asked Kate.

Beatrice nodded.

"Yes. We've found it. Well, you did. Thank you."

Beatrice suddenly stood up and gave Kate a heavy hug. The girl seemed taken aback by the gesture, and her arms hung in the air for a few moments behind Beatrice's back before she returned the embrace.

"You're welcome. I didn't really do anything though."

She released Kate from the hug and they turned away from each other. An awkward silence pervaded the room, as if a barrier between the mentor and trainee had been broken. Beatrice should have been angry at her lack of discipline, but the unexpected bounty that they had discovered had salvaged an utter disaster, and not only that, there was an an extra pen and plenty of ink for her own use.

"You did though. Anyway, let's book it out of here before the Guild realizes what they've missed."

"Sure. But what's the Guild?"

Beatrice's thoughts again drifted to that moonless night in the Park.

"You don't want to know."

The wine was red tonight. A bottle of Carignan from their last trip to the South of France. Beatrice had mixed memories about that vacation. On the one hand, who could be unhappy lounging on a Mediterranean beach? But on the other hand, it was the last time that she and Garrett had had sex and the result of that act was quietly sleeping in the other room.

Garrett's glass remained full, for no sooner had he poured it than his work phone had rung. That was two hours ago and he still hadn't returned from the bedroom. Well, whatever. If he didn't come back soon, she was going to be forced to drink his glass, as the bottle was nearing its end.

Her marriage might not have been firing on all cylinders, but at least Kate's progression had been going smoothly. The girl had performed admirably on the raid, although Beatrice was glad that they hadn't actually run into the Guild, not just because that was always a bad time, but also because she could just picture Kate inadvertently getting both of them killed. Maybe some krav maga and light weapons training was in order.

Beatrice took another sip of the Carignan and closed her eyes. She thought about the latest spoils of the raid. It was a little too perfect and that worried her slightly. Was the Guild that dense to have overlooked the mattress? Were they looking for something else? After all, if the old woman had the ink, who knows what else she was hoarding in that apartment? But Beatrice couldn't dwell on such things now. Still, a test of the ink was in order before she made any more plans.

Doreen's letter was currently soaking in alcohol downtown, which would separate the ink from the paper. That would give Beatrice a little bit to perform some trial runs without wasting the pure ink left in the bottle. Now that she actually had a sample in hand, Kate's research with the diary would likely bear more fruit. Speaking of fruit, Beatrice made a mental note to start lining up preparations for the fall, as her apple stash was running low. But that was a longer term project and she hoped Kate would be ready in a few months with a little more seasoning.

The buzzing of Garrett's phone on the coffee table brought Beatrice back to the present. Which was odd. Because Garrett was still in the other room. It vibrated again and she picked it up to bring it into the kitchen so she could get back to her brainstorming.

That ended up being a mistake. Because as she put it down on the kitchen counter, another buzz went off and Beatrice saw the string of text messages that had caused all the commotion.

"When is this call going to be over :("

"If it keeps going any longer, how u going to come over 2night?"

"dont worry ill wait up for u :)"

Beatrice stared at the messages. She wanted to take the phone and chuck it out the window. Or smash it with a hammer. Or go over to that little tart's apartment and shove it down her throat. Instead, she picked it up, walked slowly over to the bedroom, and opened the door.

Garrett was sitting on the bed in his boxers in front of a laptop, talking too loudly about shutting down some factory in Malaysia. He looked up at her and gave a half wave, and then when he saw the phone in her hand, his eyes went wide. Beatrice let the phone drop from her hand, and then, without another word, walked out of the apartment and escaped into the night.

The warm morning light washed over the bedroom. Well, it would have, if the one window in the room actually looked out onto something other than a brick wall. Still, a tiny ray of sunlight usually crept into the tiny "den" of Beatrice's Bowery apartment and it was enough to rouse her from her sleep. Her reward for waking up was a pounding in her head and a dry throat. She sat up and opened her eyes, trying to remember why she was here instead of in her much larger bed uptown.

The half-naked man beside her let out a loud snore. Oh, right.

She had stormed out of the apartment, hopped in a cab downtown, and then had started texting the Quester guys in her phone to see if anyone would meet up for a drink and then some. Let Garrett deal with Jack Jack by himself for once, she had thought. If he was going to be so blatant about flouting their marriage vows, then she didn't feel bad at beating him at his own game. From the presence of whoever this guy was, and her own half-state of undress, she surmised that she had succeeded in some part of her plan.

Beatrice scooted down to the middle of the mattress. A set of built-in cabinets ran along the adjacent wall, with a clearance of maybe four inches from the bed. It made the tiny room feel even tinier and she had to move back onto to the bed to even open the doors. What clothes did she even still have here? The answer was one full-length black dress and one old down coat. Beatrice sighed and bent down to pick up her sweater from yesterday off of the floor, but it was nowhere to be found. She settled for the blue button down at the foot of the bed and walked to the bathroom.

Her reflection in the mirror could have been from ten years ago - the bags under her eyes, the hangover headache, the shirt that wasn't hers. She had been a typical wild child living it up in the city: out most nights, a new guy every other week. That was before the Quests though, before the curtain had been pulled back and Beatrice had discovered a truth about the world, a truth that would have made most people curl up into a ball on the ground and never get up. Except she was made of sterner stuff. Working her way up from the bottom, grinding out Quest after Quest after Quest, piling up all those tokens. Sure, she had caught a few breaks along the way, the diary being one, but if anything, that had made her work even harder.

Beatrice turned on the tap and let the rust-colored water turn clear before splashing some on her face. It didn't do the trick, and she tried to remember if she had anything in the other room that would help get rid of the throbbing in her head. She could deal with the aftermath of last night if she could just get in the right mindse--

Three successive pounds on the front door broke her train of thought.

Fuck.

It was Garrett, although she didn't know how. She'd already moved to a different apartment by the time they started dating and she never told him where she used to live. Maybe he had tailed her last night after she stormed out of the apartment. She laughed at the image of Garrett racing out of their building with a sleeping Jack Jack in a baby Bjorn, and decided it must just be the annoying old woman from across the hall complaining again.

Beatrice walked back into the bedroom, where the mystery man was still asleep, and tiptoed into the living room. The front door shook again. Too loud to be the old woman, she thought. A flick of the peephole finally revealed the perpetrator: it was Kate.

She unlocked and unlatched the door, and the pounding stopped.

"Just a second," said Beatrice, slowly opening it with a creak.

Kate stood in the hallway, her hair a tangled mess, her eyes bloodshot, and her mascara running down her face. The girl was visibly shaking, as if she had just been mugged.

"Kate, what are you doing her-"

The trainee pushed past Beatrice, walked into the apartment without saying a word, and sat down on the couch just past the large wooden bookcase. Her body continued to shake, and she stared unresponsively across the room. Beatrice walked into the kitchen to get a glass of water from the tap, so she could stall a bit before confronting Kate. She hadn't told her about this place, had she? Was she stalking her? Whatever was going on, it was one less thing she wanted to deal with now, so hopefully she could steady the girl and send her on her way.

Beatrice set the glass of water down on the coffee table next to her pocketbook and waited for Kate to do or say something, but the girl didn't respond.

"Kate."

"Kate."

"KATE!"

She shouted the girl's name, but that too received no response. Beatrice wanted to slap her upside the head, but she settled for throwing the glass the water all over the trainee.

The girl stirred back to life, looking down at her soaked shirt and then up at Beatrice, before finally settling on Beatrice's pocketbook.

It only took a split second for the thought to percolate in her head, but it was a second too long, and before Beatrice could react, Kate dove toward the bag and wrenched something free.

Once, a long time ago, Beatrice discovered that not only did her knife pierce through skin as if it were jello, but also that it had the neat ability to cause the person on the receiving end of the said piercing to turn to stone. Beatrice was as shocked as her would-be assailant was when he saw his forearm turning grey after she had slashed him in the dark alley, but she hadn't had any occasion since to witness what the knife was truly capable of. That was, until the present moment, as Kate held the blade pointed at Beatrice, the girl's hand shaking violently.

"More. I need more."

Kate's voice was barely above a whisper, which gave Beatrice some measure of reassurance.

"More what, Kate? You know, you could have just called. Now why don't you just give me that-"

"The buffs. I need more."

"Oh."

"I made the last one into a powder, so it would last longer and you wouldn't think I was an addict by asking for more so soon. Bought a mortar and pestle at Goodwill. Snorted a little bit to see what would happen and passed out. Woke up, did a little more, tried to finish a paper. Then it wore off again. But not before a thought occurred to me. I needed to inject it. So I went down to the health center, got into the exam room, and then took off with some syringes and tourniquets before the nurse came in. That did the trick. But I only had a little left, so I needed to find you."

"Kate, again, you have my number. You didn't need to come down here and-"

"Wasn't expecting you'd be here. Took me all night at the city records department to find this place. Knew you wouldn't keep the good stuff at your actual apartment. No. You keep your lives separate. Smart. So I'd like the stuff now, if you wouldn't mind."

On a normal day, Beatrice would have been able to handle the situation, if it were any other knife. But this particular morning, she was hungover, running on two hours sleep, and facing down the blade of a horrific weapon, and that left her with only one option.

"Ok. Fine. I'll give you more. Just put the knife down first."

The girl's brow furrowed and her eyes went from Beatrice to the knife, as if she hadn't realized that she was holding it. With a flick of her wrist, Kate rotated the knife around and presented the handle to Beatrice, who slowly wrapped her fingers around the ivory.

Beatrice looked down at the point of the blade. It would be so easy to just push it forward, to rid herself of another failed trainee. But as quickly as the thought arose, she quashed it. Too messy, she thought. And in any event, she didn't have a garden in which to store a statue of poor petrified Kate. No. She would have to figure out another way.

Beatrice sheathed the blade and put it back in her pocketbook, which she slung around her shoulder. No sense leaving the bag unattended again and having to repeat the whole exercise.

"Now that we've dealt with that little situation, just sit here and I'll get you what you came for."

Kate nodded and went back to staring off into space, as Beatrice got up and walked over to the towering bookcase that stood right next to the couch. Her eyes scanned the multi-colored rows of books until she found the two that she was looking for. Not that she needed to look so hard. She knew where they were by heart.

With one hand, she grasped the spine of *A Tale of Two Cities* and with the other, the spine of *The Lion, the Witch, and the Wardrobe* on the shelf above, and pulled both at the same time. A satisfying click sounded behind the bookcase, which Beatrice pushed forward to reveal the hidden second bedroom. This was no bedroom though.

The musty smell hit Beatrice's noise as she stepped inside, and she smiled. This was where the magic happened. The far side sported a long table that ran the length of the room, which was partially covered in wax paper. The rest of the walls were lined with shelving and bookcases, holding all manner of jars, books, tools, and other oddities that Beatrice had picked up along the way. Even the windows had been sacrificed on the altar of space, although she had left a tiny sliver of one window uncovered to prevent the room from being completely cut off from the outside world. As much as she wished she could have a nice little cottage out of the city, there was something satisfying about having this hidden nook right here in the Guild's backyard.

Beatrice turned around to see if Kate had followed her into the room, but the girl evidently remained planted on the couch. That would make things go smoother. She had hoped one day to show Kate this room, to work side-by-side with someone who could become almost equal to her, but she knew now that her search would have to continue.

She started walking over to a bookcase on the right side of the room where she kept the full-strength buffs when something on the desk caught her eye. It was the green-tinted mason jar where Doreen's letter was currently soaking, the second pen from the raid sitting next to it. Beatrice walked over and looked at its contents. The letter was still somewhat intact, but more importantly, a thin black film was visible at the top. A different idea now formed in her head. The perfect way to test the potency of the ink. It would solve at least one of her immediate problems, and if it failed, well...

No, she thought. She needed certainty, she needed closure.

Her pocketbook began to vibrate. No doubt it was Garrett, trying to find out where she had gone and whether she would be coming back soon and where did they keep the diapers, and it's not what you think, I swear, blah blah blah. She'd heard it before, but frankly she didn't actually care anymore. She had moved on long ago from the idea that her marriage was anything but a convenient front. Still, she needed to send a message to him that she expected a certain level of discretion. Which brought her thoughts back to the ink. Her eyes lit up. Now there was a good experiment.

Beatrice opened the drawers in the desk until she found one that had some paper, which she brought over to the jar. Pen in hand, she carefully unfastened the lid and dipped the tip in the black liquid, swirling it around counterclockwise, before withdrawing it. She quickly went to work, dipping the pen back in the jar as needed, and soon, the note was complete. Perfect. She set it down to dry and walked over to the closet, sliding the door open to reveal a pair of mahogany armoires. It had been a long time since she had crafted this particular item, and she hoped it hadn't lost its potency in the intervening years. Well, only one way to find out, she supposed. The bottom drawer on the right armoire held what she sought and she brought the container over to the desk to assemble her little care package for tonight.

Beatrice emerged from the hidden room a few minutes later with a sealed envelope, and pulled the bookcase back in place. If Kate had noticed her prolonged absence, or even the hidden room, it didn't register on the girl's face.

"Here," said Beatrice, handing Kate the envelope. Kate stared at the envelope with a puzzled look on her face.

"What's this?"

"Your next task. Make sure this letter gets delivered and I'll make sure you're taken care of by the evening."

The girl's expression didn't waiver as she considered the envelope, and Beatrice held her breath, steeling herself for another outburst. But somewhere the gods of fate and chance were smiling upon her, as Kate stuck the envelope in her pocket and walked out the door.

The girl was late. Ordinarily, Beatrice Taylor would not have cared, and this morning was no different. The baby was at her mom's, Garrett's little analyst had inexplicably been transferred to the West Coast office last week, and one story in the paper had particularly caught her eye.

"Kate O'Laughlin, 19, found dead facedown in dorm room," the headline on page 14 read. Beatrice folded the paper and put it on the table, as a chipper redhead ran up the street and sat down across from her.

"Sorry I'm late! The subway was a complete disaster."

Beatrice smiled.

"No worries. I take it you have the book?"

MEMORIA

INTRODUCTION TO MEMORIA

Memoria begins a year and a half prior to the events of *Trainee*.

CHAPTER ONE

KATE

As much as I like to think it was the opposite, in reality, the Quests found me.

I was walking one afternoon through Brooklyn Bridge Park with some friends from my hall when, on a fencepost, I noticed this little vial. It looked like a tiny beaker that stood on its end and had a cork stopper in it, sealed with hand-dripped red wax.

So I left my friends and walked over and I could see inside was a tiny paper scroll.

It looked like something left by a wood nymph who had escaped from a Grimm fairy tale.

And I remember thinking, "Maybe I've stumbled on some viral scavenger hunt or a prize. Or even a prank. Maybe I'm being filmed for some weird Internet TV show."

I glanced back at my friends, who were deep in conversation about some profound nonsense our history professor had said during yesterday's lecture. And, rather than share this discovery with them, I instead opened the vial and turned it upside down. The scroll fell neatly through the neck of its container and I unfurled it slowly.

Written on the paper was tiny, tiny writing in red ink. It said:

"You're here because you know something. You've felt it your entire life, that there's something wrong with the world. You don't know what it is, but it's there, like a splinter in your mind, driving you mad."

I stared at the scroll.

All that build-up for a fucking quote from The Matrix.

Sorry, I don't usually curse, but someone clearly had too much time on their hands. At least, that's what I thought at the time.

If I had known then what I know now, then maybe I would have rolled the scroll up, stuck it back into that tiny vial, and chucked the thing into the East River.

But I didn't.

And what a mistake that was.

CHAPTER TWO

KATE

The boy next to me was snoring.

Which was annoying, because we were currently sharing the twin bed in his small-even-for-New York dorm room, leaving me with few options to escape.

It's not that I didn't like him—I probably did—although we had only hung out a couple times. But there are some things that I just couldn't tolerate and this was one of them.

I gently lifted Zach's arm up over my waist and slid out of bed, looking back to see him turn his body to face the other way. It was four in the morning and the autumn sun wouldn't be up for at least a couple hours.

I considered my options. I could quietly get dressed in last night's clothing, slink out of the dorm, and take a long subway ride back down to the Village, and hopefully not get mugged or worse. Or, I could quietly get dressed in last night's clothing, slink out of the room, flick through the channels in the lounge at the end of the hallway, and pretend I had been admitted to this stupid preppy school.

The computer monitor on Zach's desk suddenly flickered to life and a third option presented itself. I wasn't one for prying into other people's electronics, but the window currently open on the screen was like nothing I had ever seen on a modern computer.

It was white with black ASCII text, and it reminded me of the rudimentary software my grandpa used to keep track of his crop rotations. As I wiped the sleep from my eyes, for a second I thought it had formed into the shape of a tiny vial. But then I blinked and instead, there was a message:

"Welcome back to the Quest Board, zach_attack," it said at the top.

A list of ten numbered entries appeared below and I swear it was like reading a page from one of those fantasy novels that lined the shelves of my older brother's room. Except instead of an imaginary world filled with elves and dwarves, the "Quests" on the screen were asking for things in New York City.

Seriously!

```
1. Feed a leaf of the Corpse flower from the Botani-
cal Gardens to one of the sea lions at the Bronx
Zoo. Reward: 17 iron.
2. A cup of dirt from Corlears Hook Park. Put it in
the mailbox on the corner of Madison and Gouverneur
and I'll take it from there. Reward: 3 iron.
3. Hiya! Could you help me out by fetching me a
handful of blueberries, a tillandsia, an orange
Popsicle, and three pounds of 80/20 ground beef
from Chelsea Market? Leave in the windowsill of 194
```

```
West 9th Street. Thanks! Reward: One wood
```

My eyes scanned the rest of the entries until I reached the bottom of the screen, where further instructions awaited:

```
"Select your Quest, or press A for the next page,
B to submit your own, C for Q-mail, D for Quester
Profile, or Esc to quit."
```

My mind was racing and all thoughts of fleeing evaporated as I clicked through page after page of these so-called Quests.

I was about to open Q-mail, whatever that was, when I heard rustling in the bed behind me.

"Kate?" mumbled Zach, half asleep. "S'hat you?"

"Yeah babe, it's me," I said, quickly turning off the monitor. "Just had to pee."

I retook my little spoon position in bed, Zach's arm soon returning to my thigh, and tried to forget everything from the past 10 minutes.

It didn't work.

So I did something rash, something bold, something the 18-year old girl who left Lincoln, Nebraska a few weeks ago would have never done.

I went to the computer, turned the monitor back on, and selected the first Quest.

We held hands all the way from the MetroNorth station. It was awkward because, well, holding hands was something couples did and I didn't know what we were, really.

I had told Zach the next morning that I had accepted the corpse flower Quest. He had stared at me blankly for about three minutes before silently exiting the room. When he hadn't come back after an hour, I had shrugged my shoulders and went back on the Quest Board to explore until he returned from his 11 a.m. class. I had bombarded him with as many questions about the Quests as I could come up with, but he had deftly deflected and demurred them all. Finally, after a different type of convincing, Zach agreed to let me complete the Quest with him, a "trial run," as he called it.

So that was how we found ourselves at the New York Botanical Gardens the following Saturday, pretending to be tourists from Sweden. It would let us linger by the corpse flower a little longer, I had postulated, but Zach was skeptical.

"Are you ready?" I asked after we handed our tickets to the stern-looking man at the entrance to the atrium.

"I guess, yeah."

"You don't sound so sure."

He grew visibly irritated and would have let go of my hand had I not squeezed it.

"Of course I'm not convinced," he whispered. "This Quest is way out of my comfort zone. I usually stick to the easy stuff. You know, like buying random shit at a flea market."

"Where's the fun in that?" I said with a smile. "And besides, you're never going to level up with that strategy. You've been stuck on level two for what, two months?"

He jerked my arm suddenly and I nearly fell into him.

"Look, I already told you the other day that you shouldn't have been snooping around on my computer, let alone looking through the Quest Board. You're not supposed to … it says I'm supposed to Quest alone. I could get suspended by the Council if they find out!"

"But they're not going to find out," I said. "I'm not going to tell them, are you?"

"Well, no."

"Good. And after this is over, I'll just get my own account and then it won't even be an issue!"

I let go of him and ran ahead to the enormous line of people waiting to get into the main section of the atrium. When he finally caught up to me, I put my finger to my lips and he nodded reluctantly. It was showtime.

We had practiced our fake accents the night before and I had decided that the best course of action was to say as little as possible. Which, given the hundreds of people who had showed up to see a smelly flower, would probably be an easy thing to do.

"Right this way, right this way," shouted a docent over the crowd. "Tickets 251-325 up here with me. The rest, hang back."

"That's us," I whispered and we quickly joined the assembled crowd.

"The Titan-Arum," the docent said, "otherwise known as the corpse flower, has a curious life cycle. Once every four to five years, it produces a flower that blooms only for a single day, before withering and dying. And in that one day, the flower produces a rather pungent smell which, oddly enough, attracts pollinators. We've had several Titan-Arums here at the Botan over the years and we're fortunate to have one in bloom again."

I felt the press of the crowd against me and I stuck my elbows out to push them back, as the docent gave us the final instructions.

"In a minute, you'll get to approach the flower in groups of five. Each group will have two minutes and then you'll need to move on to the rest of the atrium."

"Hold back," I whispered to Zach. "And then you'll distract the docent when your group comes up."

He nodded and stepped back while I slowly approached my quarry. The docent stood guard in front of a roped off section of the garden, with the flower towering behind him. Its odor already threatened to overwhelm my nose, which, after spending every summer on my grandpa's farm, took a lot, but I needed to get closer.

I now appreciated the irony of the docent's comment about the flower attracting pollinators despite its horrid smell. Were all of us here not also pollinators, but in a different way? We would leave the atrium and tell our friends that we had seen the magnificent corpse flower and then they too would try to visit, and then tell their friends and so on, and the flower's legend would continue to grow.

I tucked that philosophical quandary into the back of my mind as my time with the flower was almost at its end. The edge of the flower's enormous petal was a few feet beyond the rope and I hoped that my nails were sharp enough to break off a piece without too much struggle. The docent raised his hand to urge us onward and that's when I heard a familiar cry from behind.

"I think someone's fainted," I said to the docent, who didn't know if he should abandon his post guarding the flower or go help the person in need, before finally relenting and scurrying away. I watched the crowd part to let him through to Zach before quickly ducking under the rope to break off a section of the petal.

Except when I arrived at the corpse flower, the chunk of the petal I was going to grab was already gone.

I suddenly felt a sharp pain in my shin and a whoosh of air hit my face and the next thing I knew, I was lying face down at the base of the plant. The smell was overpowering at this close distance and I struggled to push myself up. But when I finally did get back to my feet, all hope of a quick escape went out the window, as I saw three guards converge on me while Zach faded silently in the crowd and walked away.

CHAPTER THREE

KORA

The woman with blonde hair observed the scene from afar and frowned. It should have been an easy mission. But her soon-to-be erstwhile boyfriend couldn't keep his pants on long enough between her visits and so he had snared himself a freshman from downtown. That in and of itself wasn't a big deal. He was a 21 year-old college kid, after all, and she could only gain control of her host body once every three weeks during a good month. The complicating factor was that this new girl had not only taken Zach to bed, but had stumbled onto his computer in the middle of the night and taken the very Quest that Zach needed to complete.

Kora had resisted her host's urge to reassert control for one more day and this had allowed her to follow the couple up to the Botanical Gardens. After some more observation, she had concluded that it might not have been such a bad idea to have Kate intercede in the Quest, as the farm girl had proven herself more competent in subterfuge than her beau. The folly of inheritance, she had now come to realize. But what Zach had lacked in intelligence, he had made up for in alchemic wealth, even if he was the third son of a third son. It was the angle she had to play in her current state, unfortunately, and she didn't know whether this extra exertion would be worth the potential price of sitting unused in a drawer for another decade.

She watched the couple enter the atrium and Kate whisper something to Zach, who nodded and halted his progression, while the redhead advanced toward the flower. The girl had moxie, it seemed. It was short-lived, however, because just as she made her move, an opposing force revealed itself, just in time to steal the prize. This was what Kora had expected and it was still gratifying, after all these years, to know that her intellect and instincts were still above and beyond most other living humans. But, just as quickly as her true target had appeared did she vanish, aided no doubt by one of her so-called speed buffs. This, too, she had predicted and it was currently one puzzle that she hadn't yet managed to crack.

That was, until she witnessed the security detail descend on poor Kate and haul her down to the atrium basement. An unexpected gift that would allow her to plant the seed earlier than she had hoped. For in this girl, she sensed drive and determination. It was just a matter of directing those energies toward their common enemy.

Kora watched the security detail depart for the main office, and she quickly descended into the basement. The hallway that greeted her ran the length of the atrium and she hoped that Kate heard her echoing footsteps as she approached. Surprisingly, there was a makeshift cell at the end, in which the poor girl was sitting on the floor, clutching her ankle.

"Hello," said Kora.

Kate looked up at her with a confused expression.

"Hi," she replied. "You're a bit young to be the head of the Thain Center."

"I'm sorry?"

"The person in charge of the exhibit. And who also maintains the forest at the center of the Gardens. The security guards said that they were going to get her."

Kora crouched down so she was eye level with Kate, which, in the heels she was wearing, would have made a normal woman's feet go numb. But she was not exactly a normal woman.

"It's a nice forest. From what I remember, I used to walk it frequently in my younger days. Maybe if they let you out of here soon, you can go see it."

"I'm confused," said Kate, who winced as she suddenly stood up. "If you're not with the Gardens, then why are you here?"

Kora grasped the bars of the cell door and pulled herself back to her feet. She had a good six inches on the girl in her heels, not that she needed the height advantage at the moment.

"I'm here because I need your help. I want you to help me find the woman who put you in this cell."

Kate's confusion grew as she considered Kora's words and she took a few steps backward into the cell.

"W-what are you talking about? The security guards put me in here."

"They did, but that's not why you're here. You're here because you unknowingly got in Trinity's way."

"I...I don't know who that is or how I could have..."

"Let me just cut to the chase," said Kora. "You were here on a Quest with Zach to take a piece of the corpse flower. So was Trinity. Unfortunately for you, you do not have alchemy-enhanced speed. So, when you tried to grab the petal, she had already beat you to it. And kicked your shin for good measure. And now she's gone and you're stuck holding the empty bag, as it were."

"You know about the Quests? Do they have something to do with that vial?"

"I know a lot about a lot of things, some of which I will tell you about, in time."

Kora felt a slight pull against her neck and instinctively grasped the green stone on the chain with her right hand while her left hand fished the letherium tablet out of her jacket pocket.

"Here," said Kora, extending her hand past the bars.

"What is that, a mint?" asked Kate, who took the golden square without question.

"I thought you could use one. You'll be down here for a while."

Kate nodded and popped the tablet into her mouth, which made Kora's lips curl up slightly.

"It tastes like—"

"Like emptiness. Which is what is filling your head right now. But, I want you to hold on to a singular thought for me, while I take the rest. Can you do that for me? Until we meet again?"

Kate's eyes widened as the letherium took effect.

"*Find her.*"

KATE

Who even knew the Botan had a jail? I mean, it seemed like the kind of place where the most extreme thing they could muster up was a stern talking to by a woman with greying hair holding a watering can.

And yet, I spent what felt like 12 hours in a holding cell somewhere in the bowels of the arboretum, probably directly below the stinking flower for an added dash of irony. When the door to the cell finally creaked open, it was nearly midnight and by the time I reached the entrance to Zach's dorm, it was almost two and he was arm-in-arm with some girl with blond hair who might actually have been from Sweden. I wanted to run up and punch him in the back of the head, but I was exhausted and my shin still ached from whatever had hit me in front of the flower.

So I did what every normal girl from Lincoln does when she finds out their sort-of boyfriend is two-timing them: I showed up at his doorstep the next morning bright and early with a heaping pile of freshly made pancakes and a bottle of maple syrup. Needless to say, the not-actually Swedish girl who answered was nonplussed at the whole situation and slammed the door in my face.

And so ended the first chapter of my Questing career.

Without access to Zach's Questing account, I had no way to access the Quest Board, no way to earn tokens, no way to find out what the hell this whole thing was in the first place. It wasn't like I could just Google "weird Internet quests" and find my way back (believe me, I tried).

As much as I wanted to believe the whole thing was some psych grad student's idea of a practical joke, there was a nagging feeling in the back of my mind that just wouldn't go away. That and the way the corpse flower petal had just vanished right before my eyes.

So I pressed on, searching for a hint or a whiff of something. Anything. But, as the weeks turned into months, I found myself ready to give up and pretend I had imagined the whole thing.

Then one day, when I was walking through Chelsea Market to pick up some tacos I had heard about from a girl on my hall, a flash of inspiration hit me. There had been a Quest that first night, in Zach's room, that was asking for a bunch of random crap from the Market. A mixture of beef, a fistful of blueberries, a fruit-flavored popsicle, and some sort of flower? The details were hazy, but I forced myself to remember.

Five minutes before closing, I left with a tote bag full of what I hoped were the right items and headed for an address I hoped was the one referenced in the Quest. The place looked boarded up when

I arrived, but I left the bag in the windowsill just the same. I returned the next day and the bag was still there and full, except for the popsicle that had melted into a pile of mush. When I went back the day after and the day after that, it was more of the same. That Saturday, I resolved to spend the entire day on the bench across the street in the hopes that whoever had posted that original Quest was still out there, waiting for someone to complete it. It being January and snowing, it was not the most pleasant way to pass the time. But, I had no other choice left really, save for breaking into Zach's room and demanding he invite me back to the Board. And, with how my pancake delivery had been received, I didn't think that had a high chance of success.

I must have passed out at some point, either from the cold or the boredom, but when I checked the windowsill at 9 o'clock that night, the items were gone, and in their place was a note:

"Impressive. You even got the beef blend right. Text me your address and you'll get the red pill soon enough."

The proverbial red pill arrived three days later in the form of a USB thumb drive in my dorm mailbox. I ran upstairs and inserted it into my laptop, only to find that the only thing on there was a text file with a single sentence that said "follow the white rabbit" followed by an ASCII picture of said white rabbit.

I rolled my eyes at yet another *Matrix* reference and was about to toss the drive in my garbage when I looked at the rabbit again. Its head was pointing down, so, on a lark, I highlighted the rest of the document with my cursor to reveal what was quite possibly the longest website address I had ever seen, hiding as white text.

I pasted the URL into my browser, backed up the contents of my laptop, and then tabbed back over and hit enter.

Nothing happened.

I hit enter again and still, the page remained blank.

Frustrated, I went down the hall to fill up my thermos at the water fountain and came back to my room to find nothing had changed. I refreshed yet again and that's when something finally happened: the string of white Christmas lights that hung on the ceiling above my bed went out. Then each of my three lamps did the same, along with my closet light, and then finally the dingy light fixture that was left over from when the dorm was first built.

The only thing left alight in my room was my laptop screen, which now sported a white window with black ASCII text splashed across that read:

```
"Welcome to the Quest Board."
```

I smiled.

Getting access to the Quest Board was only the beginning. I spent the first few days on a bender, doing Quest after Quest after Quest. It was like a new designer drug that only I knew about. Not that I really knew about drugs. I was pretty straight-laced as they came back home, and the only thing that I did that was "against" the rules growing up was sneaking out once to watch a midnight showing of *The Princess Bride* at the local drive-in theater. By the end of that first week, I had to take a break to protect my sanity and also my grades, as spring finals week had arrived.

I tried to throw myself into my studies with the same rigor I had applied to the Quests, but the thought of reading one more analysis of Freud's essay on the uncanny paled in comparison to the actual uncanny Quests that were waiting just a keystroke away. In the end, though, I kept my head down until the last essays were turned in and then immediately ran to the nearest coffee shop to log back onto the Quest Board.

With classes done and a mind-numbing but thankfully predictable summer job at one of the college's vast number of administrative offices freeing up my off hours, my initial pile of seven wooden tokens soon swelled. Earning them had taken me across the city a dozen times over, out of my Greenwich Village bubble. Their craftsmanship was quite stunning and I posited that they each must have taken several hours to carve. As my loot grew and the summer waned, a nagging thought kept tugging at me from the back of my mind. Who was this mystery benefactor and what did they want? Why had they sent me the Quest Board invite only to recede back into the shadows?

Finally, at the beginning of August, a sliver of an answer arrived. I was in the middle of yet another week sorting old faculty files when a yellowed piece of folded and taped paper fell free and lazily drifted to the floor. Before I could absent-mindedly stick it back inside the folder, the front of the paper caught my eye.

"Kate," it said in neat block letters.

Probably a coincidence, I thought. Maybe this professor's name was Kate. Except the file belonged to one Glenn Marle. Fine. Maybe it was a note that Professor Marle meant to send to a colleague. Except I now knew the list of business school faculty from the past 30 years and there was no Professor Kate or Katie or Katherine or even Kitty.

"Oops," I said as my fingers tore open the tape and unfurled the note.

"StarCityCutie42," it said at the top.

What the hell? How did they know my Quest Board handle?

"First, get a better handle," the note continued. "You're not in middle school anymore."

Hey, I liked my handle, even if it was from my old Tumblr site.

"Second, you're overdoing it. Slow down."

A fair point. I had recently pulled an all-nighter collecting refuse from behind restaurants in all five boroughs in the pouring rain and was rewarded for my troubles with one whole bronze token (even though I was promised 10).

"Third, FFS, get a Q-Mail account. Who knows if you're ever going to find this letter."

I remembered seeing Zach's Q-Mail account that first night but had never figured out how to create my own. Noted.

"Fourth, if you really want to know the truth, about everything, then be at Belvedere Castle on August 14 at 10:45.

Cheers,

Trinity"

Who was "Trinity" to talk about handles when she (assuming she even was a woman) was just borrowing her entire persona from *The Matrix*? But if Trinity wanted me to slow down, giving me yet another Quest to complete hardly seemed like the way to do that. Luckily, August 14 was only a week away. Maybe then I would finally get some answers.

CHAPTER FIVE

KORA

Summer in New York City was hit or miss.

Fortunately, for Kora, she had missed most of it. After seeing Kate show up at Zach's doorstep the night after their meeting in the basement, her host had re-exerted control that lasted well through the spring semester. And so Kora was forced into a role she had played frequently over the years: that of the compulsory bystander. Unlike in decades past, when some of her hosts had been right in the thick of alchemy circles, this one left much to be desired. Instead of using the gift of the glamour for something interesting or intriguing, this host had been using it to fornicate. It made Kora want to roll her eyes, if she still had them. Finally, by mid-July, the host had over-indulged to such an extent on a trip to the south of France, that Kora was ready to reassert herself when the time was right.

The plane landed at seven a.m. and when the striking blonde in 2A who had flirted a bit too much with the flight attendant named Francois awoke from her mid-afternoon nap, she found herself back in the pit of her own mind. Kora wasted no time in utilizing her reacquired body and had marched down to Kate's dorm room and rapped on the door around 9 p.m. The girl opened the door with trepidation, no doubt alarmed at the visage of Kora in her peephole.

"Look, I didn't know he was your boyfriend, but we haven't seen each other since that night and—"

"Don't care, not why I'm here. Can I come in?"

Kate was visibly shaking and her eyes were bloodshot, despite the early evening hour, but she acquiesced to Kora's request and stepped aside to let her pass. The dorm room was covered with papers and books, which was odd, because it was the summer, and Kora knew that summer was not normally a time that college students focused on such academic matters. She made herself comfortable on Kate's unmade bed and surveyed the room.

A picture of a castle taped to the wall above Kate's computer drew Kora's eye and she smiled. Her words were doing their job wonderfully, but she needed to know how far the girl had come in these long months. Had she already found Trinity? Or was she still in the middle of the woman's arduous training program?

"You've been busy. That's heartening to see."

Kate stood just at the edge of the room, not knowing what to make of her, not knowing what to say.

"I ..."

"Need a mint. Yes, where are my manners? Here you go."

Kora withdrew a thin circular mint from her pocket. It had a silver sheen and tasted terrible from what she had remembered of the others.

The girl took the mint with trepidation, unlike last time, but ate it quickly just the same.

"It tastes like—"

"The truth."

Kate's eyes rolled into the back of her head as the morarium tablet removed the effect of the previous mint and when she finally regained what had been hidden from her, she clasped her hand over her mouth in shock.

"You! You were there, in the basement at the Botan. But, I didn't realize it. When I saw you in Zach's room. I thought you were just—"

"His girlfriend. But how fortunate for me that you fell into his bed."

"I told you, I didn't know! Or else I never would have—"

"Relax, Kate. Do you think this is all about some stupid boy? No. There are more important things we need to discuss. Such as your search for Trinity."

That last part got the girl completely flustered, and her knees nearly buckled. So Kora directed her over to the desk chair and then re-took her spot on the bed.

"How…how do you know about that?"

"Do you remember what I told you that night?"

"No," said Kate. "Wait, I remember it now. You found me in the basement. Told me about Trinity and alchemy, and the Quests. And then you gave me a mint. But after that…"

Kora watched as Kate tried to piece everything together and she didn't envy what she was going through. Having remembered one version of the truth for so long only for the real truth to spring forth from inside her mind like Athena emerging from Zeus's skull? Well, she had to imagine it was giving the girl quite a headache.

"Even though everything has come back to me, it's like whatever you told me at the end is just out of reach in my mind. And that's what scares me the most."

"Hmm. The only thing that seems to be missing is the end of

our conversation, in which I told you not to worry and that we would meet again."

This was a bold-faced lie. The reason that Kate had so much trouble remembering those two little words was not because of anything wrong with the morarium tablet. No, it was because Kora had spoken those words directly into Kate's subconscious. It was a powerful piece of alchemy and one Kora reserved for situations such as this. What good was a mind-wiped supplicant if they couldn't remember what the hell they were supposed to be doing for her?

"Oh, OK. But how do you know about Trinity then?"

"I've been hearing whispers about her for some time. But it's been difficult for me in my present circumstances to track her down. Much like her namesake in that movie. I don't care for the handle. I mean, can't she come up with something more original?"

Kate's features finally relaxed and her mouth curled into a soft smile.

"That's exactly what I was thinking! It's not like *The Matrix* came out yesterday! And I didn't even tell you about the vial I found with a *Matrix* quote in it. Oh."

The girl paused for a moment and Kora let her sift through the newly resurfaced memories.

"Actually, you did. But it's OK. Your mind will eventually get used to this process."

"What do you mean?"

"I want you to keep looking for her. But she can't know that your search for her is anything other than your inner drive to discover the truth about magic."

"Magic?"

Kora sat the girl down and explained more about alchemy than she would likely learn in her first six years of Questing. But she felt she owed Kate something for what she had done and would continue to do to her. And the girl's mind was like a sponge, soaking up every bit of knowledge and even surprising Kora with some of the connections between the disparate disciplines. Unfortunately, it would do her no good in the weeks ahead.

As the clock struck midnight and their time together had come to an end, Kora placed a golden square on Kate's desk.

"When will I see you again?" asked the girl, who took the mint willingly and began to chew it slowly.

"Not for a while. It will take you some time to work yourself into Trinity's good graces."

"OK. I guess I'll see you when I see you then? Thank you for telling me the truth."

Kate's eyes widened just the same as the first time and Kora considered what command to implant this time.

"*Don't give up.*"

CHAPTER SIX

KATE

There was a castle in Central Park.

This was news to me.

And not just one of those pretend castles on a playground covered in kid snot and who knows what else.

A real, honest-to-goodness castle, with ramparts and a tower and everything. It reminded me of the "castle" at Renaissance Faire Ground in Antelope Park, except that it wasn't made of rubber and filled with air.

I studied Belvedere Castle from afar, as it would be uncouth to perform a scouting Quest, especially when I suspected this was yet another tryout from my mysterious benefactor. But I learned enough about its layout that I was certain I could escape in any number of ways if need be, save for jumping out of the top tower into Turtle Pond below. And even that seemed like a 50-50 proposition.

Finally, August 14 arrived.

I spent the morning aimlessly scrolling through pages of Quests while flicking a wooden token into the air over and over again. And then I spent the afternoon going backward through the Quests until I arrived at the first page again. In between, I scarfed down a pint of Goodrich peanut butter fudge ice cream that my mom had sent me last week. By 6 p.m., my nerves were already shot, and so I collected my token stash, deposited it into the secret pocket I had sewn at the bottom of my pink knapsack, and departed for the upper hinterlands of the island, armed with a small can of mace and my wits. I thought about bringing my pocket knife or maybe a regular knife, or even some sort of sword. I was going to a castle, after all, but had decided against it.

The journey was nevertheless fraught with peril. First, I battled against the raging humidity that had descended over Manhattan, only to finally prevail when the heavens opened up and I found myself soaked from head and backpack to toe. My purple NYU t-shirt clung to my body like an oil slick on a lake, and eventually I discarded it in a hopefully empty alleyway, donning an "I ♥ NY" tank top I had purchased just north of Times Square from a leering street vendor.

Then I tussled with the security guard at the Met, who wanded me more times than I wanted to count in search of my token cache and mace secreted out of sight. I spent the remaining hours until closing time wandering the Museum's seemingly endless hallways of awesome artifacts, trying to psych myself up for the task ahead.

My last opponent of the evening was darkness itself. Even in the city that never sleeps, with its endless lights, there are still pockets of emptiness. And Central Park at dusk seemed to be the nexus. I traversed the tree-lined path away from the Museum, past the statue of a king, until finally the tower of Belvedere Castle crested into view. I circled around to the courtyard on the opposite side and waited for the appointed hour.

My phone buzzed. It was time.

I brought up the Quest Board and found an unsigned message waiting in my newly acquired Q-Mail inbox:

"COLLECT MOSS FROM THE CASTLE."

Well, that was pretty anticlimactic. I was expecting something a bit more challenging, like fighting the undead guardian of the keep. Or standing on one foot at the top of the tower for the entire night.

But there was moss growing on the plaque on the base of the castle wall, and so with my dorm room key, I scraped off as much as I could and responded to the message.

"Done."

Several minutes passed before the reply materialized.

"LEAVE THE MOSS BEHIND THE WITCH."

What?

Thankfully, the magic of the Internet provided a quick answer to the riddle. There was a carving of a witch near Bethesda Fountain, which was conveniently located on the other side of something called the Ramble and across a body of water called the Lake. I set off immediately, hoping that the mace would be enough to defend myself from anything lurking in the night. But the trek southward was uneventful, and as I crossed a stone bridge and the Fountain came into view, I breathed a sigh of relief.

I stuck the handful of moss into the crevice behind the witch and reported back that the second task was done. This time, the response was almost instantaneous:

"COLLECT YOUR TOKEN AT THE NEW YORK PUBLIC LIBRARY."

You've got to be kidding me! The note had promised the "truth," whatever that was, not another worthless coin. But after getting this far, I had to find out what all my effort had earned me, and so I quickly exited the park and hailed a taxi on Fifth Avenue.

It was nearly midnight by the time I passed between the lions guarding the library and, it being midnight and everything, the library was obviously closed. But I strode up to the giant front door like Dorothy approaching the gates of Oz and knocked, not knowing what else to do.

To my complete shock, out of the metal mail slot fell a little brown satchel. I furiously undid the satchel's strings and pulled out one shiny and more importantly, silver, token.

"Hey," said an accented voice behind me and I nearly jumped out of my still-soaked tank top.

I turned around slowly and was greeted by the sight of a girl with dark black hair dressed in a black sweater, a black skirt, and knee high black boots, holding a flannel tote bag around her shoulder. She couldn't have been more than 16.

"Nice outfit," said the girl with a smirk and a decidedly British accent.

"Thanks," I replied, my voice nearly cracking. "It's new."

"As are you, it would seem," she said.

"What do you mean?"

"Don't know anyone else stupid enough to show up here, alone, but it is what it is."

"I'm…sorry?"

"You will be if you don't hand it over."

My pulse began to quicken. Was I being mugged?

"Hand what over? My wallet? My phone? You can—"

"No, neither. It's your tokens I'm after."

I froze.

"I…don't know what you're talking about. Look, I don't want any trouble. I don't have too much on me but—"

"Fine, we'll do it the other way, I suppose."

The girl dropped the tote bag to the ground and it landed with a clang for some reason. I quietly began fumbling with my backpack zipper in an attempt to retrieve the mace, when the girl reached her arm deep into the bag and pulled out an impossibly long and very real metal sword. She held it aloft and the blade seemed to repel the darkness, an otherworldly glow beating back the night and the remains of my courage. Then she brought it down in one smooth arc until the point of the weapon was aimed directly at the heart on my tank top.

"Who are you?" I asked, my voice trembling.

"I'm Emma Patel, head of the Black Vultures. A pleasure to meet you. Now, which arm should I lop off first?"

I threw up.

It wasn't the proudest moment of my life, but fortunately it took the girl named Emma completely off guard, and she lowered the sword ever so slightly as the vomit slowly made its way to a drainage grate next to one of the library lions.

"I think there's been some sort of misunderstanding," I said, wiping the remainder from my mouth. "I'm just here to collect the token I earned for completing the Quest up at the castle."

"Right," said Emma. "And I'm here to rob you. It was my Quest and that's my silver token."

"What?" I asked, taken aback.

"A robbery, a holdup, a filching, a…what else do you Yanks call it? Or maybe con job is more accurate. I list an easy Quest with a way-too big reward, and relieve whoever shows up of their valuables. It's pretty straightforward. If the mark refuses, *Solais* here usually gets us to a satisfying conclusion."

Emma stuck the point of her sword into the ground and leaned on it like it was a cane, and I noticed the panoply of rings on almost all of her fingers. Her face wore a smirking teenage grin and if I wasn't so overly outmatched, I would take a run at her, even if she did have

10 pounds on me.

"I don't understand, I thought this was supposed to be a test. I was going to—"

"Don't know nothing about a test," said Emma. "But whoever put you up to it does not have your best interest at heart, I'm afraid."

I looked down at the silver token nestled in my palm. It gleamed in the moonlight, the etched number one in the middle looking particularly regal compared to the other tokens in my bag. What it was really worth, I had no idea. But I knew someone who did.

"OK," I said, holding the token out in front of me and walking slowly in a semicircle toward the nearest lion. The girl and her sword still cut off any hope of escape, which was exactly what I was hoping for, as I reached the statue without incident.

"I have a question, though," I said, my foot gently tapping against the grate as I slowly extended my token-holding arm out over it.

"What?" said Emma.

"What happens if I drop this token down the drain?"

Emma's eyes widened and she quickly raised her sword back up.

"You wouldn't dare, you stupid little git. I swear, if you do, I'll—"

"Hey, hey, hey," I said, trying to maintain my composure while my insides turned themselves into peach jelly. "I'm just talking hypotheticals. And I think I know part of the answer. You really want to slice my arm off with that giant sword of yours, it seems, but that won't get your token back and probably bring a whole lot of attention down on you. Am I right?"

The girl considered the question, her sword still aloft. I should have been more afraid, but it was like I had stumbled onto a movie set and my subconscious didn't want to believe anything I had just seen.

"OK," said Emma.

"OK what?"

"I'll treat with you. What do you want?"

I almost blurted out that I just wanted to get out of here alive, but now that I had some sort of leverage, I decided to get some answers.

"I was promised something by the person who told me to complete this Quest and seeing as how that turned out, I doubt they are going to fulfill their end of the bargain. So I may as well get it from you."

"And what's that?"

"The truth," I said. "The truth about all this. The Quests, the tokens, the whole thing. I mean, I've seen some interesting things since I started, but pulling an enormous sword out of a tote bag? That's something that just shouldn't be possible."

"You're right," said Emma with a smirk. "It isn't possible. And I bet it's making your little head hurt just thinking about it?"

"Maybe," I said, and oddly enough a dull pain in the back of my head had suddenly materialized. "So, is that a yes?"

"It's a yes," she said. "Now, if you'll just gently place the token on the ground, I'll put away my sword and we can get down to business."

"I don't think so," I said. "There's nothing stopping you from telling me what I want to know and then committing your unspeakable act of violence anyway. No, we'll reconvene at a more appropriate hour, no weapons, no magic tote bags, no funny business."

"Fine," said Emma. "Where did you have in mind?"

KATE

"Why of all places did you want to meet here?" said Emma, the next morning. It was Saturday and the adrenaline from the previous night's events had almost worn off to the point where I could start imbibing food again.

"Because it is known that the Central Park Children's Zoo has a strict no-murder policy," I replied with a smile and Emma rolled her eyes. She was dressed in a similar ensemble as the night before, except now her fingers featured an additional half-dozen rings. "What with the children and the delightful farm animals. It reminds me a bit of home."

I scattered a handful of animal feed over the fence and several eager goats scampered over to eat it while Emma scowled.

"Will you cut that out? You're acting like if we met at the seals over at the regular zoo, I'd already have cut your foot off or something."

"Well, you did threaten to 'lop off my arm,' did you not?" I replied.

"Fair point. But sometimes, it's fun to get a reaction when I take out *Solais*. It's much more impressive looking than the *White Hilt*."

"Do I want to know what that is?"

In my mind I pictured a much longer and sharper sword, obviously with a white hilt.

"No. No you do not. Anyway, can we get down to it? I really need my silver token back."

I reached into the inner recesses of my bag to retrieve the token, only to come up empty. Panic began to set in, as I could have sworn I had stowed it in the zippered side pocket, but the only thing in there was a tube of lipstick and some breath mints. Not wanting to admit I didn't have the goods, I quickly ad-libbed, again.

"I don't have the token with me," I said, hoping to buy myself a few seconds.

"What? Why am I here, then? I could have been sleeping. Or I could have been just coming home after not sleeping. I thought we had a deal."

"We do have a deal. The token for the truth. But I don't have any assurances from you that once I give you the token that you'll hold up your end of the bargain. So what we're going to do is—"

Emma's right arm was suddenly around my shoulder and she let out a playful laugh, as if we were old friends recounting last night's adventures in the Village. Except then her black-painted fingernails began to dig into my skin through my t-shirt, and I suppressed a yelp of pain by biting my tongue.

"We may be in a children's zoo and I may have left my weapons at home, but I still have ways to hurt you. Now cut the shit and give me back my token, or you'll be lucky if the only thing bruised by the evening is your shoulder."

She withdrew her arm quickly and before I could even breathe a sigh of relief, the rings on her fingers started to buzz as they brushed against the back of my head.

"What was that?" I asked and Emma slowly took two steps away from me and looked at the stones in her rings, which had changed to a brilliant shade of turquoise.

"That," said Emma, whose whole demeanor had changed on a dime, "is the signal to me to get the hell out of here. Keep the token, it's yours. Consider it both a gift for outwitting me and a payment."

"A payment for what? I don't understand."

"A payment so that if you ever see me again, you will quickly turn and walk the other way."

Emma strode off toward the pigpen and I wanted to run after to ask what the heck was going on. But then I thought about the one sword I had already seen and the other that was somehow even worse, and decided to stay put feeding the animals.

The silver token gleamed in the mid-morning light as I sat at the table outside the coffee shop. There was nothing unusual about this particular caffeine dispensary other than that it served a delicious almond milk cold brew drink with honey that I hadn't come across at any other non-chain establishment in the city. Oh, and this was the meeting spot where Trinity was finally going to reveal herself (or himself).

I had sent Trinity a Q-Mail note after getting home from the zoo yesterday morning, informing her that I had retrieved the silver token, per her instructions, and leaving out the harrowing ordeal I had faced. By noon, I had a response back:

"Meet at Bleecker Street Grounds tomorrow at 10 a.m. Sit at the table to the left of the door. I'll be wearing sunglasses and a white hat."

I had arrived 20 minutes early and spent each of those minutes scanning the sidewalk for anyone wearing the designated outfit. By 10:15, I was beginning to worry that Trinity wasn't showing up and by 10:45, I was ready to call it and go pick an easy Quest to kill the rest of the day.

But then a black Suburban pulled up in front of the shop and the door slowly opened to reveal a woman with large, black sunglasses and a large, white sun hat holding a braided leather bag. As she stepped down onto the street, I couldn't help but notice that she was severely pregnant. And for whatever reason, instead of the flowing summer dresses I had seen other pregnant Manhattanites sporting, she had decided to wear a tight black lycra tank top, which was straining to stay in one piece as she slowly walked past the front gate and sat down at the empty chair across from me.

"Hello Kate," said the woman, sweat dripping down the sides of her neck. She withdrew a small cloth from inside that fancy designer bag and patted her brow and her neck clean. Somehow, it was still impeccably dry when she stowed it away.

"Trinity?" I asked. "How…how do you know my name?"

"I know a lot about you," she said. "I know why you're here. What you've been doing. Why you hardly sleep. Why night after night, you sit at your computer. You're looking for something. An answer to a question. It drives you—"

"Can I just stop you for a second?" I interjected. "Is this all necessary? I mean, I found the vial with the Morpheus quote. Which was a bit weird, but fine. Then I track you down and now there's a Trinity. And just now, you lifted your entire speech from the movie. So can I ask you a question? Is this all some ridiculous casting call, or is there something more going on here? Do you even want this token? Because I've seen some things and I just want the truth."

"The truth…is complicated," Trinity said. "Too much of it will break your head. Not enough of it and you'll find yourself seven years into the Quests with only a pile of worthless tokens to show for it. That silver one included. In the middle, there is what you currently need. But time is short, so for now, I'll give you my name, a job, and a task, and hopefully you'll find some truth through your own efforts."

"Oh … OK."

"My name," she said, "is Beatrice Taylor."

I felt something push against my leg under the table.

"Your job," she continued, "is to sell every last dose of knock-off Adderall in that duffel."

"And your task," she concluded, withdrawing a folded piece of paper from her bag, "is to find this."

I gingerly took the piece of paper, unfurled it, and was greeted by a string of numbers encased in brackets.

949.278, I read. "What does it mean?"

"That," said the woman now named Beatrice, "is for you to figure out. Suffice it to say, it's something I've been searching for for a long time and given my current state, I'm not sure I'll be able to find it anytime soon."

Beatrice rubbed the top of her belly slowly before withdrawing a little vial from inside her bag. She unscrewed the top and took a small sip of the contents, which made her head twitch uncontrollably for a few seconds.

"What was that?" I asked, my curiosity getting the better of me.

"Something I probably shouldn't be drinking. But it keeps me going. Anyway, hopefully by the next time we meet, I'll be back to my college weight and you'll finally be ready to help me."

She slowly pushed herself up from the table before I could offer her my arm and walked out of the cafe, where another imposing black SUV was now waiting. I left the duffel bag under the table and trotted after her.

"That's it?" I asked. "A few sentences of nonsense and a menial job? Do you know what I went through to get that token?"

"Are you a doctor?" she answered.

"No," I said. "I'm about to be a sophomore, so—"

"Good. Then we're on the same page. So let me get to the hospital now, please, as my water just broke and I don't feel like explaining myself to you while an eight-pound human pushes his way out of my body. Take care!"

KORA

Kora awoke in an unfamiliar bed next to an unfamiliar man and an unfamiliar woman. In the dim light of the room, she could see that all three of them were in various states of undress, most of all herself, who only had on the glamour at the moment. Such debauchery was unbecoming and this episode had pushed her to the conclusion that her host had become unsuitable. Unfortunately, due to the long list of items on her plate and her limited time in which to complete them, she had not made any progress toward finding a new one.

The woman at the edge of the bed began to stir and a thought percolated quickly in what passed for Kora's mind as she quickly surveyed her prey. This one was tall, lean, and athletic, a far cry from the slob of a person who had found the glamour at the bottom of a bin of rusting magical items at the Night Market in a back alley in Paris. Her ties to alchemy were likely none, but her essence, at first blush, was most likely an improvement.

"Hi," said Kora, placing her hand on the small of the woman's back.

"Hey," she responded in an unexpectedly high-pitched voice. "I… umm…I like your necklace."

Kora smiled.

"It is quite something. And I am feeling a bit too overdressed with it on. Would you like to borrow it for a spell?"

The woman, who Kora surmised was in her late 40's but exuded a surprisingly vigorous energy, stared down at the green colored stone and then back up at Kora's eyes, before nodding.

"Then it's settled," she said. This would be the riskiest transfer she had ever attempted. Normally, her stone changed hands when she was dormant and she had little say over who put her on next. Once, she had tried something similar and it had not…gone the way she had hoped. But hopefully she had learned from that experience and this time would be different.

Kora gently pulled the woman's hands, which were adorned in several silver rings, toward the necklace until they had a hold of the chain.

"No peeking," she said with a wink and the woman closed her eyes as she lifted the glamour free of Kora's current host.

If the third member of the prior evening's activities had been conscious, he would have witnessed a peculiar sight, as Kora's body somehow enveloped his wife the moment the chain fell around her neck, and in Kora's place on the other side, now there was only a decrepit looking woman with mangy hair and loose skin.

Kora opened her eyes and stared down at her former host, ignoring, for a moment, the buzzing sound in the back of her mind that was the new host, now trapped somewhere deep beneath the active glamour.

"You," said the woman in a barely audible whisper. "Give it back. It's mine."

"I'm afraid not," said Kora, now firmly in control of her new host. "When you first found me, you had so much promise. And I was willing to provide you with a road map to untold power. And what did you do? You sacrificed everything for depravity and hedonism."

"I …" the woman tried to continue, but her vocal chords had atrophied away to almost nothing. To be honest, Kora was surprised that the woman was still even able to sit up. But the complexities of glamour alchemy were less interesting to her in the moment than her immediate task: to find Kate, and ultimately, Trinity.

"I wish it could have turned out differently, but such is the way of things. Enjoy the remaining hours of your life, if you can."

With that, Kora strode out of what turned out to be a SoHo loft and into the bright light of the morning sun. Despite what she had told Kate last time, she wanted to check up on how the now-almost sophomore was doing before her new host clawed her way up from the subconscious abyss and threw the glamour in the river.

"Hush, woman," Kora said in the back of her mind. "I promise you won't end up like that hag back there if you just do what I tell you. But right now, I have some urgent housekeeping to take care of. So just ride along in silence, please, and you'll have your body back in due course."

The protesting stopped and Kora nodded in appreciation. A stop at the local newsstand established that it was August 16, which meant that Kate should have been done with her mission at the castle. After a brief stroll to the Village, she found a bench located an inconspicuous distance away from the girl's dorm room, and pretended to read the paper until Kate returned sometime in the late morning. She left briefly to grab lunch and a coffee, but after that did not emerge again. By nine, Kora had given up on learning anything particularly useful that day and instead walked across Washington Square Park to a particularly decrepit bench in front of a particularly decrepit mid-block walk-up.

Kora closed her eyes and the woman underneath the glamour appeared to her, cowering in a corner of her mental space like a frightened tabby.

"Listen very carefully. When I am done speaking in a few moments, I am going to squeeze the stone around my neck and you will get control of your body back for the rest of the evening. However, tomorrow, you will wake up and be back on this bench no later than 6:30 a.m., at which point, you will squeeze the stone again. You will feel the weight of what was once my body envelope yours, but you will still be in control. I will permit you a few minutes to experience what it is like to have been me, but at 6:47, you will relinquish command again to me. If you follow these instructions to the T, I will make the same deal that I made with the woman you saw back in the loft and I pray that you will not squander the opportunity like she did."

Kora paused and waited for a response from the woman, before finally receiving it.

"Good. I am glad I did not have to explain what will happen if you do not comply. I suspect this partnership will be a fruitful one. Until tomorrow."

Kora grasped the glamour stone with her fingers and squeezed.

CHAPTER NINE

KATE

It was a surreal scene, watching Beatrice stagger into the SUV sopping wet. I half-considered climbing in after her, so at least she wouldn't have to be alone until she got to the hospital. But from what I had learned about her during our brief conversation, she didn't seem like the type of person who wanted any help at this particular moment.

I returned to the table to fetch the duffel bag and mysterious note and instead was greeted by the familiar face of Zach's girlfriend, who had plopped herself down in Beatrice's seat and was sipping hot coffee from an oversized mug.

"You again?" I stammered. "It's been nine months, leave me the eff alone!"

"Of course, but first, I wanted to offer you a mint."

I stared at the strange woman as she extended her open hand across the metal mesh table. In the middle of her palm was a small, silvery mint. Given that it was broad daylight and we were seated in a crowded cafe, I didn't think there was anything particularly nefarious afoot, and so I gingerly took the offering, put it into my mouth, and started chewing.

My head exploded in pain, forcing my eyes shut, while the rest of my body from the neck down felt like it was encased in a huge ice cube. I watched in the mental space inside my mind as Zach's girlfriend approached me down in the makeshift jail in the Botanical Gardens basement. I watched as she spoke to me and then handed me a golden mint, which I had taken so innocently. Then the scene shifted to my dorm room and a knock on the door.

Again, it was her, and again, she offered the silver mint. Remembering the pain from that first time I had regained my memories made the pain now even worse. I watched out of my own eyes as she explained why she was doing this. It was all about Trinity. Or Beatrice. Or whoever she was. It wasn't about me. It had never been about me. And then she had handed me the gold mint and tucked these memories back into the recesses of my head like a lost box forgotten somewhere in a dusty attic.

I opened my eyes and stared at this woman with newfound hatred.

"Why are you doing this to me?" I asked.

The woman, who hadn't even bothered to give me her name, took a long drag of her coffee before answering. She looked different from before, even now that I had these extra memories of her floating in my head. She seemed more youthful and livelier than last time, even though she couldn't have been more than two years my senior. Her hair was preternaturally blonde although there was now an out of place streak of brown hair running down her brow.

"Like I told you twice before, I need you to find Trinity."

"I did! She literally just drove away to the hospital to have a baby! And her name is Beatrice Taylor, in case you were wondering."

"Well, that complicates things," said the woman. "What did you two talk about? Did she give you anything?"

"No, no, no," I said, feeling the fire of rage that this woman had ignited within me. "I'm done with this. With you. Give me three of that other mint so I can forget all of this and go back to my simple life."

I slammed my fist down on the table and the oversize mug toppled on its side, sending the hot coffee through the metal slits and onto the top of the duffel bag that Beatrice left.

"What is that?" asked the woman, and before I could do anything, she had retrieved the now-sopping bag, unzipped it, and began pilfering its contents. What Beatrice had described to me as drugs were actually brightly green colored squares wrapped in plastic, and the blonde woman quickly freed one from its casing and held it up to her face.

"Interesting," she said, giving the candy-like item a lick, which made her recoil.

"What?" I asked, drawing a raised eyebrow from the woman.

"Oh, now you want to talk? You want to know what I think these are? Tell me, what did she say to you about them?"

"Nothing. She just said that I had to sell every last dose of that. She called it knock-off Adderall. Then she gave me a cryptic note and drank something out of a weird vial."

At this, the woman's eyebrows raised even higher.

"Trinity didn't happen to say whether what was in the vial was the same thing as this?"

I shook my head.

"She's explained about as much to me as you have. Why is she so damn important?"

Instead of answering my question, the woman popped the square into her mouth and began to chew.

"Hmm, tastes like socks and bananas, and is that molasses? I wonder why she added…oh."

The woman's voice suddenly went monotone and her eyes went glassy. After a few moments, I noticed her breathing had slowed to once every 10 seconds, and then after another minute, I couldn't tell if she was even breathing at all.

"Are…are you OK?" I asked, waving my palm in front of her face several times. "What's going on? Why aren't you—"

Her hand suddenly lurched up and grabbed mine, and it felt like it was made of pure ice. Then she turned her unblinking gaze toward my face and a small whisper escaped her lips.

"Focus on the past," she said. "Focus on the past. Focus on the past. Focus on the past."

The patrons around us started muttering and I gave them a shoulder shrug as if to say, "I know, right?" Finally, I did the only thing that made sense and slapped her clean across the cheek.

The woman let out a deep breath as I made contact and when she locked eyes with me again, her old self had returned.

"You…you slapped me," she said softly.

"I…you didn't leave me any other choice! It was like you had become a statue. Or you were having a severe allergic reaction. Then you started muttering to yourself."

"What did I say?" she asked, her voice slightly trembling.

"You said 'focus on the past' over and over and over again."

"I see."

Without warning, the woman got up from the table, nearly knocking it over with her knees. For the second time that morning, I chased a strange woman down the street to get the answers I felt I was entitled to.

"You forgot something!" I nearly screamed and the woman turned back at me.

"What?"

"My memories! Don't you want to wipe them again? Can't have Beatrice know what you're up to, right?"

The woman turned around suddenly and before I knew it, she was inches away from my face.

"Keep quiet!" she hissed in my ear while hooking her arm around mine and steering me back to the cafe as if we were old schoolgirl friends. "You're angry. I get it. Whatever. But that doesn't mean you can go around broadcasting everything that you know to the world . That's a quick ticket to the Mooney House basement. Now sit and finish your coffee."

She pushed me back into my seat and I noticed, strangely, that the brown streak in her hair had spread down either side of her face and was now somehow mixing with her blond hair to create a reddish hybrid.

I took a sip of my now lukewarm coffee and froze as the now-familiar taste of the dissolved golden mint registered on my tongue. But something about it was different this time.

"You noticed the change?" asked the woman with a sinister smile. "You're very perceptive, I like that."

I felt my body lock up and my eyes seemed to focus only on the woman's lips as she continued speaking.

"As this little episode has demonstrated, after a few times of being reawakened with a standard letherium tablet, the subject will start to rebel. And that's not conducive to a proper working relationship. So a higher dosage is now necessary. It's for your own good, you see. I hope when we see each other tomorrow though, you'll be in a better mood. But if not, then I have one more thing to say to you."

The scene in front of me froze, as if someone had hit pause on my brain and then everything from the past 20 minutes began playing in reverse. The only constant was the blond woman in front of me, from whose lips a single word now escaped.

"*Comply.*"

I nodded and closed my eyes.

CHAPTER TEN

KATE (AGAIN)

It was a surreal scene, watching Beatrice stagger into the SUV sopping wet. I half-considered climbing in after her, so at least she wouldn't have to be alone until she got to the hospital. But from what I had learned about her during our brief conversation, she didn't seem like the type of person who wanted any help at this particular moment.

I returned to the table to fetch the duffel bag and mysterious note and trudged back to my dorm room to contemplate my next move, trying my best to ignore the stabbing pain that had suddenly materialized in my head.

CHAPTER ELEVEN

KORA

Kora regained consciousness on the bench at the appointed time and smiled. It seemed that her new host was smarter than her last several and this pleased her. She quickly unlocked the front door of the walk-up building in front of the bench with some deft finger work, and bolted up five flights of stairs to the top floor. A set of three doors greeted her on the landing, but they all went to the same place: her home for the past 100 years.

One by one, she had been hosted by each of the former residents of the three apartments on this floor and the four on the floor below, and at the end of their usefulness, she had made certain arrangements to transfer ownership of all the units to a Bahamian shell corporation that she had set up in the 1930s. In terms of square footage, her abode was spacious, but other than her bedroom, she had deliberately kept the premises almost entirely spartan so as not to attract the wrong sort of attention. That, and there was no point in investing in interior decorating when there were years where she spent less than a fortnight here.

Kora made her way to the study, which encompassed all of the C unit on the fifth floor. Mismatched bookcases lined one of the walls, and on the opposite wall was a long work bench that she had fashioned together from various pieces of wood over the years. Several jars were grouped together in one section, each containing different iterations of the golden letherium, for forgetting, and the silver morarium, for remembering. But there were obvious variations and twists she had developed.

For example, increasing the amount of letherium in the mint extended the temporal range of memories to be forgotten. Or more, accurately, buried within the subconscious. And increasing the potency in turn increased the amount of morarium needed to resurface the memory. That was particularly helpful in the case of a similarly equipped adversary. Still others left the subject with a hint of what had happened, almost the equivalent of a lucid dream.

Right outside her study was a small nook, where a laptop rested on a nightstand tucked inside. Kora was not one for technology, as it was hard to keep up with the non-stop developments when you might spend years locked at the bottom of a chest and wake up to find that MySpace was no longer a "thing." That was one reason why she appreciated the utilitarian esthetic and features of the Quest Board, which had largely remained unchanged in the years since the Board's creation.

Having long since infiltrated Kate's Q-mail inbox, she nearly squealed with delight as she read the note from Trinity instructing the girl to meet her at the cafe that morning. With an assortment of mints stowed away in her bag, Kora quickly exited the apartment and headed to the meet-up. She contemplated showing up early, so that she could observe Trinity for herself, but Kate's continued recollection of her from that one night in Zach's dorm room put a damper on that plan.

Instead, she had arrived just in time to watch a very pregnant and sopping wet woman stumble into an SUV and drive away. Good, she had thought. Trinity wouldn't be going anywhere far with a new baby to take care of.

Her subsequent conversation with Kate wasn't as positive. The girl's anger at continually being memory-wiped had finally materialized, as Kora had feared, and the whole enterprise was now teetering on the edge of the abyss. Fortunately, Beatrice, the blonde's true name, had provided a solution to the problem in the form of the concoctions she had left under the table. Kora had hoped beyond hope that the green-colored square was a distillation of the liquid in the vial that Kate had mentioned, but when she bit down on the gummy and tasted molasses and ageratum, Kora realized the truth.

And then she fell into the depths.

The alchemy at work was not designed to have such a pronounced effect on the subject, that she surmised later. Surely Trinity was not so stupid as to proliferate such powerful prima materia in a random manner. But because of her uniquely situated consciousness and—to put it bluntly—current lack of an actual brain, the gummy had plunged her straight into the maelstrom of borrowed memories and energies that she had survived on for so long.

But then she heard her own voice, her true voice, from ages past, slice through the cacophony.

"Focus on the past," her voice said. And she did. She focused on a singular moment, one that she had forgotten in her waking life. It was summer and the winds were warm. She raced along the shore of her little isle, hidden from the larger surrounding islands and the mainland by a gentle rolling fog that always seemed to frustrate ship captains no matter how favorable the conditions. It was here she lived and studied and loved and all she wanted to do was to stay within the confines of the island for as long as she could.

But this was the day that everything had changed. For when she had returned to her cottage at the top of the hill, the door had been shattered into a thousand splinters, and the intruders had already laid waste to her possessions. But it wasn't until she ran through the destruction and out the back door that the real horror revealed itself. Because staked down in the dirt, his wrists and ankles and torso bloodied, was the man she had loved for years too numerous to count. The invading trio stood at three separate points around him, and underneath were elaborate markings that must have taken weeks to construct.

As they muttered words of ancient power, she unleashed a torrent of her own. But they had been prepared and it ricocheted harmlessly off of their protective barrier and had instead destroyed a nearby tree. She continued while they continued, but the strength of her magic and the shriek of her cries could do nothing to stop their perverted ritual.

When it was over, he was gone, and even though she knew she should have run, she could not abandon him. And although she was strong—had been from the very beginning—there were three of them and only one of her. It had taken them more effort than they had anticipated, but they subdued her as well, driven the stakes into her skin, circled her prone body, and placed a small necklace around her neck, a ring on one of her fingers, and a small metal bead into her mouth, which she had involuntarily swallowed. As their incantations reached her ears, she felt a sharp pain across her cheek.

Kora opened her eyes and took in a huge breath of air, as if she had just surfaced from hundreds of feet below the waves. She was back at the cafe and the girl was staring at her.

"You slapped me," Kora said, softly, while trying to grab hold of the memories she had just experienced.

"I...you didn't leave me any other choice! It was like you had become a statue. Or you were having a severe allergic reaction. Then you started muttering to yourself."

"What did I say?" she asked her.

"You said 'focus on the past' over and over and over again."

"I see."

Already the details of that day on the isle were fading, and Kora knew if she sat here any longer, they would be gone. So she fled, taking a few more of the gummies with her, and dropping one of the more powerful golden mints into Kate's coffee to wipe this morning's meeting clean. But the girl was persistent and would not go willingly into the night. And so, as a parting gift, Kora imparted the ultimate command and left her new thrall to ready the final stage of her plan.

CHAPTER TWELVE

KATE

My headache finally went away the next morning as I was jogging up the West Side Highway path, and it's there that I saw her again. Zach's girlfriend, running the opposite way. Except her hair was now a mix of strawberry blond and brown and although I wanted to yell at her for stalking me, somehow the only thing I could manage was a meek hello.

"Kate," she said. "Let's have a jog together. After you freshen your breath. Here, take a mint."

"OK," I said, ignoring the insult and quickly chewing the silver mint. I keeled over as the waves of memories flooded back into my head from our prior two meetings, and when I finally straightened up to scream at the woman for her manipulation, I felt all fight go out of me as soon as she held up her hand.

"Not today," she said. "Today we will get off on the right foot. Let's go."

The woman started running south and I turned to follow her.

"OK," I replied, not really knowing what she meant. "But…"

"We need to be efficient while Beatrice is out of commission," she said. "Do you know what she named the baby?"

"I…how do you know…"

"As I told you before, in your dorm room, I've had my eye on Beatrice for a long time. And you as well. I saw what happened yesterday. What did she say to you?"

I wanted to protest the barrage of questions, but every time she asked me something, it was like something in my brain said I needed to just answer.

"She told me to sell some weird bag of drugs. And to find a random number. I don't know what one has to do with the other, though."

"Did you use the drug yourself?"

"No, I didn't. I don't do drugs. Well, sometimes, but not that kind of drug."

"If you haven't tried it, how do you know what kind of drug it is?"

"Good point, I guess."

"You'll be a much better saleswoman if you actually use the product, you know? So just try one when you get back to your room."

We jogged the rest of the path in silence, and by the time we reached Battery Park City, I was drenched in sweat and filled with a desire to run back to my room and try one of the green squares.

"This was fun," said the woman. "Let's meet same time tomorrow."

"Umm, OK?" I replied and Zach's girlfriend squeezed my shoulder gently, which was weird.

I walked back to my dorm room, puzzled both by the woman and by the memories now floating around in my head from months ago that didn't seem quite real and yet were just the same. Opening the duffel bag, I found it stuffed to the brim with mountains of individually wrapped squares. What the heck were these things? I freed one of them from its plastic and tentatively put it into my mouth. It tasted completely horrendous, but I couldn't focus on that for very long, because for the second time that day, my brain started going haywire.

I glanced around the room frantically before my eyes locked in on one of my psychology books from last semester. Opening its cover, I began to read it, paragraph-by-paragraph, page-by-page, as if it was the most interesting thing in the entire world. But then about 10 pages in, I felt something click off in my mind, and I slowly closed the book. What the hell had just happened?

I recounted the experience to Zach's girlfriend the next morning during our run.

"Sounds intense," she said. "Like a souped-up version of Adderall."

"Yeah," I said. "But it didn't last that long. I was going to take another one to see if the same thing would happen, but didn't want to waste them."

"Try one more this afternoon," the woman said. "This time, while holding the piece of paper with that number Beatrice gave you. See if you can direct your focused brain onto the number, maybe you'll get a clue as to what it means."

"OK," I said. "That sounds like a good idea."

I returned to my dorm room, put on a timer, and did what she said. As my brain went into overdrive, I held up the piece of paper in front of my face.

"949.278," I said out loud. "949.278."

I repeated the number a few more times before quickly opening my laptop. Soon, my browser history was littered with random searches, Wikipedia articles, and numerology theories. But before I knew it, the drug wore off again, just as the timer hit 10 minutes, and I was no closer to solving this puzzle than before. So against my better judgment, I ate another one. The now-familiar feeling of intense focus blocked out all other thoughts and I sunk back into the research with a renewed vigor.

I eliminated geographic coordinates, substitution ciphers, and bank account numbers. The problem was there were so many numeric systems that I feared I would have to eat the entire contents of the duffel bag before the solution would reveal itself. After the effect wore off again, I held firm on eating another until I reported back to Zach's girlfriend.

"Did you count how many doses are in the bag?" she asked the next morning as we jogged through the light rain.

"No," I said.

"Might be a good idea. She wants you to sell them, not use them."

"Right," I said. For whatever reason, I always found myself agreeing with everything she told me.

"If you bring me one tomorrow though, I can try to analyze it myself and maybe figure out what she used to make them."

"OK," I said. "That makes sense."

"Don't use any more until I tell you, OK?"

I nodded and did as instructed. A week later, Zach's girlfriend, who had oddly still not given me her name, showed up to our morning jog with a huge smile on her face.

"I think I've finally cracked it," she said. "But I'm going to need you to do some experiments for me."

"Sure, but what happened to selling them like Beatrice wanted?"

"I have that covered," she replied, handing me a thick envelope. "She just wants the money, I think. So we'll give it to her and keep the squares for ourselves. Now, here's what you're going to do when you get home."

She explained in detail the tests she wanted me to run, which all involved me taking various doses of the drug, which she said contained a substance whose name she told me to forget. I took half a dose and it predictably lasted 5 minutes. I took two doses immediately back-to-back and spent 20 minutes accidentally staring at my toenails. Things got interesting when I moved onto the more complicated part of the assignment.

Taking two at a time didn't make me focus twice as hard; instead, I woke up an hour later with no memory of anything that had happened in-between. She wanted me to run that test twice, and another hour went into the waste bin of my subconscious.

But it wasn't until the final phase that I had a real breakthrough. This involved creating a concentrate made by heating up a dozen doses until they liquified on my dorm room hotplate. When the mixture cooled, I poured it into an empty water bottle and made my way to the student health center. I complained of light-headedness, dizziness, and a lack of energy to the nurse on call, and soon was hooked up to an IV in an exam room. Then, when I was sure that no one was coming back soon to check on me, I poked a small hole in the IV bag and poured some of the green concoction into the saline.

I watched as the liquid slowly made its way out of the bag, down the tubing, and into my arm. For someone now used to having their mind regularly altered by magical substances, I still wasn't prepared for what happened next.

I felt my eyes roll back into my head and then I was falling through pure darkness. Or maybe I was just floating. It was hard to tell. Then I heard it. What I had been focusing on, what had been bothering me ever since Zach's girlfriend restored my memory during our first jog. Why were there still pieces of our conversations that were just beyond my recollection?

Tiny orbs of light floated around me and I finally remembered what she had said to me:

"Find her."

"Don't give up."

I reached my hand into one of the orbs and the words echoed in the void of my mind. It was soft and gentle, not a command, but a suggestion. She had started small, urged me to find Beatrice and keep at it. It had fueled and encouraged my many months of searching. But then everything had changed somehow. I brushed against the last command, but all that came out was an undecipherable whisper. And unlike the other two, it was rock hard, like an over tempered piece of steel, brittle and cracked. Holding the orb a little longer, I was shocked at what I heard next.

It was a conversation between Zach's girlfriend and me at the coffee shop where I had met Beatrice earlier that morning. I saw myself storm out of the cafe after her only to be steered back to my seat. I saw what my distracted self had not: her closed fist hovering over my coffee while I had stared at her reddish hair. I heard her lecture me while I sat there helplessly and finally heard the word contained within the orb:

"Comply."

The command reverberated in the inner recesses of my mind, and while it still held power over me, I saw in its absoluteness a way out.

I opened my eyes and was back in the exam room. Despite feeling like it had been days since I was last awake, only a minute of time had passed. I quickly unhooked the IV from my arm, fetched a couple of bandages from a nearby drawer, and snuck out of the health center through a back staircase.

The memory of the new conversation replayed over and over in my head as I walked back to my dorm room. She had been so confident and so cocky that she had absolute control over my memory and over me that she had gotten sloppy.

And I was going to make her pay.

CHAPTER THIRTEEN

KORA

Kora stared at the 1870's-era mirror in her apartment, its silver frame nearly dull. The same could not be said for her hair, which was now nearly red to the roots. This troubled her greatly. It had been so long since she had been able to stay in control for weeks-on end, that she wondered whether her host was even still alive. She couldn't remember the last time one had died while she was in control, but she was quite certain that she went dormant soon after it had happened. As much as she wanted to interrogate the brown-haired woman underneath about her unusual pliancy, Kora had other things on her mind.

Her morning jogs with Kate had been productive, but she felt like the girl was holding something back from her. After a month or two more of testing, Kora had concluded that the focus enhancer was incredibly watered down, her own experience with it notwithstanding. Whatever other alchemy Beatrice had at her disposal, it was not on full display here. So the duo had moved on to the mystery of the six-digit number. But not before Kora had done a full memory wipe on the girl back to that morning at the cafe. A fresh start was what they needed, she had decided, and besides, Kate probably didn't even want to remember all the different ways she had been experimented on.

Once they fell into a new routine-spinning classes in a basement studio in Alphabet City-it had only taken a few more weeks for Kate's brain to finally seize upon a promising lead: a Dewey Decimal number.

Except that was only the beginning.

Because as it turned out, there was no electronic record of any book in any library in the city with that number. Poor Kate spent more weeks, under Kora's firm direction, visiting almost every public and private library. The girl hadn't complained, as she had no say in the matter, but Kora had eventually noticed a tiny shift in her demeanor, which troubled her.

Finally, they had struck pay dirt in March: a professor had checked the book out of a tiny research library in SoHo that had not been properly documented. Kora had sent Kate to the professor during his office hours, posing as a student interested in taking his class next semester. She had complained that he was more interested in her physique than her mental acuity, but Kora had coaxed her back to his office for another session the following day. Incredibly, the old man kept the book lying out in the open, and Kate had nabbed it when he had stepped out to go to the bathroom.

She glanced down at the armoire below the mirror at the aged leather-bound book. Inside were the diary entries of Rita van Asch, one of the founders of the Worshipful Company of Alchemists, better and simply known as the Guild, from 1777. Its contents were somewhat interesting, but for Kora, who had lived through a portion of that year, it was a disappointment. She could see why Beatrice had been interested in finding it, though. If one were industrious and cunning enough, one could piece together the secret ingredients of Rita's compulsion ink. But Kora had no need for such sophomoric alchemy.

A twinge of pain suddenly erupted in her thigh, and Kora nearly doubled-over. She instinctively grabbed the stone to steady herself and the sting dissipated. So the woman was alive after all, she surmised, and not happy about her prolonged imprisonment. She could empathize with the feeling of powerlessness, but now was not the time to hand back over the reins. Not until she learned what Beatrice had drunk from that vial.

CHAPTER FOURTEEN

KATE

It happened at night the first time. Zach's girlfriend had shown up at my dorm room door with a cup of tea and a pep talk to get me through her latest crazy experiment. Except that when I had finished the tea, I felt my mind go numb and when I woke up the next morning, I couldn't remember anything about her apart from that same night after the corpse flower quest.

But fortunately, I had been waiting for this moment. The next afternoon, like every afternoon for the past several months, I went down to my mailbox and found a letter addressed to me and sent by me. Inside were the same set of instructions I had been sending myself every day as a contingency plan. They told me how to access the inner recesses of my subconscious, where my lost memories were waiting like an old friend.

Another trip to the student health center later and my mind had been restored. Unlike the first time, when she had only tried to take one memory, this time there were dozens. Every morning we had gone jogging and afterward she had commanded me to do something. But although that command still lingered in my head, this latest mind wipe had washed away some of its power.

I pushed the command to the limit as Zach's girlfriend pushed me to find the book. Yes, that stupid number was for a book, hidden somewhere in the city. After weeks and weeks of trudging into every single library in all five boroughs, I had finally found it on the desk of a dirty old professor in my own department.

"I found it," I had written to Beatrice on Q-Mail, but not before handing the book over to Zach's girlfriend for her to study first. A week later, I received both a response back from Beatrice and the book back from the now-completely redhead, who showed up unannounced at my dorm room with a bottle of rum to toast the results of a successful scavenger hunt. One sip later and I woke up the next morning with a pounding headache and without any knowledge as to how I had acquired the book.

After yet another round of memory reacquisition, I locked myself in my room to prepare for my second meeting with Beatrice. The chipper girl who had randomly stumbled into this world of Quests and magic had sadly been destroyed by the schemes of a woman drunk on her power over me. But in front of Ms. Taylor, I needed to play a different part.

The morning of our rendezvous arrived and I of course slept through my alarm. I quickly stuffed the book in my pink backpack and ran the entire way to the coffee shop.

"I'm so sorry I'm late!" I said, as I nearly collapsed into the empty seat across from Beatrice. She looked decidedly not pregnant this time, and so there was no risk of her running out on me before I got some answers.

"It's fine. I take it you have the book?"

"Yep!" I said in my fake eager voice as I dumped my backpack on the table and began rifling through it, before withdrawing the diary.

"Excellent. How is the old professor? Still a disgusting lecher? I hope he didn't leer at you too much. You're just his type."

My eyes widened.

"Wait, how did you know that he had…oh. This was just a test. Again."

A test that had wasted months of my life. And for what? So she could impart her precious wisdom to me? I wanted to wipe the smile she flashed me off her face by punching her right in the jaw.

"Of course. You think you're ready for the big time already? Did you read the book?"

"I did. Was up all night. Then tried to take a quick cat nap but slept through my alarm. That's why I was la—"

"Then you know that this wasn't something I would leave to the likes of you if I didn't already know I could get it back."

I almost lost it at this last comment. The arrogance of this woman nearly rivaled that of my other favorite person, and between the two of them, they had made my life a living hell. But now was not the time to lose my temper, not when I had finally made some progress.

"Oh don't be so sensitive. You did well regardless. Here's your reward."

Beatrice set a stack of iron tokens on the table and took the book. I stared at the coins for several seconds and again contemplated violence, before grabbing the lot of them and stuffing them into my backpack.

"Thanks."

Clearly my displeasure was still very much evident because Beatrice cocked her head slightly as if I should be grateful for the worthless pile of metal.

"And because you were up all night, here's something extra."

She withdrew a small green square wrapped in plastic from her pocketbook and slid it across the table. It looked identical to the other green squares she had given me last time, of which I had eaten probably three-quarters.

"What's this?"

"A little something to help you next time you need to finish a paper. It lasts only a couple of hours, so don't waste it, but it's one of my better buffs, if I do say so myself."

A buff? Was that supposed to be clever? But the promise of a couple of hours of focus got me intrigued and I played dumb.

"You don't know what a buff is?"

I shook my head.

"OK, fine. Think of it as a magic version of the Adderall you've been dealing in your dorm for me. Which it is."

"Oh. OH. Wow, thanks!"

"You're welcome. Don't waste it, though. I don't hand those out to everyone for free you know."

"I won't. So, what's my next assignment? Do you have the next volume of the diary? I have so many questions!"

"Easy there, tiger. I'll be in touch. Go get some sleep. You're beginning to sound like a chipmunk."

I nodded, grabbed my stuff, and left the coffee shop. It took only a few blocks for the other woman to appear in the distance, and I cursed under my breath as I approached her.

"How did it go?" the redhead said.

"It was…" I started to answer, but paused and instead waited for the familiar echo of "comply" in the back of my head to sound. But it didn't.

"Fine. It was fine."

"What do you mean 'fine'?"

Again, no command. I smiled on the inside, but decided to answer anyway.

"She was the one who hid the book. It was all a test."

"I see," said the woman. I couldn't tell if it was the repeated memory wiping I had undergone, but it seemed to me that other parts of the woman were also starting to change in addition to her hair. "But, you passed?"

"Yes, I did. And then she sent me on my way. Put me in a holding pattern."

"That's not ideal, but I suppose it's the best we can do right now. Let me know when she contacts you again."

Finally, at that direct imperative, the command reappeared, and I heard the word "OK" escape from my lips.

"Good," said the woman, who turned to walk the other way, but then suddenly pivoted and looked back at me.

"Is there anything else you're not telling me?" she asked, as if realizing that she wasn't as precise with her prior questioning as she should have been. Had this been several weeks ago, I would have been forced to answer truthfully. But not today.

"Nope, that's it."

Satisfied that I had obeyed her, the woman turned back and walked back to whatever hell had spawned her.

CHAPTER FIFTEEN

KORA

Kora woke up at 4 a.m. in her four-poster 19th century bed covered in sweat. Quite frankly, sleep was not something she was accustomed to, after so many years of unsuitable hosts. There had been too many times where she had closed her eyes in one decade and opened them in another, that she preferred to spend the limited time that was usually at her disposal in the service of her goal. But nothing had been usual about the last six months. She couldn't recall a time when she had found a host that made her almost feel like a real human again. And that worried her.

The copy of Rita's diary that she had transcribed by hand sat next to her, half-buried under the cotton sheets she had bought in Scotland during the tail-end of the Industrial Revolution. It took a second for Kora to recall that she had been reading the book in bed before she had drifted off into what had become an amalgam of nightmares.

Some were familiar: an extended interrogation in an underground black site somewhere in Eastern Europe that had ended with her arm being hacked off; that beheading during the French Revolution; and then of course that time she was burned at the stake in Salem. The only positive thing about her current state was that any physical damage to her glamour self was erased just as soon as the next time she was activated. But the pain still remained afterward. Always.

Yet other nightmares were foreign to her. Kora still had lifetimes of memories she had yet to reclaim, but still, these were not hers. But, like hers had, they stretched back beyond the normal lifespan. A woman, stabbed and left for dead in an alleyway in Five Points. Another woman, waking in an unfamiliar room with the taste of blood in her mouth. And then the last one, the most horrific of all, a woman screaming in the dark as her life-force flowed out of her.

Kora shuddered and pushed herself up from the bed. She had little time to dwell on the past when the present was already fraught with so much unknown. Three train transfers later and she was walking up the up staircase at the random half-empty middle school where the Council had recently relocated the Raid Board to. After listening out for any other potential Questers, she approached the bulletin board and began perusing the latest jobs, which were mostly busts. But then she saw it and nearly did a double-take.

"Urgent! Need retrieval of ink and pen from estate sale in Bed-Stuy. Contact me for more info."

Kora couldn't afford to believe in coincidences and was therefore troubled by the confluence of the discovery of the diary and this Raid suddenly appearing. And it wasn't as if she needed the ink to achieve the power of compulsion. But the thought of someone else acquiring that power troubled her. Or a collection of someones.

And so, she took the note and replaced it with an identical one, save for replacing the contact information with her own.

Three days later, when she saw Beatrice approach the dead drop, where she had left the altered Raid instructions, Kora smiled. A few blocks away, she found Kate waiting next to the W. 4th Street subway, as instructed.

"The first part of the trap is set," Kora said. "And now we go to set the second."

"OK," said Kate, who seemed nonplussed by the plan. Not that she could blame her. In time, most of her external conscripts had wilted under her hand and it had been long enough where the same would be expected from the girl.

After a silent train ride, the pair reached the five-story walk-up a few minutes before 1:30 and Kora hit the buzzer for 5A. Upstairs, a wrinkly old man in glasses greeted them at the door.

"Hello," he said in a raspy voice. "You here for the estate sale?"

"Yes, we are," Kora replied. "Can we come in?"

The man peered at Kora through the thick lenses of his glasses before noticing Kate standing silently behind her.

"Yes, just need to get a name for the ledger."

Kora frowned. She didn't like giving out her name to random strangers, and in fact, Kate still didn't know it. But a thorough cleaning after this Raid was in order anyway, so she complied.

"I'm Kora, and this is Kate behind me."

"Hmm? There's two of you? You're a looker, aren't you?" he said, pointing at Kate. "And you're not so bad either. Must be my lucky day."

Kora shook her head at the insult. By any century's standard of beauty, she was at least twice as attractive as Kate, but didn't have time to argue with the old geezer.

"It sure is," she simply said instead and walked past him into an apartment that made her own look spartan.

Every inch of the small foyer was packed with mismatched bookcases, bureaus, hutches, and shelves, each holding collections of the most random assortment of items and knick knacks one could imagine.

"How do you live like this?" Kora said to the man when she returned from the equally crowded bedroom.

"I don't," croaked the old man, who had settled into a weathered chair near the door. "This is—was—my sister Doreen's apartment. Hadn't seen her in years and I guess I won't see her again. Good riddance."

"That's a nice story," said Kora, ignoring the old man's subtle prompting to ask about his awful relationship with his sister. "But we're looking for something in particular. Do you know where Doreen kept her ink and pen?"

"Oh, sure! It's right next to the 6000th pile of crap over there! You can't miss it!"

The man grinned at Kora and she resisted the urge to punch him in the face.

"Fine, I'll do it myself."

Kora walked into the bedroom and closed her eyes. She would have preferred to do this another way, but time was of the essence and she surmised it wouldn't take very much energy to perform the necessary ritual.

A buzzing sound suddenly permeated throughout the small room, as if a small colony of bees had woken up from their slumber. Kora followed its trail over to a rolltop desk in the corner of the room, pushed it open, and stepped back just in time to avoid the stacks of crap that had been stuffed underneath. Still, the buzzing got louder as she tossed piles of paper, faded envelopes, and old issues of TV Guide until at last she discovered the prize: four fountain pens paired with four bottles of dark black ink that were tucked away in the back recesses of the desk.

"What's that?" asked Kate, and Kora nearly jumped at the girl's sudden appearance.

"You read the diary, right?"

Kate nodded.

"Then you know what this is, what Rita van Asch used this for."

"But how…"

"… did this crotchety old woman manage to acquire so much of it? Good question, but that's a puzzle for another day. Right now, we have work to do."

Kora picked up a couple of the pieces of paper she had tossed aside and set it on the desk. She then unscrewed the fountain pen, poured a good portion of the ink into its reservoir, and reassembled the implement. The ink flowed easily from the nib, but she had to be careful in her word choice.

"What are you doing?" Kate asked.

"Writing a note to your erstwhile employer. To set a meeting."

"And you think she's just going to show up?"

Kora smiled.

"Of course. That's the beauty of the ink. Take a look."

She handed Kate the note, who read it out loud:

"Beatrice, meet me at the Belvedere Fountain on April 10 at 10 p.m."

"That's it? Nothing happened."

"Well of course not. It's not directed to you, is it? But the one under that is."

Kora gently pulled the note free from the girl's hands, revealing a second piece of paper underneath. Unfortunately for Kate, the ink's alchemy began to work almost instantly, as her eyes registered that her own name was written at the top of the missive. She walked out of the bedroom without another word and Kora heard the front door slam shut a few moments later.

"See you around," said Kora with a smirk.

Truth be told, she was beginning to come around on the ink's usefulness. It paled in comparison to her own power, but being able to issue commands from afar did have its own set of positives, and would certainly help facilitate her meeting with Beatrice. That reminded her, she needed to complete the last part of her ruse. She was eager to unleash a bit of chaos into the Guild's careful planning, and outfitting one of their adversaries with a bit of leftover ink was just the ticket.

After stashing a half-filled bottle of ink and two of the fountain pens inside the box spring, Kora returned to the living room

"Where'd she run off to?" asked the old man, who seemed disappointed that only Kora remained.

"Term paper," she said. "Anyway, I'll take it."

"Take what?"

"Everything. How does $400 sound?"

The old man paused for a second before his nearly toothless mouth broke into a smile.

"It sounds perfect."

"Great. I'll be back tomorrow morning to get everything. Can I get your name for the check?"

"Sure, it's Morten. Morten Ryerson."

"Well thank you very much, Morten. It's been an absolute pleasure."

Kora withdrew the pen and a third sheet of paper from her pocket and added the man's name to the top of the already-written note, before setting it gently in his hands, and walking out the door.

CHAPTER SIXTEEN

KATE

"Go back to your apartment and forget what happened today during our Raid," the note had said.

Simple, but effective.

But even after 15 minutes of the IV drip, which I now administered myself, I still didn't remember being forced to leave that hoarder's dream of an apartment. Everything up until reading that piece of paper, I eventually recalled though.

Including her name.

Kora.

It troubled me that there was more magic out there of such strength. It was bad enough being memory-wiped one way, but now I had to worry about this ink too? I knew that I was in over my head and I knew that I needed help. Fortunately, I already had acquired a second mentor, one who was powerful in her own right, and one from whom I was going to take every ounce of power when the time was right.

Beatrice's next task for me after locating the diary was piecing together evidence from other sources of Rita's handiwork at Valley Forge. That had meant pouring through nearly indecipherable microfiched pages from the diaries of various Revolutionary War generals, and then cross-referencing those entries against Rita's own. It was mind-numbing work because Rita had been very good at keeping out of sight—and of course, her own husband's diary had coincidentally not survived the intervening centuries.

At 6 p.m., I had regained enough of my faculties and memories to resume my research, which is exactly when I received a message from Beatrice.

"Meet me at W. 4th Street station tomorrow at 9 a.m."

"What 4?" I texted back.

"Going to Bed-Stuy for a raid."

No. It had to be a coincidence. There was no way that Beatrice also knew about…but of course she did. She had read the diary, probably many times. She knew about the ink and she had probably been waiting years for this opportunity. And so had Kora. Which is why we had gone there today. It was a game of cat and mouse and I was the unfortunate piece of cheese in the middle. Or a ball of yarn. Or maybe I was the mouse and they were both cats? Honestly, my brain was too fried to process this latest development.

But thankfully, I still had one final trick up my sleeve that I had been hesitant to use.

The little green square had sat in my desk for weeks now, untouched and unused. Because of what I had been able to do with the diluted one, I was admittedly afraid of how powerful the full-strength version would be. But now was not the time to be timid.

I broke off the tiniest of corners of the buff and started to chew it. It tasted even worse than the ones I had been eating for months, if that was possible. I finally swallowed and waited for the effect to kick in.

Nothing happened.

Throwing caution to the wind, I cut the thing in half with a knife I had stolen from the student cafeteria and ate one of the pieces. Even conditioning my mind so many times still didn't prepare me for the intensity of what followed. It was different than the tunnel into my subconscious I had been creating with the IV drip, almost as if someone was placing my brain into a vise and forcing a single thought into it. That first time, it was the photocopied pages of the Valley Forge journals that were resting nearby. I tore into them with such vigor that I had pieced together the dozen hidden references to Rita that I had missed during my first review.

After an hour, the effect had still not worn off, but fortunately, I redirected my focus elsewhere. My friends had papers due this week, so I wrote them. Then, I found a random freshman struggling with calculus in the lounge on the third floor so I did his problem set too even though I didn't even pass pre-calc in high school. After that, it was still only 1 a.m., and the focus buff still showed no signs of wearing off, so I returned to the room to tackle one final project.

The note that Kora had written to me in the compulsion ink was locked away in my bottom desk drawer and I gingerly removed it, careful not to glance at the writing. I was no engineer, but at the moment I felt like I could take on anything, and so I spent the next 5 hours poring through scientific papers on the solubility of gallic acid, until I must have passed out.

When my phone alarm went off at 8:30, I slowly opened my eyes and it was as if someone had stuck silly putty in between the neurons of my brain. I couldn't focus enough mental energy to change into new clothes, to figure out how to get to the bathroom, or even to tie my shoes. It was as if the focus buffs had overwritten the proper workings of my brain chemistry.

Fortunately, I still had one piece left, but I knew I couldn't handle another bender like last night. So I quickly turned on the hotplate and dropped the buff into my little pot. After several minutes, it eventually liquified and I poured the substance into a flask that my friend Lanie had bought all of us on prom night. I took a tiny sip and the gears in my brain finally started cranking again. Securing the flask inside my jacket, I ran off to meet Beatrice at the subway.

She wasn't mad at my tardiness, said she had built in some extra time for us to get to our destination. After several subway transfers and several surreptitious sips of the liquid buff, Beatrice asked about my research and I told her, perhaps a little too eagerly. I made a mental note to keep quiet, lest I accidentally reveal what else I had done, but not before asking for more buffs. Beatrice glared at me and I could tell whatever trust existed between us was slowly eroding. Still, she handed me her last one and chided me not to waste it.

Don't worry, I thought. I won't.

We disembarked in Bed-Stuy and for the first time that morning, Beatrice was in a rush. I wanted to tell her that there was no need to run, that she was already too late. Instead, I played dumb.

"Where are we going anyway?" I asked, matching her now brisk strides.

"The Requester wants us to procure certain items from an estate sale," Beatrice said.

"That's it? Couldn't they have gone themselves?"

"Sure, but when you're flush with tokens, why would you stoop to such labor yourself when you can sit back in your comfy chair and let others do the dirty work for you?"

Makes sense, I thought. But whose dirty work we were doing was what worried me. I had no idea what Kora had ended up doing with the ink. She didn't need it, as she had other means of magical control, but she clearly didn't want Beatrice to find it.

"We're here," said Beatrice when we arrived at the familiar five-story walk-up with a rusty fire escape. She rang the buzzer and we walked into the deserted lobby, where Beatrice approached the stairway, before stopping.

"What are you doing?" I asked.

"Listening. Shhh."

After a minute, Beatrice retreated and walked towards the mail-boxes at the back of the lobby, and began rummaging through her purse. With her momentarily distracted, I took the opportunity to recharge with a quick sip of the green liquid. I hoped that after this Raid was over, I could just sit in my bed and let my mind return to normal on its own. But if not, I needed to start thinking of a back-up plan.

"Why aren't we going up?" I asked.

"Because I need to give you something first," said Beatrice. "I said that our employer probably was just using their money to hire us instead of getting their lazy ass down here, but there's also a chance that someone else knows what's for sale here, so we need to be adequately prepared for that probability."

She removed what appeared to be a knife from her bag and un-sheathed it from its leather scabbard. The smooth metal of the blade caught the light from the dirty fluorescent fixture overhead and suddenly the vestibule was five times brighter. After a few quick stabs in the air, Beatrice resheathed the weapon.

"Here," she said, handing the knife to me, and my eyes widened as I grasped it. It wasn't that I was afraid of weapons; I had fired my fair share of shotguns out on my grandma's farm when I was younger. No, *this* weapon was something else entirely. Maybe it was because of the buff or something else Kora had done to me, but I could *feel* the power the knife possessed and it scared me to my core.

"W-what, why are you giving that to me?" I asked. My mouth began to tremble and my thoughts began to slow as I continued holding the weapon. Thankfully, noticing my distress, Beatrice quickly intervened and took back the blade.

"You know what, on second thought, why don't you let me hold onto that?"

I was both relieved to be rid of the weapon but disturbed that this woman had something that *felt* so powerful. How did she get it and what did it do? But now was not the time for such direct questions, and as Beatrice climbed the stairs ahead of me, I took another sip and focused on shutting my mouth.

The door to 5A was slightly ajar when we arrived and when we stepped inside, I couldn't believe my eyes. The place was empty, bare. All of Doreen's crap was gone. Except that ugly leather chair and her brother sitting in it. My pulse quickened as I worried whether he would recognize me from yesterday and ruin everything. But when he called me a looker for the second time in two days, I breathed a sigh of relief. Kora had taken care of one loose end by wiping the old man's memory from yesterday and another by apparently buying the entire contents of the apartment lock, stock, and barrel. But she hadn't taken care of them all.

We interrogated Morten for a bit and he coughed up his sister's letter written in compulsion ink that had forced him to deal with her estate, which I so wanted to get my hands on, but Beatrice beat me to it. Afterwards, she sprinted off into the bedroom hoping that somehow Kora had been dumb enough to leave the ink here for her to find.

I found Beatrice sobbing when I walked into the bedroom a few moments later after another refill of focus and immediately took back what I thought about Kora.

"Hey. Look at that."

My mouth blurted out the words before my brain could tell it not to. What the hell was the matter with me?

"What?" asked Beatrice.

"There's a bulge in the box spring. Right next to you."

Again, mouth word vomiting, brain not thinking.

Beatrice sprung back to life and tore open the top of the box spring with her knife to reveal a ziploc bag underneath with two fountain pens and a small bottle of ink. My heart sank. The power of that ink could have been mine and with it, I could have guaranteed my freedom from Kora's puppet strings.

My internal brooding was interpreted by Beatrice suddenly giving me a huge hug. I was so shocked by the sudden display of affection that my arms hung in the air behind her back, before I eventually returned the embrace.

"You're welcome. I didn't really do anything though."

Except, well, everything.

"You did though. Anyway, let's book it out of here before the Guild realizes what they've missed."

"Sure, but what's the Guild?"

I didn't care about whatever the Guild was. I only wanted to get the hell out of here and recuperate before Kora paid me another visit. And before Beatrice started using me to experiment with her newly acquired alchemy.

"You don't want to know."

It took the rest of the vial to get me back to my dorm room. A few times, I cut it close, and watched the world go in and out of focus. A quick sip restored everything to its normal working order, but as the green liquid gradually decreased, my heart started racing more and more.

I collapsed into my bed just as the last dose ran out and let the confluence of the last two days pull me down into slumber. But when I awoke at 4 a.m., it still felt like a 100-ton weight had lodged itself in my head. I would have gone back to sleep had I not noticed an envelope that had been slipped under the door. Literally crawling on my hands and knees, I reached the intruding object, and discovered a dozen green gummy squares inside to go with the one Beatrice had given me. I greedily unwrapped one as quickly as I could and was about to eat it whole when I stopped myself.

How did I get here? How had I fallen so fast? And what would happen if I continued down this path?

I left the envelope by the doorway and somehow pulled myself back into bed. Trying to collect my thoughts was like trying to catch a jar of fireflies with nothing but a torn net. The focus buffs taunted me from across the room, like a siren taunting Odysseus. Sleep eventually reclaimed me, but by the next morning, still nothing had changed.

As I saw it, I had three options. I could keep eating the green squares indefinitely. I could tell Beatrice the truth, and admit that I was a mole sent by a mysterious blonde-but-now-redhead named Kora. Or—and this was the least appealing choice—I could tell Kora the truth and ask her to use her power to fix my head.

I spent another day in bed, subsisting on a frozen TV dinner I had bought my first week of school and the half a bottle of vodka, which was the only liquid left in my mini fridge. By the second morning, I was running out of time. My stomach ached from hunger and my brain couldn't come up with any other ideas because I was expending all my energy just trying to think the simplest of thoughts.

Finally, I gave up and retrieved the envelope. While one of the buffs melted down into liquid, I ate half of another and it was as if I had been plunged into a pool of frozen water. I snapped to alertness and directed my focus onto temporary and long-term solutions to my problem. One trip to Goodwill later and I was grinding one of the buffs with a mortar and pestle into a fine powder. I snorted some of it and it got me through almost the entire day before I came back down. Setting aside a quarter of the buffs for memory recovery and another quarter for research purposes left me with about two weeks' worth of powder. So I went to work.

I spent a day in the bowels of the chemistry library, finishing my research on gallic acid solubility. Then the following day in a purloined lab testing ink extraction methods and procedures on notes I had written with ink purchased from a flea market under the Brooklyn Bridge. After a day wasted hemming and hawing, I retrieved Kora's note from the bottom of my dresser. Using a pair of tweezers, I gently lowered the paper into the mixture of water, sodium carbonate, isopropyl alcohol, and a sprinkling of other reagents. When the beaker didn't immediately shatter into a thousand pieces, I breathed a little easier and left for a few hours to attend to other business.

Beatrice's Upper East Side apartment was incredibly easy to find, which made me wary. I watched the front of her building for the rest of the day, and all I found out was that her very attractive nanny was most likely sleeping with her husband. The next morning, with the ink still very much adhered to the note, I returned to see a different woman pushing the blue baby carriage around the block. Night fell and finally Beatrice appeared, exiting the building through the service door, before quickly stepping into a waiting car. As much fun as it would be to engage in a high-speed chase through the city, I left her to her evening escapades and retreated for the time being.

Days passed and the ink still hadn't separated. I had used up the buffs set aside for research and was perilously close to finishing the ones in the memory recovery reserve. So one final experiment was in order. Wrapping the tourniquet around my arm was like old hat at this point, and I didn't even flinch when I stuck the syringe into my arm. Unlike the original, watered-down buffs that had made me retreat into my subconscious, I was wide awake when this version kicked in. Like a thirsty desert traveler searching for a single drop of water, my mind spun, looking for a thought to focus on.

More, I thought. I need more.

CHAPTER SEVENTEEN

KORA

Kora left the note with Beatrice's doorman and took a stroll through the upper reaches of the park, before making her way back down to the rendezvous point. Sure, she could have used Kate as an intermediary, but she wasn't yet ready to burn her mole. Besides, she wanted to give the girl and her mind a break for a few weeks, lest she crack under the multitude of stresses she was under.

The pond was quiet today as Kora walked across the bridge toward the fountain. She recalled a day here long ago that had not been quiet, when a different woman had worn her necklace and she still had her blonde hair. But today the only blonde was the woman waiting for her on the bench, who was staring straight ahead at the figure on the top of the fountain.

"Hello, Beatrice," said Kora as she sat down on the other end of the bench. At the sound of her words, the woman's eyes finally blinked again.

"The ink," Beatrice said, her breathing forced and her voice quivering. "How did you get it?"

Kora smiled.

"The same way you got it. You should really be thanking me. I did all of the dirty work. I doubt you would have found it in that mess."

"So you're the one who beat me to it. Why didn't you take all of it?"

"Because I don't need it. You do."

Beatrice's facial expressions turned to confusion.

"Then why don't you just give me what you took?"

"Nice try," said Kora, laughing. "I gave you just enough so that you won't use it as a crutch. Too much power would easily go to your head. You need to be resourceful if you're going to have any hope against them."

"Who?"

"I think you know."

Beatrice slowly shifted her weight back, as if she was planning to run. For all the good that would do her.

"Relax, I'm not with them. In fact, you and I are working toward a mutual goal."

"Which is what, exactly?" asked Beatrice.

The woman's hands drifted slowly to the purse at her side and Kora wondered whether the Relic that Beatrice was rumored to have found was inside.

"The complete and total destruction of the Guild. They tried to kill you, right? Not far from here actually. Yes, I know all about that, don't look so surprised."

"Why do you need my help then? You seem to know everything. You have your own supply of the ink."

Kora considered the question. It was true that she had more than enough power at her disposal, that was never the issue. Time and agency were what she lacked, but both she had full measure of recently, thanks to her incredibly compliant host. Still, there was always the gnawing feeling in the back of her mind (if she still actually had a physical one), that in an instant, those would be taken from her, like they had been so many times before.

"The Guild has many pieces on the board," she said. "I've been trying to gather my own to counter them for many years. Unfortunately, it's been a non-linear process. But you, you could change everything."

It was an exaggeration, to be sure, but Kora had spent lifetimes learning the subtle art of manipulation, and ego stroking was among her most useful tools.

"I'm glad you think so highly of me," said Beatrice. "But I'm still not sure what you want me to do. I don't feel like getting stabbed again."

"Don't worry," said Kora. "I'm not asking you to step into the lion's den. Not yet, anyway. We're both playing the long game here and there are still many moves left to be played. I just wanted to meet you face to face to take my measure of you."

Beatrice scoffed, before abruptly getting up and starting to walk away.

"I don't need anyone taking my measure, I'm getting along just fine, thank you."

"*Sit down*," said Kora and the blonde nearly staggered backward onto the bench. "Do I have your attention now?"

Beatrice nodded, a look of trepidation in her eyes.

"Good," said Kora. "As I said, I don't need anything from you now, only that you will be receptive to my help and aid in the years to come. Is that going to be an issue for you?"

"No," said Beatrice. "I'll talk all the help I can get."

"That's what I wanted to hear," said Kora, cracking a smile.

"Oh-OK," said Beatrice. "Can you at least tell me why you hate them too?"

"You already know too much about the world," said Kora. "Best you don't know any more. But suffice it to say, they took *everything* from me. And I want it back."

Kora pushed herself up and headed to the passageway that ran under the terrace, and as expected, Beatrice trotted after her.

"Wait," said Beatrice. "When will I see you again?"

"You won't. This city has many eyes and ways of hearing, and too many lead back to the Guild. In the future, I'll be in touch through more subtle means. Mint?"

She extended her hand toward Beatrice and in her palm was a red flat disc. The woman took it without further prompting and Kora watched as the last two hours of Beatrice's memories dissolved into a wisp of smoke.

CHAPTER EIGHTEEN

KATE

I don't remember much from that night.

I remember the feeling of desperation as I poured the second-to-last portion of the focus liquid into the syringe. I remember sticking the needle in my thigh. I remember frantically pouring through print-outs in a dingy government building basement that I had snuck into. I remember the feeling of the cold water hitting my face and finally coming to in the living room of Beatrice's downtown apartment.

I looked at her and her unkempt hair and the men's shirt she was wearing before my eyes fell upon her pocketbook. The same thought that formed in my head also formed in Beatrice's, but I was faster, and a second later, I was pointing the unsheathed dagger at her, my hand shaking almost beyond control.

"More. I need more."

The dagger's ivory handle radiated an uncanny energy and I so wanted to drop it on the floor and never touch it again.

"More what, Kate? You know, you could have just called. Now why don't you just give me that—"

"The buffs. I need more."

"Oh."

"I made the last one into a powder, so it would last longer and you wouldn't think I was an addict by asking for more so soon. Bought a mortar and pestle at Goodwill. Snorted a little bit to see what would happen and passed out. Woke up, did a little more, tried to finish a paper. Then it wore off again. But not before a thought occurred to me. I needed to inject it. So I went down to the health center, got into the exam room, and then took off with some syringes and tourniquets before the nurse came in. That did the trick. But I only had a little left, so I needed to find you."

Even in my unnerved state, I was still able to twist the truth to my will. She didn't need to know how far I'd fallen, how much my mind was now subservient to the magic she had created.

She pleaded with me to drop the knife and of course I wanted to. I didn't know how she could stand to hold the thing or keep it so close to her, but I held firm until she agreed to my demands.

I flicked the knife around and offered her the handle, and the energy emanating from this end of the weapon was even more terrible. In the corner of my eye, I saw a look forming on Beatrice's face and for a split second, I thought I had made a critical mistake. But instead, she resheathed the blade and walked toward the nearby bookcase.

I pretended to stare vacantly ahead while watching Beatrice grab two books off the shelf at the same time, generating a click from somewhere behind the wall. She then pushed the bookcase forward to reveal a secret door and a secret room beyond. As much as I wanted to trail after her, I stayed put, calming my breathing and concentrating on staying in the moment.

Beatrice returned several minutes later and handed me an envelope.

"Here," she said and I took it. It was completely flat, unlike the one she had sent me earlier with the last supply of buffs, the name of a woman and an address somewhere in midtown written on the front.

"What's this?"

"Your next task. Make sure this letter gets delivered and I'll make sure you're taken care of by the evening."

I considered the envelope and its contents. I could feel the traces of something inside, something that was more than just a letter that needed delivering. There was alchemy in there, and, if I had to guess, it was a note written in the ink that I had found for her. Fine. I would jump through the hoop like a good dog and get my reward.

I pocketed the letter and walked out the door. It was almost 10 a.m. and I had another 12 hours before I would literally be down to my final, emergency back-up buff. The NYU fitness center was conveniently a few blocks north of Beatrice's apartment, and a brisk jog later, I was walking to the back of the locker room showers, the sealed envelope in hand. After running the hot shower for 10 minutes, the resulting steam easily freed the glue and I carefully removed the note.

My suspicions were correct, as I recognized the same black ink from Kora's notes. Unlike those, this one was incredibly mundane, directing the recipient to transfer a random woman to the firm's West Coast office. Whatever. I didn't have enough spare brain cells to figure out what Beatrice was doing, but as long as it didn't involve me, I didn't care.

An hour and a half later, the letter had been delivered and I was back in my dorm room, waiting for the promised resupply of buffs that night. I stared at Kora's note suspended in the solution I had crafted. Despite all my best efforts, the ink was still firmly attached to the paper and I was firmly headed for a complete breakdown.

The hours ticked down. My focus-seeking brain searched for new avenues to explore. It didn't find any. So I dove inward.

I focused on my memories of the past year. Of the initial excitement of discovering that vial in Brooklyn Bridge Park and the Quest Board soon after. The exhilaration I felt hunting for Beatrice. The danger I felt confronting Emma and her swords and stealing away her silver token. The humiliation I felt being under Kora's thumb. The anger I felt after taking back control. That first promise of adventure had turned into a living nightmare as I was throttled by this trio who thought they were better than me because they had power and I did not.

But I was going to change that.

CHAPTER NINETEEN

KORA

Kora woke up and her apartment was on fire. The four posters of her bed were lit up like burning stakes and her mind flashed back to a cold night in Salem and the villagers' vain attempt to burn her alive. They had succeeded, in part, but after the mayor's wife had fetched her necklace from the charred corpse and put it around her neck later that night, the town was quite surprised to see Kora still alive and well.

They had burned her again and then after yet another woman foolishly put on the necklace, and after yet another burning, someone finally came up with the bright idea of locking Kora away in a wooden box. 100 years later, when Kora awoke again, the witch burning craze had fallen out of favor and she had learned a valuable lesson in humility. But over the last century, she had grown complacent, and now she was evidently paying the price.

The billowing smoke forced a reflexive cough from her host body, jolting Kora out of her daze. She threw herself through the fiery bed curtains and was aghast at the blaze that greeted her. There was heat and ash everywhere, and, crawling on the ground to the bedroom door, Kora let out a loud cry of anger as decades of work and planning were incinerated before her eyes. Her laptop sat thankfully untouched on the desk and she grabbed it before making one last mad dash out into the hallway and down the stairs.

As she walked down the street opposite the wailing sirens of the firetrucks, tears ran down her face and she collapsed on the cobblestones of MacDougal Alley.

"Think," she commanded herself. "You planned for this eventuality, set redundancies, even if you don't remember where they are right now."

Of course. She had not been naive that she was invincible. It would just take time to rebuild. But she had the tools and knowledge and a malleable host, and all she needed—

Wait.

She pushed down into the recesses of her mind, where the poor woman was huddled into a dark corner, like a malnourished street dog.

"You!" Kora yelled. "What have you done?"

"N-n-nothing," said the woman, who seemed half-asleep. "I did like I was told. Didn't want to end up like the other, I swear!"

Kora couldn't remember the last time she had even let the woman have control back. The weariness of the months she had spent awake had finally caught up to her and she realized that in her lust for freedom, she may have doomed herself.

"Fine," she said. "You'll be free of me soon enough."

"Wait!" cried the woman, but Kora had already resurfaced and had now broken into a sprint. She needed someone she could rely on, someone she had trained over many months, someone who could be counted on to carry on her work while she rested.

The light in the dorm room was on despite the early morning hour, and Kora threw a flirty smile at the security guard, who buzzed her in without a second thought. On the walk up the seven flights of stairs, she clutched her stone tightly in her right hand, a reminder of who and what she was.

But not forever, she thought.

KATE

A sharp rapping sound stirs me out of my pensive reflection and I open my eyes to see an envelope wedged between the ugly dorm room carpet and the cracked bottom of the door. But my hope soon turns sour as I open it up to find not a cache of the familiar green buffs, but a lone square of dark green. Its texture is as rough as sandpaper and it looks barely edible, and when I lift it out of the envelope, I yelp in pain from its touch, before dropping it on the ground.

I bend down and lower my hand just above the would-be buff and focus. Pain erupts across my palm, as if a crazed griffin has mauled me with its talons and I curl my fingers tightly around the wound. I open my eyes and slowly open my fist, fully expecting to see my blood seeping forth from the violent claw marks. But there is nothing there except the five lines of my life.

For a moment, I consider running after Beatrice or whoever dropped off this trojan horse. Did she think I was that stupid that I would willingly eat this poison? Perhaps. She didn't know how I'd been changed, how I could now sense the alchemy around me. And that would be her undoing.

A wild thought enters my head and before I push it back down, my hands are unscrewing the jar holding Kora's note. I carefully scoop up the buff with the empty envelope and drop it into the liquid and brace for an explosion. But instead, the green square that would have been my death slowly dissolves into solution and I nearly shriek in delight as a few minutes later, the ink is freed from the paper at last. With the purloined equipment I borrowed from the chemistry lab, I filter out the ink, careful not to spill any of the now-probably deadly liquid, and am soon holding a tiny container with the power to bend anyone to my will.

Another rap at the door and I think I know who it is. I pause for a moment, trying to recall what I am supposed to remember and what I am not. On the way to greet my guest, I quickly hide the ink in my little walk-in closet, and then slowly turn the aged metal knob and pull.

It's Kora. But not like I've ever seen her. She smells of ash and fire and her magnificent red hair, which used to be blonde, is singed on the ends.

"Hi," I say quietly, trying hard not to say her real name. "You look—"

She pushes her way into the room and nearly knocks me over, before collapsing into my desk chair.

"Are…are you OK?" I ask and Kora looks at me with her piercing green eyes.

"I will be," she says. "Just need a minute to gather my thoughts."

I lean awkwardly against my dresser and watch as this woman, who had made my life a living hell, seems to be on the brink of collapse. Her breathing is heavy and I see dried streams of tears that have partially cleaned away her soot-stained cheeks. Finally, she straightens up and slowly turns her head toward me, a hungry gaze now manifest on her face.

"I want to give you something," she says.

"Umm, OK," I say mildly, but inside I'm absolutely terrified. She's clearly not in her right mind and based on her past track record, I can't imagine that this is a generous gesture. And I realize quickly, that I can't let her do whatever it is she intends to do. So I stall.

"One sec," I say and run into my closet before she can respond. My hands nimbly unscrew the fountain pen I bought the other day and I carefully pour the little bit of ink I managed to retrieve into its nib. I set the tip of the pen onto a small scrap of paper and write the letter K.

And that's when the buff runs out and my mind turns to sludge. All I can do I stare down at the incomplete note and the pen that is mightier than any weapon I can imagine. But it's as if I am frozen in a block of ice. My thoughts form at a wild pace but my brain cannot focus their energy to move my fingers even an inch. Time slows to a standstill and I wait for Kora to find me in here, a veritable statue.

But then something happens. My hand begins to move. It sets the pen next to the "K" and writes another letter. "o." And then a third, "r," before the final one, "a."

I don't understand why this is happening until I hear someone's voice inside my head and it isn't mine. In fact, it's the last person I want to hear right now. But her words, which she impressed into my subconscious so long ago, now compel me forward.

"Don't give up."

I won't. Not now. Not ever.

I blink and somehow I've completed the note. I stare at the words and nod to myself, before the voice in my head brings me to my feet and back outside to where Kora is absent-mindedly looking out the window.

"Hey," I say, and as she turns toward me, I close the gap between us and hold out the note, like the tip of a sword.

Her eyes are immediately transfixed to the words, and she repeats them in monotone.

"Kora, give me your power."

The woman nods and stands up from the chair. My body and mind are on the verge of collapse as she approaches, and I don't know whether to try to run or hold my ground.

Kora grabs my hands, interlacing our fingers. Her skin is cold to the touch and then it isn't. It's warm and then hot and then burning and then suddenly my whole body, my whole being is aflame.

My eyes snap shut as Kora feeds her power into me and it's as if I'm being hurtled down a never-ending roller coaster. But as I'm lurched downward, I feel the ill-effects of the focus buffs fading away and in their place is something else entirely.

I open my eyes.

Kora is kneeling in front of me with a mixture of fear and exhaustion on her face. A blinding light casts an intense green glow over everything in my little room and it takes a few seconds to realize that it's coming from me.

"*Get up*," I command and Kora lurches to her feet. "*Why did you come here tonight?*"

She tries to fight my question, but in the end, my power is too much for her.

"To...to give you this."

She holds up the green stone locket around her neck. Its shimmer matches my own and for a moment, I think about pulling it free and taking it, but then I stop.

"*Sit*," I say to her, and she awkwardly falls to the floor, her legs crossed as if she is a second grader listening to her teacher.

"You used me like a dog, made me jump and bark at your commands, but now it's my turn."

I snap and a ball of flame appears in my palm. Another snap, and a crackle of lighting erupts from my fingertips and shoots toward Kora. She can only yelp in pain as the electricity goes through her to the floor.

I hold my hands down at my sides and push down against the air, and suddenly I'm floating half a foot above the ground. It's as if every childhood fantasy is possible, I only need to make it so.

"What else can I do? *Tell me.*"

I see Kora struggle to refuse the command, but I put my fingers on my temple and concentrate, and she lets out a wail as if I've punched her in the stomach.

"Anything," she says with a whisper. "But…you can't…you won't be able to…"

"Don't tell me what I can't do!" I yell and grasp her throat with my mind. Her hands lunge up to her neck, trying to free her next breath and I release her after a moment.

"You, you will teach me how to use this power. And then you will serve me until you are no longer useful."

I concentrate for a moment and a silver dagger materializes in my hand from the ether. I flick it forward, guiding it with my thoughts, and it nicks a lock of Kora's hair before finding its mark in the wall behind her.

"Or maybe I'll kill you. I can't decide what would bring me more pleasure."

I stick out my hand and the dagger wiggles itself free from the wall, flying end over end through the air back to me. I grab it with a flourish and let out a maniacal laugh. After all the suffering I've endured, I finally feel a sense of joy at the absolute power of creation at my fingertips.

But then I stumble.

The dagger slips from my fingers and before it can reach the ground, it evaporates to nothing. My vision is suddenly fuzzy and my legs feel like they are made of jelly. The familiar feeling of the synapses in my brain slowing to a crawl

"What's…what's happening?" I scream, but only a whisper escapes my mouth.

"I told you," says Kora, who deftly lifts me up and places me face down onto my bed. "A mere mortal such as yourself has no ability to control the power that I possess."

"What are you?" I croak out, barely able to turn my head to face her.

"Someone who used to be real," she says. "Good bye, Kate O'Laughlin."

She grabs my hand. It is cold, like a statue. I feel my remaining power recede back into her, and before it's all gone, I desperately try to conjure up something, anything, to stop her. But it's gone.

And so am I.

I close my eyes and think about the vial on the pier.

The night air whipped against the ramparts of Belvedere Castle, but the man at the top didn't seem to mind. He grasped the stone railing and watched the rippling of the moon's reflection on the surface of Turtle Pond below. It had been an interesting year, but he had the oddest feeling that everything was about to shift again. Which was fine. He was used to such things. It had been nice, though, to operate on his own terms, even if it was only temporary.

Finally, a visitor appeared. The woman had red hair, which was odd, as the last time he saw her, she had blonde locks, but he was sure an explanation was forthcoming.

"Hello, Kora," he said with a smile. "It's been a while."

He waited for her to commit whatever act of violence she had planned. But reading her face, it seemed she only wanted to talk.

"Is he in there, still?" asked Kora, a desperate longing in her voice.

"Who?" replied the man, trying hard not to laugh. "Oh, him. That's a good question. I can't recall the last time I heard his voice. Maybe it was right before I split his stone in two."

"You did what?" Kora screamed and the man who had been called Gilbert braced himself against the railing, waiting for her to charge forward. But instead, the woman slumped down to her knees. Sensing an opportunity, he walked over to her and crouched down next to her.

"To be honest, I wasn't sure it would work. You homunculi are at once so powerful and yet so fragile. I ended up having to use *Ukonvasara*, which was really ironic, if you think about—"

The woman headbutted him, which wasn't entirely unexpected, given what Gilbert had said. But in her current state, all she had managed was to bloody his nose.

"You're lucky I always carry a handkerchief," said Gilbert, wiping all the blood away without a trace from his face and clothes, before returning the still pristine fabric to the top front pocket of his blazer. "Otherwise, I would be really mad."

Kora slowly rose to her feet and began mumbling something under her breath. A green glow appeared from the locket around her neck, which slowly radiated over her entire body and then outward. Gilbert extended his hand and felt the tendrils of the homunculus's power. It filled him with a sense of longing and sadness, but he quickly brushed it away and returned to the present.

"We're really doing this?" asked Gilbert. "Here? Now? This is the moment you've selected, after all the centuries you've been waiting?"

"*Shut up,*" said Kora in a language that Gilbert wasn't sure still existed.

"OK then. Suit yourself."

He withdrew a set of small, silver darts from his inner jacket pocket, and with a flick of his wrist, he scattered them in a staggered row between himself and Kora. The woman's energy pushed forward again, but the faint golden barrier that had formed between the darts easily dispelled it.

"Ready when you are," said Gilbert, as he watched Kora manifest a ball of green energy in her right hand, a look of pure malice on her face.

But then a curious thing happened. The woman's left arm, seemingly independent of her body, rose slowly from her side and with a snap of her fingers, the alchemy dissipated.

"Huh," said Gilbert. "Having second thoughts?"

"No," said Kora, but her intonation of her voice was somehow different yet the same as moments ago. "I've let this go on far enough."

Kora's hands reached up to the chain around her neck, and although her eyes seemed to scream in desperation, the rest of her face looked unconcerned with what was happening. As the chain rose over the head of the red-haired woman, Kora dissolved in an instant, and a different woman stood in her place.

"Mother," said Gilbert. "There you are. I wondered where you had run off to these past several months."

Gilbert squeezed the stone that was tucked inside his collared shirt, and a moment later, in his place, was a teenage girl, wearing a smaller version of the business casual ensemble.

"The things we do for research," said Dalia de Wyck, chairman of the Guild, caressing the green stone in her hand. "I don't know how you stand to wear his stone for so long, Ty."

Ty shrugged her shoulders. She was so used to traversing the city as Gilbert that she didn't give it a second thought. And after the splitting of the stone, it had been even easier to assume the homunculus's identity, with his pesky voice relegated to the other stone and her new protégé. It was too bad, really. She would have liked him to be here when she crushed his wife into a pile of dust. But her mother had spoiled that fun.

"Tell me," she said. "What has little Kora been up to?"

"Many things," said Dalia, holding the stone's chain out in front of her, as if she was afraid that the woman would suddenly appear again. "But I saw to it that all of them are no longer viable. Well, almost. I have to admit, I was impressed with my own resourcefulness with the limited hours I did have. The woman had built up quite a collection in that building. I took great pains to catalogue everything properly before burning the place to the ground."

"Good," said Ty. "I worry, though, that you fed her too much. That red hair…"

"Yes, I know. It was unavoidable. I was sure she would realize immediately what was going on after she gave me the necklace that morning bed, but she was so happy to have her freedom that I don't think she gave it a second thought."

"What of her acolytes, though?"

"Don't worry about them," said Dalia. "The newer one is gone. She got the jump on poor Kora, used up a good deal of her accumulated power in only a matter of minutes. It was actually quite spectacular. But it was too much for the girl's body to handle. The morgue will do an autopsy and chalk it up to a drug overdose, so nothing more we need be concerned about."

"Are you sure about that?"

Ty had observed the girl named Kate a few times over the last several months from afar and was surprised by her resourcefulness. It was too bad that she was dead, as she would have complemented her other puppet. But things didn't always go the way you planned, even if your plans were painstakingly crafted. She was loath to let that cache of memories go to waste, though, even if her mother was. That would be a good project for the next several weeks, now that her mother was back and could cover the Guild's administrative responsibilities that Gilbert had been doing.

"And what about the other?"

"Oh, that's the best part," said Dalia. "Beatrice will think herself so clever that she disposed of the poor girl, but will never know how close she came to losing everything. I say let her be for now and wait to see where she goes from here."

"Fine with me," said Ty, recalling how the last direct encounter with Ms. Taylor had gone. Enforcers like Rufus didn't exactly grow on trees and she was years away from molding another one just as talented. But she could afford to wait, now that her mother had delivered her a gift on a silver platter.

"May I?" she asked and Dalia relinquished the green stone to her.

"It may be ready for a splitting," said her mother, "though I do wonder if it is wise. Her righteous anger toward you may complicate things when she next awakens."

"Oh, that's where I disagree, Mother. It's exactly what I need. Because if this little jade," said Ty, stroking the edges of the stone, "ever wants to see her husband again, she'll do exactly what I tell her."

"Suit yourself," said Dalia, who turned toward the stairs leading down to the base of the castle.

"Leaving so soon?" asked Ty.

"Yes, my dear. I deserve a rest in my own bed after so many months away. We'll talk after the next Guild meeting."

"Fair enough. Until then."

Ty walked back to the castle railing when her mother was well and gone, and held both glamour stones in her hand. If she listened hard enough, she thought she could hear Kora's voice screaming from deep within the recesses of the alchemic shell that her mother had created so many long years ago.

She smiled.

"What am I going to do with you now?"

ENFORCER

INTRODUCTION TO ENFORCER

Enforcer takes place six years prior to the events of *Guild of Tokens*, and four years prior to the events of *Trainee*.

Garrett was late.

That wasn't anything out of the ordinary in Beatrice Taylor's experience.

Her husband couldn't be counted on to be on time even if he only had to walk across the street.

But tonight was different.

Tonight was their first wedding anniversary and the snickers of the waitstaff at Joel Daniels were becoming too much for Beatrice to bear.

She sighed and swirled the wine in her glass, a pinot noir from a winery in New Zealand that she and Garrett had visited on their honeymoon. Had a year passed already since they were two newlyweds off on an adventure halfway around the world? At the time, Beatrice had no illusions that the trip was going to accomplish what many years of dating had failed to do: turn their relationship into something more than a marriage of convenience. And she had been right. But for one night at least, maybe they could pretend they were a happily married couple.

Beatrice glanced at her watch and wondered what was keeping Garrett.

A last-minute call from his boss, asking him to move a text box up a quarter of an inch? Despite him being named a vice president last year, she was still surprised at how much grunt work he was still expected to do.

Maybe he had gotten stuck in traffic? It wasn't yet holiday season, when hoards of tourists would descend on the city like barbarians at the gates, but Manhattan's roads still managed to slow to a crawl with the slightest bit of provocation.

Or, and Beatrice hoped that tonight of all nights that this wasn't the reason, Garrett had decided to indulge in a bit of extra-curricular activity with his newest sidepiece? It wouldn't be the first time that he had stood her up because he was off with some 23-year old he met out at a bar.

There was that time he failed to show up to *Silver Linings Playbook* and when he crept into bed later that night, he had smelt of gin and Coco by Chanel. Then there was his firm's summer outing three years ago, when one of the summer analysts could not stop making eyes at him. After the party, an inexplicable "emergency" had popped up and, wouldn't you know it, Garrett and the summer were the ones who had to rush back to the office to finish it. The brazenness of the whole thing had been so off-putting, that when Garrett finally rolled into their apartment at 8 a.m. the next morning, she had nearly thrown a wine bottle at his head. Instead, she had tried to play the oblivious girlfriend card and offered to brew him a fresh cup of coffee, which he happily accepted. Except instead of half-and-half, Beatrice had added three drops of the truth serum she had been testing downtown.

As he sipped the coffee, Beatrice had debated what to ask him. The serum only lasted so long and she needed to be precise.

"How was she?" seemed too blunt and Beatrice had no desire to know the actual details of Garrett's fornicating.

"How did the 'assignment' go?" seemed too wishy-washy. For all she knew, there was actually an assignment but maybe it had taken a total of five minutes.

In the end, Beatrice had gone with the simple route.

"Did you hook up with Laura yesterday?" she had asked him.

"No," he had said, his voice monotone. "It was a few minutes past midnight."

"Oh," she had replied. "Did you use protection at least?"

Beatrice was surprised that she had chosen that particular question, but she had later surmised that it was her subconscious deflecting her away from the query she wanted to ask: why?

"Yes," he had said.

"Well, at least you're not a total idiot. Here, let me refill your coffee."

She had practically ripped the mug from his hands and rushed into the kitchen, where she had poured in a smidge of coffee along with a different additive this time.

Garrett's face had born a look of confusion when she had returned and handed the mug back to him. Whether the look was from the line of questioning or why he had answered truthfully, she would never know, because as soon as he swallowed the first sip, the memory serum had begun to work its alchemy. His pupils had dilated and he stood there, without blinking, for more than a minute, before his mind had come back to him, only without the memory of the last five minutes.

"Sorry I was out all night B. We needed to completely rework the financials of the breadstick manufacturer acquisition before the investment committee meeting this afternoon."

"It's OK," she had said. "Hope you got it done in time."

"We did. Laura was terrific. One of our best summers in a long time."

"I'll bet she was."

She had walked out of the kitchen before the urge to slap him across the face returned and had spent the next hour sobbing silently in the bathroom. She bemoaned her lack of fortitude in fully confronting Garrett, but then had convinced herself that maybe deep down she didn't want to know why he had done it. If she didn't know the truth, she could pretend that it wasn't that Garrett found her lacking, that he wasn't just using her to placate his parents and their country club set. Maybe one day she would be able to recreate Rita's ink and she could make him be faithful.

Tonight she also wished she had some of that ink, if only to ensure that Garrett would actually show up. She took her phone out of her clutch and shook her head. He wasn't coming.

Beatrice gulped down the rest of her wine and left the restaurant without another word. The dinner was already paid for and she didn't need to suffer any more embarrassment at the hands of her husband tonight.

As she exited the building, Beatrice began to raise her hand to hail a cab, but then stopped as she saw that the road just south had been blocked off with a string of construction barriers. Fine, she thought. She walked one block west as quickly as her heels would allow to find the east side of Broadway similarly blocked off.

Beatrice threw up her arms in exasperation and began crossing the street for further points west, before abruptly turning around and doubling-back toward the restaurant. She had no desire to return so quickly to her empty apartment, to eat the top of her frozen wedding cake alone, to wait for Garrett to trudge in at some ungodly hour, to harp on him for being a complete and total jackass for standing her up without warning.

Fortunately, the restaurant was located at the western edge of Central Park and Beatrice quickly decided that a scenic walk home in the brisk autumn air would go a little ways toward salvaging a terrible first anniversary.

The walking paths of the park were well lit but empty as Beatrice made her way into the interior of the urban wilderness. She didn't make it a habit of walking alone in the city at night, but she had enough confidence in her alchemy that she could handle an attempted mugging in a pinch without resorting to her trump card.

That trump card, the Medoblad, so named because it turned whoever was stabbed with it to stone, was unfortunately stashed away in her lab downtown. Not that she needed it, but it provided an extra air of reassurance that the handful of buffs in her bag did not.

And of course there was the useless ring on her finger.

Not the engagement ring, which might as well be a cubic zirconia, for all the anguish her marriage had brought her.

But the other ring, the simple silver ring slotted above the obscene diamond, that contained a small purple stone. The stone that had held so much promise, but in the end, Beatrice had not been able to unlock its secret. So there it sat as a reminder that she was still an infant alchemist compared to the might and knowledge of the Guild. Some days, today especially, she wanted to walk into that jeweler's shop and throw both rings down on the counter and demand her money back.

No, maybe the better idea would have been to skip her meeting with Doug on that muggy July afternoon two years ago.

D oug was late.

Ordinarily, Beatrice would not have cared, but the humidity was doing extreme damage to her just-blown out hair, and she didn't feel like wasting another $30 today getting it fixed back into place.

Finally, she spotted her trainee sprinting down the block toward her table, as if he was trying to outrun the bulls in Pamplona. It made her think, just for a second, that something was genuinely wrong, that they were both in danger. But then he calmly walked into the outdoor cafe, his reddened face glistening with sweat, and Beatrice almost chewed him out for making her worry for no reason.

"You're not that late," she said. "No need for the 100-meter dash."

Doug hunched over in his seat, breathing heavily, before wiping the sweat off his brow.

"So-sorry T, needed to get here to tell you that..."

T was short for Trinity, a *Matrix* reference she thought was funny at first, but she had begun to worry that Doug was beginning to actually believe she was Trinity, come to save him from the doldrums of the real world.

"Tell me what?"

"That your boyfriend is cheating on you."

Beatrice stared at him blankly and took a long drag of her coffee. She was of course plainly aware that Garrett had begun another dalliance. All the familiar tells had recently resurfaced for the first time since she had interrogated Garrett the previous summer, but the identity of the new girl was something she hadn't sussed out yet.

"With his boss."

It had been, in retrospect, a bad time to take a sip of coffee, for it took all of Beatrice's willpower and determination not to spit the contents of her mouth all over herself and then pour the remaining contents of her cup on top of Doug's head. Instead, she forced herself to remain absolutely calm, as if Doug had merely informed her that it might rain later.

She considered her trainee with a wary eye. How did he know all of this? It was clear now that he had started stalking her, and Beatrice was annoyed with herself at being so clueless to that fact. And that he was apparently infatuated with her and trying to be the white knight to save her from the horrible asshole she had shacked up with.

Beatrice contemplated, just for a millisecond, giving in to Doug's transparent plan, but quickly decided that sleeping with him was not only a lousy choice for revenge sex, but also would open up a whole can of worms that she didn't want to deal with. Frankly, she wasn't sure she wanted to keep Doug on as a trainee if he was going to pull stunts like this. That was an issue for another day though. Right now, she needed to put a stop to this particular affair once and for all.

40 minutes later, in the elevator up to the 50th floor, Beatrice started to waiver.

It had seemed like a great idea initially, when she had run out of the coffee shop without saying a word to Doug. But now that she was moments away from striding angrily into Garrett's boss's office, she was having second thoughts. It wasn't like she was Rita van Asch, with vials of command ink at her fingertips that would allow her to bend her adversaries to her will. If she had even a smidgen of that ink, all this would be over in a few seconds.

No, her alchemy wasn't going to do her much good here. The few buffs she had managed to perfect were all about enhancement and the truth and memory serum combo would be less than useless. She already knew the truth and wasn't confident she could selectively wipe the memory of the affair from such an unwilling subject. The mind-linking apples might do the trick, except her supply had dwindled over the past several months and getting Amelia to eat one would be a challenge in and of itself.

That left only the Medoblad, the most powerful and most impractical item in her arsenal. How she would love to see the look on Amelia's face as the stone streaks worked their way up her body until she was nothing but a statue. But the thing about turning someone to stone is that it's hard to move a two-ton statue inconspicuously, let alone find a place to put it.

The elevators doors finally opened on the 50th floor, but Beatrice quickly hit the lobby button before anyone could see her. As she descended, she kicked herself for being so impulsive. A direct confrontation was never going to be the right approach. And how could she have forgotten that she was not the only aggrieved party here?

Beatrice had met Amelia's husband last December at the holiday party. He was a chemistry professor at Columbia in his mid-fifties with an endearing British accent and a hearty disdain for his wife's profession. Beatrice wasn't sure how he and Amelia had ended up together. Maybe he had just needed a green card back in the day and had therefore given Amelia free rein to sleep around. If that was true, then merely confronting him with Amelia's unfaithfulness was going to go down in flames immediately. But maybe there was another way. She did always have a thing for men with accents.

The night had grown chilly and with half of the park still to traverse and her heels beginning to make her feet throb, Beatrice was beginning to regret her decision. She was also regretting the decision to wear the skimpy leopard print dress with black sequins in place of spots, the garment providing no barrier to the night air.

Grey clouds dotted the sky and the moon was barely a sliver, so the only illumination guiding her way home were the intermittent bulbs of the street lights that adorned the path. Which had all begun to flicker for some reason. She quickened her pace, but the flickering continued, until, one by one, the lights began to disappear and Beatrice was enveloped in darkness.

"Hello," said a raspy voice from behind her and Beatrice nearly toppled over before slowly turning around. She could barely make out the figure, who was standing several strides away from her, but he was large, that much was for sure. The man stepped forward a few paces and Beatrice's pulse began to quicken. He was holding a small lighter in one hand, its glow providing the only source of light and illuminating the contours of his body.

It wasn't just that the man was gigantic, with arms the size of tree trunks and broad shoulders that would make fitting through most doors problematic.

No, what really made Beatrice start sweating was the smile on his face. It was a wicked, malicious, knowing smile, the kind worn by a person about to commit a heinous deed and then walk away afterward like nothing had happened.

Beatrice took a deep breath and tried to compose herself. She was not the defenseless little girl that she once had been. She could do this. Besides, maybe he was just a fellow nighttime walker.

"Hi," she said, slowly reaching her hand into her bag dangling at her side.

"Pleasant evenin' for a stroll, ain't it?" said the man with a half-cockney accent that nearly made Beatrice roll her eyes.

"A bit too chilly for my taste," she said, her fingers now trying to determine which of the buffs was the one that she needed. She cursed herself for wrapping them all in identical plastic. If she grabbed the wrong one, she wouldn't get a chance to correct her mistake.

"Your man run out on you tonight of all nights? Probably just as well. Seemed like a git."

A smirk formed on the thug's face and Beatrice's eyes widened.

"Don't know what you're talking about. I'm just trying to walk home."

Her courage was flailing along with her fingers, which couldn't seem to grasp any of the buffs. She didn't want to look down into her purse, in case the man thought she was pulling out a weapon and made a move first.

"Sure, sure. Wouldn't want to delay you. Just here to deliver another message."

Beatrice unwrapped one of the buffs inside her bag and grasped it with her fingers, before slowly bringing her hand up to her mouth in a fist, as if she was deep in contemplation. She gently pushed the buff into her mouth and ran her tongue over it, its sour taste making cringe just a tad.

"And what's that?" Beatrice replied, resting the buff against the inside of her mouth, ready to release its strength at any moment.

The moon may have been but a sliver that night, but the knife that appeared in the man's left hand was an adequate substitute, for its blade shone so bright that Beatrice nearly had to shut her eyes. She bit into the buff and steadied herself as she waited for the power to flow through her. The thug regarded her with a curious expression before his mouth broke into a half-toothed smile and he stepped forward.

"Gilbert sends his regards."

The rows of diamond rings under glass were so overwhelming at first that Beatrice had no idea where to begin. Truth be told, she had been fine with Garrett never getting around to proposing and even the affairs, as long as they were kept relatively out of sight.

But this latest transgression had been too much. Not only was Amelia Garrett's boss, and thus, directly in control of his future earnings, but from the few times she had met her, Beatrice had been taken aback by her domineering personality. It would only be a matter of time, she had surmised, before Amelia would either chew Garrett up and spit him out, or, and this worried her even more, she would convince Garrett into cutting Beatrice loose.

And that, simply, was unacceptable.

Beatrice did not need their engagement to be a gesture of Garrett's undying love for her. Far from it. She needed the engagement to send a message to Garrett that she would no longer tolerate any behavior that could jeopardize their future.

It had been relatively easy, in the end, to bed the professor.

Beatrice had been wrong about the green card and that had made things much easier. She had called his office, pretending to be a reporter from an obscure trade journal, her chemical engineering degree had provided the necessary bona fides to be convincing enough to set up a meeting at a bar near campus.

Gerald had recognized her as soon as she sat down, which she knew was a possibility, and he had nearly fled, before Beatrice forcefully convinced him that he should stay. Him being married to a domineering bitch had given her an easy template to follow and she was surprised at how effective it was. It had only taken three more clandestine meet-ups before Gerald was infatuated with her and she had brought him back to her downtown apartment for a mid-afternoon romp.

As they lay together in her small bed afterward, Beatrice had contemplated revealing their significant others' treachery, but then she saw the look of shame forming on Gerald's face and knew that it wasn't necessary. A week later, Amelia had called Garrett into her office and explained that it was probably a good idea that the two of them cease their fornication and also she would be happy to recommend Garrett for the open position at one of the other big PE shops in town.

Beatrice had waited a few weeks after that to broach the subject of marriage. The interview process had gone quickly, most likely thanks to Amelia's recommendation, and Garrett was soon set up at a cushy new job with a cushy new title and, unfortunately, surrounded by a whole new group of young analysts to go after. So one afternoon, she had surprised him in the office, dressed to the nines, and dragged him out to lunch nearby, where she delivered her ultimatum.

Beatrice was surprised at how easily the conversation had gone and surmised that Garrett's parents must have been getting too embarrassed up at their country club in Greenwich that their son had been dating the same woman for so long and wouldn't it be nice to have grandkids before they were too old to run around with them. She had shuddered at the thought of producing offspring with Garrett, but she would have to deal with that eventuality later. Right now, she had a ring to select.

"See anything you like?"

The jeweler looked straight out of central casting, with tiny spectacles perched at the end of his nose, patchy tufts of white hair on the sides of his head, and a very pronounced slouch that made it difficult for him to look her directly in the eyes.

"Just browsing for now, thanks," she said.

Beatrice was not the type of woman who had spent her 20's dreaming of the ring she wanted and after dating Garrett for so long without even a whiff that a proposal was forthcoming, she was utterly uninterested in the entire process. Nevertheless, she didn't trust Garrett not to come home with a tiny solitaire from one of the stores on Fifth Avenue and so she had taken it upon herself to find a jeweler deep in the Diamond District where she could get a rock for the same price.

"Ok, just let me know if something catches your eye."

Something did eventually catch her eye. It wasn't terribly big and it wasn't actually a diamond. The stone was purple-amethyst if she had to guess-and was wedged between two enormous hunks of glittering carbon, almost as if it wasn't even there. The way the stone caught the light gave Beatrice pause. There was something different about this ring and she wanted to know what.

"Sir, could I take a look at that one?"

"Oh, that's a recent arrival. Close to four carats and superb color. It's-"

"No, not the diamond. The one next to it."

The jeweler looked up from the case with a furrowed brow and frowned.

"Oh. That one. Didn't realize that was still out. I'm afraid that's most likely out of your price range, no offense ma'am."

"I don't know about that. My future fiancé gave me a pretty substantial budget and–"

"I'm sure he did, but, still, the problem remains that you do not have the correct funds to purchase that particular ring. Now, if I can direct your attention to–"

The word caught Beatrice off guard.

"Correct" funds?

He couldn't have been talking about tokens, could he?

In her years of Questing, she had met many people hawking alchemic wares in exchange for tokens, but those transactions had always occurred in the shadows. In a trash-filled alley, or a back corner of a random flea market, or that one time where Beatrice waited for seven hours under the Manhattan Bridge.

This was different.

This was brazen, out in the open.

And that intrigued Beatrice even more.

It was fortunate for her that she even had the bronze token with her that day. She normally didn't travel with any tokens unless she had specific business to attend to.

With a flourish, she flicked the token into the air. It landed after several flips onto the top of the glass case, where it wobbled a bit before finally settling down. The jeweler, his curiosity piqued, leaned over to examine it with his loupe before picking it up.

"Hmm," he said. "Interesting."

"What?" asked Beatrice. "It's a bronze, but there's more where that came from."

"No, no. Not the token, which you can have back by the way."

He put the token back down on the glass and slid it across to Beatrice, making a horrific scraping sound in the process that made her cringe.

"It's you I'm talking about. I've heard whispers of a blonde alchemist whose buffs are second to none. Never thought though that she would come walking through my door wanting to buy a piece of shitty carbon."

"What's that supposed to mean?"

"It means, my dear lady, that your reputation precedes you but mine didn't. Were it not for Providence, we might never have crossed paths. Anyway, that's an issue for me to deal with some other time. For now, we must discuss the terms of your purchases."

The taste of the buff was acerbic, as if Beatrice had washed her mouth out with fetid lemon juice. She had contemplated waiting a few moments, to see if maybe the thug could be reasoned with. With only one strength buff in her bag - another stupid oversight, she realized - she didn't want to waste it right out of the gate. But the enforcer had made his intentions clear when he had uttered that name.

Gilbert.

If you walked by him on the street, he would be the last person you'd notice, even if he was the only other person in eyeshot. He was so unassuming that he would blend in at an all-women co-working space. The man was just so … ordinary. From his nondescript brown hair to his simple dress, his entire air screamed: "I'm not worth noticing."

But his appearance was the only thing about him that was unremarkable.

The man was, in a word, unnerving. Beatrice had only ever met him one time, but that one encounter was enough for her to know that he wasn't someone you wanted to run into alone in a back alley.

It had been a short meeting, at the Greenmarket in Union Square. She was considering the ripeness of some green tomatoes when he had sidled up to her in his unassuming way, and it took a rather pronounced throat-clearing before she even noticed him.

"Yes?" she had said, turning to look at him.

"Hello Beatrice," he had replied.

"Umm, hi. Do I know you?"

"Not directly, no. Your reputation precedes you, though, so I wanted to come size you up myself."

"I'm sorry, not sure what you mean. I-"

A silver token had appeared in between his fingers as if he had grabbed it out of thin air. She had never seen that denomination before, as at the time, she was flush with only bronze. But the gesture was obvious: this man, whoever he was, knew about the other half of her life.

"Come, let's take a walk."

Beatrice had put down the tomatoes and followed behind him, into the interior of Union Square. Even though they were only a stone's throw from the gaggle of hipsters perusing produce at the market, it felt like they had entered another world within the park. The few people around were all … different in some way and Beatrice suspected that if she started screaming, no one would come help her, or even hear her.

They had sat down on an empty bench and faced each other, and it felt like the most awkward first date Beatrice had ever been on.

"Gilbert," he had said, extending his hand. Beatrice had returned the gesture, but when she had touched her palm to his, a chill suddenly ran up her arm that had nearly made her recoil in horror.

"Nic-nice to meet you, Gilbert."

"No, the pleasure is all mine. I had heard rumors about a new alchemist who was churning out some interesting stuff and, well, I make it my business to know the people who should be known.

I was even able to procure a sample of your wares and I have to say, I'm impressed. Very impressed."

"Thanks. Are you with the Council or something? Did I do something wrong?"

"No, I'm not with the Council. And the answer to your second question depends on how the rest of our conversation goes. I'm curious, how did you come up with the strength buff?"

"What? Oh. It was just a lot of trial and error. I-"

"Sure, sure. New alchemy always is. But you obviously found a … unique source of prima materia for the strength enhancement."

Beatrice had seen several steps ahead of where this conversation was headed and had tried to put an end to it quickly.

"Salamanders. In Swindler's Cove up in Inwood. But there's not many left after I finished up there, so-"

"Ah, I see. Well then, if you happen to come up with any more interesting alchemic breakthroughs, I'd love to hear about them."

He had grabbed her hand again suddenly with such force that Beatrice had nearly been pulled forward onto him. His second handshake had been just as cold and clammy as the first, and when he had finally withdrawn and walked off without another word, Beatrice had breathed a sigh of relief. It was then that she had noticed the business card that was now in her hand.

It was cream-colored, no different than any of the hundreds of other business cards Beatrice had received in her lifetime.

"Gilbert," it had said on one line, with "The Guild" on the line below, followed by a random PO box number that she had later traced to somewhere in lower Manhattan. She had turned over the card to see a raised red sigil of what at first glance was a pigeon. But upon further inspection, she saw that it wasn't a pigeon at all. The bird had no beak and wings that were more befitting a hawk than the lowly vermin that Beatrice had been killing over the years.

She later determined it was something called an alerion.

Only two of the mythical birds were said to exist at one time, laying eggs every 60 years, and after those eggs hatched, the parent alerions drowned themselves. It was a rather morbid and sad symbol and Beatrice had wondered why the Guild hadn't chosen a more majestic creature to use, like the phoenix or the roc.

But the answer to that question was furthest from her mind at the moment, as she steadied her footing and waited for the right moment to knock out the knife-wielding idiot in front of her with one blow. She finally felt the familiar surge of strength flowing through her as the buff went into effect. It was exhilarating and Beatrice couldn't help but smile.

"Well, let's get this over with," she said. "You just going to rob me of my effects or is that knife intended for other purposes?"

"The latter," the enforcer said. "Nothing personal, just business."

"Oh. I don't suppose I can convince you otherwise? Because if you think I'm going to let you just stab me to death, you're going to be severely disappointed. I-"

"Just ate of one your little strength buffs and are gonna knock me out with a single blow, eh?" The enforcer's grin widened as Beatrice recoiled in horror. "Oh, don't look so shocked. You didn't think there were going to be consequences to defying the Guild? Didn't think they told me exactly what you were capable of before sending me out here tonight?"

Beatrice's body began to tremble, her confidence shattered in an instant. She tried to steady herself, tried to pretend that it would all be fine, but as the seconds ticked and her strength began to ebb away, she came to the realization that she was most likely not going to walk away from this encounter alive.

"Now, I can do this the easy way: a quick poke to your abdomen and I'll be off. You'll still bleed to death nice and slow on the ground, but at least you'll look pretty in the casket. Or, I can slice you up real good that it'll take a few weeks before they figure out who you were. Your choice."

"Sorry, I choose option three," she said, surging forward. It didn't matter if he knew what was coming. Even a brute like him was no match for her strength.

Beatrice screamed as her eyes closed and she felt her left fist connect cleanly with the enforcer's jaw. He hadn't even tried to block her, the big dope. But then she opened her eyes and was greeted by the enforcer's crooked smile and her hand exploded in pain. She swung her right fist forward only for it to be blocked by the man's forearm.

Before she could stagger backward to safety, he had her, his left hand lifting her body cleanly off the ground like she was a little kid. Beatrice flailed in the air, trying desperately to land a kick in the enforcer's midsection, but he just laughed as Beatrice's heels flew off her feet and hit him with a whimper.

"Hold still, girl."

The man's grip on her shoulder tightened like she was caught in a vice and she screamed from the pain as the arc of the knife came down toward her. She pleaded with the amethyst ring to do something to help her, to lend her its strength.

But it remained silent on her finger, a worthless hunk of rock that she had sacrificed so much to obtain.

Beatrice watched as the crooked blade completed its trajectory and time seemed to slow. It was as if she was watching a movie of her own life in a darkened theater and the director had decided to draw out this last moment as long as possible. Well, she had seen enough, and closed her eyes to wait for the life to drain out of her.

Except that conclusion didn't come.

Instead, Beatrice heard the impatient grunting of her would-be murderer, and she hoped beyond hope that maybe someone had come to her rescue.

She wasn't that lucky, but somewhere the goddess of luck must have been smiling down on her just a little, because when she opened her eyes, the knife was not lodged in her stomach but caught on the black sequins that coated her dress just above her thigh.

The enforcer cursed in some foreign language as he tried to pull the knife free, his grip on her left shoulder loosening just a tad. Beatrice tried in vain to turn her body away so that he couldn't grab it, but he grabbed the handle with a quick thrust of his arm.

Beatrice screamed as the enforcer forced the blade through her dress into her thigh and slashed downward before pulling the weapon free. He released his grip on her shoulder and she crumpled to the ground. Her hand instinctively went down to her thigh and she felt the warm blood spilling out of her.

Her eyes drifted up to the man, who was now crouching over her with that same stupid smile on his face and the red-coated blade in his hand, and she braced herself for the end.

The sky was blue, the water was warm, and Beatrice was drunk.

It was the last day of her bachelorette and a part of her didn't ever want to leave the sun-soaked Bahamian beach to return to the miserable February snow and to the aftermath of Garrett's likely debauchery in Las Vegas. She thought about drugging him so full of memory serum that he wouldn't even remember what transpired, but hoped that alcohol had done the job for her.

She finished her third mojito and signaled to the waiter further down the beach for another. The rest of her compatriots were still passed out from the previous night's festivities, and Beatrice would have been too if she not had cranked out an extra batch of vitality buffs before the trip.

As much as she appreciated the anti-hangover effects of the buff after a hard night of partying, what she really found intoxicating was the feeling of rejuvenation that came with it. It was like she was a goddess in ancient Greece, not bound by the rules of physiology that applied to the mere mortals around her.

Beatrice absent-mindedly fiddled with the ring on her finger while she waited for the waiter to return. She had left her engagement ring back home for safekeeping. If this whole engagement became an intolerable disaster, it would at least provide her with some cash to live on for a year or two.

No, the only ring on her finger was the amethyst ring that had cost her an even greater fortune than Garrett had spent.

The jeweler had extracted a princely sum for the ring, not just in tokens but in bags of buffs and jars full of memory and truth serum. The transaction had wiped out her existing stores and then some. It had taken Beatrice nearly five months to make enough of what the jeweler wanted, and when she finally delivered the last installment, he had simply handed the ring over to her with barely an explanation of what it did.

"She'll lend you her strength in times of need," was all he had said before disappearing into the back room and not returning. Beatrice had put on the ring and wasn't surprised when nothing had happened. But as the weeks passed and she still hadn't figured out the ring's secret, or why the jeweler had referred to it as a "she," Beatrice was beginning to suspect she had been had.

Her suspicion was confirmed when she had returned to the jeweler's shop just a week before the bachelorette to find a Cluck-A-Wing restaurant in its place and the neighboring shop owners having no recollection of there ever not being a Cluck-A-Wing there. She had half a mind of reporting the incident to the Questing Council, but had decided against it, as she had already drawn too much attention to herself.

Beatrice closed her eyes and listened to the gentle lapping of the waves on the sand. She needed a new ally and fast to help her sort through all the Questing intricacies, for two reasons.

First, without a second Quester, she was cut off from the Raid Board. Not that she had seen any enforcement mechanism of the "two or more people" rule for Raids, but their complexity necessitated another pair of hands. She had a few promising leads working their way up the ladder she had created and hopefully one of them would bear fruit, but that took time.

And second, it was only a matter of time before she got a new tip from her source about an especially important Raid. She still had no idea who this person was. One day several years ago, she had been minding her own business, looking for another seemingly pointless Quest to complete, when her Q-Mail inbox flashed open with one unread message. It was a short one, just a set of numbers, which Beatrice thankfully copied down because the message deleted itself after a minute. After spending hours trying to figure out what the numbers were, she finally narrowed it down to a library call number.

Which was all well and good, except that there were probably over a hundred libraries in the city and if the call number wasn't in the online catalog, which she suspected it wasn't, she was looking at untold hours of work. But Beatrice was nothing if not relentless and so, after almost a year of digging, she had finally found it: Rita van Asch's diary and along with it, the secret of the magic flowing through the world.

That had been the catalyst, that had ignited the spark of her burning desire to ascend to the top of the Questing ranks, to become the best alchemist the city had ever seen. The mysterious notes continued appearing in her Q-Mail, leading her to more discoveries. To be honest, she resented the amount of help the notes had provided her. Sure, she would probably still be wandering around aimlessly fetching junk for lazy Questers without them, but Beatrice had spent most of her entire adult life pulling herself up by her own bootstraps.

It was part of the reason she resented Garrett, whose entire life had been one giant handout. She had tried to make peace with it, that she deserved the comfort and stability that Garrett's money would provide her. But instead all she felt was an even bigger desire to prove herself, to not let that cushy lifestyle make her soft. That had meant late nights in her lab, days spent in dusty library archives, weeks spent trekking around the small bits of wilderness still left in the city. And of course that trip to Corfu, where all on her own she had found the crown jewel of her arsenal, the Medoblad.

Beatrice opened her eyes, hoping to see a full mojito on the table next to her. Instead, her empty glass was gone and in its place was a small ivory envelope set under a small rock. An envelope sealed with a wax seal bearing a familiar sigil.

Beatrice shot up from her chair and ran down the beach, hoping to catch a glimpse of whoever had left the envelope. After jogging nearly halfway back to the hotel beach bar and finding no trace of anyone, she walked slowly back to her chair. The alerion in the sigil glared up at her with its singular eye and Beatrice felt her heart skip a beat. She tore open the envelope and pulled out the small piece of paper tucked inside.

Which was blank.

Beatrice turned the paper over and found the back blank too. She ran her fingers across both sides, trying to feel for impressions left by a pen or some other substance that had been surreptitiously applied, but there simply wasn't anything there.

A shiver rippled through Beatrice's body and she felt exposed in a way that she hadn't felt in a long time. She kicked the sand and cursed herself for being so careless. Was she that naive to really think the Guild was going to just leave her alone? After she had lied to Gilbert and flouted her alchemy prowess by buying that ring? She wanted to scream, to take the ring off and toss it in the ocean and just run away. But the Guild had just demonstrated that it could track her wherever she was, so what would be the point?

No, she wouldn't be cowed so easily. She was Beatrice Stallard, master alchemist. And she wasn't going to let someone like Gilbert push her around.

The ground was cold and Beatrice was dying. Whatever strength still remained in her body was fleeing as fast as the blood was pouring out of the gash in her thigh, an unfortunate consequence of the misused strength buff. Even now, in her darkest hour of need, the stupid ring sat there dormant.

It was her own fault, really. She should have forced the jeweler to explain the inner workings of her purchase. After all, who buys a half-million dollar piece of factory equipment and doesn't make sure it comes with an instruction manual? What was she supposed to do, ask the ring for help as if it were a real person?

"*That would be a start, yes,*" said a voice.

Beatrice opened her eyes to see the boots of the enforcer turned away from her, but the pain was too great to look any further for the source of the new voice. She shut her eyes again and concentrated on a thought.

"Who said that?" said Beatrice in her mind.

"*I did,*" said the same voice. It was a woman's voice, that much Beatrice concluded, but the words were laced with an unplaceable accent.

"Who … who are you?" she asked.

A flicker of light appeared in the back corner of Beatrice's mind. It was purple, the same color as the stone. The flicker slowly gained shape until Beatrice could make out the faint figure of a woman.

"I am nobody. Well, I was somebody, once. That was a long time ago though. Now I am nothing more than an essence distilled into a rock perched upon the finger of a woman who is about to die."

"I don't understand," thought Beatrice. "How can you be a-"

"As much as I would love to have this conversation right now, if I do not lend you my strength, that very large man standing above you will begin slicing you open and letting your insides drain out of you."

"Oh," thought Beatrice. "Then, please, lend me your strength."

"That is it?" said the voice. *"No, that is not sufficient. I have been trapped in here a long time and I am not going to give you my power simply because you said 'please.'"*

"What then?" said Beatrice. She felt the anger building inside her and her head began to spin, a haze beginning to envelop the internal world in her mind. Beatrice tried to suppress it, tried to return to the stoic frame she maintained day in and day out, but she couldn't. Instead, she unleashed the torrent of rage that she had been holding back for so long.

"You want me to beg like a dog? To plead on my knees for you to save me? Is that it? I didn't kowtow to Gilbert or his brute or anyone else in my life and I'm certainly not about to do so to an incorporeal voice in my head. So either give me your strength or let me just die already!"

The figure in her mind crystallized for just a moment and Beatrice could barely see the face of the woman. Her eyes shone with the same color as the ring and her mouth curled upwards in a smile.

"Gladly."

Beatrice felt her right hand begin to tremble and she opened her eyes to see the amethyst stone glowing softly. The light continued to brighten and she felt a surge of power pour into her body. It was similar to the strength buff but only as a tabby and a lion are both technically cats. This was raw, undistilled power, not the pale imitation that Beatrice had created in her lab.

As strength poured out of the ring, so too did the purple glow. It spread over her like a protective shield and Beatrice finally pushed herself up from the ground. She held her hands in front of her and they shimmered with the purple aura of her mysterious benefactor.

The enforcer turned around to face her once again.

"You're still alive." He stared at the light enveloping her, a look of confusion on his face. "What's this about then? You eat another one of your little candies?"

Beatrice smiled, the wound in her thigh nothing but a pinprick. "No."

"Oh," he said, pointing the blood-stained knife toward her. "Then it shouldn't take long to finish."

She shook her head.

"I don't think so."

The brute laughed.

"We already went through this song and dance. Now if you don't mind, just let me kill you so I can get on with my evening."

He lunged forward clumsily with the blade, but Beatrice was ready. She caught his knife-wielding hand with her own and dug her fingers into his wrist like she was squeezing a tomato. The enforcer screamed, dropping the knife to the ground and trying to wrest his hand free, but Beatrice wouldn't let him. She tightened her grip, heard the crunch of bones breaking, and saw the man's hand go limp. Now it was the brute who was cowering with fear.

"Please," the enforcer said. "Can't you just-"

"Just what?" asked Beatrice. "Let you go? After what you were going to do to me with this?" She bent down to pick up the knife and pointed it at him, her outstretched arm gleaming with power

The man's body began to tremble as he nodded slowly, and Beatrice relished the role reversal. She felt invincible, unstoppable, unbreakable.

Still, the nagging pain at her side was slowly returning, and she looked down briefly to see blood seeping down her leg. A minor inconvenience that she would deal with shortly.

"Sure, but I want you to deliver a message for me to your boss."

"Any-anything," said the enforcer, practically whimpering.

"You tell him that Beatrice Taylor is under nobody's thumb."

She reversed her grip on the knife, stepped forward, and smashed the handle into the man's neck with all of her strength.

The enforcer collapsed onto the ground and Beatrice tossed the knife at his crumpled form before turning and walking away.

She only made it another 20 feet before the purple aura suddenly evaporated and with it, Beatrice's consciousness.

The room was white.

White walls, white sheets, white drapes, and a white tray of food perched on a stand next to Beatrice's bed. She stared at the unappetizing cup of jello and the small carton of juice and frowned, before a shooting pain erupted along her thigh.

The door opened in that moment and in walked Garrett.

"B, you're awake!"

Beatrice looked at her husband with a blank expression, trying to recall how it was that she ended up in a hospital room overlooking Central Park. Her head hurt, which was odd, because she could have sworn the reason she was in the hospital had something to do with the throbbing on her thigh.

Then, like the morning fog on the water burning off from the rays of the rising sun, it all came back to her: the dinner, the walk in the park, the ambush, and the ring.

"You're late," she said matter-of-factly. "I waited for you at dinner and you never showed."

"What are you talking about?" said Garrett. "I waited for you at dinner and *you* never showed."

"No, I was at Joel Daniels for over an hour and you were definitely not there."

"What? Why did you go there? You changed the reservation to Cafe des Arts last week, remember? You texted me that you were able to get a table off the waitlist."

"I most certainly did not, why the hell would you think I . . . oh."

The events of the evening suddenly all snapped into place.

This second reservation. The blocked-off roads. It had all been a set up so Beatrice would walk right into the trap that Gilbert had sprung for her.

"S-sorry," she said. "I must have forgotten. What time am I getting discharged?"

Garrett looked at her like she was an insane person.

"B, do you not realize? You've been in a coma for a week. The doctor said it was lucky that the jogger found you when he did, otherwise you might have bled out."

"Oh. Well, lucky for me then, I guess. What about the guy who did this to me? He locked up somewhere?"

"Not exactly," said Garrett, who lowered his eyes toward the floor.

"What?" she asked.

"Well, he's, umm, he's dead. Paramedics found him close to where you had collapsed, a knife wedged into his abdomen."

Beatrice's eyes widened. She hadn't done that, had she?

"It's OK. I already talked to the police days ago. They're not going to charge you, obviously it was self-defense. They just want to talk to you when you're up for it. I think they want to know how a 5 foot-nothing like you managed to take out a guy four times your size."

"No, I mean, I didn't hi-"

Before she could finish the thought, Garrett had wrapped his arms gingerly around her and began stroking her back, which made her almost want to vomit.

"It's all right, everything's going to be OK. I'm just glad that you're awake. I thought I had lost you!"

Garrett began to sob into Beatrice's shoulder and she found herself comforting him, which was odd, given the circumstances. Her body was still too weak to return the hug, so all she could do was rest her chin on his head.

"Sorry, didn't mean to . . . just need to get some fresh air. I'll be right back."

Garrett quickly stood up from the bed and walked out of the room, leaving Beatrice alone once again.

Not wanting to deal with the mental fallout of having killed yet another person, Beatrice closed her eyes and tried to fall back asleep.

It didn't work.

She eventually heard footsteps approach her bedside and quickly retreat. The orderly, she suspected, clearing her uneaten food. Except when she opened her eyes a crack a few minutes later, the tray of food was still there, along with a small ivory envelope sealed with a wax sigil.

Beatrice jolted upright and grabbed the envelope, sending another stab of pain through her body. She ignored it and broke open the seal to reveal a piece of paper with a short message written in blood-red ink:

"Message received.

Best regards,

Gilbert"

RELIC HUNTER

Introduction to Relic Hunter

Relic Hunter takes place nine years prior to the events of *Guild of Tokens*, seven years prior to the events of *Trainee*, and three years prior to the events of *Enforcer*.

T he tour guide was late.

Ordinarily, Beatrice Stallard wouldn't have cared. She wasn't one of those people who planned their vacation down to the millisecond, who visited a dozen different places in a day just to snap a picture before heading off to the next attraction.

And this trip to Corfu had been no exception, at least for the first week. Beatrice had arrived the previous Thursday evening, tired from a day spent running through several airports, eating horrible airplane food, and waiting several hours for a rickety bus to show up to take her to the hotel.

But all that travel angst had been washed away by the rays of the morning sun reflecting off of the blue waters of Corfu Bay. She had spent most of that first day lounging on the deck of her palatial suite, enjoying the view and the breeze off the crystal blue waters. And the next day. In fact, she hadn't done much of anything the entire weekend.

That was perfectly fine though.

She had given herself the entire month to accomplish her task here in Corfu and if she front loaded her R&R, so be it. On Monday morning, she had finally begun her reconnaissance, slowly moving outward from the hotel a little bit more each day. The island was large as far as Greek islands went, nearly three times the size of Santorini, which she had visited once on spring break in college. It also had a plethora of historical sites, which would have been great if she were here purely on a sightseeing trip and not trying to track down an ancient weapon of unimaginable power.

And so that was why Beatrice had enlisted the services of a multitude of tour guides over the course of the next two weeks, sometimes two or three in one day. There were too many leads to track down on her own, even if she stayed a second month. At the same time though, she didn't want to be at the mercy of a single guide's knowledge, which had necessitated visiting each site at least twice.

Beatrice took a long final sip of her coffee and set the mug down on the bar. The hotel restaurant was still relatively empty this early in the morning and she tried to savor the beauty of the view just outside before another day of fruitless touring. Except there was someone now occupying the stool directly to her right.

The woman was dressed in the typical tour guide costume: a light long-sleeve white blouse, a blue backpack slung around her shoulders, and dusty sneakers. Except this one had somehow forgotten that shorts were not an acceptable garment choice on the Continent, even if they were technically on an island.

"Molly?" said the woman in a chipper voice and in unaccented English.

"Yep, that's me," said Beatrice, who had adopted a different pseudonym with each guide. "And you are?"

"Leah. Leah Pallas."

The guide extended her hand and Beatrice shook it, her palm pressing sharply against the many colorful rings adorning Leah's fingers.

She took a moment to survey today's guide. Leah had curly brown hair that spilled forth from underneath a faded white hat and down the back of her neck. Her skin was a healthy bronze, no doubt from the days spent touring around the island and her neck was adorned with several gold chains that descended into her blouse.

"Nice to meet you, Molly. I hope you're ready for some walking. There's a lot to cover in the old city and I want to get us up to the Venetian fortress before it gets too hot."

"Sounds good to me," said Beatrice, who suppressed a frown at the guide's lack of any noticeable accent. It's not that she wanted a born-and-bred Corfiot to show her around. She would be fine with someone from the mainland or one of the other islands. But the thought of wasting a day strolling around the cobblestoned streets of old Corfu with an ex-pat from the West Coast was beyond the pale.

They exited the hotel to find a black sedan parked outside, the driver leaning against the passenger side door smoking a cigarette. Leah nodded to the man, who flicked the half-finished butt onto the street and reluctantly opened the door for them.

As the car sped down the coastal highway towards the city, Beatrice decided to press for more information about her American guide.

"You're not from here, are you? I'm sorry, I don't mean to be rude but…"

"What gave it away?" said Leah with a wry smile, her words now tinged with a pronounced Greek flavor. "Most of the time I talk like that, but you seemed like someone who's used to bullshit, so I dispensed with the fakery."

"Ah, well, I appreciate the honesty. How long have you been in Corfu?"

"For a few years now, but my family has deep roots here. Used to come here a lot in my youth. Although to be honest, I prefer Kasos."

"I'll have to check that out on my next trip."

———

Beatrice squinted through the high noon sun at the old city below her as beads of sweat trickled down her face. The buildings were purposefully built to maximize their number, given the extensive fortifications that had previously encircled the town. It made for winding, cobblestone-filled roads threaded between beautiful but old Venetian-style houses leftover from when the island had been a province of the City of Canals, and it would have all been very impressive to Beatrice if she had not already been through the city two times already.

"Quite a view, huh?" said Leah, who offered Beatrice her canteen. She accepted and proceeded to greedily gulp down the citrus-flavored water. The guide frowned at her as she handed back the almost-empty vessel and Beatrice offered a quick apology.

"Sorry, didn't realize I was so thirsty," she said.

"No, it wasn't that," said Leah. "You've already been here, haven't you?"

Beatrice stood straight up and tried to keep her features calm. Her mind raced in a hundred different directions, but she settled on a simple cover.

"You got me, was here the other day with another guide. Bit of a history buff, so I wanted to get a second walk through the city," she said with a smile. It's not like it was against the law to tour twice and there was no way that the guide knew her true purpose.

"You're looking for something," stated Leah matter-of-factly.

"I'm sorry, what? I don't know what you're talking about. I'm not looking for-"

"The Medoblad. But don't worry. I'll help you find it."

In the dusty basement of a dusty library on a dusty shelf, there was a book. It wasn't a particularly noteworthy book. It had pages, as most books tended to have. And a cover, one that opened and everything.

To the ordinary observer, and there were few because as it was this book was in a not very-well trafficked corner of this particular library, it was just an old book on a shelf, indistinguishable from any of the books to its left and its right.

But to Beatrice Stallard, it was more than a book with crinkly pages and a worn cover. It was the book that had changed her life.

Before she had discovered it, she had been like almost every other Quester, grinding out laborious tasks for a pittance of tokens. Then one day, she received a random message in her Q-Mail in-box with an even randomer string of numbers that turned out to be the call number for said book. It had taken entirely too long for her to find the tome, but once she had, nothing was ever the same again.

That book was a diary written by a woman named Rita van Asch. Beatrice had devoured Rita's daily recollections of New York and its surrounding environs, circa 1777. It was a momentous time for the fledgling nation and for Rita too, as the Guild she had steered through many tumultuous years was facing its biggest challenge yet. The historical accounts were interesting enough to Beatrice, but the real value of the diary was its musings on alchemy.

Alchemy was the science of magic, which was actually real, as the diary had divulged. Once Beatrice had gotten over that shock to her system, she realized that thanks to her chemical engineering degree, she was particularly well-suited for developing new alchemic creations. The diary provided a good basis on ingredients and theory, but it had taken a lot of experimentation, a lot of wading into smelly swamps and wild forests, and of course, a lot of harvesting organs from pigeons and rats, for her to get where she was now.

Those latter tasks were a necessary evil, as vermin were excellent carriers of prima materia, the unfiltered raw material of alchemy, because of their status as the most well-traveled species on earth. The amount of prima materia one could extract from a pigeon or rat was small, but it was the closest thing to a constant that Beatrice had come across in alchemy.

The culmination of her alchemic research to date were several small squares that looked like ordinary gummies you might find in a random jar in a candy store. Except that the green one, when eaten, imbued the ingester with preternatural focus. The effect had certainly helped Beatrice refine and perfect her recipe for that flavor and the low-level strength gummy, or buff, as she called it, although there were several weekend-long benders that she would have liked to forget. Maybe after she perfected the memory-erasing serum she was also dabbling with.

Today's task, though, was the beginning of a new project, and it had coincidentally brought Beatrice back to the library where she had first found Rita's diary. Of course, she hadn't bothered to return the diary after her initial borrow. That would have been the equivalent of giving back the Rosetta Stone and Beatrice wasn't that stupid. Also, she had applied for a library card under a fake name, so there was no risk of the book cops coming after her.

The third floor of the Seward Park Library was seemingly empty when she arrived, and Beatrice set her backpack down at one of the tables before pulling out one of the green squares from her pocket. She undid the plastic wrapping, held her nose shut with her fingers, and popped the gummy into her mouth.

The taste left something to be desired, but Beatrice powered through and counted down the seconds until the buff initialized. That was always the hardest part, the waiting. The buff turned her ordinarily driven self into a manically focused crazy person, who would easily forget to eat and sleep and perform other necessary bodily functions until the effects wore off. And after that happened, when her mind had tumbled back down into its normal state, the whole experience always felt like she was remembering an old spaghetti western she watched late at night on her mom's black-and-white TV.

The buff activated without Beatrice feeling it. It was an improvement over the previous times, when she had felt like her head had been placed into an ever-tightening vice, but at least that had been a good signal. This go-around, it took Beatrice several minutes before she realized that she had been intently staring at the library table, trying to determine what type of wood it was made of. Her brain would have continued down that path until the buff eventually wore off had she not noticed her backpack sitting still unopened on the far end of the table.

Beatrice slowly got to her feet, careful not to let her vision fixate on something else, and walked to the book-filled bag. She freed its contents and laid out the volumes she had tracked down from used bookstores, estate sales, and even one from a coffee shop lending library. These were just the stepping stones, the first notes of the symphony she was writing. The rest of the knowledge she needed was somewhere in the sea of books surrounding her. It might have taken her years to track down the right snippets and cross-references and random handwritten notes hidden on the dozens of shelves. But thanks to the buff, today would be the day she finally discovered the location of the Medoblad.

Beatrice stared out the window as the black sedan made its way down the coastal road. This day was turning into an outright disaster and not even the gorgeous blue waters could make her feel anything but a sense of hopelessness. All those weeks of planning after she had uncovered the location of the Medoblad and she had still managed to make a complete jackass of herself in the span of a few hours. Beatrice had briefly considered making a run for it when the car had come to a halt at the last traffic light, but thought better of it and decided to at least wait until they had reached their destination.

After about ten more minutes of awkward silence, the car finally pulled off of the narrow road and onto a patch of grass opposite a large green expanse bounded by a metal gate. Before Beatrice could open the door to step out, Leah said something in Greek to the driver and he exited the car.

"So," said Leah, turning to Beatrice. "You going to sulk like a teen-ager who got caught out past curfew or do you actually want my help?"

"Who are you?" said Beatrice.

"I'm Leah. We've been through that. And you're Beatrice Smith."

Smith obviously wasn't her last name, just the boring pseudonym she had come up with years ago when she didn't want to particularly stand out. But the fact that Leah had teased that out worried her nonetheless.

"No, you must have me confused with someone else. I told you my name was Molly."

"Yes, I know that's what you told me. But I also know that a blond American woman has been going on tours for the past two weeks, asking peculiar questions, going to the same sights over and over. And to each guide, she's given a different name."

"And?" said Beatrice, not wanting to give an inch.

"And we're not idiots. All the guides talk. Maybe if you had a bunch of wigs or could wipe our memories or something, then it might have been a different story."

Beatrice froze. She did, in fact, have a serum that, when imbibed, erased the last several minutes of the subject's memory. There were several vials of it buried in her suitcase, along with a bag of the focus buffs, one of the stronger strength buffs she hadn't yet perfected, and a second version of the memory serum.

That one still needed work. It was designed to selectively remove a particularly event or person from someone's memory, but sometimes it made you just pass out and wake up with the memories still intact. And other times, it would heighten recollection of the memory, which obviously wasn't very helpful. But her boyfriend Garrett had been a good if unknowing subject and Beatrice was certain that another few rounds of refinements would do the trick.

"Fine, you're right. In retrospect, it was a bit foolish. But you still didn't explain how you know my name, or how you even know about the Medoblad."

Leah smiled.

"Oh, that first part was easy. I just flashed the guy at the front desk a ten Euro note and a smile. You'll have a nice fruit basket waiting for you in your room when you get back tonight by the way. As for the second part, let's just say that I keep an eye out for up-and-coming Questers and as much as you're trying to stay under the radar, you've been doing a terrible job so far. Now, let's get going."

The Temple of Artemis hadn't been a temple for more than a thousand years, but although all that remained of it were several clusters of stone and a dissembled altar, to Beatrice it was still impressive.

After all, she couldn't think of anything that she had created that would even be around in 20 years, and yet these ruins still stood in the green field. Of course, the impact was lessened by the fact that she had already been here three times, but she hoped that this visit would be more fruitful.

"Can I dispense with the formalities or do you want to learn about how the Temple was the first Doric temple built exclusively out of stone?" said Leah, opening the metal gate at the front of the complex.

"You can skip the history lesson, I've heard it already. Unless you have something new to add?"

"I do. Do you know why we're here?" asked Leah, who hustled down the raised wooden plank path that ran along the edge of the ruins. Beatrice broke into a slight jog to catch up and they soon reached the end.

"Well, I know why I went to the museum up by the fortress. It's where they keep the surviving pediment of the Temple. It would have stood above here, right?" said Beatrice, pointing to the row of stones just to their left.

"Yes. And I'm sure it wasn't lost on you why that pediment is important?"

Beatrice rolled her eyes. She felt like she was back in elementary school being lectured by a patronizing teacher. But she humored the guide for now, if it meant learning something that would aid in her search.

"It depicts Medusa. Quite magnificently, in my opinion."

"Yes. It's not a coincidence that the Medoblad is hidden somewhere in Corfu, which has the only temple in Greece depicting the Gorgon herself."

"My thoughts exactly," said Beatrice. "But don't tell me that the blade is just buried somewhere in this field? That would be disappointing."

"It's not. Which is a good thing too, because Kaiser Wilhelm had a particularly strong affinity for the pediment. He was the one who excavated the temple a hundred years ago. Can you imagine what would have happened if he had found the blade here? Fortunately, someone beat him to the punch by about 300 years."

"How do you know that?"

"Follow me," said Leah, and she stepped off of the wooden plank and began walking across the grass back toward the entrance. Beatrice glanced around, waiting for a nun from the nearby monastery to appear and scold them harshly for straying from the literal and figurative path. But evidently they were all occupied with other tasks, and so she followed the guide, who had already made her way back to the front of the enclosure, where a rectangular arrangement of stones that stood about three feet high and extended toward one of the monastery buildings awaited.

Without warning, Leah gingerly vaulted over the stones and set herself down in the structure's interior, which descended below the ground. Beatrice was now certain they were only moments away from being attacked by a horde of angry nuns, but after a minute of awkward silence, no such mob had emerged.

"Come on," said Leah. "Before the afternoon tour buses start arriving."

"OK," said Beatrice. She tried to follow the guide's precise footwork, but hadn't counted on there being a lower lip of stones at the bottom of the enclosure and nearly smashed her head trying to avoid them, before Leah righted her.

"So now that we are both desecrating this thousands-year old ruin, can you tell me what the hell any of this has to do with the Medoblad?"

"Gladly," said Leah. "This was an altar that stood outside the Temple when it was still intact. The Medoblad was used here for various ceremonies, and it doesn't take much to imagine how those must have gone. Then, the Temple was destroyed, the remains buried, and of course the keepers of the Medoblad didn't have the good sense to take it with them when they fled. So there it was left, until the daughter of the Castellan of the Angelokastro sought the blade during the Ottoman siege of 1537 and single-handedly turned the tide against the invaders."

"And how did she do that?" asked Beatrice, wondering when this long lecture would finally end.

"How do you think? She snuck into the enemy camp one night and turned a hundred soldiers to stone. It is said that Suleiman the Magnificent, who was personally commanding the siege, was so horrified at what he saw the next morning, that he withdrew the entirety of his forces almost immediately, citing a mysterious plague."

"Fascinating," said Beatrice, who let a yawn overtake her.

The guide's eyes narrowed.

"Watch what you say," said Leah, her jovial tone suddenly turning harsh, as if Beatrice had insulted her best friend. "That woman might have saved all of Western Europe. And how was she rewarded by the governing Venetian high council? By being thrown off the walls of the Angelokastro for the high crime of 'witchcraft.'"

The guide turned away for a moment, and Beatrice thought she saw tears welling in her eyes.

"I'm sorry, I didn't mean it that way. History was not exactly my favorite subject in school."

"It's OK," said Leah, wiping her eyes. "Besides, you'll know her well soon enough."

"What?"

Leah ignored her and bent down at the far end of the altar and began aggressively digging into the stone wall.

"Great, more desecration."

"Shh. Save your moral judgments for tomorrow. Ah, here it is."

The tour guide removed her dirt-covered hands from the hole she had created and held up a tiny metal sphere.

"What is that?" asked Beatrice.

"This," said Leah, "is a bead of orichalcum."

"I'm sorry, what?"

"Orichalcum," repeated Leah. "An artifact of the lost city of Atlantis. Scholars have debated for centuries whether the beads acted as a power source or imbued the wearer with mystical powers. But they're way off base."

"You expect me to believe that not only was Atlantis real, but that you just happened to find one of its leftover magic beads here by chance?"

Leah shook her head.

"No, but that would be worth an extra star in your VoyageGuide review that you're going to write later, wouldn't it? The bead I found years ago, this place just makes a good hiding spot because everyone's afraid of the nuns next door for some reason. And yes, Atlantis was real, but that's a story for another day. Here."

Leah handed the bead to Beatrice. It was heavy, despite its small size, and the metal was practically ice cold.

"So if it's not a power or magic source, what is it?"

"Memories," said Leah. "Through a particular alchemic ritual that is now lost to us, a person's memories and knowledge could be transferred into the bead at or near the time of death. Except the Atlanteans took it a step further and compounded the effect by combining memories from multiple people and multiple generations. Which ended up being very useful when the city was destroyed."

"And this ties back into the Medoblad because?"

"I'm getting there. The castellan's daughter, Eliana, besides being brave beyond measure in facing the Ottoman army alone, knew what was likely to happen to her even if she succeeded. So right before her uncle had her captured, Eliana hid the Medoblad and, being a descendant of Atlantis through her mother's line, performed the transfer ritual on herself."

"Wow," said Beatrice. Her head was swimming with all the new knowledge Leah was casually tossing around. Atlantis. Memory transference. She had so many questions, but hoped there would be time later for her to extract whatever else the guide knew.

"So we just put this bead in some sort of magic projector and it will show us where this princess hid the Medoblad?"

"Not exactly. You can only access the bead's memories by eating it."

Beatrice practically threw the bead back at Leah, but the guide pushed back her outstretched hand.

"You're kidding, right?"

"Afraid not. Do you want something to drink? It will help wash it down."

"What? Oh, no. No, no, no. I'd like to think I've become more of a go-with-the-flow type of person after I learned the truth about magic and alchemy. But this is just ridiculous. There's no way you're going to convince me to swallow this and become some sort of reincarnation of this dead girl."

"It's not like that. The bead is just her memories, not her essence."

"Still a hard no."

Leah nodded her head slowly.

"I figured you would say that. Just know that I do have some unpleasant ways of making you go through with it in my arsenal, but it's probably best if you take on the task without reservations. Go back to your hotel and relax, and we'll reconvene in the morning."

The fan in Beatrice's room spun slowly, its white blades contrasting against the aqua blue ceiling. She could still hear the raucous chatter from the restaurant downstairs, where she had spent much of the evening imbibing copious amounts of table wine in between gulps of fish stew. The exercise had served its purpose of distracting her from the events of the day, and she had probably been a wink and a nod away from the additional distraction of the particularly handsome waiter, but had thought better of it.

The bead of orichalcum had never left her person, as she had awkwardly concealed it in the small of her back, where her flowing summer dress wouldn't betray its presence. She now had two small red marks from where she had pulled the duct tape free from her skin, but it was a small price to pay for not having to hide it in her undergarments like something reminiscent of a bad spy novel.

Leah's words echoed in her mind, preventing Beatrice from drifting off into the welcome embrace of sleep. She still didn't know what to make of the woman. She obviously knew about the underworld of magic but how she came to that knowledge, whether it was through the Quests of New York City or some other avenue, she couldn't say. What was clear, though, was that this whole business of alchemy and magical items went back a lot further in time than Rita van Asch and her Revolutionary War antics. There was an entire world out there, filled with the fantastical and Beatrice had only scratched the surface of the surface.

She wondered what would happen if she refused Leah's request. Was her threat an idle one, or would she unleash a magical torrent of pain through Beatrice's body until she gave in? Or worse, did the guide somehow have a vial of Rita's command ink at her disposal? With that, if the diary was to be believed, there would be no stopping Leah from getting what she wanted.

Which was still a mystery to Beatrice. Sure, who wouldn't want a magical dagger that could turn someone to stone, but the practicalities of actually using it made it more valuable as a deterrent against a more powerful foe, such as, say, the Guild. Her only run-in with the shadowy organization had been a brief one: a man by the name of Gilbert had accosted her for the secret behind her strength buff. She had lied and made up some story about salamanders, but she knew it was only a matter of time before he and the Guild caught on. And when they did, she wanted to be ready.

Beatrice was also having major doubts that even if they somehow plumbed the depths of Eliana's memory and found the lost blade, Leah was just going to let her up and leave the island with the prize. So that thought had added yet another notch in the "don't swallow the magical memory bead" column that she was tabulating in her head.

And the prospect of this woman's memories somehow being injected into her cortex made her stomach wretch. She didn't even want to think about what *that* would feel like. Beatrice had discovered a lot about the world of magic and alchemy since her initiation several years ago, and from what she currently knew, which she admitted, was nothing in the grand scheme of things, was that this bead was beyond comprehension. Even the Medoblad and its powers she could get a handle on: stab someone and turn them to stone. Of course, that was also horrific to consider, but she hoped not to be on the receiving end of that occurrence anytime soon. Or ever.

The music downstairs suddenly reached a crescendo and Beatrice covered her head with a pillow to block it out. She wanted to block out everything that had happened on this trip and just go back home and continue on with her life. She could forget about the Medoblad, forget about Atlantis and the tragic story of Eliana and stockpile her strength gummies until she could withstand anything the Guild could throw at her. But she knew deep down that it wouldn't be enough. The Guild was hundreds of years old and surely had means of counteracting her alchemy.

Beatrice bolted up straight and glared at the Atlantean relic on the table. It reflected the light of the full moon seeping in through the window with an uncanny shimmer, adding to its mystique. She cursed under her breath and slid over to the nightstand to consider the bead further. It was the size of a shelled walnut and she figured she could swallow it without gagging too much. Then what? Leah hadn't been exactly clear on the details of how the whole "memory storage" thing worked. The prudent thing to do would be to wait until the morning, which was only several hours away at this point, and wait for further instructions.

But fuck prudence.

Maybe it was the alcohol talking but Beatrice had had it with the waiting and the uncertainty and the doing what she was told. If she was going to be used as a pawn in whatever game Leah was playing, then it would be on her terms.

Beatrice slid off the bed and walked briskly to the mini fridge embedded in the credenza below the TV on the opposite side of the room. She opened the door and pulled out an overpriced bottle of spring water, unscrewed the light blue cap, and took a sip. The clear liquid was a welcome palate cleanser from the remaining traces of wine, but as she brought the bottle up to her mouth again, she realized she was stalling.

She found her feet carrying her body over to the table, and her hand, also seemingly with a mind of its own, grabbed the bead in one fell swoop and brought it to her lips. The metal was cold to the touch and her sober mind surfaced just for a second, shouting that this thing was wrong in every way and that she should open the sliding glass door and chuck it into the water.

A laugh escaped Beatrice's mouth as she subdued her logical self and swallowed the bead whole with a gulp of water. She stood there for a few moments, while nothing particular noteworthy happened. Maybe the "orichalcum" was some sort of poison-filled vessel, and Leah's story was nothing but a fanciful tale that she and the Guild had cooked up to get rid of her while she was off in some far-flung place.

But Beatrice couldn't think such thoughts now, because at the moment her mind was being beset by a torrent of ancient memories.

"You look like shit," said Leah, after Beatrice had finished drinking her third cup of coffee of the morning. The two of them were sitting at the patio outside the hotel restaurant, overlooking the beach and a nice little garden that grew the herbs that had seasoned her stew from the prior night's dinner.

Beatrice hadn't grunted more than a few words at both Leah and the waitress in the half hour they had been dining. Her thoughts were occupied elsewhere, trying to hold at bay the deluge of memory she had inserted into her head through that stupid bead. Which was, in addition to the brain-scrambling properties already mentioned, giving her a terrible stomach ache at the moment.

Her shaking hands nearly knocked over the remaining plates on the table as she slowly picked up her coffee mug and tried to signal the waitress for more caffeine. It was then that a look of realization appeared on Leah's face.

"No, you didn't," she said, her voice raised slightly. "You wouldn't have been so stupid as to have swallowed the bead by yourself?"

Beatrice nodded her head slowly and reached down to retrieve one of the green buffs from her bag. Then, with all of her remaining mental strength, she forced the gummy into her mouth. The effects kicked in after a few seconds and she breathed a sigh of relief.

"I did," said Beatrice, smiling meekly.

"How… how are you still here?" asked Leah. "The bead, it's so concentrated with memories that a normal person would be buried beneath their weight."

"I know. But fortunately, I packed wisely for this trip."

"What did you just eat?"

"I call it a focus buff," Beatrice said. "It's a mixture of prima materia, khat leaves, and some other ingredients I don't care to mention. The important thing is, it's the only thing letting my mind keep the contents of the orichalcum at bay."

That wasn't entirely true. There were parts of her memory that now contained vivid recollections of places she had never been, people she had never met, and languages she had never spoken. But there were also strangely other sections that weren't as foreign, but they seemed so trivial compared to the others that she had let them fall away.

The surge of memories had nearly overwhelmed her within the first minute, but Beatrice Stallard was nothing if not determined. And so, she had held herself together, like an acorn bobbing against the currents of a mighty river, until she was able to crawl over to her bag and retrieve the buff.

Leah regarded her with a mixture of suspicion and awe before finally letting out a long sigh.

"Well, this has not exactly gone according to plan, but I suppose there's nothing to do now but go-"

"Wait a minute," said Beatrice, who grabbed Leah's wrist as she tried to get up from the table. "How were you going to keep me from drowning in memories? Or were you going to let the bead destroy my sanity just long enough for you to find the blade?"

"Not destroy," said the guide. "Just temporarily disable. You'd be conscious and aware, and even retain some of your sparkling personality, but without any sense of who you really were. And when we were done, I would have taken back the bead and your real self would have re-surfaced."

Beatrice released her grip and Leah pulled back her arm.

"That's why you need me, then. If you just swallowed it, you would be the one who would be consumed."

"Yes, and I also know what memories we're looking for. So if you're satisfied that I wasn't about to let you waste away into an empty shell, then let's go."

They spent the rest of the morning in the black sedan winding their way slowly up the mountain toward the supposed resting place of the Medoblad: the Angelokastro, a castle on one of the island's highest peaks. Leah recounted with great detail how the castle had never fallen and how it had been instrumental in holding off several rounds of Ottoman invasions, including the one where Eliana's hero-ism had turned the tide.

It was also conveniently where Eliana had died, and Leah was confident that the bead would reveal where in the mountain strong-hold the castellan's daughter had stashed the weapon before she had met her end.

Beatrice tried to listen, but it was a bit difficult with the pressure of a thousand memories pushing against her own in the back of her skull. She ignored the pain, but it would only be a matter of time before she would need to let the dam break and be flooded by Eliana's past.

The car pulled to a stop in a small parking lot at the foot of a stone-lined path that disappeared up into the woods. As she stepped out of the car and stared up at the top of the hill that held the remains of the Angelokastro, Beatrice felt a sharp stabbing pain shoot through her head. Her vision became blurry and when she opened her eyes again after wiping away the tears that had suddenly formed, the sun was gone, the moon was pale, and the castle was magnificent.

Fires lit the looming walls, adding to the spectacle, and she felt her body, now draped in unfamiliar fabric, taking the long steps up the hill in two strides or fewer. Her breathing was hard and as she ran, she felt the press of something hard and leathery and yet also smooth against her thigh.

It was then that the force of Leah's palm landed on her cheek.

The experience was entirely disorienting, because she could have sworn that she had some urgent business at the castle, but looking up ahead, she saw that it was the daytime but that couldn't be right as she had just trave-

"Get a hold of yourself, Smith!" Leah said with a growl, and Bea-trice looked up to see the tour guide with a distraught look on her face.

"What ... what happened?"

Her face stung from the slap and she wanted to curse out this woman who had brought nothing but misery and strange ancient substances into her life, but she held her tongue for the moment.

"You slipped. Drifted into a memory."

"No, I didn't," said Beatrice. "I was running up the steps and-"

"You weren't running anywhere. You had stopped entirely and were standing there like a statue until I brought you back."

"Oh, but the focus buff shouldn't be wearing off for another hour."

"Doesn't matter," said Leah. "We've come to the place with the most significance for Eliana. She lived here. She died here. Her memories are pushing through the barrier you've put up and they won't be denied."

"So what can I do?"

"You trust me. I will guide you up the rest of the mountain. Here."

Leah withdrew a red scarf from her bag and handed it to Beatrice.

"Cut yourself off from the present and the past won't try to force its way in. My voice will keep you grounded until we reach our destination."

Beatrice regarded the would-be blindfold with as much suspicion as one should have after the happenings of the last 24 hours, but it wouldn't do Leah much good to push her off the castle ramparts if the bead hadn't been retrieved first. So she threw the tiny bit of her remaining caution to the wind and blinded her deceiving eyes.

"Step forward but keep your body taut," said Leah, but her voice was far away for some reason. Beatrice's world for the past hour had been the red fabric pressed against her eyes and Leah's words. It had worked well enough to keep the memories at bay, but she felt that at any moment, she would slip and fall into a bottomless pit from which there was no return.

And now Leah was asking her to do just that.

"Where are you?" asked Beatrice.

"If I told you, you wouldn't like it. Hurry, before someone sees you."

A week ago she would have laughed at the things she had done in the service of this stranger, but once again she blindly trusted Leah's instructions and took one step forward.

As she suspected, there was nothing but empty space in front of her and she fell through the supposed opening. It could have been five seconds or five minutes, but eventually Beatrice hit something soft and her body tumbled forward.

"Keep your blindfold on, please," said Leah's voice, as Beatrice began to push herself up from whatever had broken her fall. She turned to where she thought the guide was standing and let everything out that she had been holding in.

"OK, but I'm done with the trust walks and the trust falls and the magic memory beads. If you want me to go any further, you need to answer my questions."

Her words echoed softly in wherever they were. That was probably a good starting question, she figured.

"Where are we exactly?"

"One of the castle cisterns. It's normally covered by a metal grate so that stupid people like us don't accidentally fall in. From here, we can get to where we need to go."

"And that is?" asked Beatrice.

"Wherever Eliana hid the Medoblad."

"You're sure it's here?"

Beatrice knew the answer to that question. She had felt the scabbarded blade rubbing against her side as she ran up the castle pathway, or rather, she remembered what Eliana had felt on that night so long ago.

"Yes, I'm sure. I wouldn't have given you the bead and brought you all the way here if I wasn't absolutely sure."

"OK. But why me? Am I the only one who's come looking for the thing in all this time?"

"Oh most certainly not," said Leah, and Beatrice wished she could see the woman's face. "There were others and they, we failed. But I had a good feeling about you and if there's anything I've learned over the years, it's that I should trust myself more."

"That's it? You had a feeling? You don't know a damn thing about me."

"But that's where you're wrong, Beatrice Stallard. You're right to be wary about the Guild, by the way. If they consider you an enemy, then you'll need more than the Medoblad to hold them at bay."

Leah's utterance of her real last name and her real purpose here made Beatrice nearly fall over. Was this whole thing a set-up by Leah from the very beginning?

"Who are you? Really?"

Beatrice felt Leah's hand suddenly grab her own and she let herself be led forward into the unknown.

"I'm the light in the darkness. Now let's get going, we don't have much time."

L eah led her through such a maze of twists and turns that soon Beatrice lost track of time and space. She felt like Theseus braving the depths of the labyrinth except that he hadn't been blindfolded and that was on an island several hundred miles to the south. All the while, the pressure in her head kept building until she guessed it was a matter of minutes until the memories would break open the door and dilute her own being to a drop in an ocean.

"Are we almost where we need to be?" she asked after yet another series of sharp turns left her feeling dizzy.

"We're close. The underground passages in this castle are extensive.

They were designed to let the inhabitants escape if the fortress ever fell. Ah, here we are."

The guide stopped and Beatrice collided into her back, the red scarf finally falling free from her eyes. They were in a dimly lit chamber, with faded frescoes painted on the walls that matched the hue of the water outside her hotel, and an opening in the opposite wall. She looked around the room for the source of the light and found it in Leah's hands: a small red rock that was emitting a strange glow. Ordinarily she would have inquired about the seemingly magical object, but she had more pressing concerns to worry about.

"What is this place?" asked Beatrice.

"This," said Leah, "was Eliana's study. She painted the walls herself. You can imagine what they would have looked like in her time."

"I don't need to imagine," said Beatrice. "I can see them, in all their former glory. It's like the room is flickering to life."

"Then it's about to happen. There's only so much I can guide you after it does. If this is going to work, then you need to hold enough of yourself together so that you can follow Eliana's path. So that you're not just a bystander viewing the past."

"OK. I can do that."

Beatrice wasn't sure if that was true, but she could make it the truth if she believed it strongly enough.

She took a deep breath, closed her eyes, and then opened them again.

The brightly painted walls nearly overwhelmed her at first, but she didn't have time to marvel at their beauty as the memory began to dictate what she saw and where she went. When Eliana turned to face the other wall, Beatrice saw a small table and chair in one corner of the room. She, well, Eliana, walked to the nook and picked up the quill that rested next to a vial of ink and an open book. The page was filled with crisply written letters interspersed with diagrams and drawings. There was a sketch of the human body that reminded Beatrice of Da Vinci's *Vitruvian Man*, except this one was of a woman and it had several additional markings: a circle at the center of the forehead and one on each wrist, with a set of lines connecting the three in a triangle.

The words dotting the page were all in Italian, but despite not knowing the language other than a few stereotypical phrases, Beatrice found she could understand what was written.

"The rituals of the three," the top of the page said. "Mastery of the three elements of being was the long-desired goal of the ancient powers. Atlantis mastered the first, memory, while-" the word was so foreign to Beatrice that she couldn't make heads or tail of it "-squabbled over whether their efforts should be spent perfecting their stones to hold essence or body. Avalon concerned itself with none of the three pursuits. I have studied extensively the possibility that-"

Essence, why did that word sound familiar, Beatrice wondered, but before she could examine the page any further, Eliana had closed the book with a thud and began walking to the opposite end of the chamber where a door that wasn't there in the present blocked the way. With one hand, Eliana slowly turned the knob and pushed the door forward, while the other she brought to her neck and began rubbing something.

It was the same bead of orichalcum that was now somewhere inside Beatrice.

A whisper suddenly permeated the memory but Eliana paid it no mind.

"You're doing it," the faint voice said. "Keep going."

Beatrice imagined that her actual head nodded in response to Leah's words and concentrated on merging her actions with those of the castellan's daughter.

The memory continued, and they journeyed through an intricate series of corridors beyond the study. It was one of the strangest experiences of Beatrice's life. She felt like a ghost haunting the halls of an old mansion, a foot in two different worlds. If she had any spare mental capacity to focus on the sensation, she might have collapsed under the weight of everything. But as it was, the current task was slowly eating away at the remaining vestiges of her sanity and she hoped that they reached their destination soon.

Thankfully, it soon appeared ahead: a solitary door at the end of the long hallway. Eliana slowed her gait and retrieved the Medoblad from underneath her trousers, but before she opened the door, something odd happened. Beatrice's field of vision began to shake and blur and she feared that she was being yanked out of the memory when she only needed to hold on a tiny bit more. But then the world steadied and she let out a sigh of relief. It was only temporary though, because when Eliana resumed her trek forward, Beatrice was standing there, in the hallway, looking at the back of the woman she had previously been joined with.

"Why... why is this happening?" Beatrice heard herself say before cupping her mouth with her hands, but it was too late, as Eliana turned around to face her.

"*What are you doing here?*"

The two women faced each other across time.

Eliana had dark brown hair that was hidden mostly beneath a piece of linen tied around her ears and tan skin that reminded Beatrice of the local women she had seen bathing all day on the beach abutting her hotel. Her face was a mixture of sadness and fear, the former because of her impending fate, and the latter from the likely discovery of the interloper in her memory.

"You can see me?" said Beatrice in English.

"*Yes,*" said Eliana, in Italian, but both women somehow understood each other. "*Who are you and what are you doing here?*"

"This is just a memory. How are you talking to me?"

"*Just a memory? Who told you that?*"

"The woman who gave me the orichalcum, the same bead that's around your neck."

"*I see. During the ordinary memory ritual, it is not possible for the other aspects to be absorbed. However, I devised a different way, as you may have seen in my diary.*"

"The door's locked," Leah called out from somewhere. "We can't go any farther."

"Shh," said Beatrice aloud to the not visible tour guide. "Something's happened."

"*Is that her? The woman who found me?*"

Beatrice nodded.

"*So, she is back. Do you trust her?*"

"I don't know. I'm not in the habit of trusting people to begin with."

"*A good quality, some would say. I too only trusted myself and my own abilities. But I still ended up here.*"

"You cheated death. How is that a bad thing?"

"*I cheated nothing. I will die this night. When the ritual is finished, I will be arrested by guards doing the bidding of my uncle. Even though I saved everyone, he will cast my heroics as the work of the devil and have me thrown from the walls of my home. Which he will take from my father too. This last piece of my essence, it is to safeguard the location of my greatest treasures: the Medoblad and my research. Tell me, which is it you have come here seeking?*"

"The former. So I can fight back against those more powerful than me."

"*And how will the blade let you do that? Will you turn all your enemies to stone and smash their corpses to pieces? Will that give you the peace you seek?*"

"I don't know. But everything I've done so far will amount to nothing if I don't do something."

"You act out of desperation, out of a desire to save only yourself. Such a person will never be worthy to wield the Relic. It was a waste for her to bring you here."

"No!" Beatrice shouted. "You don't know what I've been through to get here. How much those I've loved have suffered because I wasn't strong enough to protect them."

She opened her mind to Eliana and everything poured out. All of her pain and loss, all of her ambition and resilience, all of her being, she laid bare. If it was not enough, then so be it, but she would hold nothing back.

Time stood still as the castellan's daughter considered Beatrice's offering, like Anubis weighing the heart of someone seeking entrance to the Field of Reeds, and eventually, a small smile escaped her lips.

"Very well. It seems I was mistaken. But do not think I will hand over the blade to you only because of that. You will still have to earn it."

Eliana opened the door and disappeared into the darkness behind it, but when Beatrice went to follow, it shut again with such force that she nearly toppled over.

As she waited at the precipice, she could hear Leah's voice back in the real world pleading with Beatrice to keep going, but she ignored it. This was her trial and she would bear it however long it took.

Finally, the door creaked open and Eliana emerged, the Medoblad conspicuously absent from her hand.

"It is done. Now your final test will begin. Go forth and claim the Gorgon's blade, if you can find the diamond in the rough."

With that, Eliana pushed the startled Beatrice into the blackness beyond.

The room was not dark.

That was odd, thought Beatrice, but the answer to her confusion soon revealed itself in the form of dozens of small slits cut into the rock walls that allowed enough sunlight to creep into the chamber.

The second thing that was odd was that Leah was standing in the room next to her, and Beatrice could only conclude that Eliana had somehow pushed her out of the memory. She still felt the familiar pressure of the orichalcum in her mind, but even though the focus buff had long since worn off, the memories were being kept at bay for the moment.

The third thing that was odd was that the walls of the room were filled with daggers. From floor to ceiling, the rusted weapons were suspended on metal hooks and each looked exactly like the Medoblad.

"You're seeing all this, right?" Beatrice said to Leah, who nodded in response.

"Yes, but how did you finally open the door?"

"What do you mean, 'finally'?"

"We've been standing in front of that door for six hours. This light that's illuminating the room, it's the from the sun setting. I was about to forcibly remove the bead from you when you-"

"Oh," said Beatrice.

The light of the setting sun was suddenly transformed into a daz-zling array of colors by the exposed blades. It was almost blinding, and Beatrice figured that was Eliana's intention.

"What now?" asked Leah, who had made several circles around the chamber before coming back to the entrance.

"No clue," said Beatrice. "We've gotten this far because of you. Don't tell me you're all out of ideas now."

"OK, I won't," said Leah. "Don't suppose we could just take down all the knives and figure out which one is the real one later?"

"Really? Haven't you been in an ancient chamber full of treasure before? If we grab the wrong one, the knives will probably rotate to point at us and the walls will close in."

"You've seen too many movies. The real world doesn't work that way," the guide said.

"Oh, you're right," said Beatrice. "In the real world, magic actually exists, so it's probably something much more terrifying than being slowly stabbed to death."

A muffled pecking noise echoed in the room, most likely from one of the song thrushes she had seen in her time on the island.

"Great, and now we have a ticking clock to aid in our deliberations."

"Go back into the memory," said Leah. "Eliana will help you."

"No, she's helped enough. This last step, it's up to me, alone."

Beatrice walked to the middle of the chamber. She wanted to believe that she was wrong, that if she pushed hard enough, Eliana's hiding place would burst forth from the wall, the promised diamond in the rough.

But there was no diamond to be found, just dozens of sparkling daggers.

The thought gave Beatrice an idea.

She spun around slowly the first time the room turned into a dazzling light show, one that only became more brilliant the faster she twirled. The fourth rotation she thought she saw it and by the seventh, she was almost positive.

Leah was yelling something, but Beatrice didn't care. She needed to keep going, just once more around and she would find the rough in the diamond. She closed her eyes as her feet did their dance, and the shining knives fought to pierce the darkness. All but one.

Beatrice opened her eyes, the dizziness a trifling concern, because all she had to do was take three steps forward and pull the one knife in the room that refused to return the sun's light. Her fingers grasped the ivory handle she pulled with all her might.

"*There is no need for that*," said Eliana, suddenly beside her. "*It is yours now, Keeper.*"

The Medoblad came free from the wall and Beatrice felt its power pulsing through her as if her heart and the weapon were one.

And then, without warning, the chamber vanished she was back in the study, back looking out into the world from Eliana's eyes. Except this time, she wasn't alone. There was another woman in the room, garbed in long pants and a flowing blouse.

The newcomer had her back to Eliana, and was bent over a large chest, frantically searching for something.

"*You have returned,*" said the woman in an oddly familiar voice. "*Are you ready then, to perform the rituals?*"

Eliana yanked the orichalcum free from the middle of her necklace, the other beads cascading onto the stone floor. She then walked to her notebook, tore out the page that Beatrice had read earlier, and fed it to one of the candles that lit the room.

The other woman didn't seem to notice this wanton destruction of what Beatrice could only speculate was priceless knowledge. Instead, she continued digging through the seemingly bottomless chest until at last she lifted a gleaming longsword and turned around to face the combined Eliana and Beatrice.

"Yes, *Alea,*" said Eliana to the woman who bore Leah's face. "*I am ready.*"

B eatrice woke up in a cold sweat.

The study, the castle, the vision of Eliana and improbably Leah, they were gone, but not the orichalcum.

She tried to sit up in her hotel bed, but her body wouldn't respond, and from her reclined vantage, she could just make out the sliver of the moon shining dimly outside her window, which gave her pause.

"*Are you finally awake?*" said someone sitting in the dark corner by the bathroom.

The words were Italian, but Beatrice couldn't understand them.

"Leah?" she said with uncontrolled trepidation. "What's going on?"

"So no," said the guide in English, emerging from the shadows. "You're not. It's just the vessel."

"I don't understand," said Beatrice. "You, you were there, in the memory. She called you Alea."

Leah walked slowly to the end of the bed, the Medoblad gripped tightly in her right hand.

"She showed you, did she?" said Leah. "You must have made quite the impression on her. Who would have thought?"

"You knew, then, that the bead isn't just memories, that there's a part of Eliana's essence still in here."

The woman pointed the knife with shaking hands at the frozen Beatrice, and for a second she thought Leah would plunge the weapon right into her heart.

"It wasn't supposed to be that way!" Leah said, her words coming out in small sobs. "She had deduced the essence ritual, the one that the Atlanteans, even with their combined knowledge, had never figured out. She knew what would happen if she used the Medoblad so brazenly, but she convinced me it was the only way to save the island, and I let her go. She told me that it would be OK, that a body was just a container, and that with her essence and her memories intact, she could live on, truly, in the body of another."

"But she lied to you," said Beatrice. "She only put enough of herself in the bead to guard her secrets."

"That's correct," said Leah, finally regathering her composure. "It was an unwelcome surprise when I put the orichalcum into one of the villagers a few weeks later only to watch as the woman's mind was instantly overwhelmed and crushed by the memories, without a trace of Eliana to be found."

"And then you ate the bead yourself," said Beatrice, the feeling in her muscles returning enough to allow her to prop herself up in the bed. "But of course Eliana would never give up the secret to you, would she?"

Leah advanced another few steps forward, her eyes filled with anger, and Beatrice realized she was powerless to do anything to stop the inevitable.

"Shut your mouth, before I shut it forever."

"*Alea*," said a voice from Beatrice's mouth, but it wasn't hers. "*Enough.*"

Alea or Leah or whoever the guide really was dropped the Medoblad, and it fell unceremoniously to the ground.

"*Eliana?*" asked Leah. "*Why? Why did you do it? You could have lived on, with me. We would have been happy.*"

It was the oddest sensation. Beatrice felt like she was back in one of the memories of the bead, watching someone else's life. Except somehow, the remaining little piece of Eliana had pushed aside Beatrice and grabbed control of her body.

"*Are you sure?*" said Eliana, fully taking control of Beatrice's body and sliding slowly down the bed to Leah. "*Would you have felt the same way about me in a new body? And then what would have happened when that one withered and you did not, would you make me change hosts again? And again after that? This was the true reason my ancestors did not seek the other rituals, as I foolishly did.*"

"I ... we would have found another way."

"*No, it is hard enough for your kind to change as it is, without me there also providing the warm comfort of familiarity that would have kept you stagnant. And I thought you had moved on when you finally hid the bead. Why did you come back?*"

Leah grabbed Beatrice's hand, but even that sensation, she couldn't feel. She wondered how much of Eliana was left in the bead and whether the woman would really return her body back to her when this was over.

"I did move on. Many times. I didn't want to come back here, but recent events forced my hand. And then I found this one, who had discovered the breadcrumbs I had left over the years. I wanted to see if she was worthy of the Relic, if she would support our side in the war to come."

"She is worthy, but she fights only for herself. I think that will change. You would do well to keep an eye on her until she is ready."

In the depths of her own mind, Beatrice was shouting at the other women, but to no avail. She wanted to know more, about the rituals, about Leah, about everything, but Eliana's essence remained in firm control.

"I'll try," said Leah, who brought the back of Beatrice's hand up to her mouth and gave it a gentle kiss.

"Thank you, Cuoro Mio," said Eliana and a tiny smile appeared on Leah's face. *"And now I need to leave you again, while there is still some of me left."*

Beatrice saw her own eyes close and a hazy figure then appeared in front of her in her mindscape.

"Beatrice," said Eliana. *"Do not make me regret my decision."*

"I won't," said Beatrice. "But I have so many questions. Wha-"

Eliana held up her hand and shook her head side to side.

"And I am afraid there will be no answers today. You still have much to learn, much to discover. I will leave you with the Medoblad, but your memories of Alea and of me, those the orichalcum will take as payment."

"What? No, you can't do that! I need to kn-"

Beatrice felt a stinging sensation as silvery strands of memory were pulled from her mind and into Eliana's outstretched hand, where they were drawn into a tiny bead that she then offered up to the giant glowing orichalcum that shone overhead like a metal moon. When the last thread had been torn free, the specter of the castellan's daughter opened her other hand, where a similar but golden-colored ball was waiting. It unwound itself into thin tendrils that snaked their way into the fresh gaps in Beatrice's memory and settled in like a bird discovering a newly abandoned nest.

She fought against these intrusions, tried to form a barrier to block their entry, but that quickly failed. She could see the mindscape collapsing all around her, the orichalcum ready to force its way out of her, and with a last-ditch effort, Beatrice formed a single thought in her head that the gold was fake.

"*Clever,*" said Eliana, pulling forth the new thought and crushing it with her palm, "*but futile. I leave you now and trust that you will find your way. Farewell, alchemist.*"

The woman faded into mist and it was then that the orichalcum came crashing down from its perch in the sky of her mind, and the next thing she knew, Beatrice was head down in a garbage can behind the bar of the hotel restaurant, vomiting her guts out.

It was morning and a woman with curly brown hair and several gold chains around her neck was standing over her, a look of concern on her face.

Beatrice pushed herself up from the ground, ignoring both the woman and the glint of metal at the bottom of the pail, and walked back to her table on the restaurant patio. Her new friend, however, was persistent and soon sat down across from her.

"Are you OK?" she asked. "I was eating next to you and you sprinted away so suddenly that I thought you were possessed."

"I'm fine," said Beatrice, her bearings returning to her slowly.

She was in fact, not fine. Far from it. This morning was supposed to be her moment of triumph but instead she felt like absolute shit.

Her last two weeks of searching had improbably born fruit the previous night, when she had discovered the Medoblad buried in the stones of the altar at the Temple of Artemis. She had been there four times already but for some reason, she had decided that maybe the simplest solution was the most likely one. And so, she had dug up the ancient site with the aid of an imperfect strength buff and had been handsomely rewarded for her efforts when she had pulled the ivory-handled blade free from the rubble.

But no sooner had she retreated into an alleyway behind the neighboring monastery was she attacked by a shadowy cloaked figure. It was almost ridiculous in a way, like a script out of a bad movie. Who the man was, Beatrice never found out because he didn't bother introducing himself. Instead, he had immediately resorted to violence. His punch to her stomach hadn't fazed her in the slightest, she was still running on the last dregs of the buff after all, but she knew that her opportunity to counter him was rapidly diminishing.

She hadn't wanted to use the Medoblad. Hell, she wasn't necessarily convinced that it was the real thing. Her options had been limited though, and if the strength buff had run out before she dealt with him, the rebound would leave her ripe for the picking. So before the attacker could strike again, Beatrice had plunged the would-be Medoblad into his right arm.

She had been as shocked as the man when stone had sprouted from the wound, so much so that she had yanked the knife out immediately lest it somehow reverse course and transfer the curse to herself. But the stone had halted at the crook of her attacker's elbow and Beatrice, with her last ounce of super strength, had shattered it like it was a delicate ice sculpture. The man had turned and fled, which was good, because a moment later, she had blacked out.

Beatrice now surveyed the breakfast in front of her and despite the rawness in her throat and the pounding in her head, she devoured it as if she hadn't eaten in days. The annoying woman remained seated across from her and finally, after she had finished the last bit of eggs and downed her fourth espresso shot, she acknowledged her again.

"You can go now, lady. I told you I was fine."

"OK," said the woman, who got up without another word and walked away.

A sudden feeling of deja vu crept over Beatrice, but she pushed it aside, along with the rest of her current ailments, and tried to bask in the glow of her accomplishment. She had, despite all the seemingly impossible obstacles, recovered an ancient weapon brimming with unimaginable power. Power that would let her move forward again, conquer the Raid Board, train an army of disciples, and finally confront Gilbert and the Guild.

Beatrice pushed back from the table and was about to head down to the beach for some well-deserved relaxation, when she noticed a piece of paper under the empty water glass where the mysterious woman had been sitting. It was trying to catch the morning breeze and fly away, but before it could, she snatched it, turning it over to find a single, handwritten question:

"If I am only for myself, who am I?"

GALLERY

JEN & JADE

BEATRICE

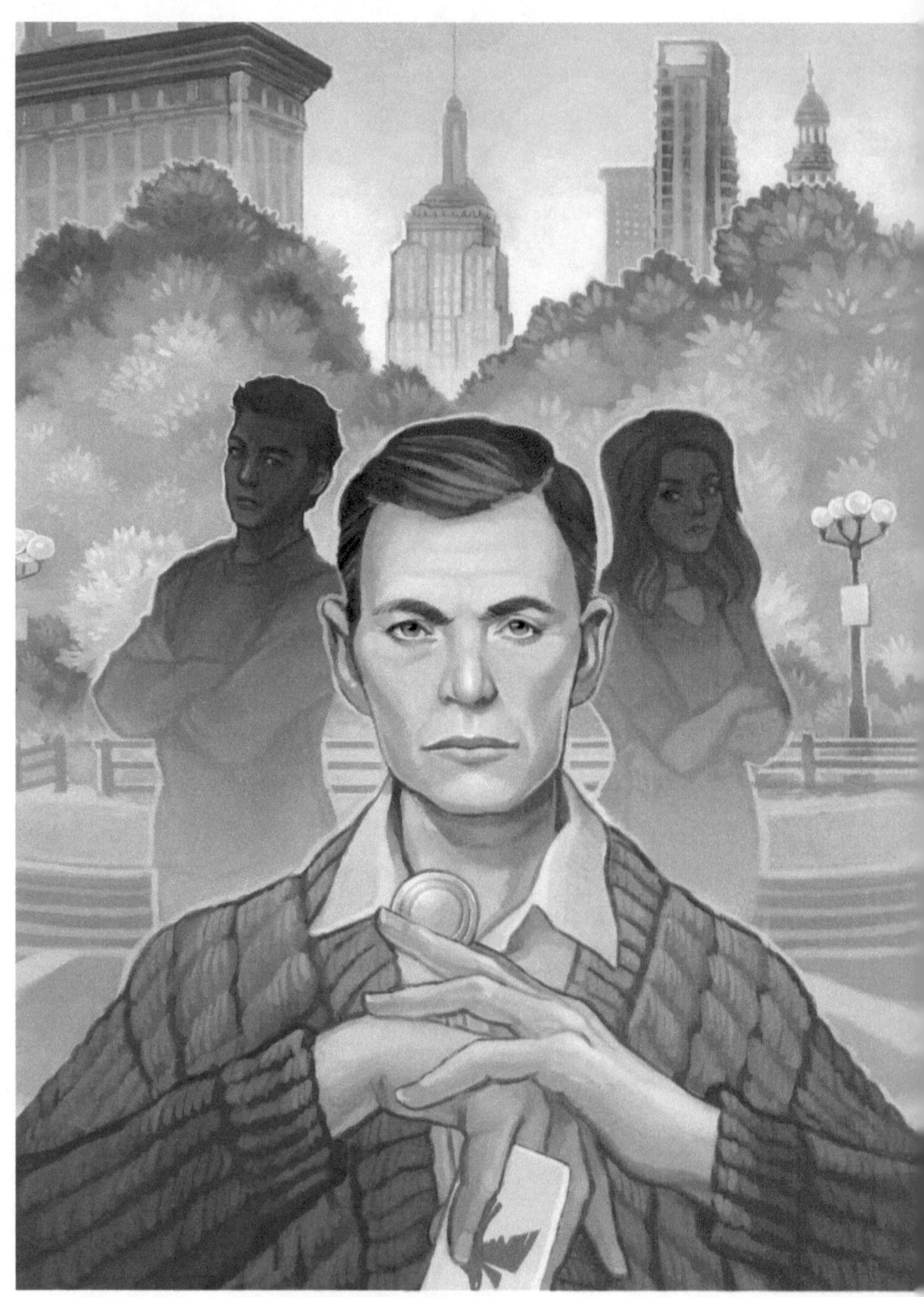

GILBERT

Vignettes

THE GUILD NEEDS YOU!

AUTHOR'S NOTE

Join the Readers' Guild by subscribing to my monthly newsletter to stay up to date on everything happening in the *NYC Questing Guild* universe, including exclusive short stories, discounts, and news.

Sign up at www.jonauerbach.com/back_matter.

ACKNOWLEDGMENTS

I would like to thank my family and friends for all of their support along this writing journey. Without their help, this book wouldn't have been possible.

- To my mom Sandi and my sister Alissa, for going above and beyond in making this book possible
- To my dad Rich, for first inspiring my love of science fiction and fantasy
- To my friend Brian Clouser, for always listening to my (sometimes) crazy marketing ideas and politely telling me to get back to the writing
- To my friend Brant Englestein, for his invaluable story help and for believing in *Guild*
- To beta readers Claudette Levy, Moe Levy, and Mikey Distenfeld
- To ARC team members Stephen Bassett, Eddie Hallahan, Charlie Newkirk, Paul Parsons, and Emma Scott
- To Stephanie Goodman for coming up with the Raid in Chapter 21

- To my author friends Angela Boord, Josh Erikson, Barbara Kloss, Devin Madson, Steven McKinnon, Richard Nell, Kayleigh Nichol, Carol Park, Travis Riddle, Phil Williams, and D.P. Woolliscroft, for all their support and camaraderie
- To Nick Borrelli for hosting my cover reveal
- To my friend Emmanuel Werthenschlag (aka Meir Srebriansky) for his spectacular cover for the first edition of *Guild*

And finally, thank you to my wife Danielle, for her continued encouragement, love, support, and excellent bookselling, and to my kids Allison, Robby, and Claire, the ARC of my world.

KICKSTARTER BACKERS

Thanks to the following people
(and those who chose not to be recognized publicly) for backing
and supporting the creation of this Special Edition.

A.J. Bohne IV • Aaron Jamieson • Aaron Morse • acolyte
Adam Auerbach • Adam Dugger • Adam Mull • Adriana Raats
Alexis Wolfer • Alexius Serefeas • Alexzander Sakamoto
Alice Klein • Alijohn Ghassabeh • Alison Mehravari
Alissa and Dan Mizrachi • Alok Baikadi • Andrew Godecke
Andrew McDonald • Andrew Pfeiffer • Andrew Powers
Andrew Tuesley • Angel Ocampo • Angela Boord
Arkyen (miguel ortiz) • Arlene Levine • Arsen Yakubov
Avi Lieberman

Beatričė Vaičekauskaitė • Belinda Crawford • Ben Nichols
Benita Kwok Benjamin & Tiffany Moore • Betty Schwartz
Blakely Infante • Brad Alan Searing • Brad Duncan
Brandon Carter • Brett H Kammerer • Brett Lewis
Brian "Smidge" Twomey • Brian Bowes • Brian Clouser
Brian R. Bondurant • Bridgette Findley • Britt Garcia

Bruno Geraldes • Bryan Geddes
Bryan, Joy, Alamea, Kai, & Millie Hill

C. Corbin Talley • C.J. Pizzurro • Caelin Johnson • Carissa Ford
Carrie Luna • Cedric Gasser • Chad Bowden • Chance Garcia
Charles Bergman • Chris Carbone • Chris Matthews
Christina Gregory • Christopher Froebe • Claudette Levy
Connor Whiteley • Corky LaVallee • Craig Cruzan
Cristov Russell • Crysella • Curtis Steinhour

D.P. Woolliscroft • Dale A. Russell • Dan Cagneux
Dana & Joe Feldman • Daniel Stephenson • Daniella Schwebel
Danielle Auerbach • Danielle Rockman Greene • Dave Baughman
David A. Quist • David Bobbitt • David Gomberg
David Holzborn • David Lundgren • David Pantirer
David Pepose • Dawn Piano • Dead Fish Books • DFarziana
Dianne Nicholson • Dipin Nayee • Doug "Kosh" Williamson
Dyrk Ashton

E. Ashby • Ed McCutchan • EePin Pang • Elisa Pines
Elizabeth Pantirer • Elizabeth Tabler • Elliot Pines • Emily Burt
Emma Mitchell • Eric Gomberg • Erica Distenfeld
Ernesto Pavan • Esther Messeloff • Evan Majzner

FanFiAddict • Fennec Foxfire • Franklin Ard • Frederick Littles

Gabe Feghali • Georgia Witkin • Gerald Patrick McDaniel
GhostCat • glenn Curry • GreenShirt52

Hannah Ormond Yip-Chuck • Hazim Awad • Heather
Hillary Griffin • Howard Schwartz •

Isabelsmad

J.M. Martin • J.R.Ruark • Jackie R Robey
Jacob & Elizabeth Pawson • Jacob Goldstein

Jacqueline & Barry Levine • Jake Hunter • James Lucas
James Richards • James S Skala Jr • James Stirling
Jamie Dockendorff • Janine Belsky • Jason & Sunisa Martinko
Jason Bush • Jason C Lund • jaymi elford • Jeff Belsky
Jenni D Strand • Jennifer L. Pierce • Jerome • Jerry Korde
Jo Munro • Jo! • Joanne R. Fishbane • Joel Singer • Johanna
Johanna Peel • John Idlor • John Jutoy • John M. Portley
John Markley • John Timmins • Johnny Ballgame
Jonathan and Brianne Haas • Jonathan Peldman
Jonathan Schwartz • Joshua Crane • Joshua Mickelsen
Joshua Spicka • Joy Meisel • Judi & Andy Marcus • Judy Elbaum
Judy Mehravari • Jules • Julie Anderson • Julie X. Ma
Justine Bergman

K. Dudzinski • Kajtryna Hanson • Kara Linna • Karen M.
Karen Mandelbaum • Katherine R • Kaylin Cullum-Lynch
Keir Alekseii • Kellie Chava Safar-Lerner • Kevin BigO Daniels
Kevin Grønberg • KHW • Kim Bedrick • Kristi Preston-Barnes
Kristian Handberg • Kristopher Horatio Mason • Kyle

Lahman Marcel • Lance Hurst • Larry Pantirer
Larson Steffek • Laurel Rom • Lauren Bochner
Lauren Himbeault • Lauren Moore • Lee W Smith • Leora Klein
Lex Wilson • Liam Charles • Lindsey and Caleb Vaughan
Liora Tarlowe • Lisa Cohen • Loren L Coleman • Louis Silverstein
Lucas Wolfgang Sexton • Lydia Fehrenbach • Lyssa Spurgeon

Machine_Galaxy • Maeira Werthenschlag • Marc Pantirer
Marcel de Jong • Marci Berlin • Marcia Kopel • Marina Shew
Marisa Regal • Mark S Randles • Mark Wahlbeck • Marko S
Marlene Brown • Martin Lingonblad • Mat Meillier
Mathias Rotestam • Matt & Camille Knepper • Matt Dean
Matt Wayne • Matthea W. Ross • Matthew Carpenter

Matthew Siadak • Maurice Levy • Megan Quinn
Meghan Asaurus • Meir Srebriansky • Michael Capraro
Michael Daniels III • Michael J. Sullivan, author • Michael Levine
Michael Luxenberg • Michael Pandolfini • Michael Park
Michał Kabza • Michele Felsher • Mihir W. • Mike Klein
Mike Tadross • Mikey Distenfeld • Mo Albertson

N. Scott Pearson • Nancy Korde • Nancy Pantirer • Natasha Liff
Nate A • Neilson Brown • Nemo Numquam Nunc
Nicholas Liffert • Nick DiMartino • Nick Long • Nicolas Lobotsky
Nicolas Mandujano III • Nicole Holloway • Noah Barral Vila
Nuvene Litefoot

Omar Escobar • Owen H. • Øyvind Nordli

Patrick Higgins • Patrick Welsh • Phil Williams
Philippe Gauthier

Quentin Christensen

Randy Eng • Ras Mitmug • Raymond J. Bull • Rella Feldman
Reuben Kopel • Rhel ná DecVandé • Rhiannon Vose
Rhonda Tayloe-Calinda • Richard Callanan • Richard Larsen
RJ Hopkinson • Rob Steinberger • Robert Flipse
Robert Zimmerman • Robertas Leikus • Rodney J Cressey
Roman Hatnyanskyy • Ronald H. Miller • Ronan Lahar
Russell Ventimeglia

Salvator Joseph Tierno Sr. • Samantha Landström
Sandi and Richard Auerbach • Sandra K. Lee • Sarah Werfal
Scott Berlin • Scott R. • Sean M Tardif
Sean Pierre Ringold Esq • Sebastián Vela (Adaby) • Serena
Shaun Kilgore • Shawn P. McMurray • Shayla Griffin
Shelagh McLean • Sheri • Signius • Simon Dick • Stacy Shuda
Stefani Wiener • Stefke Leuhery • Stephanie Nina Pitsirilos

Stephannie Tallent • Stephen • Stephen Ballentine
Stephen Kostantini • Steve Locke • Steven Hall
Steven McKinnon • Susan J. Voss • Sylvia L Foil

Tactical Tokens • Tali Pines • Tamara Case • Tania
Thaddeus Watulak • The Masked Ferret • The Nickels • thedave
Tim Stroup • Timothy O • Travis M. Riddle • Trevor Parkinson
Tristan Retzlaff • Ty

Uriah Robins

Vic Casados • Victoria Heath • Vince Martin • Vince Thanh Vo

Wendy Snyder • Weston Davis • William Rivera
Winston Roberts • Wolf

Yosif Behar

Zach Bolin • Zach Sallese

夏谷実

ABOUT THE AUTHOR

Jon Auerbach's love of fantasy began at the tender age of six, when his parents bought him the classic 1977 animated version of *The Hobbit*.
He hopes to pass on his stories to the next generation, including his kids, who have their own copy of *The Hobbit* that they lovingly call "the Bilbo book."

JEN JACOBS WILL RETURN IN

GUILD
OF
MAGIC

Beatrice Taylor walked up the hill as the sun set over the picturesque valley, a bag of groceries slung over one shoulder and the Medoblad affixed to the small of her back with a special adhesive she had recently developed. Her blonde hair was long gone, as were the distractions of her family, the Guild, and the woman who had betrayed her. But none of that mattered to her at the moment and she wasn't sure when it would matter to her again.

After unceremoniously dumping the contents of her shopping haul on the linoleum kitchen table, she changed into something more comfortable in her small bedroom before unlocking the back door of the house with a particularly important key.

Beatrice stepped into the waiting darkness and then immediately stepped out of it at the top of a rickety staircase hundreds of miles away. She descended into the basement of the abandoned warehouse she had purchased sight unseen for a briefcase of cash at a bankruptcy auction and flicked on the light switch at the bottom to reveal a football field-size expanse of concrete that she had only just begun to utilize.

As she walked the various metal shelves arranged in neat aisles, a muffled cry interrupted her wandering thoughts, and Beatrice walked over to a nearby table draped in a cotton sheet. She pulled the covering free with a flourish to reveal a man shackled to all four corners, a sock taped clumsily in his mouth. The local gang leader had been easy prey for her, now that she had had plenty of practice, and Beatrice was hopeful that the results of tonight's experiment would obviate the need for future acquisitions in the near term. Not that she remembered the prior ones at the moment, but the echo of them still bothered her. But that was a problem for another night.

Beatrice withdrew one of the vials slotted neatly in her tool belt and let loose a droplet of the liquid speed buff onto her tongue. Five seconds of real time later, the setup was complete and her subject was screaming through the dirty sock.

"Hush," she said. "I'm trying to work."

The man continued on with his desperate cries, but they stopped just as soon as Beatrice flipped the knife switch next to the table and the electricity broke free from its cage. After a few seconds, it made its way into the wire wrapped around a specially crafted piece of metal lodged in her subject's stomach and the real agony began. She busied herself with some other housekeeping tasks, aided by another drop of speed, and then finally returned to the now-carcass, where a gleaming light now shone from the end of the impaled metal. Shielding her eyes slightly, Beatrice unscrewed the glass bulb from the top of the stake and peered inside.

The tiniest drop of glowing liquid sat at the bottom and she excitedly, but carefully, ran to one of the nearby shelves, withdrew an aluminum cylinder wrapped in multiple layers of special insulation, and unscrewed its top.

The light that greeted her inside made the new drop's radiance look like a dull flashlight. For just a moment, Beatrice considered using tonight's harvest now, remembering with wonder the fleeting experience of that first ascension. But instead, she dutifully added it to her collection, resealed the storage device, and went about the messy but necessary work of cleaning up what had a few minutes ago been a horrendously evil man. With that finished, Beatrice sat down at the wooden desk next to the stairs, retrieved her writing implements, and removed the memory of the deed from her head and onto the page. The pain of this process would last the rest of the night, a necessary reminder of what was no longer there, but she relished it nonetheless.

Several minutes later, with the ink dry, Beatrice completed the ritual and grasped the newly created ring in her hand, its form as solid as silver. She glanced at her watch and, apprehensive of the late hour, quickly walked up the stairs and back through the darkness to her simple house in the simple town, and into her simple bedroom, where she removed a wood panel from the wall to reveal another cylinder resting into a small nook.

Beatrice peered down at the pile of rings in the glass jar and placed the newly minted one with the others. She couldn't remember which one held the memory of her son or which one held the memory of her philandering husband or which one held the dozens of other memories that she had dutifully extracted. But she didn't particularly care. She had permanently shelved that that edition of herself, and in its place, she was slowly rewriting, reconfiguring, and rebuilding a new version of Beatrice Taylor from the ground up. And woe unto anyone who would stand in her way.